DOWNWARD DOG

EDWARD VILGA

DIVERSIONBOOKS

Diversion Books
A Division of Diversion Publishing Corp.
443 Park Avenue South, Suite 1008
New York, New York 10016
www.DiversionBooks.com

All illustrations by Laura Grey (www.lauragrey.net).
All quotations from several Rumi poems herein are from *The Essential Rumi* (translated by Coleman Barks, HarperOne).
In Chapter 24, Monique quotes one line from The Gambler, a song written by Don Schlitz and recorded by Kenny Rogers.

For more information, email info@diversionbooks.com

First Diversion Books edition June 2013.

Print ISBN: 978-1-62681-323-6
eBook ISBN: 978-1-626810-15-0

Adho Mukha Svanasana

Downward Dog … God knows I've been called worse things.

I lovingly dedicate this book to
Leslie and Susan—
Two extraordinary women who have enriched and blessed
my life in countless extraordinary ways.

I've had it with chicks.
They're like an occupational hazard.
Warren Beatty, *Shampoo*

CORPSE POSE
(SAVASANA)

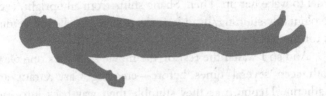

Who doesn't like a nap? Like a flashback to kindergarten, this is how a yoga class ends. Technically, even though you're lying down, eyes closed, hands at your side, you're not really supposed to fall asleep. Instead, you hope the mind and body will quiet and rebalance.

When the attention wanders—and it will—it's helpful to bring it back to the breath. As always, breath is through the nose, with the belly expanding on the inhale. After ten minutes or so, you stretch a bit (hug your knees into the chest, or twist side to side, that sort of thing), then sit up and chant Om a few times.

Corpse Pose sounds like no big deal, right? Then what's so difficult about this spiritualized snooze? Forget about getting your feet behind your head. Just try lying still for ten minutes. With nothing left to do, you're finally forced to come face to face with yourself.

The first time Shane sleeps over isn't after the first time she and I make love. (That would only happen months later.)

Instead, one rainy Saturday night in October, after a

passionate round of Scrabble—that she wins as always—Shane accidentally falls asleep on my shabby sofa while we're watching The Philadelphia Story together.

Somewhere about an hour into her favorite black-and-white '40s comedy—right around the time Katherine Hepburn's getting drunk at her own engagement party—Shane's head finds its way onto my shoulder, followed by a moment of the lightest possible snore.

I wonder for a moment what I should do. It just feels cruel to wake her up. Then, Shane shifts from an upright/eyes-involuntarily-shutting/head-jerk sleep state, to silently settling in for the night.

And so I watch the rest of the movie solo—it's one we've both seen several times before—enjoying Cary Grant and Katherine Hepburn as they stumble their way back into each other's arms, exactly where they so obviously belong. (I just wish real life could be half so forgiving when it comes to the possibility of second chances.)

The lights are already dim and when the movie ends, I gently reach for the remote on the coffee table and flick off the TV.

For a while I just sit there in the dark, listening to the rain, and holding Shane. Right before drifting off to sleep, I realize something: more than I can remember ever being before, in this moment, I'm happy.

CHAPTER 1

This is a very bad beginning.

I wish I were not the kind of guy who finds himself totally hungover in a yoga class on New Year's Day.

Unfortunately, I am that guy. Or at least, that's the guy I've become.

I have a massive throbbing in the front of my head. I am still dehydrated. Despite my nausea, I need something to eat, but it will have to wait. I realize that I forgot to shave, but at least I'm reasonably clean, and my mouth has been swabbed of its mealy, alcoholic sleep state. Despite a continuous blur of New Year's Eve vodka martini toasts, I know I made it back safely to my apartment last night. I can only hope my foggy state means that last night's debauched memories will get blurrier. (Why am I here, you might ask ... because given my life these days, yoga is the only thing keeping me sane.)

Right now, if we're being truthful, rather than retrieving best-forgotten drunken memories, I'm trying my best not to indulge in ogling any of the hot women surrounding me. But brother, it's damn hard not to. They are everywhere. Slim, yogafied bodies. Median age twenty-five. Minimal makeup and even more minimal layers of clothing. Everywhere my roving eye wanders, there's someone fair and fetching dead in my sights—and I am one of only five guys in a room of forty-five women, a wolf let loose amongst a flock of comely sheep. I want to be on my best behavior here—I don't want to screw up the one corner of my life that's working—and I suppose I could close my eyes and pretend to meditate, but honestly, given my miserable condition, I'd probably just fall asleep.

As the students file into the room, Gigi, my yoga teacher (and rock-and-roll guru) and the co-owner of the Thank Heaven Yoga Center, greets us, one by one. Her recall of names—unlike my own—is encyclopedic. She hugs me with profound conviction—she hugs nearly everyone, yet I still feel special—and wishes me a happy New Year.

"Rough night, baby doll?" A long-lost echo of Creole drawl flavors each word. Her once-over of me is nonjudgmental but nonetheless thorough.

"Reasonable enough," I reply, assuming (and hoping) that she's just teasing me, in a half-knowing way. Yet again, I regret my best friend Hutch's steering me toward that fourth, fifth, and sixth vodka martini.

"Well, you picked the absolute perfect place to be this morning, is all I can say," Gigi soothes. Her sprightly Asian girlfriend, Calypso, gives me my second hug of the year. Thank Heaven indeed for the hospitality of lipstick lesbians. Generous, feminine, and totally sexy, but never demanding or accepting anything in return.

As always, Gigi's music is fantastic. Today, once we start moving, she has some wild up-tempo stuff at the beginning, everything from Janis Joplin to Mary J. Blige, and then over the next hour and a half, she segues into music that is slower in tempo and mood. Stevie Wonder, Miles Davis, Marvin Gaye, something classical (Fauré's Requiem perhaps), and then a lot of Coltrane at the end. Sadness in sound.

A legendary '70s groupie, in her sixties now, for ten years Gigi was "with the band," accumulating a trunkload of stories of brilliant musicians, famous concerts, tragic overdoses, and narrowly missed plane crashes. As she says over and over, it's a miracle she's still on this earth. Hence her yoga center's name: Thank Heaven.

And, thank heaven, but I fuckin' love being in class at Thank Heaven. This is yoga for the hardcore crowd. Although yoga is supposedly noncompetitive, I can't help that my Alpha nature requires that I go for the hardest variation of every pose, always pushing my limits as far as possible.

We're balancing upside down when Gigi offers a super-challenging headstand variation: switch the position of your hands while inverted. This requires not only balance but real balls. I'm willing to take the risk.

I manage—almost—but come crashing down a few seconds later. My basic headstand is rock solid, so I'm back up and balancing immediately, and once I feel steady enough, it's only one deep breath before I give it another try. And this time—Shazam!—I nail it.

This is exactly why I love yoga so goddamn much. The physical thrills, the challenges, and the tests are endless. Three years ago, in a typical quest to get laid, I let one lovely lady drag me to Gigi's yoga class, thinking it would be easy, breezy stretchy crap. Once the sweat started pouring out of me—and I saw that despite my workout routine, Gigi seemed about a thousand times stronger, more balanced, and of course infinitely more flexible than I was—I was hooked. I plunged in, becoming instantly addicted to the vigorous, hyper-athletic style of Thank Heaven's classes.

This style of yoga is called vinyasa, and it basically means "flow." You breathe in harmony through fast-flowing sequences until, after getting extremely warm and energized, you start lingering in shapes and moving inward. Always going deeper. By the time the last forward bends are done, by the time the final twist is taken, we are all drenched, yet calmed, from over two hours of movement. Sweetly exhausted, we are totally ready for rest. It is then that we lie down and let ourselves go into Corpse Pose, Savasana.

Gigi comes around, her hands smeared with a scented lotion—something embarrassingly cheerful, like "Peaches" from Kiss My Face. Her warm hands hover over my closed eyes so I can detect her presence, then she presses down expertly on my shoulders, releasing tons of tension I didn't even know I had. Then she's gone, moving on to the next student in the crowded room—maybe Lavender Tights Over Perfect Butt, the beautiful woman who's only a foot or two away from me.

The scent does its job: automatically I deepen my breath.

The simpler, reptilian areas of the brain—the ones that process smell, the ones that guide my loins—are addressed. Surprisingly, the smell of this Duane Reade beauty product brings something back to me. My bargain-brand madeleine, as it were.

The one—the last and only one—to break my heart ... Shane.

As I take another deep breath, a vast, open, empty corridor of fuzzy memory opens until it comes back to me: Shane was never a big fragrance girl, but I know I've smelled this on her at least once before ... last summer at the beach, an impromptu day trip to Montauk.

Spontaneously, we decide to stay the night. We luck into a vacancy at the East Deck, a groovy beachside motel straight out of the '50s. In town, just as it's closing, we find a drugstore for toothpaste and saline and, because Shane's had a bit of sun, some peach-scented lotion to sooth her slightly pink shoulders. As we polish off a very cold bottle of a nice chardonnay (an essential that I did remember), I slather the cool, slick moisturizer on her warm back as she reads aloud recipes from an old issue of Gourmet.

The next morning, while she's in the shower, I return to the drugstore to grab a copy of the Sunday Times so that we can do the crossword on the drive back together. Then I procure some surprisingly great iced coffee and breakfast burritos plus an awesome sesame-noodle salad from the Ditch Witch, a local food stand.

Driving home, Shane does most of the puzzle herself, asking me only an occasional question, mostly just to include me out of politeness. Shane's actually much better than I am at the crossword. While I come from blue collar, TV-watching roots, she grew up in an intellectual family that played word games compulsively, with endless string quartets playing in the background. On multiple levels, she doesn't need my help. Curled up in the front seat, I find her intense concentration and autonomy charming, sexy even.

I remember how, two months ago—the morning after our first night together, lingering in bed—Shane tried to tutor me on the finer points of crosswords but ended up scolding more than instructing.

"Stop! You're definitely not ready to start doing them in pen yet," she chides me, smiling. "You can't just jot down the first answer that pops into your head that fits and commit to it in ink. That kind of impulsiveness will get you into tons of trouble later on in the puzzle. The whole thing will end up a total mess."

I yield to the overwhelming impulse to kiss her again. "Oh, will it?"

Shane holds her ground as I nuzzle her neck. "You're not giving your brain a chance to find other solutions, look for other meanings, explore other possibilities," she warns me. I continue kissing her as she lectures: "Plus, skipping around isn't good unless you're really stuck. It's better to work one corner and see where it takes you." I continue my quest to disrupt her concentration.

"And there are some frequently used words that you really should memorize," she tells me. I take my sensual exploration further. "I mean, you'll never use them in real life—take 'ret,' which means soaking flax or hemp—but it's used all the time, and …" She moans softly. Puzzle temporarily abandoned, Shane's back in my arms. "Okay, you win this round," she concedes. I've won indeed.

(Please note, before we go too much further, that these are my shining moments. In the mornings, I am apt to be groggy and hungover, not a hunter-gatherer of impromptu picnics, much less ever clear-headed enough for the crossword. In fact, these are probably the only episodes in my narrative where I am the stand-up, responsible good guy you're rooting for, instead of the loser who totally fucks everything up with Shane.)

But the truth is, six months ago, if Shane had asked me, in that rental car, high on the smell of sand and surf and with the sweet scent of peach lotion rising from her shoulders, I might have considered switching gears and given up my dreams of nightlife glory and hipster moguldom. I'd have started studying for the LSAT or whatever, striving for respectability. But then again, Shane would never have asked or even wanted me to become a corporate drone. Anyway, it's all just theory now. Even if it was only six months ago, I was a lot younger then.

Now the lesson's tattooed across my forehead with the invisible, indelible ink of experience: Never, ever get near Shane territory again. Never invest so much in anyone romantically that you lose your head. The Buddha of casual sex, I remain detached at all costs.

Minutes later, Savasana ends. I have contented myself with Coltrane and steady breathing and fantasies that Shane will someday forgive me. Today, I have gone no further in Corpse Pose than jazz appreciation and the potent, painful nostalgia brought on by a cheap, peachy fragrance. Not profound peace. At best, aimless drifting.

And probably that's as far as I'll ever get.

Chapter 2

After class, I can't wait to eat something. A greasy bacon cheeseburger and an even greasier platter of onion rings call out my name.

Yet another contrast between my yoga comrades and me is that I'm a carnivore through and through, especially when hungover. Thank Heaven usually has some after class "offerings" donated by earnest vegan yogis—shapeless homemade lumps that I suppose are probably some sort of indigestible granola/oatmeal/molasses cookies designed be washed down with well-intentioned herbal tea. This is NOT the meal I want to start the new year with—not by a long stretch.

Before you know it, still sweaty against the January cold, I'm at the Knife & Fork, perched at my favorite counter stool. Sully, the owner, stands guard over the grill while his son, Sully Jr., takes orders and works the cash register.

The Knife & Fork is totally Classic with a capital C. Twelve seats at the Formica counter, each covered in red Naugahyde. A neon sign out front. Stainless steel panels and terrazzo floors reveal how little has changed since the '50s, including some gnarly old dudes who seem suspiciously close to homelessness, always sipping the abundantly refillable bad coffee.

Granted, there are four giggling Asian polysexual hipsters just coming back from clubbing, but beyond that, there's no way to tell which decade you're in. I may be a bit of a food and wine snob, but still, it's damn hard to trump a good diner.

My Pop runs a small family joint in Goshen, a small town of 13,000 people in Upstate New York, called The Grill. Unlike the Knife & Fork, The Grill is completely lacking in style. Fresh from the Marines, Pop bought the place just before I was born, and it never occurred to him to change one iota of its beige, '70s non-décor or its nondescript menu. The food is actually pretty decent although mostly pretty bland. Nothing there would ever surprise you, particularly as nothing has changed in thirty years. Imagination was never Pop's strong suit. Nonetheless, beyond the total lack of style, Pop does keep the place afloat—maybe because he's totally content with being Small Time. Unlike me, he's pillar of solidity and dependability.

At the Knife & Fork, I start with a milkshake, hoping it will quickly sop up any remaining alcohol and provide the simple sugar rush that I need after Gigi's class. It actually does help, but when my burger arrives, I decide to be honest and order a little hair of the dog, too. Thank God the Fork serves beer. Two Heinekens later, I've devoured everything in front of me, including a slice of Boston cream pie. Over a cup of coffee on the house—Sully Sr. is on autopilot after years of sobering me up and getting me through hangovers—I'm feeling relatively civilized again.

By now, it's almost four in the afternoon. Time to head home.

As completely delinquent as I am, I manage to be reliable towards one woman; on the way home I call my Mom, as I do like clockwork on Sundays and every major and minor holiday. Not the chatty type, I don't think Pop has ever answered the phone in his life, but I know my mom takes real pleasure every time I check in with her. We're generally low on "safe topics"— gone are the days of discussing my classes, and obviously my love life isn't "Mom Material"—but nonetheless, no matter how briefly, I actually do feel a little better every time I speak to her.

As I listen to Mom's recounting of her New Year's Eve at home with her grandkids watching the ball drop in Times Square on their TV, I'd like to say it was an accident, but it's an accident that happens on a pretty much daily basis: On my way home, I stop by the bridge gallery (the lowercase thing is their idea, not mine), which is five blocks from my pad, and gaze inside. Of course, on New Year's Day the gallery is closed, but

I usually don't go in anyway. Arty video is projected on Mylar on the front window: an endless loop of a man and woman blowing smoke into each other's faces. It's kind of hot and kind of creepy at the same time. I pretend to check out the current exhibit of some postmodernist, neo-Expressionist whatever … but that's not why I'm here. It is legitimately on my way home—although probably going directly down Essex, the way I always used to go, would be faster—but I somehow always end up on this block.

It was at this gallery that I last saw Shane, three months after things collapsed. Andrea, her college roommate, was having her first group show of paintings, something I would probably have blown off but knew that Shane would not. Andrea's relatively talented, enormously ambitious, and fiercely loyal to her friends—which is weird when you consider that most everyone I know feels that Andrea doesn't really like them. It may just be her art-snob superiority, but she somehow gives you the feeling that she disapproves of you, yet is also too cool to really express the true level of her disdain. Unlike me, Shane is one of the few people who meet her standards.

Looking at Andrea's large canvas but feeling my gaze on the back of her neck, Shane turns to me, almost in slow motion. Her look is atypically enigmatic—one of Shane's many virtues is her directness in all things—yet, in this moment, a galaxy of contradictory emotions is hurled my way—anger, hurt, and regret are the most luminous constellations—but before I can respond, she pulls back. She turns to her group and departs with them, somewhere between flight and hauteur. I sense it would be unwise—even life threatening—to chase after her, so I stay there, entrenched in stationary retreat. And now, like DiMaggio putting daily flowers on Marilyn's grave, I find myself compulsively drifting past here every day in a vigil that only reinforces my unredeemability.

As I climb the five steep flights to my apartment, the wafting smell of Peking Duck mixes with the smell of dirty sweats, letting me know I'm home. Although the curtains are drawn tight, I can still make out the sad details of my dingy, 450-square-foot Chinatown pad.

Astutely, I realize that I'm not alone. There's a warm, seemingly very hot, curvy female body asleep in my bed. I try to remember what her name could possibly be, but frankly, I already know I haven't got a clue.

She's a souvenir from last night. Having had a massive fight with my snooze alarm and barely able to make it to Gigi's class, I offered to let her stay under the covers and leave when she awoke. I'm surprised—make that annoyed—to find she's still hanging around. Experience has taught me that it's infinitely easier for me to ignore even the possibility of there being any moral consequences for my prowling when there are no traces left behind, no chances of sincere morning-after pillow-talk moments that could so easily weaken my supremely steadfast resolve to stay detached. Conflicted as I am between my behavior and my secret ideals, it's best to at least pretend I'm working with a clean slate.

Yet apparently Miss New Year's Eve has showered, made coffee, and then returned to her spot under the covers, cozy and smiling at me like the Cheshire Cat.

I vaguely recall her having a connection to Anderson Becker—the king of upscale nightlife and my unofficial role model. As a failed Becker wannabe, however, I'm sure I kept my résumé off the table last night. Fortunately, the gold "Monique" necklace dangling over the curves of her awesome breasts gives her name away.

Kissing Monique hello, I'm calculating how I can get her out of here without a messy scene. Yet, the necklace bobbing over her exposed curves really does it for me. Within minutes, we're seriously fooling around.

Monique, besides being totally beautiful, is completely uninhibited. Little sex-game tricks that I play to see if they'll shock her—tiny bites to her neck, a tug of her hair, and other things I won't go into just yet—merely make her want me more. She somehow manages to give the impression that she's a classy gal who has nonetheless seen and done it all before. I have to admit that I find the combination extremely hot.

We chat briefly afterward. I realize that both of us were so drunk last night that, besides not really registering little details about each other (like first or last names, much less occupations), we didn't have sex. We made out, stumbled into bed, and collapsed. Now that we've gotten the sex fantastically out of the way, both of us seem to feel a little bit of artful backtracking might be in order.

Monique does indeed work in some executive capacity for Becker, the embodiment of Big Time. Restaurateur, hotelier, and reformed compulsive modelizer, decades ago Becker made his first fortune in the disco '70s, turning his talents to increasingly bigger venues and ventures. He's moved from party promotion, through nightlife domination, to a hotel and real estate empire. Hovering in his late fifties, he's seriously rich with a spectacular career and a trail of gorgeous women behind him.

Shane still works for him in one of his five-star midtown joints. She is, however, thanks to me, stuck in the garde de manger position of salad washer. Frankly, in some ways, Shane was lucky to be rehired at all after I lured her away with the promise of being head chef for my ill-fated venture, the failure that's sent me wildly into debt. After my investor pulled out, I wound up owing over $100,000 to various restaurant suppliers and, worst of all, $15,000 to Shane. (Note: it's not like Shane has piles of cash. Hoping to advance her career as a chef—and as a foolhardy gesture of faith in me—she took no salary at all and even invested the sum total that an aunt had left her the year before.) It's all a big, sorry mess, one that I'd give anything to clean up.

At first pass, with Monique, I manage to gloss over my six-month hiatus of extended wound licking. But when I'm pressed—and Monique is a clever girl, she gets it out of me—she quickly puts together exactly who I am and the entire story of my failed nightlife venture. Sadly, my failure even made Page

Six: "WE HEAR that a certain UP-AND-COMING BAD BOY, a BECKER Wannabe, got caught in the sack with his investor's wife—and that a certain much anticipated hipster HAVEN won't be opening its doors next month after all." I'm shocked that elegant sexpot Monique (the gold name chain, I now realize, is meant to be ironic in a Sex and the City way) actually snorts when she puts it all together. I can't hide the fact that I'm not thrilled by her reaction.

"I'm not judging you," she says. "I just think it's funny."

"It's a little hard to find the humor in my shabby situation," I tell her. "Sliding down the slippery slope of public debacle, right into bankruptcy. It's pretty lame."

"Oh, don't take it like it's the end of the world," she tells me. "God knows how many failures, how many oceans of red ink and lawsuits Becker's swum through."

I don't protest, stating that my compulsive Becker research reveals that out of the gate he scored a bunch of massive successes that skyrocketed his reputation and his wallet. Unlike my failure to launch, his own non-triumphs are mere footnotes in a brilliant career.

"So, what are you working on?" Monique asks. She's as direct in business as in sex, but while I find the latter a turn-on, the former depresses me.

"Nothing. I'm outta the game."

Once again, she smirks.

"What's so funny?" I ask, moderately provoked.

"Oh please. 'Outta the game.' Come on. A guy like you may get his ass kicked, but you know you're going to get back in the ring. You'll stumble on some hot new place, some cool location, some new venture. Then you'll rope in all your hipster, after-hours friends—not to mention all the babes you never call back—and you'll get something off the ground."

"Nope. I don't think so."

"This is the life you're going for then?" Monique removes from my bedpost my laminated Sweatshop entry-access badge, dangling it on its silver chain in front of me.

Sweatshop hours are long and hard, the pay miserable,

and the bosses (the investment banking division of Dugot & Burnham) rich, abusive assholes. Okay, The Sweatshop (technically "Presentations") requires nothing physically difficult or more dangerous than cranking out PowerPoint slides. And yes, the temperature is perfectly climate controlled, and except for occasional traces of bad music leaking from someone else's iPod and the perpetual, obnoxious glare of fluorescent lighting, there's nothing too tortuous. I grant you that it's not quite Dickensian, but nonetheless, it's a brain-deadening, soulless way to earn twenty-five bucks an hour on the 4 p.m. to midnight shift four nights a week. Most importantly, as a temporary wage slave, I'm barely making ends meet, with no discernible path towards repaying Shane, much less launching any of my former Big Time Dreams.

Softening, Monique smiles and, as though it were a diamond necklace, she slips my plastic ID over her head. It's oddly erotic against her soft, naked skin. "Listen," she charms, "I'm a West Village gal. I saw the spot you had for Haven and swung around. I thought what I saw, albeit abandoned and incomplete, had the makings of something great."

"You did? Really?"

"Totally. The oversized booths. That racy mural. A well-done, revitalized classic. The size of the bar and the layout of the open kitchen—all of that worked perfectly for that street, that location, that size space. I saw your crowd last night—I'm sure you would have filled it with the right types to make it a hit."

Monique sidles up next me, presumably for Round Two. "I know you've had the shit kicked out of you, with your first venture imploding. But trust me, the rules have changed," she continues. "Things that used to ruin a person forever are now just sound bites. I think we're at the point where absolutely none of the content of PR matters. To paraphrase McLuhan, the coverage is now the message."

She starts nuzzling my neck. "Everything is cyclical. Business. Sex. I hate to sound like a James Bond punch line, but trust me, things will rise for you again."

When I open my eyes, I find that Monique has left, writing her number on a Post-it. Such is the level of correspondence with a New Year's Eve fling.

I crumple the Post-it and trash it, but then, feeling residual, retroactive horniness, I reconsider. You never know … Still, Rule #1—Always Be on the Prowl—must be obeyed.

Basically, post-Shane, I abide by a Three Fucks and You're Out policy. I know that this will NOT endear me to Oprah, but I like to keep things simple. I will almost always sleep with a chick only once, helping to illustrate the literal meaning of "one-night stand" for the lady. On rare occasions—if the sex is particularly great, or conversely, if she's remarkably hot, but I still feel she deserves another chance to prove herself in the sack—I will go a second round. But a third time … well, my friend, the third time is definitely not the charm.

With tryst numero trois, the inevitable "relationship" talk arises. Until that point, you're more or less in the E-ZPass lane. Only the deeply needy or the foolhardy will push for that conversation before the third go-round. On the rare occasions when I'm somehow cornered, I find it hard to disguise my baffled look of surprise that we are discussing something—like Santa Claus, the Easter Bunny, or the Tooth Fairy—that, for me, simply does not exist.

(And just so you know that I'm not totally heartless, 95 percent of the reason I've got to avoid these conversations entirely is that if Superman had Kryptonite as his undoing, I have no defense against a woman's tears.)

Anyway, with Monique gone, I've slept the rest of the day away, and when I awaken, no longer hungover and feeling more or less refreshed, it's very dark outside. I look at my alarm clock and see that it's 1 a.m. The neon lights from the Chinatown restaurants and merchants glare in my window even at this hour, but especially under the haze of alcohol, it's possible to see my crash pad as a little more glamorous by moonlight than it is in reality. Those off-the-map qualities of Chinatown—undefined animal shapes (duck? boar? peacock?) dangling in the shop windows—are still creepy, but they have a little more allure, a little dose of hipster chic to them, at this hour. Like my life, the scene manages to be vivid yet depressing all at once.

I log on and against my better judgment, I examine Shane's Facebook profile, a ritual I now limit myself to doing only once a week (with dispensation for coming in drunk after 3 a.m.). Of course, she immediately unfriended me after things blew up, but if I log on with a bogus email account, I can still read the contents of her Wall. (She's not gone all the way with her privacy settings, whether out of ignorance or neglect, I cannot say.)

There's a new photo of her, although it's more interesting than flattering, given that she could easily have gone for something more traditionally hot. She has a reasonable number of friends—356, meaning they're all definitely actual friends and not just bizarre Internet losers looking for pen pals—and I've come across almost all of them in real life. I'm spared the torture of her being one of those people who shares their every drab moment or coy thought with the world. Even in cyberspace, Shane is one of the few people who are actually consistently real.

As usual, this is a total and really painful waste of time. I am not the New Year's resolution type, but nonetheless, I make a vow NEVER to check out Shane online again; that's another kind of guy I really don't want to be.

I notice that my cell phone's flashing that I have missed messages. There are a few pals calling to wish me a Happy New Year. Chloe, a very hot two-night stand from last week, called; I erase her message without listening to it. Integrity. Integrity. Integrity. I must remain steadfast and hold to my principles.

Then there's a message from my best friend Hutch: "Urgent, Dog. Call me ASAP." And after that there's a message from someone who's a stranger to me, someone named Brooke Merrington.

Brooke commands with a hint of purr, "This is Brooke Merrington, calling at Jason Hutchinson's suggestion." Then she speaks her phone number clearly, repeating it should I not have had the intelligence to have caught it on the first try. Brooke says nothing more than that, but oddly, I sense that she's somehow irritated that she's speaking to a machine, that I've offended her by not being present on New Year's Day to receive her unexpected phone call.

Hutch leaves another two messages: "Dog, where are you? Pick up!" Here is a guy who graduated magna cum laude from an Ivy League school—like me, as an English major, no less—yet "dog" and "bro" and the occasional "dude" constantly pepper Hutch's speech. (FYI, our code of reverse snobbery requires us to avoid mentioning our academic pedigree unless we absolutely have to, and never, ever using SAT words in our daily dealings. As always, Über-Waspy Hutch takes things further, riffing endlessly in wannabe gangsta-speak.) "Oh, shit," Hutch spouts, bar noises in the background. "I have a great gig for you. Serious Benjamins. Call me."

For better or worse, Hutch is someone you can actually call at 1:15 in the morning. Weekends, he's definitely out carousing, and weeknights, if he's not, he wishes he were. On the rare chance that he's grabbing some sleep—something that he feels his first five years as an investment banker have trained him to do just as well without—his cell rolls over to voicemail. He'll buzz you back at the first available moment that's convenient to him, no matter the hour. Just as I start to dial Hutch, however, a second message from Brooke plays. And, yes, there's definitely irritation in her voice.

"I'm sorry I'm having such difficulty reaching you," she remarks, "but I had wanted to start tomorrow. Eight a.m. sharp. I have a 10 a.m. committee meeting, but that should give us enough time. Let me give you the address. I'll assume we're on unless I hear otherwise. You may call me until 9 p.m."

This strange woman's arrogance is dazzling. We've never met, and I have no idea what she wants from me, but I can tell that she is already irritated at my poor performance, my lack of total availability to meet her unknown needs. Whatever the hell she wants from me must remain a mystery because, out of nowhere, there's an extended and passionate buzzing of my doorbell. I know from the insane insistency that it's Hutch—or else the world's most impatient, misguided, 1 a.m. Domino's delivery man.

"Dude, the cab is waiting. Get your lame ass down here!" Hutch blasts into the intercom.

I comply. Although it's been barely twenty-four hours since we've seen each other, Jason MacCondrey Hutchinson,—aka "Hutch"—my beloved Yale roommate, comrade in carousing, and professional preppy bad boy, greets me on the cold Chinatown street like a long-lost brother.

Hutch directs the driver to Pastis, the Meatpacking District's classic scenester bistro, open until 3 a.m. (steaks frites for us, with a side of babes picking at their endives), and then launches in with a shaggy-dog pride at being able to help me out.

"Dude, yet again, I've saved your sorry ass. Time to supplement that temping income in a serious way."

Out of nowhere, it seems, Hutch has gotten me my first private yoga client. Forced by filial obligation, Hutch was at some Park Avenue New Year's Day luncheon, and the topic of yoga came up. Apparently, Hutch says, Brooke Merrington was bitching about her former teacher moving to India and "selfishly" abandoning her to work for the Peace Corps, and she requires an immediate replacement. "Brooke is richer than Bill Gates and better connected than Bono," Hutch tells me. "This will open a lot of very swank doors."

Hutch gets a call on his cell, and I'm grateful since frankly, I'm not sure what to say to him. I did go to yoga school in the fall, mainly as an escapist way of working out while dodging bill collectors from restaurant supply stores. Actually, that's not true. Doing yoga was the only time I felt good; in fact, it was the only thing in my life that didn't suck. My attending yoga school (basically, boot camp training for teacher certification) was more or less Gigi's idea. She noted that I was coming to the center every single day at least once, and just as my unlimited monthly pass was about to run out, after they heard about my debacle on Page Six, Gigi and Calypso graciously volunteered to let me slip into yoga school on an outrageously generous deferred tuition plan combined with several discounts for repainting Thank Heaven's outrageous florescent walls late at night

Look, I'm not the suicidal type—I may drink too much, but overall I think channel surfing is my most destructive vice— yet only that kind of extreme immersion could have gotten me through the misery of losing Shane and my dreams of Step One towards the Big Time. But let's face it: given my sorry state (both now and then), I have no business teaching anyone anything.

We arrive at Pastis—in full swing at 1:45 a.m.—and as I enter, I make a mental note of how well their signature red awning works out front. Immediately, Hutch orders a round of drinks and two steak frites, and waves to a group of Brazilian models he thinks he recognizes from a Maxim party. This kind of joint is prime hunting ground: ladies, liquor, bistro fare, and a buoyant, boozy vibe that anything can happen.

"Dude, did you do the redhead?" Hutch asks me, trying to be cool.

I glance over her way. "No. I know who you mean, though. She does look a lot like that publicist chick, the one who was obsessed with PETA."

"Yeah! That's who she reminds me of," Hutch exclaims, totally relieved, as though correctly filing away a one-night stand of mine is as important as confirming the balance sheet of a megamerger. "Ellen was her name, right?"

"No, Rachel, I think. Or maybe Sarah. Anyway, it was something from the Bible."

"Dog, I know it was last month, but you gotta at least try to remember their names."

"Great tip, Hutch. Why don't you start a sideline consulting biz as the Miss Manners of Hooking Up?"

Hutch smirks. "Genius suggestion. Anyway, let's get back on track here. So, did Brooke make her first appointment already? She said she was calling you right away. I made it clear you were totally available during the day. FYI, I did NOT mention your whole evening secretarial career."

"Look, Hutch, I don't know if this is such a great idea. Thanks, but I'll call her tomorrow and take a pass."

"What? Are you shitting me?" Already a few scotches into the evening, Hutch's usual party-boy, laissez-faire attitude vanishes. "Dude, you've been fuckin' sitting on your ass for six months creating flowcharts for assholes like me for barely the minimum wage—what the fuck else are you doing tomorrow morning?"

Unfortunately, he's right: I have no excuses, no conflicts. I have nothing to do except channel surf until my cable gets cut off. But still, me as a teacher feels dead wrong.

"Look, Hutch, I know I'm certified to teach, but yoga's a little more than that. It's about having your shit together, and I just don't."

"Exactly. That's why you need to earn some extra loot—so you can get your shit together. Jesus, Dog. Didn't they teach you anything about being fucking proactive in that yoga school? What the fuck good is standing on your head if you can't make a little bread from it?"

"I know it sounds lame, but I actually try to take yoga, I don't know … seriously."

"Well, Jesus Christ, Dog. I get that you love all that yoga shit. So why don't you put it to use to bail you out of the hole you're in and make some money? That's my definition of enlightenment. Okay—I never thought I'd say this but … forget about the money. You've got to do something to get over fucking things up with Shane before you're fifty, fat, and totally unemployable."

In his non-mushy way, he's doing all he can to get me back on my feet. Hutch is one of the very few people still in my corner of the ring. And the dude's right. I'm a man overboard, drowning in shark-infested waters and here I am questioning the only hand that's offering to pull me into the lifeboat. Time to get off my high horse. My decision's made.

"Okay, Hutch. Of course, you're right, man. I'm in."

Hutch softens back to Preppy Best Friend. "Sorry to get on your case, bro. You want another round? This one's on me."

"Hutch, I just agreed to teach yoga at 8 a.m. tomorrow."

"I know—let's celebrate."

"That means I have to get up in five hours. No offense, but I really don't think my hanging out with my brother boozehound right now is your best idea ever."

Hutch chuckles. "Oh, yeah, maybe you're right." Then I smell the sexy, unmistakable scent of a Brazilian supermodel, a soft cloud of South American fragrance appearing nanoseconds before she reaches in to nuzzle Hutch's neck.

Like all guys, I know that the visuals around women—the way they look and move—occupy the control center of my brain. But sometimes I think the way they smell—the deep, sweet reality of their perfume—grabs my groin at an even deeper level. (And although I forget every chick's name in five seconds, I never forget their scent.)

Hutch kisses Soft Cloud of South American Citrus Fragrance back. It's obvious he doesn't need a wingman now.

"I'll leave you two alone."

I reach for my wallet. Hutch stops me. "You buy once you get paid." A friend to the end.

As I put on my coat, Soft Cloud of Citrus kisses him more intently. I head for the door, deciding it would be wise to stop by the bathroom first. Right in my path is one of the hotties from the redhead's table.

This little honey dip is smoking hot, but I can tell she knows it. She looks at me with one of those "Don't Hit on Me" looks that's probably totally successful at intimidating the mass of sheep-men out there. But I fancy myself a wolf, in fact, like Hutch, an Alpha out on the prowl. (As an aside, I truly believe this is my total true nature, even though it took years of intense practice for me to get over every nerdy impulse in my body to run for cover, totally intimidated by every beautiful woman I meet. In the same way, although I'm perpetually rooting for my inner Bad Boy Hedonist to win the battle for my Sorry Soul, I'm constantly trying to get the former altar boy within to pipe down and just please let me have my goddamn share of guilt-free fun.)

Steeling my reserves, I don't wait for permission, or an introduction, or even eye contact or a smile. That's low status. I walk right up and approach.

"Hi." No corny opening line. I give her a strong gaze and just a touch of smile, inviting but not overeager. She does not return it. In fact, her manner is decidedly unfriendly. I do not let this faze me in any way. I smile more warmly to build a little comfort, but she still does not return the smile.

And then it dawns on me. The redhead I was right about, but one of her party whose back had been to us is, indeed, my biblical adventurer Sarah/Rachel/Rebecka/Leah. In fact, through a blurry alcoholic haze I remember working this exact routine on her, with tremendous one-night-stand success, just two months ago.

"Hi, there. How have you been?" I try for a breezy, casual feel.

"Well, if you really wanted to know how I was, you could have called me anytime this fall."

I'd like to make a smooth getaway and avoid a scene, as Bible Girl seems about to erupt with Old Testament fury. I already have my coat and scarf on. The bathroom can wait until I'm home.

"Well, it's late, and I should be heading out. Happy New Year … Sarah." I don't know why I venture a guess at her name. It just sort of slips out of my mouth.

Bible Girl shakes her head as though I've uttered the lamest thing a person could ever say. And then she slaps my face. Somehow the intensity of her vehemence, combined with the slap, is enough to draw the stares of an uncomfortably large number of diners. Then Sarah/Rachel/Rebecka/Leah pauses dramatically and delivers what is, to her, the "smoking gun" of my moral turpitude.

"It's Eve, you bastard."

Stunned, I fail to even mutter an apology about at least knowing it was something from Genesis. Bible Girl's about to slap me again for good measure, but Hutch, spying the encounter from his banquette, is already by my side, not so much to break up the fight but out of instinctive fraternal supportiveness. Dropping a wad of cash on the table, he eases me out the door to the street.

It's just a slap, but he nonetheless readjusts my coat and scarf, unruffling me from the fracas inside. Somehow it helps me feel normal again. He follows this with a brotherly pat on the back. He looks to hail a nonexistent cab just as Soft Cloud of Fragrance exits the restaurant with his coat.

"Dog, we've gotta wash that slap away with one more stiff drink. In fact ..."

Hutch produces a sterling silver hip flask—an awfully old-fashioned, preppy affectation from some great-grandfather—and offers me a swig of straight scotch. I exchange the sting of the slap for the sting of the whisky. It's a good trade.

Hutch smiles broadly, a shit-eating, bright-eyed smile. I return the flask to Hutch, and he partakes heartily. Then, out of nowhere, he does our crazy wolf howl. I can't help but laugh. And, bizarrely, in this case, his wail actually helps us grab a cab—except we don't need it. Hutch has hatched a new plan and ushers us around the corner to Cielo. I murmur further protest, but Hutch will have none of it.

"Seriously, it's totally on your way. Besides, it's just one drink," Hutch tries to convince me, "and then you're home."

I pause for a moment and then give in. "You're right—I just can't start the new year being bitch slapped."

Cielo has got it right when it comes to music and dance. It's true to its groove: the sunken dance floor is surrounded by banquettes of brown and beige suede, a timeless albeit hipster take on a seventies aesthetic. I wonder where Nicolas, the owner, got those banquettes and start texting him, realizing as I press "Send" that I'm supposedly out of this game. Still, a little information to file away never hurt anyone.

Two hours later, I look at my watch, and once my eyes refocus enough to tell the hour, I'm more than a little dismayed. It's 4:15. And I have to be up by 7 am. I find Hutch on an overstuffed sofa, working his best moves on Soft Cloud and a nubile friend of hers, no doubt trying to negotiate some interesting way for the three of them to greet the dawn intertwined.

"Dude, I gotta go."

Hutch barely takes his eyes off the two prized beauties.

"Call me first thing and let me know how it goes with Brooke."

"Sure."

"Oh, and one more thing." I have his attention for a full moment.

"Whatever you do, Dog—don't fuck this up!"

Triangle Pose
(UTTHITA TRIKONASANA)

Triangle Pose has magic in it, just like that perfect first martini.

You know, the one that's completely refreshing with just enough of a sharpness to the alcohol that it somehow feels cleansing, almost medicinal. Pure liquid therapy.

Stand with your legs about four feet apart. Your heels should be in a straight line with each other. Turn the back foot in slightly. Exhale, bending to let your lower hand rest wherever it lands—most probably on the shin. Your top arm reaches up. Rotate your chest skyward. Hold the pose for a half-dozen breaths, then inhale to lift yourself back up to standing. Repeat the pose on the other side.

Like that first martini, Triangle Pose invigorates as it

loosens you.

And, to the best of my knowledge, no one has ever woken up feeling like shit from one Triangle too many.

It's not like I dream about Shane all the time, but at least in my dreams, I have the pleasure of looking at her again.

Shane has classic features that veer a few degrees away from Great Beauty towards the better land of Unbelievably Hot and Really Interesting. A slight bump in the aquiline, elegant nose that make it even more worthy of nuzzling. (She will never realize that her so-called "flaws"—like that nose—are actually her best features.)

It was rare, but every now and then Shane would make an offhand disparaging remark about her appearance—like her nose, or wanting to lose a few pounds, or that her feet were too big—and it always took me aback. For me, she was like one extended Hirshfeld line, a mile-long curve starting with graceful, feminine slope of jaw and endless neck, and gliding sleekly along her perfect frame. But what most draws your attention are her eyes; they contrast their soft, mossy green palette with flashes that are tiger fierce. Interestingly, when still, her lips are actually quite pouty, but more often than not they're intensely engaged in banter, a kissable blur.

She's not someone who suffers fools, but she's also the person you'd definitely call to bail you out of jail, no questions asked. You always knew she was being real with you and expecting the same in return. Just because she liked you, you felt a little more special, as though someone who had really great taste saw some potential in you that you secretly hoped was really there.

In short, she was amazing.

And I fucked it completely up.

CHAPTER 3

Little could prepare one for the grandeur of Brooke Merrington's apartment building. While I have many friends from college whose families reside on the Upper East Side, mind you, those are not my roots.

I am a clever enough guy whose dad grills cheeseburgers and flips pancakes. In fact, were it not for scholarships and student loans, my father's entire earnings would have just about covered my annual Yale tuition, leaving my two sisters empty-bellied, perhaps, but proud. All three of my college roommates were affluent, with the richest by far being Hutch, with his complete Mayflower pedigree and Waspy, untouchable trust fund. He's at Jefferson Filbank Investments and doing very well as a Master of the Universe-in-training.

Yet, Hutch's family wealth was constantly understated, even denied. His father's an adjunct professor at Columbia Law and on the boards of a bunch of financial concerns, while his mother works with several charities. Despite the respectable townhouse in the 90s address, sometimes things were so genteelly shabby in their pad that I half wondered if maybe all the money was gone. Perhaps, somehow, mismanagement (or inbreeding) had left them with little more than maintenance money and Waspily downplayed chic. Brooke's lobby, however, while smacking of Old Money, has no such air of restraint. It reeks of ready cash.

I give my name and destination to the doorman. I throw in that I'm Brooke's new yoga instructor, trying, I suppose, to bond with him as a "man of the people" and not of Park Avenue. "Of course, sir," he nods, dialing up, confirming everything. "Very good. I'll send him up," he concludes.

Yet the doorman—his brass plate reveals his name to be Wallace—seems hesitant. "Is something wrong?" I ask. He considers for a moment, then decides to level with me.

"Forgive me, sir, but this is your first time here, correct? I've known Ms. Merrington for quite some time and have a sense of how she likes things."

"I see," I reply, not sure where this is going. Wallace seems kindly, but I'm confused.

"I'm sorry, sir, but might I suggest that Ms. Merrington can be, well, quite particular about certain things."

"Okay. I'm not sure I get it, but …"

"Sir, may I speak freely? Your pants are wrinkled. Your hair is uncombed, and your collar has dandruff on it. And I believe your shirt is on inside out. Ms. Merrington will make note of such things."

I'm stunned. No one's paid this much attention to my appearance since my mother on my first day of school.

"I'm sorry, I guess, but I'm not sure what I can do about any of it, though," I stumble, now feeling totally outclassed by both the lobby and the doorman.

"Jimmy, stand in for a moment," Wallace signals to his second in command. "Follow me," he continues, leading me down the hall to a private door and alcove.

From his modest doormen's locker, Wallace offers me a comb. Over the years, I have perfected my "just rolled out of bed" style by, more often than not, just rolling out of bed. I've cultivated the look since I've found that ladies like my messy hair—it's an excuse to run their fingers through it. More important, it's yet another component to my whole strategy: nothing works better in a wolf's quest for getting laid than looking like you've just gotten laid. While my general dishevelment successfully reads as insouciantly sexy to most chicks on a night out clubbing, Wallace reacts to my cowlick with the quiet but intense horror most folks reserve for pedophilia.

He dusts off my collar, whisks my sweats under the iron, and even insists on swapping my T-shirt for a fresh one of his own. He urges me to quickly shave with a disposable razor and is quite vehement about my using a little mouthwash.

"Better go again," he insists after round one with Listerine, "just to be safe."

Wallace spritzes me with two dashes of his discrete Green Irish Tweed, no doubt to remove the alcoholic fumes seeping through my pores. Then, following my three-minute, Jeevesian makeover, Wallace—looking me over like a good horse trader—silently deems me presentable.

Entering Brooke's apartment, I get it at once. I'm completely grateful to Wallace. It's like the Museum of the Wealthy—everything perfectly in place and on well-lit display. Without his help, I fear that the apartment itself might oust me. More than a bone marrow transplant between mismatched donors, a scraggly boozehound like me is an abomination to this environment.

Unlike the gilded excesses the tacky Trump likes to display in the press, this place—despite both Trump's and Brooke's shared fetish for gold—is relatively tasteful. While indulging in opulence, it remains on the safe side of tacky, and yet I can still entertain myself by speculating on just how many things one could uselessly plate in gold—toothpicks, cell phones, chopsticks, nail clippers, staplers—purely for the hell of it. And I wonder if Brooke has purchased all of them.

The tuxedoed butler has left me alone for a few moments, so I look around a bit more. I am very careful not to touch anything or allow myself to be in a position that might be embarrassing should Brooke appear from behind a secret passageway in the wall. It's that kind of an apartment; rotate a torchiere accidentally, and who knows what will happen.

I smell Brooke's jasmine fragrance (she's wearing Joy—a scent I remember from a particularly label-dropping fashion victim I "dated") a moment before she appears. I am caught behaving well, as I admire a gold-framed family portrait of two girls and their mother.

"My mother, myself, and my half sister, Phoebe," Brooke

offers, extending her hand. Her smile is warmer than her phone voice. Her eyes are bright. She's a woman in her late forties (I suppose), maybe early fifties, entirely trim, perfectly composed, with a society woman's photogenic profile. Her shoulder-length brown hair bounces nicely in the perfect bob. She's wearing clothes that might be appropriate for yoga, but somehow she looks so put together, so composed, that I wonder if she'll mind sweating or only want to do poses that won't muss her hair.

"Welcome," Brooke says to me. "Can Gerard get you anything?"

Tuxedoed Gerard has miraculously reappeared—Is Brooke telepathic? Does Gerard have a cochlear implant?—and I question for a second if she will object to my own plastic bottle of water. Will it be offensive to Brooke if I sip from that instead of a Waterford goblet?

"Madame, the flowers for tonight's dinner have arrived," Gerard informs Brooke.

"Finally," Brooke replies. "I'm sorry," she says to me. "This will only take a moment, but it's rather urgent."

She leads—on Park Avenue, Brooke is clearly used to being the trailblazer—followed by Gerard and me, directing us toward an alcove where twenty buckets overflowing with dozens of white roses await her inspection.

"These will not do."

"What shall I tell the florist, Madame?"

"That she failed to deliver what I wanted and that she must correct the problem before the caterer arrives," Brooke commands, and Gerard vanishes. Brooke mutters something about "never again" with icy formality. I half wonder if Brooke will have Gerard take the florist out in a rowboat in the Central Park reservoir.

"You didn't want white roses?" I ask. It seems a rather large error to send several dozen blooms if that's the case.

"I wanted Iceberg white roses. These are French Lace."

They are among the most beautiful flowers I have ever seen, transforming the harsh fluorescent hallway outside the service elevator into an urban garden overflowing with snowy, long-stemmed beauty. Brooke notices my small reaction.

"Icebergs are unscented," she explains. "Even if I wanted scented, these are far too fragrant. And Icebergs are pure white. The little blush of pink on the edges marks these as a different hybrid. Now that I look at them, they're probably Nicoles."

As she ushers me into her sitting room, I make a mental note that Brooke wants her roses, by any other name, not to smell as sweet.

The flower debacle soundly behind her, she gives her attention to our meeting. "I've been told you're a wonderful teacher," she says. "I had just started with someone else, but after three weeks my instructor abandoned me for India. So, naturally, I was quite pleased when Jason"—God, it's so funny to hear Hutch called by his given Christian first name—"mentioned he had a Yale friend who was certified to teach."

On his way to his trainer this morning, Hutch called because he figured that any old-school bonding might require some explanation about my unconventional career path. In other words, why I'm not a banker, a lawyer, or living off a trust fund, but rather a failed nightlife impresario/temp. Between sit-ups, Hutch fed me my lines, offering that I should be deliberately vague and mutter something about "weathering the storm of this difficult economy." I realize that this suggests that my capital gains have been marginally reduced rather than that my cell phone's about to be cut off, but I follow my drinking buddy's, and now yoga mentor's, advice.

Brooke nods sympathetically. "Yes, these are very challenging times. I'm sure Jason has told you we alternate summers in East Hampton and in Europe. Quite frankly, with things so rocky financially for everyone we know, I'm not sure we're going to be able to rent out the villa in Tuscany this year."

While it's rather trippy that anyone with a spare villa in Tuscany feels that they can bond with me about economic woes, I do not mention this—or the fact that my Chinatown landlord, ever the charmer, cornered me in the hall at 6:30 this morning. Instead, as I assume any good yoga teacher should, I ask Brooke about any health issues she might have.

"My right hip has some stiffness. Actually, that's part of the reason I wanted to start again. I know they replace them like used car parts these days, but I'd prefer to avoid surgery."

"We can definitely try."

"And of course, I'm interested in weight loss."

I glance at her with sincere incredulity. Brooke seems perfectly trim, her body as sleek and tailored as a racing yacht.

"That's ridiculous. You're obviously amazingly fit."

"You're being kind."

"No, I honestly don't think you need to lose any weight. We'll definitely add more strength and length through practicing, but you seem quite toned already."

"There's no need to be reassuring. I expect you to be totally ruthless with me. I want to tone here, here, and here." She pinches aspects of nonexistent fat on her belly, thigh, and backside. "And although no one promises spot reduction but plastic surgeons, I still cling to the hope that we might be able to accomplish something."

Her conviction and delivery are so direct that I realize that arguing about her imaginary cellulite would be pointless. Dangerous, even. This is a woman who brings new meaning to the cliché about stopping to smell the roses: Brooke stops to smell them, then sends them back to the florist for being too fragrant. Instead, I'm inspired to utter a rare statement of smiling, neutral politesse: "Yoga certainly is a wonderful workout."

"Well, then," Brooke says, rising. "Why don't we get started?"

I realize that she's very accomplished at this, interviewing someone in a manner so relaxed and polite that it belies the fact that she is concisely stating her expectations while confirming that you are the right one to fulfill them. It is interview masquerading as chitchat.

I follow her through the apartment's labyrinthine corridors. Brooke has a vast room—I realize that it's twice the size, in fact, of my entire apartment—devoted to exercise. Half of the room is filled with free weights and exercise machines. Satisfied, I unfurl the mat, but she stops me. "No, not here."

She opens another door, and we enter a smaller room (this

one also still larger than my apartment). She's clearly had this room decorated exclusively for yoga and meditation. There's some kind of celadon-colored wallpaper that looks incredibly expensive, finely patterned but with a sense of texture. The floor is sisal. There's a very beautiful Japanese fountain offering the constant, soft sound of a ripple of water flowing over rocks and stones. Orchids are tastefully displayed. The entire room is a Zen fantasy of soothing tones, textures, and sounds. It's incredibly calculated, but it works. I do feel calmer within seconds. (Obviously, I am on compulsive autopilot re: creating a vibe. Even though I don't see myself opening a club ever again, much less a Japanese tearoom, I can't help but make a million mental notes on her décor.)

Brooke has all her yoga equipment neatly stacked in a corner: mats, blankets, foam blocks, a strap. She turns on the Bose CD player and your basic New Age music starts to play. Brooke doesn't like to waste time, I realize. We sit and I direct her breathing, inviting her to deepen it. We center, chant three Oms together, and move through some easy stretches.

My hands-on assists in the yoga poses are purposefully gentle in the beginning, becoming stronger as we continue. Gigi has taught me how to use my hands well, yet at first I am hesitant about touching Brooke. Her body is perfectly shapely—her formfitting outfit could almost be considered revealing—and yet her inherent aloofness seems to discourage human contact. "Look, but don't even think about touching," proclaims her hyper-manicured appearance.

It's only when we get to Triangle that my hands significantly alter Brooke's energy in a pose. I stand beside her, rotating the slim barrel of her socialite ribcage upward so that her heart center yearns skyward. As I do this—and I do this very gently and with deliberate slowness so that she can feel the motion as an opening, not a correction—she lets out an audible sigh.

The sigh is not an intellectual response; the brain's understanding comes second. The sigh Brooke lets slip is purely physiological. It's simple, anatomical release like a lover's moan. This is the first moment Brooke and I have shared that hasn't felt controlled, scripted even.

Although we continue practicing, there are no more moments when I feel that Brooke releases nearly as much as she did in Triangle Pose. Perhaps, taken aback by having let go, she wills herself not to lose control like that again.

Although the mat and the other props I brought have not been needed, for Corpse Pose I have had the foresight to bring an eye pillow to place on her eyes as she rests. Before running out my door this morning, I also grabbed some rather terrific-smelling massage oil a rather steamy "bodyworker" had left behind in my pad. I put some on my hands like Gigi does, briskly rubbing the palms against each other. My hands hover inches above Brooke's face so that the warmed fragrance encourages her to breathe deeply as I perform a few simple massage strokes to her brow, neck, and shoulders. Brooke seems pleasantly surprised by this—clearly I have given her something her other teacher had not—and drifts off into Savasana.

Brooke's so composed in her Upper East Side persona that, for all I know, while resting perfectly still, she might be planning the agenda for her next committee meeting (or maybe just listing other people she can fire by midmorning). There is a moment, however, where I notice that at rest, her face does have an imperial beauty to it. A bit cold perhaps, like a profile on a coin, but nonetheless, the features are admirable.

I glance at my watch a handful of times to be certain that exactly ten minutes have passed. Leading her from Corpse Pose, I make sure my voice is at its most soothing. I realize, as I do so, that this low, whispery softness is something one only uses to awaken a lover. Brooke gently stirs and comes to sit for our final Oms together.

Opening her eyes, she smiles and thanks me. Immediately, I can tell I've passed her test. "That was lovely," she declares, gently rising.

Exiting the yoga room, I follow her back towards the sitting area of our interview.

"How do Tuesdays and Thursdays at this time work for you?" she asks me.

I'm too startled to even play coy. I have no imaginary datebook to check. I labor at The Sweatshop in the evening, and I take yoga classes during the day. I have absolutely no morning obligations whatsoever.

"Fine," I reply. Brooke opens a Chippendale desk drawer and produces a checkbook. She confirms the spelling of my last name, adding, almost as an afterthought, "Jason didn't tell me what your rate was."

I realize I do not have a rate. I haven't thought that far ahead. Somehow, my gut tells me I needn't fear; Brooke is way ahead of me when it comes to these kinds of transactions.

"I'm very comfortable paying you what I paid my last yoga instructor. Frankly, I think you're much better. It's a little more than my trainer, but …" She hands me a check. "This will be for ten lessons. That should cover us until the first week of February."

I nod, looking at the check. Brooke has written it out for $1,500. $1,500! That's $150 a lesson. It's six times what I make an hour temping—more, considering that no taxes are taken out of it. Now, I know that one $1,500 check is too small a shovel to dig myself out of my $120,000 hole. Even if I were to take the high road and sign over the full amount to Shane, that would only dust ten percent off my debt to her. I'm no lottery winner, but nonetheless, this allows me to start scraping away at the basics—shelter, food, cell phone, and martinis—that my urban survival requires.

"I have a great feeling that you're going to be quite a success as a teacher," Brooke tells me. "You're just the sort of person I feel quite comfortable recommending to my set of friends."

"That's very kind of you."

"Not at all," Brooke smiles. "It'll be my pleasure to help establish you with the right kind of clients. And, of course, I'm looking forward to getting back into shape."

I don't respond with a compliment. I sense she doesn't want or need one. And I do not want to be sent away, like the white roses, never to return in the service elevator.

The fifteen hundred feels like helium lifting my wallet's

heavy heart. I will teach Brooke, even if it means indulging her quest to remove the shadow of a micron of that hyper-resilient fat molecule that can somehow avoid liposuction (much less the human eye).

Knowing that I can travel home and give my landlord a check—albeit one he will have to hold for a few days—I'm astonished at my sudden burst of good fortune.

MOUNTAIN POSE
(TADASANA)

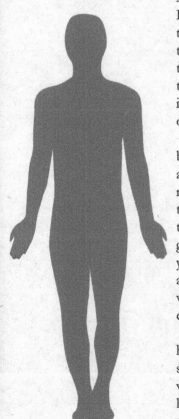

At first, just like with Corpse Pose, I thought they were kidding. What's the big deal about standing? But then one day, Gigi drew my attention to my feet. To the subtle shifting of the weight and the balance. I zeroed in on what she was saying, grooving on the intricacies of simply standing.

Big toes touch. A little space between the heels. Legs active, thighs and kneecaps lift. Shoulder blades melt down the back. Slight tuck of the tailbone. Head gently floats on the neck. Face softens. Finally, I got it. It's not just hanging out, as if you're waiting to get the bartender's attention. There's an awareness of what you're doing that makes all the difference in the world.

Mountain Pose becomes a home base where you feel grounded, secure, and able to take on the world. Even the strongest of us have moments where we need to reconnect with our reserves of inner strength, our own inner mountain.

Indeed, it's entirely how you stand—be it presiding over a board meeting or cruising a late-night lounge—that distinguishes the Alpha from the pack, the Wolves from the Sheep.

Shane practically takes a swing at me when I tell her that I think her crab cakes are a little too salty. Annoyed, she takes a bite herself. Then another, to pause and consider. "Okay. Maybe you're right."

We're still just friends at this point in my story. Shane's recently arrived in the city and through a buddy of mine has found some survival gig as a cater waiter. Ambitious as always, two weeks into the job she's tried to convince the chef to let her get into the kitchen.

"Is that what they make you wear?" I ask offhandedly, eying her catering uniform.

"No. It's completely my choice to wear an ill-fitting, gender-concealing white oxford shirt with sad black pants and flats. Soon, every hot young girl in the club scene will be copying this exact outfit."

She returns to the kitchen and I go back to channel surfing.

Ten minutes later, Shane's whipped up three more crab-cake variations, each with different seasonings. She waits expectantly as I sample them.

"This one is totally awesome. Definitely perfect."

Shane smiles as I finish off the platter. "Even though that's coming from someone who's pretty much always hungry, I'm still relieved."

"Well, I may be an omnivore, but that doesn't mean I don't have taste."

CHAPTER 4

Thanks to Brooke, for this month, at least, the rent is paid. (Okay, technically it's actually October's rent, but at least it's a start.) On second thought, given my paltry Sweatshop wages versus my massive debt, since my plastic is long maxed out, it seems far wiser to be at least reachable by phone and email and enjoy the benefits of electricity and cable, even if it means eviction. To celebrate I treat myself to dumplings from a Chinatown storefront dive (five for two dollars), check my email, and then nap until a few hours later, when Hutch calls me back.

"I'm like the greatest pimp daddy of all time," he boasts. "On Sunday you're coming with me to Honey's brunch." ("Honey" is what everyone, including Hutch, calls his mother.)

"I thought you said those things were geriatric conventions. I'd rather sleep in, thanks."

"Dude, we're onto a goldmine here. We've got to go trolling for more clients for you."

"Bonus check bounce? Is it the commission you're after?"

"I already asked Honey if she wants to take yoga with you, but she's so into her Pilates instructor, it isn't funny."

"Maybe they're banging."

"Dude, we are so totally not going there. Anyway, she said I could bring you to her Sunday shindig, and you could 'tastefully' work the room. Just like she lets all her divorced friends who need sugar daddies."

"You make me sound like an escort."

"Hell, the classy ones make great money. No joke. Listen, I gotta hop. Biz calls." And then, just as unceremoniously, he's off the line.

Until I face the 4:00 lash of The Sweatshop, the day is mine, so I take Gigi's noon class at Thank Heaven. She's brilliant as always.

Part of what I love so much—and what got me hooked on Thank Heaven—is that this style of yoga means that no two classes are alike. Yes, there's a basic sequencing from easier poses to more difficult, from warming up, to sun salutes, to standing poses, then revolved ones and so forth. But unlike my former weight routine, NOTHING is ever the same here. I've yet to see Gigi substantially repeat a class, and I've been coming almost daily now for two years.

During every class of hers I take, I try to commit to memory her sequencing of poses, but within ten minutes, I'm forced to abandon that entirely. Beyond the physical challenge, I'm too lost in the movement to analyze it midflow. It would be like graphing a Miles Davis concert rather than just letting it wash over and through you.

Slogging in at The Sweatshop at 4 p.m., while I'm still invigorated from the yoga, more than ever before, my heart isn't in it. Well, my heart was NEVER in it, not for a millisecond, but nonetheless, I realize that I am even more resentful of the sixty-odd hours I will work here to match Brooke's blessed check.

Facebook is blocked on computers here, so whenever those odd intervals occur where I'm waiting for an assignment, I surf. I google Becker compulsively. I'm not so much interested in the gossip column stuff—of course he's going to be at some premiere or gala at the Met whenever he's in town—but instead, I focus on his latest corporate exploits. I monitor his progress from afar, keen on knowing how, where, and why he's expanding his empire. (Once again, like an alcoholic touring taverns, but swearing he'll never touch another drop, I'm hooked. With over a hundred grand in debt from Failure #1, the last thing I need is to contemplate getting back on the horse that threw me. In this case, that horse should be shot.)

Sometime in my early teens, something of The Grill's greasy residue must have seeped into my blood—or maybe it's just genetic. It was never a conscious decision—I never woke up one morning and said, "I shall become a barkeep!"—but somehow the role of tavern owner and host just made sense for me. It seems I can't live without the excitement of the party vibe at its peak, that amazing "plugged in" feeling of being at the very center and source of where my community congregates. I realize that for some smarter guys, that rush can be found on the floor of the Senate or ringing the bell on Wall Street. For me, it's in the electricity and energy that are created by the right lighting, music, and crowd in the wee hours of the morning.

These dreams, however, are NOT supported by my paternal role model. Growing up, it's not like Pop gave all that much thought to my future; certainly he never thought his boy would go off to a fancy college. In fact, having failed to explain to Pop the concept of "need-blind admission," I practically got into a fistfight with him in order to get him to sign the required financial aid forms. (He did, but only because of Mom's gentle persuasion.) Only when I got to Yale did Pop even begin to "get" what it all meant.

I don't know if my randomly assigned first-year roommate Calvin Goldstein's parents—they had been grooming Calvin for the Ivies since his Scarsdale birth—took Pop aside for a Freshman Orientation field trip to set him straight on the correlation between income and higher education. Nonetheless, by sophomore year, no one was more in favor of setting me on the fast track towards a joint MBA/law degree than Pop. And other than me, probably no one is more disappointed that six years later, I'm working for the Calvin Goldsteins of the world as a temp.

My self-tutorial in Failed Banker/Failed Becker Wannabe, however, is interrupted as Diane approaches my desk. A fifty-something Staten Island matron who runs Presentations with the intensity and commitment of a Crusader of Investment Banking Spreadsheets, Diane knows how to invoke the corporate lash. Indeed, Diane is amazingly immune to my charms. Beyond accurate data input in the New Template, there's nothing she wants from me.

This past New Year's Eve, some lame multinational merger required a bunch of Excel charts reformatted to the New Template. She refused to release me (or anyone) one minute before the 4-to-midnight shift expired on December 31st. So up until 11:59 p.m. on December 31st, when I could join Hutch and posse mid-plastering, I clicked my mouse and converted shades of grey, navy, and crimson into slight variations of themselves so that a $2 billion merger (one apparently vitally contingent on color-coding) could roll forward as scheduled.

Diane offers me a smile that we both know is totally fake.

"Please make sure that the pie graphs are 3-D," is all she says as she hands me a presentation to work on. I note with chagrin that the junior banker who created it is Nathaniel Phelps, a cliché nerd (with pimples even), since I believe he harbors a targeted resentment towards me. Nathaniel—aka "Pimples"—was probably high school bully target #1 and as such, as he rises towards potentially stratospheric income levels, the world must suffer his nasal wrath.

Five minutes into charting and color-coding his presentation, Nathaniel is literally breathing down my neck, appearing out of nowhere to complain, "No—you've got to put the Earnings Ratio column in a larger font."

What I want to say is, "I did not attend your high school, Pimples, but if I had, I swear I would definitely have been the jock who said, 'Hey, leave the kid alone.'" Instead, I reply, "Sorry, Nate. No can do. That's just not allowed in The New Template." FYI, I honestly couldn't give a flying fuck whether the font sizes correspond—although if I did this of my accord, Diane would have me publicly crucified, no doubt complaining that I wasn't bleeding in the right shade of New Template Crimson. Honestly, it's just hard to resist when someone's chain is just so easily jerkable.

Before I know it, Pimples has brought over Diane to plead his case. The two of them hover over my desk, negotiating whether it might be enough just to bold the column (that's allowed) or to select another New-Template-approved color (that's debatable). Finally, sensing perhaps that Pimples will stop at nothing save the Supreme Court or the CEO to get his way, she authorizes me to bump up the font two points. Such is life at The Sweatshop.

I honestly like Hutch's parents. Every time I inquire after Hutch's father, I learn he's on a rafting trip in the Amazon or at the base camp of Everest. From his example, it seems there's very little to do at the top other than attend a few board meetings a year and appreciate the miracle of compound interest.

Hutch's mother, Honey, could star in an Emily Post instructional video for good manners and breeding, but an undercurrent of wry amusement runs beneath her every smooth move. You can see the wicked gleam in her eye—one that Hutch inherited and has made the cornerstone of his rakish charm. Honey's not bad looking for a mom either, a cozy, fifty-something bottle blonde with a bourbon-soaked laugh. And, for an Über-WASP affair, the food is reasonable.

I'm standing at the bar, waiting for the uniformed bartender to refresh my vodka martini, when a Traffic-Stopping brunette crosses my path.

"Jesus," I hear a husky bass voice with an upscale accent mutter to me. I turn and see this mountain of a man—sixties, craggily featured, elegantly dressed—scoping out Traffic Stopper. We acknowledge each other.

There's a momentary crisis at the bar. They're out of champagne, but the bartender protests that he can't leave his station to secure replacements.

"Allow me," says the Mountain. "I think I can manage to fill in for a few moments." The grateful bartender scoots off to the kitchen to replenish the bubbly. The Mountain deftly mixes two martinis with an almost balletic swiftness and elegance, shaking and serving them with such aplomb as to make them a breezy sacrament. I take my martini from the Mountain as he raises his glass. Already, he's my hero.

"Cheers," he offers. "Here's to the lady."

"Who is she?" I inquire.

"Nicky Tremaine. Third wife of a colleague."

A man of about a hundred and twenty helps Traffic Stopper with a fur coat. She really is stunning, wearing some kind of supremely upscale, amazingly clingy dress that seems just about to deconstruct. I can't help but stare at the two of them. She exudes life-transforming sexuality; he radiates the need for life support.

"Tremaine really must be doing well to afford that."

I don't know what to say. In some ways, we are acknowledging the obvious, but spelling out the relationship seems like I might be transgressing on Hutch's assurances of my "tasteful" behavior.

"Andrew," says the Mountain, as he extends his hand. "Andrew Harding." I introduce myself back. Andrew's impressive, without being stuffy or arrogant. He wears his man-of-the-world confidence in a way that includes you, rather than intimidates. And he makes a fantastic martini. The guy has got game to spare.

Andrew refreshes the white wine spritzer of a grandmotherly woman of seventy in a bright pink Chanel suit, disguising, I fancy, his manly distaste for diluting something as viable as alcohol. Then he resumes conversation with me, dismissing the heartfelt thanks of the bartender returning to his post.

Andrew is—like many in his circuit, I'm learning—quite adept at polite conversation that gets your stats down quickly. He deftly elicits that my connection to the hostess is via college roommate Hutch, and if he reads Page Six on the sly, at least, unlike Monique, he doesn't snort.

I inquire about him, and he sidesteps the question, as if I'll come to my senses in a moment and recognize him. He smiles and says he's involved with a handful of companies. (In other words, I feel like I've asked Lady Gaga at a cocktail party if she has something to do with entertainment.) I leave well enough alone, especially when the rather cute catering waitress offering us a plate of shrimp catches his ever-roving eye. (FYI, I tend to avoid yuppie house parties like the plague, as I live in terror that some urbanite less on my side than Hutch will hire Shane's fledging catering operation.) Without exerting any visible effort, Andrew lures the cute little caterer toward him with the strength of his charisma. It's almost mystical, like Dracula captivating a spellbound virgin, the way this very cute, early twenties cater-chick is transfixed by Andrew.

Andrew's appeal runs way beyond looks and even beyond his wealth. He radiates a striking confidence, perhaps stemming from worldly assets, but manifesting as personal charisma. He's a Matterhorn of a man, a cuter Kissinger, a corporate Nicholson. I, of the infinitely lower income bracket, sadly have no such wealth or power to trade upon.

When I look into the mirror, I see a face that, if not destined for the cover of GQ, is at least formed along a mode that most people would label traditionally handsome. Mind you, I am not particularly vain about my appearance. I know that I am lucky and that while super-athletic yoga keeps me in fine shape, I have good genes to start with. Hutch even has a running joke about it. He suggests that my universal response for any praise or criticism should be: "My father was a Marine."

Why am I always on time (no matter the hangover)? My father was a Marine. Why am I so commitment-phobic (i.e., such an asshole)? My father was a Marine. Why do I have such a workout ethic (i.e., obsession) about being strong and fit and having pumped biceps? My father was a Marine. Why can Andrew bond with me about being a virile man of the world? One guess: My father was a Marine. Take that Marine gene pool, refine it through four years of Yale, and add a half-dozen years of player training on the field and you've got ... well, the compelling disaster that is me.

Andrew's inquiries as to the waitress, namely Aspiring Allison, and her fledgling (make that nonexistent) acting career are cut short by the arrival of a stunning blonde. "Hello, darling," Andrew intones. "Shrimp puff?"

The blonde (hovering just a few years over my own late

twenties) declines politely, displaying no reaction other than the pure pleasure of returning to Andrew's side. He kisses her with the perfect display of public passion. Andrew introduces me to his "lovely bride," and Danielle smiles sweetly and extends her hand. I barely notice that Aspiring Allison has taken her cue and vanished.

Danielle has the graceful, gravity-free glide of the former ballerina I later learn she was, with the long mane of hair and freshly scrubbed quality of the horsey set. I do not read Town & Country, but if she has not graced the cover, I'm sure the editors are pursuing her ardently. While Andrew is a supernova of charisma compared to the geriatric Tremaine, I can barely suppress the desire to compliment him slyly with, "You must be doing well, Andy, Old Boy, to afford this amazingly hot young thing."

Suddenly, I have a new life goal, besides being Becker. I also want to be Andrew: confident, charismatic, worldly, and while hovering in his baronial sixties, still able to have a woman as hot as Danielle craving him (not to mention sampling little canapés like Aspiring Allison on the side). Somehow, the idea of settling down—albeit in my sixties—doesn't seem that bad. Basically, Andrew's another Becker, triumphing in the world of finance rather than nightlife and luxury, offering a lusty Model of Maturity I can actually appreciate, even envy.

Andrew shares my scanty biographical details with Danielle, then reveals for the first time that he's been shopping for a yoga teacher, no doubt as part of some conjugal New Year's resolution. (I'm right: a breezy but probative interview technique thrives among the upper social stratum) Danielle, ever the former dancer, adores yoga and sparkles at the notion that I start teaching Andrew. As a capper, when Andrew mentions Brooke Merrington's name, she practically genuflects.

Almost immediately, it's settled. We make an appointment, I get their address, and they're off to another function. The party is winding down, so I seek out Hutch and share my good news about scoring a new client.

Allison returns with a tray of mini-quesadillas, deeply

engrossing Hutch with her search for a representative monologue. When Hutch leans one arm against the wall, cozily framing them close together, I merely nod to him and he to me, as I take off toward home.

Leaving the party, I check my cell for messages. Brooke has called twice (as always, she seems vaguely irritated that I'm not waiting by the phone for her). On the phone, she's her usual polite, direct self. "I've spoken to my sister, Phoebe, and she'd like to start taking yoga with you. Thursday morning at 7:30 would be good for her." She doesn't ask, mind you, if I'm available, but when I call back, I tell her that I am and that I'm grateful.

"I also dropped by Epitome today," she tells me. "The new spa on Madison."

"Uh huh," I reply, wondering if they offer a deluxe treatment for invisible fat cells. I can see it: Invisible Fat Removal by highly trained laser/sonar/herbal aestheticians at $350 an hour. Destroy the fat you cannot see—the most dangerous kind—before it blossoms into visibility.

"I've known the owner, Marguerite, for years," Brooke says, "and I strongly suggested they hire you for some classes. She'd like you to call her and arrange a meeting."

I stroll down Park Avenue, reflecting on my fate. Somehow, in less than three days, I have gone from being one step shy of becoming a Homeless Hipster to (with Phoebe's presumably commensurate check tomorrow) suddenly having three clients, each paying $300 a week for yoga. Even without counting potential income from Epitome, I realize that this is a far cry from financial security, but I feel quite prosperous. This is only three clients, and only mornings, but if it proves sustainable, then I am miraculously halfway to a six-figure income. After six months of self-pity (which pays surprisingly poorly), the perfect solution has fallen into my lap.

Do other people know about this yoga-teaching goldmine, I wonder? I almost feel I must be quiet about it; otherwise, New

York will suddenly be flooded with waiters and temps bursting into yoga schools so they can get these cushy Park Avenue gigs.

Of course, I realize that, for once in my life, I have been lucky. I have been hired because I have a well-connected friend in Hutch and, in Andrew's case, bolstered by my Marine-scioned mien. But I also know that I can do this: I can teach well. Brooke's lesson showed me that.

Yes, I am truly a yoga teacher. I am a guru, albeit one in a muscle tee, making—for me—big bucks on Park Avenue.

Walking along, out of nowhere, into my head comes the only advice my father ever gave me, taken from a World War II Nat King Cole song: "Straighten up and fly right." For once, maybe I am.

HANDSTAND
(ADHO MUKA VRIKSASANA)

I learned early on that most yoga poses are about showing off.

You find something amazing you can do, and suddenly, Shazam—you're a guru, ready for your groupies. Handstand's great for that. (Although it does go to show you just how far the original Yoga Dudes were willing to go in their quest for enlightenment. They wanted to change their perspective on life so much that they experimented with doing that quite literally, flipping themselves upside down for spiritual kicks.)

Practice handstand a few inches from the wall, coming from up downward dog. One leg lifts, and the other follows. Arms have to stay straight, and shoulder blades should gather together on the back. In time, you can flirt more and more with moving away from the wall and trying to balance on your own. Every second you hold the pose is challenging.

In the end, who needs enlightenment when a good head rush will do?

"You are such an idiot!" is what I hear as I come crashing down and splash Shane.

I've persuaded her to snap my picture with her camera phone as I attempt to nail a handstand on the beach at Montauk. Without a nice yoga studio floor, it's a lot harder than I thought. The wet sand has a lot of give to it, plus I've got to land the pose before too big a wave comes crashing through. The only advantage is that when I tumble down, the ocean is a bit more forgiving than a hardwood floor—and infinitely more than Shane getting splashed!

"Why are we doing this again?" Shane asks, but she's laughing.

"Facebook. And because I can!"

Somehow, the elements of earth, water, and air cooperate, and I find my balance. Shane gets the shot.

"Wait, I've got an idea!" she shouts. "Just hold it!"

"Easier said than done!" I yell. But somehow I'm steady.

Grabbing the lobster-red suburban dad who's been watching us, she steps beside me for him to get our picture. She puts one arm around my feet, pretending to lean on them but actually assisting my balance. Then a decent wave comes crashing through and I get a mouthful of salt water.

But Lobster Dad got the shot. It's the perfect photo. Me upside down and smiling. Shane goofy and beautiful. The wave about to hit. For the rest of the summer, both of us use it as our Facebook profile photo.

A perfect moment of balance before everything comes crashing down.

CHAPTER 5

It's a quarter to midnight and again, I can't sleep. I see my cell phone flashing, as I've turned the volume down so as not to be distracted by Hutch's latest cavorting call. The message, however, is from luscious Monique, of New Year's Eve fame.

She's called me at 11:10 p.m., a little late to initiate a conversation with someone you barely know. From that alone—and from the purring tone in her voice, and by the fact that we have nothing to say to each other—it's obvious what she wants. I hesitate for only a moment. I do have Brooke at 7:30 a.m. But that's a whole 7 hours and 20 minutes away.

What the hell, I justify, knowing full well that this is a booty call, a hit and run, pure and simple. She picks up, her caller ID clearly reading my name. "Sorry, is it too late?" I ask.

"Not tonight," she replies, an inviting amusement to her voice.

Truthfully, in general I don't have that many booty calls. In fact, I've never found that perfect woman who's willing to show up on my doorstep, have sex, and leave. As Hutch points out, they have a technical term for them: escorts. And sadly, even with my recent cash-positive reinvention as guru to the rich and famous, until the rent's paid up, I think it prudent not to be dabbling in hookers.

Fortunately, I learn that Monique lives in the West Village, a mere seven-minute cab ride away. Our phone flirtation (more like an illicit negotiation) is intense and to the point. Just after midnight, she appears at my door. I half expect her to be wearing a fur coat with nothing underneath. It doesn't matter because barely one minute after she knocks on my door, we're immediately and intensely making out while tossing off items of clothing.

Total time between placing the order and delivery of naked female sex object: sixteen minutes. Even Domino's can't beat this kind of service.

It's just before 2 a.m. when we're both finished. Good, I think, knowing that without excess alcohol in my system, I'm reasonably functional on five hours sleep and a triple espresso (Thank God Starbucks opens at 6:30.).

My only fear is that I'm going to have to spend more time talking or cuddling or in some way managing Monique. I can't really ask her to leave, although right now, I'm more than ready to just roll over and doze off. So imagine my delight when she kisses me sweetly, gets out of bed, and starts dressing.

"You can stay," I offer, demonstrating what I feel is enormous gallantry given that I'm beyond thrilled she's leaving.

"No offense, but I sleep much better in my own bed. And I've got to get up practically at dawn tomorrow."

"Me, too," I reply, and for once, this is actually true.

She moves with sexy efficiency, sliding into her scattered clothes and slipping on her shoes. "Good. I didn't think you'd want cuddling or anything like that. You're not the type," she tells me. I wince politely, as though wounded to be found out.

"I thoroughly enjoyed myself," she says, putting on her coat. "And I mean that." She leans in to kiss me goodnight.

"I know you did," I reply confidently. "And so did I," I second, kissing her again.

"So maybe again sometime …" she replies, hesitating only briefly.

I register the pause. "Except?"

"Don't take this wrong, but I'm only interested in you sexually. Definitely not as a boyfriend. In fact, I really don't want any kind of emotional involvement." I don't know exactly how to respond, although frankly, since this is a slightly watered-down version of exactly what I always say to my conquests, you'd think I'd be less perplexed.

"Meaning … You want a fuck buddy?"

Monique laughs. "I've never been crazy about that term, but frankly, more or less, yes."

"I see," I reply, wondering if this could possibly be true (And if this is actually something I really want.).

"I've already got tremendous friends and a not-too-insane family. My sisters are great. My career is exploding. I'm traveling all the time and I'm about to move to the next level with Becker. My plate is full with great stuff; I just don't have time for any boyfriend shit." She pauses for effect. "Although I wouldn't mind some uncomplicated hot sex on the side."

I consider for a moment. "Monique, are you proposing to me?"

This elicits a smirk from her. Putting on her earmuffs and gloves, she leans in for a final kiss, her gingery perfume mixed with the scent of our lovemaking (Okay, make that screwing.). It completely envelops me.

She's totally captivating as she whispers, "Do you take this woman, not to have, but to screw with passion and gusto, so long as you both don't get bored?"

I kiss her back, and God help me, I reply, "I do."

"By the authority vested in me … by, I suppose, me—a confirmed, career-consumed total narcissist—I now pronounce us 'Fuck Buddies.'"

I smile back at her but treading lightly, decide to ask, "What exactly does this mean to you?"

She tosses off the question with a ready answer. "It means that while it's still hot between us, we can call each other for sex whenever it's convenient. We dispense with all the social foreplay involved in dating—I can buy my own dinner and flowers, thank you very much. I'm sure, by the way, that soon enough you'll be back on your feet with some new nightlife venture that will take up all your time."

"That's pretty unlikely."

"Oh please—it's only a matter of time. You'll ride the right wave when it comes in. Say—have you seen The Genevieve since it reopened?"

"I liked the whole decor thing they did with the waves, but I wasn't crazy about the tiles in the bathroom. Plus I thought the menu was too cute, too girly. They're never going to attract bankers who want to shag models, and at that price point, that's clearly their target."

"I rest my case. You're one of those guys who just has this stuff in your blood. Anyway, while it's fun, I wouldn't mind dropping by here occasionally and screwing your brains out."

"Is that all?" I ask, both stunned and elated.

"Yes, there's one thing, and perhaps it's the most important: we have sex, but we sleep in separate beds."

Smiling, without further adieu, she's out the door.

And I have to admit, I'm surprisingly conflicted. On the one hand, I feel like I just won the sex lottery: beautiful, intelligent Monique wants to have a no-strings-attached situation with yours truly. It's like the answer to every Player's Prayers.

And yet … well, it's not like I'm consumed with guilt, it's that I'm feeling a little … incomplete. I'm not sure what more I want, except there's this lingering, absent feeling of "And Now What?" that I can seem to shake.

And so, ten minutes later, I break my three week resolution and log on to Facebook (no major Shane update to report other than two unremarkable tagged photos of her at a Super Bowl party thrown by someone named Josh)—and then I'm under the covers and rapidly and (relatively) blissfully sound asleep, alone in my bed.

I take Calypso's afternoon class and it's awesome. Her dancer background and flowing music makes even a military-spawned dude like me feel he can move gracefully. I plant my mat in the back row, asking her if she minds if I sneak out right before Corpse Pose as I have a teaching interview. Calypso says, "Of course not," and hugs me twice for luck, offering an elegant and inspired ninety minutes of bliss.

Once I arrive, I find that, quite frankly, I don't blend in with the rarified spa atmosphere of Epitome at all. The preternatural calm, the sense of oasis within New York City, despite all the references to sea and sand, ironically feels particularly artificial. Especially after the Flower Child brightness of Thank Heaven, it's all too bland for me, a symphony of tasteful neutrality, of earth tones gone stale. I half listen as the desk staff upsells moisturizers as though they were miracle cures. Maybe it's all just too damn girly; in more ways than one, I am not the demographic and I am not at home here.

I'm offered herbal tea while I wait, with three varieties (Stimulating, Calming, and Neutralizing) to choose from. I opt out, wishing I'd had the foresight to have downed a double tall latte before landing in decaffeinated Spa Land.

Marguerite emerges, her face and form a glowing, perfect advertisement for Epitome. "I'm sorry I'm late. I was just observing one of our Centrifugal Force classes."

"Centrifugal Force?"

"It's our brand of core strengthening with some stretching, aerobics, Pilates, and a few yoga moves. My husband, Pete, and I invented it."

"Okay. Sounds interesting."

"Take a class sometime. It's free for teachers here. Okay, then, did you bring two forms of ID like I asked?" she smiles. I nod. "Great," she replies. "All you have to do is fill out some tax forms then watch our sexual harassment video, and we're set. Oh, unless you want direct deposit. Then I'll need a voided check."

"That's all fine. I just wasn't sure if you wanted me to teach a practice class or something first."

She shakes her head and smiles as though the idea of actually having me teach something—or having more than one reference or, frankly, any actual experience—is outlandish overkill. "Brooke Merrington's endorsement means the world to us. I'll do a little juggling, and we'll get you started with a class next week. You'll have a mix of students, but everyone wants a challenging workout."

"That's fine with me. I trained at Thank Heaven, and it was incredibly intense."

Marguerite smiles, and then, as though confiding in rather than hiring me says, "That's terrific. I've heard great things about their classes, but … we've found our clients don't really want chanting or anything like that. In fact, I'd go easy on all that spirituality stuff."

God knows I'm hardly pious, and definitely quite far from a monk, but even a guy like me's gotta have a little spirituality with his yoga. It's like a martini without the olive. (Okay, I know I reference liquor and ladies all the time, but I'm sure in conversation the Pope probably brings up Jesus a lot, too.)

"I mean, you can say some positive things, if you want," Marguerite continues. "Just generally life-affirming stuff, but I'd keep anything too vibey or Hindu or Buddhist out of it. Unless it's ayurvedic—that stuff goes over pretty well, thanks to Aveda. Oh, and when the Dalai Lama's in town, people like to hear about that, too—but not too much."

This isn't the conversation that I'd been expecting, somehow. And yet, having taught exactly one person, it's not like I'm attached to my nonexistent methodology. I suppose teaching yoga-lite—yoga without all the annoying little things such as the fact that it's fundamentally a spiritual practice and a philosophy, and not a workout—will be doable.

"Just keep it physically challenging, particularly on the fast-moving aerobic side so they can feel they're burning calories, and I'm sure you'll be a huge hit. Our base fee is $75 a class, but after ten students, we add a $3 commission by the head." (I note that my starting salary here is three times my Sweatshop wages.)

Marguerite rises and leads me to an empty, neutral room (neutral wood floors, neutral beige walls, neutral mats, neutral baskets). It seems Epitome's decorator felt that the appearance of an actual color might cause guests to suffer extensive visual and emotional trauma. Behind the tastefully neutral velvet curtain, there's a complicated stereo system with a monitor on top.

"Why don't you just watch the video now?" Marguerite offers. "It's about forty minutes, and the next class isn't until 5:15."

She sets it up and leaves the room. In three minutes, I'm bored out of my skull watching the bad acting and writing, and half wondering if Aspiring Allison ever found the right monologue so she could launch her career in just such industrial videos.

As glaring sexual harassment scenarios play out before me, I decide it's enough that I coexist half listening in the same space with the video. That seems a worthy compromise. So I start to practice my handstand, first up against the wall, then moving my legs away from it. Today feels like a good balancing day—I'm in the groove, as it were—and so I begin practicing in the middle of the room, managing to hold the handstand for several breaths. Suddenly, there's some applause.

Two very hot thirty-something women wearing white terrycloth overstuffed robes and towels wrapped around their heads smile at me. They're clearly en route between spa services, moving to and from massages and manicures or what have you.

"That was impressive," one of them—the one wearing a huge, jeweled pendant at her cleavage—says.

"Thanks," I reply. Diamond Cleavage smiles.

"You've done this before," her friend—no necklace but Serious Earrings and even more Serious Breasts—chimes in. Apparently these ladies can't leave their jewelry at home for fear of running into a competitive socialite, and they can't very well leave it in a locker, either. They're like Olympic torchbearers for Money; they must keep the Flame of Wealth alive.

"I'm going to start teaching yoga here," I volunteer.

"Wonderful," Diamond Cleavage replies. "I love Centrifugal Force, but I've been wanting to try their yoga workouts."

"I've been doing yoga for six months and love it," Serious Cleavage chimes in. "Steven—that's my husband—says it's done wonders for my ass."

"My ass is fine," Diamond Cleavage remarks. "I'm looking for something to tighten up my thighs. Can yoga do that?"

I'm a bit startled. This is not the kind of conversation I'm used to hearing at a yoga center. People want the physical benefits, yes, but I've yet to hear someone at the front desk of Thank Heaven sell a class with an "It'll be great for your ass!" endorsement.

A heavily accented attendant appears and mercifully whisks Diamond Cleavage off, no doubt to some thigh-tightening treatment. Serious Cleavage lingers.

"So what kind of yoga will you be teaching?" Serious Cleavage asks. "I want something that'll burn up a lot of calories."

"I'll try to make it challenging."

Serious Cleavage moves in even closer. "Good. I like a bit of a challenge with a man." I comically wince at the cheesy dialogue that passes for repartee here. And I notice she's wearing a wedding band (along with a massive diamond engagement ring). She notices me noticing but ignores it. I like confident women, and even though she's really hot in a late thirties, rich-chick way, this whole thing isn't turning me on. Maybe it's the incongruous bathrobe or the sexual harassment video still playing in the background. Or, that she's sipping a cup of herbal tea or that I don't have a martini. Mostly, it's that as a wolf, I like to initiate the chase myself. I don't know whether to laugh or fast-forward to reference an appropriate chapter on the sexual harassment DVD. Fortunately, just then, another heavily accented aesthetician calls her name. I note that all the cosmetic workers are foreign here; Americans, it seems, must have no flair for the Science of Beauty. Given the mushy accent, I can't tell what Serious Cleavage's name is, and she doesn't bother to introduce herself formally. "Well, then. I'm sure I'll see you in class," she says. "I'm looking forward to working up a sweat with you."

I turn as she exits, and then Serious Cleavage totally surprises me by grabbing my ass for a second. It's a pretty ballsy move, especially for a married lady in a spa robe, but I suppose that's what makes it safe. Am I, I wonder, just another Epitome spa service? Papaya facials, laser lipo, and instructor gropes?

I return to the video's equally obvious, yet disapproving, take on pickup scenarios. Just as the credits are rolling, Marguerite resurfaces, opening the neutral wooden door to the room and letting in the Centrifugal Force crowd.

At Thank Heaven, I really do restrain myself and maintain my best behavior. There's something in its yoga roots that allows me to stay, more or less, a little high-minded. Even if I'm not contemplating joining an ashram or become a vegan, at least I'm able to restrain my basest impulses.

At Epitome, however, the vibe is quite different. This place is designed for the consummate upscale consumer in us all. Somehow the emphasis on ass-perfecting, sheep-embryo moisturizers, and instructor gropes, leads me to indulge in moments of outright checking out the upscale hotties that march into the room. And I notice several very cute ladies checking me out in return.

I stop myself. This is now a place of employment for me. If I want to maintain my miscast position as a Yoga Shepherd, this wolf cannot snack on his charges. Hutch and I have all of New York City in which to roam and satisfy our appetites; I cannot allow my hungers and my habits to ruin things for me here. I'm thankful that Centrifugal Force is about to begin.

"Welcome to Epitome," Marguerite says, as she shakes my hand after escorting me to the elevator. "I think you'll be very happy here."

"Me, too," I reply as the elevator doors open. Once inside, however, I think it wise to recall the mantra my guru Hutch gave me in a sacred moment on the first day of the new year. "Don't fuck this up … Don't fuck this up … Don't fuck this up!"

For now, the chant sends me safely home.

GODDESS POSE
(SUPTA BADDHA KONASANA)

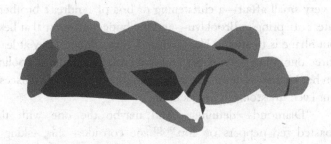

A soothing, restorative pose that opens the hips, groin, chest, and heart … and God, how I hate it.

You just lie on your back. Then draw the soles of your feet together, knees diamonding out to the sides. I remember to smooth my lower back down, even gently butterflying my knees a few times. But honestly, I still hate it.

Somehow women especially love this pose—hence the nickname. Indeed, for many women, this pose is actually an effortless, soothing favorite and a way, perhaps, to encounter a connection to their simultaneous combination of softness and strength, to the goddess within. (Kali, the fiercest goddess, who wears a necklace of human skulls, is often said to be simultaneously the most benevolent and the most vulnerable.)

As for this pose's goddess energy, if my hips do feel more open afterward, for me, this kind of vulnerability feels more like, well, pain.

"Equally excellent," I honestly reply, as I taste a fourth variation of a mushroom polenta hors d'oeuvre Shane's perfecting.

"But which is your favorite? And do you think I should go with the square cut or the diamond shape?"

I have been happily drafted into the role of food taster, although I'm beginning to wonder how many extra workouts I'm going to have to put in to balance out Shane's creativity and perfectionism. Andrea has gotten Shane her first catering gig and, fully in character, Shane has swung into action full force. It's for a very small affair—a christening or bris of Andrea's brother's latest offspring in Brooklyn—and the budget is minimal at best, but Shane is treating it like a White House dinner. I spy at least three dumpling possibilities and five crostini variations cooling on her kitchen counter. I'm all for passionate and sensual excess, but even my stomach has its limits.

"Diamonds, definitely. And maybe the one with the roasted red peppers on top." Shane considers this, taking a second bite herself. As with her crab cakes, she's always striving for perfection.

"Relax, Chef," I say, cleansing my palette with a sip of sauvignon blanc. "Everything is absolutely killer. You are a culinary goddess. They are going to be blown away."

Shane smiles and seems to genuinely relax a bit. The oven timer rings.

"Let's hope," she says, removing two trays of mini cheesecakes from the oven. "I just hope you've saved room for dessert."

CHAPTER 6

Phoebe lives merely five blocks from her sister, but everything about the apartment is more modest, more human scaled. Although I am once again let in by a servant, Phoebe's is Bernice, a Jamaican woman of about fifty with a warm smile and sweet eyes who wears street clothes as she goes about her housekeeping chores.

When Phoebe enters, I am surprised. Unconsciously, I had been expecting a Brooke-clone, and while Phoebe is also delicate, they bear little resemblance to each other, whatever strands of DNA they might share. Whereas Brooke seems like polished stainless steel (sorry, make that platinum), Phoebe is pearly, soft, and vulnerable, smelling of tea roses, just like the first girl I made out with in junior high. She smiles, tilting her face upward slightly. She wears a little makeup and a touch of lipstick even though it's early morning. It's endearing somehow, and totally unnecessary. Her skin is perfect, with her thick black hair tied back in a ponytail. Unlike Brooke, Phoebe seems actually waiting for me to take the lead.

"Where would you like us to work together?" I ask.

I realize as I travel through Phoebe's apartment, that although it's similar in size to her sister's, it's designed not to intimidate, but to welcome. It's upscale but slightly overstuffed and cozy. Phoebe leads me into an empty corner room, sun-drenched with light from windows in front and on the side. She's done little to the room—there are only a few pieces of furniture on the hardwood floors—but it has a simple, serene feel that I like. She sits down on her mat and I face her.

"Have you done any yoga?" I ask her.

"Yes," she tells me. "On and off for several years, but now it's time I got serious about it. Brooke thought you were a wonderful teacher, so I was excited to meet you. I really want to improve my practice."

"That's great," I say, beaming back a smile, one I hope is not too inappropriately broad. "Let's begin."

We start to move through Sun Salutations together, and I'm impressed with her practice. She's an ideal student: She knows many of the poses, but her form is often slightly askew. Her gracefulness is lovely—she moves very fluidly and with ease—but her muscular strength could be increased. I find myself making mental notes about future practices with her and poses I want to try. Once again, the teaching possibilities excite me.

And at the same time, I'm increasingly drawn to her physically. When I take class, I work against being distracted by feminine curves. In fact, half the time at Thank Heaven, I practice with my eyes closed, tuning into my breath, bones, and muscles and away from the distracting hotties. But now, I cannot focus my attention away from Phoebe. In fact, my job requires steadily observing and touching her.

When I place my hands to frame the sides of her torso in Triangle Pose, as I did with Brooke, I realize that my fingertips are perilously close to her breasts. I am appropriate, yes, in my touching, but I am also a half inch away from caressing her as a lover would.

My hands linger for a beat, and then I retreat, allowing her to move back into Warrior II. For better or worse, I know that in another minute, we will be doing Triangle on the other side, and for five breaths, I will again have my fingers so close to roaming where they would so willingly travel.

Despite myself, my nose is saturated with her tea-rose innocence, and my hands are eager to turn rogue. I am one step away from actually moving my fingers toward lightly cupping her breasts, a step that—if I lingered for more than a breath—would clearly be an advance and not an assist, or an accident. (You can't put a plate of lamb chops in front of a wolf and not expect him to nibble.)

Damn it, but I'm suddenly aware of how remarkably conflicted I've become in the last half hour. Part of my brain—the part I usually listen to—just wants to give in and make a move on Phoebe in the most obvious and hedonistic way. And yet there's that other part of me—some combination of common decency, common sense, a touch of residual Catholic guilt, all combined with Hutch's "don't fuck this up" warning—that hovers over me like Mother Marie Arthur during sixth grade catechism classes, reiterating that this is my student AND this is my new career.

Fortunately, before I get the chance to see if I'll listen to the angel or the devil perched on either shoulder, in walks a barrel-chested, squat man in his sixties, loudly clearing the phlegm in his throat.

"Phoebe told me not to eat anything first, but I was starving," he says. He licks his lips and brushes away crumbs and powdered sugar from his mouth, clearly having polished off a Krispy Kreme or three outside the door.

"That's all right, honey." The lovely Phoebe smiles beatifically at this strange, omnivorous beast who's intruded on our session. This vinyl-scratching, needle-lifting interruption of our flow leaves me startled, especially when, astonishingly, Phoebe says, "Let me introduce my husband, Phil."

Phil pumps my hand heartily—"Nice grip." I suppose he thinks that teaching yoga would make me limp-wristed. I can't help myself and automatically reply, "Thanks. My dad was a Marine." Somehow the semi-non sequitur makes sense to Phil, reassuring him that I didn't arrive here on a carpet of lotus petals.

Phil takes a farewell bite of his Krispy Kreme, wincing slightly, and draws his hand to his lower back.

Phoebe asks, "Phil, is your back bothering you again?"

"Same old shit, honey. What ya gonna do? Part of growing old."

With Phoebe in her late thirties, at most early forties (every million in net worth seems to be able to subtract a few years, it seems), and Phil in his late sixties, they are easily more than twenty, perhaps closer to thirty, years apart in age. And that's not the only difference. Phoebe is luminous, fit, and effortlessly upscale. Annoying self-help reference aside, she is from Venus, whereas Phil … Phil, I learn soon enough, is from Newark. It's no doubt my attraction to Phoebe that makes me player-hate Phil, but I can't help but see him as heavy-handed Darwinian proof that we did indeed descend from the apes.

"Okay, then, let's have at it!" Phil says. He smacks his hands together as though he were about to carve a turkey. Unfortunately, beyond my bewilderment that somehow the lovely Phoebe has anything to do with this squat bullfrog, I have no idea how to teach them together.

For one thing, Phoebe and I have already been working for forty minutes. Phoebe is completely warmed up, whereas Phil probably hasn't been warm from exercise in thirty years. For another, not only do they have such obviously different bodies, but Phil plainly has never done any yoga.

Suddenly, Phil's tracksuit pocket begins to buzz, and he whips out his cell phone. After three seconds, he covers the receiver, mouthing, "Gotta take this. Next time." He exits the room.

Phoebe smiles at me, and, by way of explanation, she says, "I really want Phil to try yoga. He's just so tense with business. It's not good for a man his age. I'd like him to join us when he's in town, if that's all right. He's in Detroit for half the week with his business."

I ask what he does for a living.

"Phil is Joan Crawford's nightmare."

"Excuse me?" Phoebe smiles. Clearly this is a question she's asked often and thus has a standard, witty reply at the ready.

"He's the country's largest manufacturer of wire hangers."

She reads my confused look.

"I'm sorry. My decorator came up with that one. It's a reference to Mommy Dearest. You know, with Faye Dunaway. The whole 'no wire hangers' obsession Joan Crawford had."

I still don't get it, exactly, but I do get her bigger point: this is a gay yardstick, and Phoebe is taking my measurement, as it were.

"Anyway, my decorator and his staff always bring it up. But I realize that's not your ... world."

And as metrosexual as I may be, it's just not. I realize, just as I'm trying to get a read on her, Phoebe's confirming my straightness. (Incidentally, more than anything else, over time I've found that a general cluelessness is the most convincing proof of my heterosexuality.)

We complete the rest of the lesson without incident or overture. After the last twist, Phoebe asks if I mind if she takes Goddess Pose. Her feet come together and her knees diamond to the side with a sense of real grace, confirming again how open her hips are. In this restorative pose, she's even more vulnerable.

I lightly slip blankets under each of her thighs to prevent the pose from becoming too much of a strain. I gently move my fingers across her brow to smooth away nonexistent frown lines. I lean in to place the eye pillow above her eyes. God help me but I find her physical and emotional openness utterly irresistible. I resist all temptation completely, however—not because I am ethical, but only because I am very aware that her husband lurks in some other corner of the apartment. Frankly, I wouldn't put it past Phil to barge back in now, interrupting the final rest, wondering if he can cram in five minutes of yoga (McYoga, as it were, no doubt while munching on an Egg McMuffin) before a factory inspection.

He does not appear, however, until after the ten minutes of rest are complete and Phoebe and I have Om-ed together. It seems that he's been waiting respectfully outside the door, peeking his head in only when normal conversation has resumed.

"I have to head to Detroit tonight, babe," he tells Phoebe. "I'll be back tomorrow. Maybe Wednesday at the latest." They quickly discuss travel and appointment logistics as Phil writes me a check from their joint account. He hands it to me and pumps my hand again.

"I don't know about this yoga stuff, son—I used to play a lot of ball growing up—but Phoebe swears by it. We'll give it a shot next time."

I smile and thank them. Phoebe walks me to the door.

"It's so great to be able to share the practice with someone who understands," she confides. "Phil is wonderful, but he just doesn't connect on … this level. It's so delightful to be able to have this kind of exchange, this kind of sharing, with someone who's so spiritually open and sensitive like yourself."

"Thank you" is what I say. If she only knew, is what I think. I was this close to feeling her up, and somehow she thinks I'm a swami. I'm simultaneously the Jekyll and Hyde of desire, and yet Phoebe can only see my most chaste, alleged guru self and not my inner, ever-ravenous, lusty wolf.

"Anyway," she stops, embarrassed. "Listen to me prattle on. I'm sure you have other appointments." She has the complete yoga glow now, her hair slightly mussed and her face relaxed and even softer, sweeter than when I entered. (In all candor, it's similar to the "Just Fucked" look—tousled but blissful—that's nearly impossible to resist.)

As the oaken doors shut, out of the power of Phoebe's sight and scent, I once again recall Hutch's prophetic warning, one I've been trying to tattoo to the center of my forehead since, well, yesterday: "Don't fuck this up."

For me, "don't fuck this up!" has a thousand times more resonance than any chant to Shiva, Ganesh, or any other multi-armed deity.

"Don't fuck this up … don't fuck this up … don't fuck this up," I continue softly intoning, nodding politely past the doorman's wary eye at my prayerful mutterings.

Why am I here at Happy Ending, a dimly lit Lower East Side former Asian "erotic" massage parlor and now hipster hangout, at 2 a.m.? With Andrew's first lesson scheduled for tomorrow at 9 a.m., it's officially a School Night. I ponder this as I search for Hutch. Although it has two levels, Happy Ending is small enough that I can quickly find Hutch in one of the set-in Red Velvet booths, holding court like Sinatra. I file away a mental note on how effectively the small locale enables two DJs to work simultaneously, creating different vibes. But I am not here to take compulsive nightlife notes tonight.

My rationale for hitting the town begins with my vibe first getting thrashed around 6 p.m. Usually The Sweatshop is just a general buzzkill downer, but tonight hit a new low. Slamming me with a stack of papers, Diane barks, "The cover sheet says the banker wants to see you before you start this. Mergers on twenty-five."

Glancing at the name, I see the presentation is from a nubile new banker named Paloma Christensen. (Note: I only pass muster with the names here because everyone signs their request sheet and also has a nameplate on their cubicle.) Paloma is some super-exotic, international combo (I think perhaps Brazilian and Danish) of beauty and brains. Even across the vast floor of Presentations, she's caught my eye whenever she drops off a project for Diane to send our way.

It's 10 p.m. and the twenty-fifth floor has a different energy than it does during the day. Almost all the secretaries are long gone, back to their families in Queens and Brooklyn, and most of the bankers have vanished as well. There's only a handful of folks involved with all-nighter work ahead, and the energy is a mix of Red Bull, Spartan camaraderie, and battle-against-time desperation.

Paloma looks up when I tap on her office door. She's totally gorgeous, more supermodel than banker. She even manages to make her conservative business suit look hot.

"You wanted to see me?" I inquire.

She nods, directing me to come over and signaling for the stack of papers. She goes through them, indicating a few specific graphics she wants embedded in her charts. Fortunately, it's all within New Template parameters—although honestly, even if she wanted an orgy of font violations, I'd have committed Presentations hara-kiri for her. Her irresistible continent-spanning accent would leave me no choice.

Paloma's reached the last flowchart, and maybe it's just that I'm a little dizzy from her terrific-smelling hair and whatever discrete fragrance she must have recently splashed on her neck, but when she looks up at me to signal we're through, I smile seductively. I pause to see if she smiles back. She does.

I've never asked anyone out from The Sweatshop before—it's 90 percent dudes and the few ladies seem mostly married or martyred. Trust me: Paloma is the only babe in this neck of the woods. But what the hell, why not?

"I … I wonder if I could get your number?" I ask with confidence

Paloma smiles back again. "Sure. Of course."

"Great," I reply, grinning at this conquest even here.

"But didn't I already put it on the request sheet? It's extension 2810."

She double-checks the top sheet, reshuffles the papers, and hands everything back to me, a cheerful, efficient gesture of dismissal. She doesn't look up to notice the tail between my legs as I depart.

I suppose I could pursue further and clarify that I wanted her digits in order to ask her out, but especially since she will probably have at least one or two sets of revisions tonight for me, it seems too pathetic. We are not, after all, in a tavern setting, and my behavior is already inappropriate.

Descending to the Stygian depths of Presentations, I remind myself that if we were in a club or a bar, I'd totally have a shot with Paloma. I might even score more than just a number at closing.

When it comes to chicks, I am a realist. And while I do damn well out in the field, I admit I also get shot down plenty. Rejection is part of the game. In fact, rejection is what makes it a game. But it's one thing to have a woman say, not in so many words, "Nope—not you. Not interested in what you're offering." It's another thing entirely to not even register as a potential sex object, like a crushed fifth grader bringing flowers to his teacher.

Slouching in my cubicle, I realize that to Paloma, I'm massively far from being a Player, much less Big Time. Here, I am a Sweatshop Eunuch, one who can only service her by excelling in Excel.

Maybe my Paloma moment alone would have necessitated a nightcap. But frankly, the reason why it took almost no arm-twisting on Hutch's 11:50 p.m. call to get me here was that my "accidental" intake of Shane's Facebook profile reveals a startling change: her status reveals she's "in a relationship" and even offers the dude's name. After a moment where I take this in, I click on the link, but from the moment I look at his profile, I can only think of him as Frame Boy.

Frame Boy looks exactly like the kind of guy whose picture is in the frame when you buy it. Handsome in a solid, decidedly All-American way, but not so pretty or contrived as to make him a model/actor and therefore unsuitable for framing, even as your best-looking relative. I learn that he's a year older than Shane, straight, single, likes Björk, Sigur Rós, Neil Young, the Rolling Stones, blah blah blah. Contemplating how and why Frame Boy and Shane are suddenly "in a relationship" while I'm permanently exiled from her life sends a rush of current through me. I hate him. And so I have to go out—immediately. Hence, my presence here now at the doubly ironically named Happy Ending.

Hutch and I hold court amongst some acquaintances and new nightlife friends as he pours me a refill from the bottle of Ketel One he's purchased. As we clink glasses, I spot two totally hot women by the bar. I nudge him, and he concurs.

"You want Heidi, right?" he confirms. "Heidi" is so nicknamed because she's woven her red hair into two cute pigtails, all very naughty schoolgirl.

I nod. He knows me well.

Heidi has one of those archetypal bimbette names (Heather, maybe? Crystal? Bambi?) that I'm forgetting as she's saying it.

I learn Heidi has to get up early—it turns out that she and the brunette are paralegals—and that's fine with me. It's 1:30 in the morning, I've gotten this little lamb's number, and I can be home and asleep by 2:15. All is well in the world.

For now, I will resist the urge to strangle Pimples and Diane at The Sweatshop. I will smile calmly for my masters. And I will continue to behave myself around Phoebe and the Epitome ladies and any other young yoga lovely who comes across me in my guru guise, accepting that (as in The Sweatshop) I must exist as an asexual being. But, thankfully, that is a role I only have to play during daylight hours.

At night, here with Hutch, the wolf still prowls.

TREE POSE
(VRIKSASANA)

Balance poses are like having a super-moody chick as a fuck buddy; you never know when you're going to get exactly what you want or go away empty-handed, maybe even slapped. Either way, you're never really on solid ground—just like in Tree Pose.

Standing firm on one leg, lift the other foot to the inner thigh. Hands to heart in prayer. Or, you can lift them overhead.

Gigi showed me that the nature of a tree is to be stable but flexible, to bend with the wind and the elements. Being balanced means being strong enough inside yourself that whatever life throws at you, you still stay chill. No matter what, you never lose your cool.

If they don't have the ability to dance with their environment, even the mightiest oaks end up snapping like twigs.

I have been drafted into working as a waiter at Shane's first gig, the one for Andrea's Brooklyn sibling. Actually, that's not true; I not only volunteered, it was also my idea.

Although she sincerely tried to scale it down, Shane's vision exceeded the micro-budget, and rather than compromise, she was totally prepared to take the financial loss and serve everything exactly as she wanted. Realizing she'd take less of a hit with a staff she didn't have to pay, I nominated myself and then even roped Hutch into the mix. As a huge Shane fan, my buddy, who now makes God knows how much in finance, eagerly drew upon memories of several high school summers spent bussing tables in Nantucket. (Apparently, a little service-industry labor is part of his family's required rite of passage before one becomes a banker and joins the yacht club.)

Shane pulls it off like a total pro. Nothing riles her. From the lack of counter space to the medieval dishwasher situation, she deftly solves every problem. And absolutely everyone notices that the food—rather than being forgettable post-church-service stomach filler—is extraordinary. Person after person compliments her, and since Shane's forgotten to have business cards printed up, a half-dozen times I notice her giving out her phone number to potential clients.

After the party ends, when it's just Shane, Hutch, and me in the kitchen, as we're cleaning up while nibbling on leftovers and sharing her triumph, I produce a bottle of icy Prosecco I've squirreled away in the fridge. Hutch and I raise our glasses to her.

"Here's to us," Shane beams, as we all three clink glasses.

CHAPTER 7

The next morning, I arrive at Andrew's building, noting that its lobby is even grander than Brooke's. It features marble floors, plush crimson rugs, bouquets of flowers more overflowing than most people's wedding arrangements, and crystal chandeliers that somehow manage not to be tacky.

The white-gloved doorman confirms my arrival. I have learned my presentation lessons, and although I'm still clad in cotton sweats and a T-shirt, underneath my overcoat, I am scrubbed and polished and buffed. Another White-Gloved Dude leads me down a hallway that's the size of half a city block, to the last set of elevators. The elevator opens directly outside Andrew's apartment. I buzz.

I'm expecting another tuxedoed butler like Brooke's Gerard, but the Lord of the Manor himself opens the door. Once again, Andrew's burly energy immediately spills over and takes up all the space between us. I'm dealing with a big bear of a man, handsome in a rough-hewn way, with an energy that belies the fact that he must be hovering somewhere in his late sixties.

His voice is like a deep, cheerful foghorn. "Hey there, kiddo. Come on in." He speaks at the perfect volume, but you sense that his chest and vocal chords would prefer bellowing out orders, like a ship's captain standing at one end of the boat, calling to his crew.

I'm struck that Andrew—the owner or CEO of several Fortune 500 companies—wears a black T-shirt and black boxer brief underwear, both by Ralph Lauren, and nothing else. I suppose this is his idea of a yoga outfit, and while it wouldn't work for a public class, I guess that it's probably fine for a home practice. I am momentarily thrown off by the contrast between the building's desire to demonstrate power, wealth, and unassailable solidity, and this boisterous resident's cheerful presence in his skivvies.

Andrew ushers me into his den. Like the man himself, the room has an easy dignity, an understated elegance born of confidence. We chat for just a moment before Danielle floats in. An Upper East Side angel, Danielle extends her hand with a pleasant "Good morning."

"Andrew, there were a few hang-ups again this morning, " Danielle says.

"Really. What did the caller ID say?" Andrew asks, seemingly unruffled.

"The usual: 'private.'"

"It's a mystery to me, darling."

"No matter. Have a wonderful lesson. Don't forget, we have drinks with the Templemans tonight and then the museum benefit."

Andrew kisses her. As before, it's an appropriate kiss, but sexy: gentlemanly, yet with passion. You can tell by the way she hovers near him, reluctant to leave and savoring the raw vitality of his presence, that not only is she in love with him, but things must also be pretty hot in the bedroom.

Danielle glides away, her blonde mane flashing behind her. Seconds after the thoroughbred has left the stable, just as the sound of the door slams shut, Andrew sighs deeply, then launches in.

"Damn it all, kid—what am I going to do?"

"I'm sorry, sir?" Why am I calling him "sir"? I guess because he's calling me "kid."

"Please, call me Andrew. About all the chaos in my personal life." Barely one exhale after Danielle's out of earshot, Andrew gushes forth, drawing me into his confidence. "This is my fourth marriage, and this time I really want it to work. I don't want another explosive situation. It's only been two months, well, six weeks actually, with Danni—we just got back from a month in Venice—and already, I know things are going to get complicated. I can feel it. Christ, why is my life so goddamn crazy?"

In the next fifteen minutes, along with mini-biographies of his four children (who are, he points out, all at least a decade or two older than his new bride), I learn all about Andrew's first three failed marriages and his current temptations. When he throws in, as an aside, that it usually takes five years and remarriage before his ex-wives fully forgive him, I wonder if that's a universal adulterer's yardstick I can apply towards a potential Shane reconciliation, realizing simultaneously that even an eight-figure divorce settlement wouldn't accelerate Shane's stages of forgiveness. Perhaps not even a medieval form of payback would suffice for me to get back into her good graces.

"The lawyer on the Cincinnati merger keeps wanting to get together 'after hours,'" Andrew confides. "Made it clear she expects nothing, but frankly, they always do. Maybe not at first, but after a little while that changes. Anyway, she's great looking. Probably just turned forty, but in amazing shape. Funny, smart. Another natural blonde, which I love. Christ, it's a bitch."

"It sounds difficult, sir—I mean, Andrew."

"You've no idea. And then there's Gloria de la Monterone, whom I dated for a few months after wife #2. Anyway, she's single again, and she keeps calling me at the office. Wants to take me to lunch at Per Se to talk about her investments, which I offered to do after she got screwed in the last settlement. But an investment lunch inches away from a five-star hotel ... we all know what that means."

Actually, no woman has ever tried to get me into bed via a $375 per person, nine-course lunch to discuss her portfolio (although I confess I'd go through a lot to sup at Thomas Keller's latest triumph) But, of course, I get the general picture.

"Kid, what am I going to do?" he implores me. "I don't know how much longer I can remain on the straight and narrow. I love Danielle, but why does my life have to be this complicated?"

Frankly, I'm completely fascinated by Andrew's stories—past dalliances, celebrity mentions, his extreme prowling—but even more strongly taken aback by his overflowing candor. Soon, we're forty-five minutes into our time together, and Andrew and I have yet to do a pose. That is, unless I count his offhand Tadasana, his organic Mountain Pose while he spoke to Danielle. His strong shoulders are majorly tight, but still he does not collapse his front body. He stands tall.

Right now, however, he is one very chatty mountain. There's no easy way of interrupting him. He clearly needs to talk, to spill out his entire saga. Beyond our unspoken bond as wolves—he the senior pack leader, me the young Turk nipping at his heels, eager to follow him down the trail—perhaps I'm the first moderately appropriate candidate to hear his confessions. Maybe there's no one else in the Forbes 500 he trusts. It makes me grateful for Hutch. While we've perfected our player bravado, he's often said after a night on the town: "Shit, Dude, I tell you everything. We're like those chicks on The Golden Girls." I have my wingman.

We are interrupted by a phone call—clearly business, as Andrew bellows some measured "buy/sell" decisions into the receiver, like Nero deciding the thumbs-up or thumbs-down fate of a gladiator, though here it's a conglomerate. Once he's hung up and before he can launch into more of his love travails, I inquire if he wants to do any poses. Looking at his watch, he shakes his head. "Next time, kid. Next time." He writes out a check.

"So this was the first, then. Let's do twice a week, Tuesday and Thursday at 9:30 a.m." Then the mountain moves towards me, handing me the check and once again shaking my hand with a firmness that makes no question of his authority in the world. "Thanks a lot, kid. I already feel better," he tells me.

Despite his Everest stature in the world, in Andrew's eyes, I see real vulnerability and genuine confusion about his complicated love life. Beyond his massive wealth and his worldly confidence and reservoirs of assets, one thing is clear: Andrew is authentically in pain.

As I gather my unused yoga props, Andrew turns away, tossing off his T-shirt and briefs to head, I presume, to the shower. I'm struck by his total unselfconsciousness, his King of the Forest stroll towards his inner lair, no doubt to some marble waterfall he washes himself under, and then to some rock on which he suns himself dry.

I show myself out. I admit to some mixed feelings about being paid $150 to listen to this Captain of Industry spill about his love life but nonetheless head straight to the ATM.

I know that $150 is nothing to Andrew. It's a fourth of the price of a bottle of Chateau D'Yquem at dinner. It's the pocket on an Armani suit at Barneys. It's probably what he tips his limo driver for getting him to an illicit rendezvous between board meetings. To him, it's meaningless. And I certainly was more than willing to actually teach him. God knows, cash is cash. But I really do hope that next time, there might actually be some yoga involved in the yoga lesson.

At The Sweatshop, I flirt with dropping Andrew's name to Pimples, as I feel I'm sure he must have a serial killer-style shrine to every billionaire in New York. Unfortunately, I find myself drifting off as Pimples is berating me for not using spell-check properly.

"You've got to go under Options and de-select 'Ignore all caps and caps with numbers.' Otherwise, this kind of bullshit mistake is going to keep happening!" he rants.

I look down at the source of his rage: FISCA, instead of FICA, is circled in bold red over and over with repeated fury. Okay, it's a mistake, but hardly deserving the outrage of genocide.

I look up at Nathaniel, feeling that I can spare an apology, but find myself staring at his skin instead. Apparently, this new deadline and my typos have caused another constellation of zits to erupt on his right cheek. I lose focus while trying to figure out if it's stress alone, all-nighter snack food, or just the lack of a skin care regime that aggravates his condition.

"Is that clear?" Pimples asks me angrily.

A thousand times more so than your skin, I think.

"As crystal," I reply.

When I arrive home, I casually sift through the day's overdue bills and junk mail. There's an almost too-cute invitation from my nephews and nieces for my dad's sixtieth birthday party next month at The Grill. I try not to be a bad absentee uncle—I'm still not sure what I'm supposed to do with the quarterly photos my sisters mail me of their expanding broods—but I tack the invite up on the fridge, as I call Mom for our twice-weekly chat.

As she's encouraging me to make the trip upstate, however, another piece of mail completely grabs my eye: a postcard with Shane's face on the front. Beyond the fact that it features Shane's face, the image itself is rather startling. It's an invite from Andrea's gallery for another group show of up-and-coming artists. Andrea's taken an image of Shane's face and doctored and manipulated it, rendering the body in with broad strokes and hand-drawn outlines, as though she were painting in frosting. Like a John Currin painting, Andrea's image manages to be both beautiful and repellant at the same time. No matter how it's morphed, though, it is still unmistakably Shane's face staring out at me. I skim the dates and the location, knowing full well that I can never attend this event.

Bringing the postcard further into the light, I study the image more deeply. There's something particularly familiar about Andrea's work. Somehow, I know I've seen this image before. Unable to toss it in the trash, I stick the invite to my fridge with a magnet, refocusing my attention on tales of Mom's triumph with the Red Hat Lady's clothing drive.

Next time, when Andrew lets me in, I'm not at all surprised by the sight of him wearing his Ralph Lauren black undies and T-shirt, reading a copy of The Financial Times. In fact, it stirs vaguely paternal feelings in me, as if I'm checking in with my dad at some exclusive men's club. (This is, of course, pure fantasy, as the closest my dad the grill-scraper and I ever got to a gentlemen's club was the local Dunkin' Donuts when he'd pick me up from junior high swim practice.)

"Danielle is out for the morning already," Andrew begins. "Something about one of her committees."

This time, taking a major proactive stride towards doing some poses, before he can really launch in, I direct Andrew to sit on the yoga mat so that we can begin with some breathing together. Not surprisingly, however, he listens to my instructions, takes one single deep breath, and rather than watching his breath silently for a few moments as directed, startles me by breaking the silence and immediately plunging into conversation.

"So, I told you about Gloria de la Monterone, right? The whole lunch at Per Se. Well, call me an idiot, but when she phoned me for the third time and messengered over the recommendations of her new portfolio manager, I felt compelled to respond. I mean, buying technology stocks in this economy—Ridiculous! Of course, everything started out perfectly fine. She was completely receptive to all of my business recommendations, and really, I feel I saved her a fortune. Of course, we lingered for one, two, three martinis together. She was getting a little too frisky—playing footsie under the table. Starting to rub her foot towards my crotch—that sort of thing."

There's no escaping what's about to happen. He's going to share everything. And frankly, it's not that I mind hearing the details, but it's disorienting. I'm here to teach, and yet I'm starting to feel like I've been transported to the most lavish locker room in the world.

Thinking quickly, I remember that today I've brought a yoga block, a sturdy piece of lightweight foam that's about the size of a small shoebox. The block is supremely useful; it can help the stiff achieve many shapes they couldn't otherwise get near. More importantly, blocks are fantastic for assisting restful, restorative shapes in which the prop does most of the work. In a way, restorative poses are sort of like having a trust fund; you get all the benefits of the money without having to actually earn it by the sweat of your brow.

With Andrew lying down on his back with his knees bent, I slip the block underneath his sacrum, and Voilà—he's in a real yoga pose. And it's a pose he can hang out in for five, ten, even fifteen minutes. Although I've spent all of thirty seconds getting him into this shape, I can tell he's totally chafing at the bit and more than eager to get on with his story.

"Well, as I was saying, we had had quite a bit to drink, and when it came time to leave the hotel, Gloria informed me that she'd actually taken the liberty to reserve a suite at the Mandarin."

I realize that I've gotten my metaphor wrong. Andrew doesn't belong in a locker room; with him lying on his back and me sitting off to the side, listening to him confess and share, he's positioned me as his yoga therapist.

"So, now she wants to see me again," he continues. "And I just don't know. They all get so needy, if you know what I mean. And even when they don't become needy or dependent, sometimes it's even worse when they start telling you things like you're the only man who's made them come in fifteen years." Again, I mutter agreement, although fifteen years ago most of the women I now cavort with were nine years old. "I feel so bad for them when they say things like that, that it feels cruel not to sleep with them a few more times. You know, just so they don't have to live like that."

Knowing Danielle's and Brooke's penchant for championing charitable causes, perhaps Andrew should enlist them to organize his own: The Foundation for the Preservation of High Society Climax? The Metropolitan Fund for Coming Together? Orgasms Without Borders?

"Honestly, when a woman tells me how unsatisfying her love life has been for the past two decades—married to some putz who can't tell a convertible bond from a clitoris—and now suddenly she's divorced, on the market again, and desperately worried she's over the hill … well, it breaks my heart each time."

"So, essentially you're merely demonstrating empathy by fucking them?" I want to ask. Instead, I reply, "I can understand that," surprising myself with my pseudo-therapist's detachment.

But the funny thing is that I do actually understand that Andrew's being truthful here. It's not the whole picture— this guy's appetite for sex must clearly rival his passion for making money—yet, I can tell he's being sincere when he says he's moved by Gloria's plight. Incidentally, that's not all he's moved by: It turns out she really is very hot. At one point in recounting his sexcapade, he tells me about her breasts, and then remembering, directs me across the room to an issue of W that Danielle has lying about. There's a photo of Gloria at some art gallery opening. She's like a Latin Susan Sarandon—great body, upscale, of undefinable age, seemingly forever desirable.

After a few more restorative shapes—I realize I can't leave Andrew in any of them for too long because he's too stiff and the shapes are too potent—I'm hoping to get at least one standing pose from him: our grand finale, Tree Pose.

In a way, it seems like standing on one leg should be child's play. You focus just a little bit on your balance and simply lift the other leg into the shape.

Andrew, however, shakes and wobbles. I modify the pose—suggesting that he be less ambitious and keep the lifted leg lower—but even that doesn't improve things much. His arms spring wide out and to the sides as though he were walking a tightrope between skyscrapers, not lifting one foot an inch and a half above the ground.

We try it on the other side, and like many people, when he's doing it on his left, nondominant leg (he's a rightie), it's even more unsteady.

This is a pose I thought he could do—frankly, I thought anyone could do it, at least a little—but it's beyond his range of coordination and concentration. Worse than the vague, unsteady approximation of the shape is the fact that it's made Andrew frustrated. Rather than having the poses open up his body, I feel like I've added another item to his list of problems.

Andrew's interrupted by a phone call. As always, he takes it.

I can tell it's Gloria calling. His voice becomes muted and flat, not so much for my sake—he's told me everything already and will tell me everything that follows—but more so she can understand that he's not exactly thrilled about getting this call at home.

He hangs up in a moment, sighs heavily, and has the most heartfelt hangdog expression on his face when he asks me, "Kid, what am I going to do?"

Honestly, I have no idea.

HALF MOON POSE
(ARDHA CHANDRASANA)

The word "half" is rarely used in a positive sense. Typically, it describes something that hasn't fully arrived, as in half empty, halfhearted, half-assed. Half Moon Pose—Ardha Chandrasana—however, is fantastic.

One foot stays on the ground; the other rises up and lifts off. At the same time, one hand stays on the ground, and the other reaches straight up to the sky.

The challenge is the balance, particularly when you try to spin open the chest fully. You're half on the ground and half off, and that's a provocative place to be.

Yet, after I nailed this pose, it always feels like floating free, half of me flying and half of me grounded. That degree of balance, however, is very hard to find off the mat. In life, it's pretty much impossible to sustain.

You feel like you're soaring for about one minute, secretly knowing you don't have the balancing skills yet and that sooner, rather than later, you're going to fall. But for a few spectacular moments, you're flying high.

Right away, Shane gets another gig from that brunch, and once again, Hutch and I are roped into service. This time, however, with a bigger budget and a little more restraint, Shane actually manages to make a profit.

At the end of the night, she's beaming when she hands me and Hutch $100 each.

"You don't have to," I insist, but Hutch doesn't hesitate for a second. Grabbing the bills and stuffing them in his pocket, he picks up the empty coolers to transport back to Shane's. "Come on you two. Drinks on me!" he says.

Later that night, with the three of us hanging out and then joined by other friends, I tell Shane again for the fifteenth time how great a job she did that night. I'm a couple drinks into the evening, but I'm still totally clearheaded when I tell her that someday soon, when I open my own place, she should definitely be the chef.

"Here's to someday, then," she says, clicking glasses with me.

"Someday soon," I correct, smiling back at her. "And just so you're ready."

For a while now, I've been searching for the perfect gift for Shane. I want to give her something specific and rare that I know she'll love. So for month, I've been scouring eBay for a copy of a first edition of Escoffier's Le Guide Culinaire, a culinary classic I know she reveres. Finally, I found one, and even though it took most of a week's salary, I knew I had to have it for her. And now's the time.

Opening her gift, for a rare moment, Shane is actually speechless. When she recovers, she's still dazzled. "I've wanted this since I was ten!"

"And now it's yours."

Simultaneously, I realize that gifting someone like Shane the perfect gift is something I've wanted just as much, if not more, than her desire for a dusty first edition.

CHAPTER 8

For lesson two, Phoebe opens the door for me herself. Expecting her maid, I find myself smiling. She returns the smile, perhaps a hair too broadly.

"It's nice to see you," comes out of me. Not that strange a remark, but it gives the impression that we're old friends who've run into each other by chance rather than that I'm just showing up on time as her hired fitness instructor.

"You, too," she replies back. "I've been so looking forward to our lesson." Phoebe and I stroll toward her exercise room, the fragrance of her innocent tea rose perfume mingling with the sandalwood incense she's already lit. There's an awkwardness to our walking, I realize. Even though I know it's ridiculous, I feel like I'm on a date to the junior prom, all unsure and eager to please. If I had my letterman's jacket, I'd rest it on her small shoulders.

Entering the room, I notice that Phoebe has a few yoga books and other spiritual works on a small shelf. I comment on the Rumi. I know it's a cliché to use poetry to get into a chick's pants, but the truth is I actually dig this Thirteenth Century Sufi Mystic Wildman.

Of course, it was Gigi who turned me on to Rumi. It was my very first class with her, before she opened Thank Heaven, when as a senior teacher, she was still frustratedly overseeing the yoga programs at various hipster gyms in the city. I'd heard great things about her class, and within moments, I was indeed lost in the movement and the music and awed by her ability to take in the room as a whole, able to notice everyone's individual needs and nuances. Like a Cosmic Cheerleader, she constantly called out to individuals. "Lift your left leg higher, Monica." "Tuck the tailbone down, Sarah. It'll protect your lower back."

Midclass, I notice Gigi noticing me and wonder what she'll say. We're in Extended Angle—a pose I arrogantly believe I've nailed. In fact, I secretly think I'm ready for the cover of Yoga Journal with it. "Breathe with your eyes" is all she says as she gently rolls my rib cage even more open than I thought possible. "Breathe with your eyes?" I wonder to myself. What kind of advice is that?

Somehow, I've inspired Gigi to start quoting more Rumi, mostly from memory. "'There's a field beyond right doing and wrong doing … I'll meet you there'—or maybe just in Downward Facing Dog," she laughs before looking up a longer poem to read from a Rumi volume buried in her cavernous hippie knapsack.

After class—trying not to gush too much, although I'm already an instant Gigi groupie—I introduce myself and ask her about what she was reading. Just like that, she hands me her highly worn Rumi anthology. For a moment, as I look for a pen to write down the title, it's not totally clear that she's actually lending me, or maybe even giving me, her book.

"If it speaks to you, keep it as long as you want, baby. He and I are old friends. I've got a feeling it's high time you two met."

I've read my share of poetry—I was an English major at Yale, after all—but my first hits of Rumi blow me away. The twists and turns of Rumi and Hafiz and the other Sufi always surprise me. They're weirder and wittier than their English Literary Canon equivalents. And they revel in things I can relate to, like wine and taverns and wild sexuality. They're all about passionate excess, "living on the lip of insanity." Hafiz talks about flashes of "Oneness with Everything"—and then descending back to being a "wine-soaked, talking rag." All in all, those are the kinds of dudes I want to hang with.

This morning with Phoebe, I spontaneously quote some lines from "Who Says Words With My Mouth":

This drunkenness began in some other tavern,

> *When I get back around to that place,*
> *I'll be completely sober.*

I can't remember anything beyond the opening three lines, so I read the next stanza of the poem, the first one in the anthology of Essential Rumi:

> *If I could taste one sip of an answer,*
> *I could break out of this prison for drunks.*
> *I didn't come here of my own accord, and I can't leave that way.*
> *Whoever brought me here will have to take me home.*

Anyway, you gotta admit that's pretty good shit. Sure, I know he's all about connecting to the Divine or the Big Cosmic Whatever. But for me, the poem underscores countless nights of me and Hutch carousing on the town, hoping I'm blessed with a competent cab driver and lucky enough to remember my address. (And of course, there's that hard-to-extinguish dream of being the owner of the Tavern, presumably the one where the drunkenness began.) When I look up, I'm startled to see that there's a tiny tear on Phoebe's cheek. This blows me away.

"Thank you. That was beautiful," she tells me.

I don't know what to say. I didn't write the lines—in fact, it's her book—and when I read them, I was thinking less about connecting with the Divine and more about connecting with a martini.

Phoebe brushes her tear away, slightly embarrassed. (Remember: this is my secret weakness, for which I have no defense. At least for once it's poetry, and not my bad behavior, that's provoking someone's tears.)

"I'm sorry. Look at me. It's just that Rumi's my favorite poet. It's not the kind of thing I can share with that many people."

"Especially Phil, I bet," I want to interject, but I don't. I don't know what to say. Even a cad like me doesn't enjoy making a lady cry—usually I just piss them off.

"I love his poems, too," I add simply so she stops feeling self-conscious. "We can definitely incorporate some of his verse into our practice."

"I'd love that," she smiles, her misty eyes already clear and bright once more.

We begin the physical practice. Once Phoebe's pretty warm from sun salutes and standing poses, I instruct her into Ardha Chandrasana—Half Moon Pose—a balancing challenge with one leg and hand on the ground, the other hand and leg lifted. She's unsteady, though. Her standing leg needs to straighten so it'll be less shaky. But it's less a muscular adjustment than facing one of her fears. She's uncertain about having only one foot and one hand to balance her. In this shape, she doesn't trust that she can stay lifted and supported on her own power.

I stand behind Phoebe's back body with my hand on her sacrum, positioning my hip to brush against her to give her a sense of support. My other hand touches the head of her arm bone, inviting her shoulder and entire torso to open upward.

I feel her lean into me for support. I'm steadying her less by holding on to her with any force (I'm barely exerting any tactile pressure at all) and more by the strength of my presence. Just by letting her know that she could fall back and I'd be there for support, I'm allowing her to find the confidence the shape requires.

Given all the roller coaster thrill rides we have in our society—all the addictions from drugs to gambling to sex—it may not seem like a yoga pose can provide a palpable rush, but trust me, it does. I can tell that Phoebe absolutely feels a thrill embracing this shape although I'm not sure if, like a devoted lover, I find even more satisfaction than she does in bringing this pleasure to her.

When we've finished, as before, after Corpse Pose, we Om together three times. Right before we're about to dip our heads toward each other with a mutual bow and salute each other with a traditional "Namaste," I manage to pull a Rumi quote from my wine-soaked memory:

> *The breeze at dawn has secrets to tell you.*
> *Don't go back to sleep.*
> *You must ask for what you really want.*

Don't go back to sleep …

I pause for a second, trying to remember the rest of the stanza. Sensing my struggle, like a lover returning a caress, Phoebe rescues me. She knows the words by heart and shares them:

People are going back and forth across the doorsill
Where the two worlds touch.
The door is round and open …

We complete the last refrain together:

Don't go back to sleep.

When we open our eyes, I see no tears from Phoebe this time. And yet, the way she looks at me is still pretty amazing. It's an expression I haven't gotten before, so it takes me a moment to identify it. I'm startled to realize it's admiration, and not for my biceps or in gratitude for a wild romp in the sack. Rather, Phoebe's looking at me with admiration that's closer to devotion, as though I have some deep spiritual connection that she wants to plug into and merge with. Wow—all those cult leaders are totally onto something. You can be an absolute bastard like me, but with a little smoke and mirrors—a few lines from a Sufi mystic, for example—you can have chicks not only willing to drink the Kool-Aid for you, but lusting after you, their guru.

My "Note to Self" about starting a cult is cut short when Phil, again showing surprising restraint given his boisterous voice and clunky manner, enters the room only after our regular conversation resumes. He tells me that he was feeling too stiff to try yoga today, and rather than telling him that that's a clear sign that he needs some yoga, I tacitly agree. The last thing I want is him thrashing the Sufi Poetry and Sex Vibe Phoebe and I are co-creating.

I catch myself immediately. This is not a seduction scenario. I'm not here to run my usual seduction games in order to get laid. I'm here to pay the bills. This is my new career.

As is traditional, I let myself off the hook. After all, I'm not guilty of anything inappropriate, unprofessional, or self-destructive. I'm just innocently enjoying the warmhearted teacher-student rapport Phoebe and I are developing.

And, until I exit the apartment and that bitter January wind slaps me brazenly in the face, I actually almost believe it.

I arrive to teach my class at Epitome twenty minutes early. Marguerite makes a point of welcoming me warmly, escorting me towards the large, tastefully neutral fitness room. "I thought we'd start you with an end-of-day class," she beams. "They tend to be our most popular."

In other words, a roomful of gainfully employed rich people, toning up and winding down after a day of productivity. Yet another aspect of Epitome I can't quite relate to. "Great," I reply. Marguerite wishes me luck and departs as students drift in. I can tell they're surprised to see me, some pleasantly, others not so. I'm approached by one of the latter.

"Where's Jasmine?" a strident brunette asks.

"I don't know. Did she used to teach this class?"

"Ever since it started. And that's how long I've been taking it."

"I honestly don't know. You could ask at the front desk. I don't know how they're changing the schedule."

Jasmine-Fan makes an "Okay, whatever" face, then snaps and unfurls her mat directly in front of me like a bullwhip. It feels like a challenge, a dare almost: "Go ahead and try to teach me ... But you're no Jasmine." I can tell she's going to be trouble.

I retreat to adjust the sound system. I whipped together a generic yoga mix on my iPod this afternoon. I now wish I had been paying more attention to Marguerite's stereo instructions. There are all sorts of "in studio" controls and levels to fiddle with, and yet no sound's coming out.

A Very Slinky Brunette sashays toward me. "Are you the new teacher?" I smile and nod. "I just wanted to let you know that my right wrist is a little sore. I went rock climbing this weekend," she continues.

I manufacture a look that tries to convey, "I'm concerned but informed," but frankly, I'm not sure what to say. Does she want me to modify poses? Is this just an excuse to talk to the teacher? Is it too forward to ask for her number? Instead, I strive for something generic and comforting, something unobjectionable.

"Do what you can. Don't push it. Focus on the breath." She nods as though I've said something original and insightful, and a smile returns to her face.

Another woman—a classic Park Avenue matron-type—approaches me to say this is her third yoga class, then asks do I think she'll be okay in it? I'm about to reply that "you're way ahead of me; this is my first," but think the better of the quip. It probably won't help me cultivate the illusion of authority I assume I should try to instill. Instead, I welcome her and repeat exactly what I told Slinky Brunette Rock Climber: "Do what you can. Don't push it. Focus on the breath." (Perhaps I should have cards printed out, good for any and all yoga occasions: "Do what you can. Don't push it. Focus on the breath.")

There are a lot of last-minute entrances to the class. People are all very, very anxious about getting their hit of serenity ASAP. The energy is more like the scrambling for bargains at a Barneys Warehouse sale. It's by no means "a sacred space." In fact, this room at Epitome will be used for seven different classes during the course of the day. The one right before me was "Amazing Abs, Butts, and Thighs"—no doubt attended by Serious and Diamond Cleavage between massages—and "Cardio Funk Blastoff" comes right after. Except now I can't figure out how to get any sound out of the system despite flipping every switch on and off a few times. Looking up at the large clock, I notice that it's time to begin. One of the latecomers—a very buff, definitely gay guy in an Epitome tank top—takes pity on me. "Both of these have to be on," he explains, indicating two buttons I've been fumbling with in various ineffective combinations.

I'm about to introduce myself and thank him, but since I've cranked the volume way too high in my previous, failed stereo fiddling, when I press the buttons as directed, the music blasts into the room. I quickly adjust the volume.

Despite the students still drifting in, I realize I have to start. I introduce myself briefly and invite everyone to close their eyes and observe their breathing.

I find myself looking out at the thirty or so students in the room, utterly distracted. Some are dangerously fit women who might give my own yoga practice a run for its money; others are clearly total beginners. Suddenly, I realize I have no idea what I'm doing or how this is going to work, but since I can't keep them sitting there silently forever, I decide it's as good as time as any to start Om-ing, hoping it's not too spiritual, but not really caring. Frankly, I need the Om to center myself. The clock is ticking, and judging from my own class's frenzied arrival, God knows I can't run a minute over or fans of Cardio-Funk Blastoff will ramrod the door.

With the first real physical direction I give to the class—they're in Downward Dog as I say, "Lift your right foot up to the sky"—I am utterly astonished that everyone complies in unison. Frankly, I feel a slight rush of power as it happens, followed an instant later by a wave of fear: they are actually listening to me, awaiting my direction.

The class proceeds, but I'm flailing around more and more. We move through some basic up-and-down Sun Salute motions, and more than once I forget which side I've done, right or left. I assume I guess correctly, or else no one bothers to contradict me.

When I glance up at the clock again, I realize my timing is wildly off. I'm taking way too long on some poses and forgetting others, and we're not where we should be according to my plan. Maybe no one cares, though. I can't tell because everyone looks unhappy—but again, maybe that's good. Gigi always encourages her students to smile, relax their faces, and even to laugh while practicing. Either it's me or it's the crowd here, but all these ladies look like they're in agony, enduring the most cruel physical-fitness humiliations for some obscure, sadistic end. But then again, especially knowing the way chicks are, maybe that's exactly what they want. (By the way, the super-buff gay Epitome guy is the only man in the room besides me.)

In Corpse Pose, I make a point of working the room to

give each student a hands-on adjustment, just like Gigi did for me. Admittedly, the last students I touch receive the barest of an assist, more like a gesture toward one. Eyeing the clock, I redirect everyone from rest back up to sitting so that we can complete with three Oms together. True to form, I end smack-dab on time. Sadly, my greatest skill as a teacher seems to be punctuality.

Before the last breath of the final Om evaporates, Gay Muscle Guy has leapt to the front of the room, plugged in his iPod, and Donna Summer's "Hot Stuff" floods its way into the room. Cardio Funk Blastoff has already begun.

I approach Cardio Funk to thank him—his name is Gary (I know this because Gary-fan after Gary-fan greets him)—but after flashing me a huge come-hither smile, he's already confidently barking out directions for students to pick up hand weights and other mysterious props.

My class strolls out to the strains of amped up Donna Summer disco. Some of the ladies half smile at me and thank me for the class. It feels like a polite acknowledgment that's only necessary because I'm retrieving my things near the doorway and they have to pass me by. I feel pathetic, like I've set myself up in a receiving line for a wedding that everyone knows is a bad match.

As I hit the Upper East Side street outside Epitome, Slinky Brunette, the one with the rock-climbing wrist injury, looks up and smiles at me. She's trying to hail a cab; it's still rush hour and the snow is starting to come down.

"Thanks for class," she says. I want to wince. In the elevator ride down, I've remembered another dozen or so errors, omissions, and misjudgments. I forgot arm balances, forward bends, and even twisting after backbending. The more I think about it, the more I realize that technically, the class was a disaster.

"You're welcome … It'll get better."

"I'm sorry?" She looks puzzled.

"It was my first class. It's going to get better. I promise."

"Oh, really. I thought it was very nice."

I want my class to be like Gigi's are: amazing, inspiring, life changing. "Nice?" Screw that—I was going for "Awesome." Nothing stings an Alpha male worse than "nice."

"I mean it. It was very sweet."

Okay … this is a new low. "Sweet" is definitely worse than "nice."

Slinky's trying to be helpful, I know, but she has no understanding of a competitive male's psyche. I don't want reassurance right now, when I know what I did sucked. I just want a drink. And, come to think of it—I want one with her.

As if reading my mind, just as a cab pulls up, Slinky demurs, "Maybe we could grab a coffee?"

Out of nowhere, from the underdeveloped—make that never-used—portion of my brain devoted to impulse control, however, I find myself responding with, "Maybe some other time."

Can this be? Or more specifically, can this be me? Am I, in fact, postponing pleasure? Hutch would be horrified.

On the other hand, maybe Hutch wouldn't feel that way. Maybe he'd be proud of me, that I'm not screwing up this situation yet—wait, more positive thinking, that I'm not going to fuck up this situation period.

Slinky's vulnerable look weakens me a bit, but for better or worse, the moment lends itself to the easy choreography of departure. Quite literally, the meter is running. Inordinately proud of myself, I hold the door open for Slinky, gently shutting it after her. And as she heads off into the flurries, I make my way toward the subway to slither myself home.

CHAPTER 9

It's the usual Saturday night scene. I meet up with Hutch around midnight at an upscale Chelsea joint where he's sitting with a flock of folks I know pretty well. I note that they are overdoing the whole velvet rope thing—I know the doorman so it's cool—but whenever I check out the reviews online, folks are pissed by the exclusivity in a way that I think detracts from the place's reputation.

Inside, I do dig the vibe, though. The exclusivity has its advantages in terms of breathing room. I make some notes on the hipster/retro décor and conclude that I'm liking the staged intimacy here, more or less

"Dude, you know Janek, right?"

I've met Janek a couple of times before, hanging out in situations exactly like these. I've always thought he was a pretty cool guy, with an amazing apartment, a lot of cash, and an awesomely beautiful, one-name model girlfriend. Sadly, her one name always escapes me. She reintroduces herself, however, and I think it sounds like "Symphony," but I remember I made that mistake last time as well. "It's Synnove," Janek offers. She tells me it means "Sun Gift" in Old Norse, as though that's going to be a helpful mnemonic.

Janek's around my age—still on the good side of thirty—but loaded. Unlike me, he's a total success story, a testament to hard work and making the American dream come true.

Janek was born in Slovakia—or at least I think so; all those countries totally blend in my mind—and a few years before the Velvet Revolution, and when he was just shy of fifteen years old, he immigrated to the United States. The kid had balls apparently, leaving behind the dregs of his remaining family and a completely non-upwardly mobile farm life. While I was dreaming of getting my driver's license, he was busy coming to a new country where he knew no one, having only some nebulous cousins to look up. To hear Hutch tell it, Janek pretty much threw himself on the doorsteps of his closest American relatives, offering to work his ass off in exchange for housing in the great land of American Idol and Survivor. His fourth cousins—a middle-aged divorced couple who still worked together every day at the low-end furniture store they owned in Queens—took him in. The divorcees would spend the day together, their bickering set at simmer, and then retire each night to their apartments in different boroughs. Somehow, taking in a distant stray cousin into such a garbled extended family made sense.

Massively hardworking, Janek also charmed them with his charisma and good looks. Urban legend has it that at one point he was even approached to model by Bruce Weber for Abercrombie and Fitch, but when Janek found out the dismal salaries most male mannequins make, he intensified his commitment to business.

Janek resurrected his extended family's dowdy furniture chain, which consisted of stores littered through Queens, Brooklyn, and the Bronx, and then started an upscale Manhattan branch. In the same way that Calvin Klein made his completely uncool, nerdy name synonymous with understated, upscale elegance, Janek turned Zilinikov Furniture into something mysterious and classy. A dozen years later, Janek's the president of the whole enterprise. Hip pad, tons of loot, supermodel girlfriend ... frankly, there's nothing about Janek that's not enviable. The dude would be easy to totally player-hate, except Hutch swears he's a really cool guy, and since I've never had a round of drinks with him that he (or Hutch) hasn't bought, my mind is open.

FYI, I've brought Heidi along with me and she's still wearing pigtails—apparently it's her signature style—and things are heating up between us. I'm not one for the whole "dinner and a movie" thing, but I figured this group event counts as seduction as long as we spend enough "quality time" together. Before tonight, I spent about fifteen minutes chatting over bullshit the night we met, followed up by a twenty-minute phone call two days later and a second call to arrange this night. Summary of time expenditure to date: forty-five minutes. I know it makes me sound mercenary, but gauging the level of our bonding now, I'm thinking that an additional hour and change translates to getting laid tonight

Don't get me wrong, I am deeply interested in "getting physical" with Heidi (aka "nailing her") and yet …

Somehow, I'm also feeling a little less carefree about this than I usually do. Maybe because I'm suddenly defining myself as a "yoga teacher," I weirdly feel like I've got this new standard to uphold. It's as though I'm contemplating running for office despite having a lot of secret vices.

Our evening proceeds as usual until there's a moment when the ladies depart en masse to the bathroom and Janek and I actually get into a conversation.

"So I hear you're not doing the whole club/restaurant scene any more, right?"

"Yup. Learned my lesson."

"Yeah, it's a very risky business. Very unstable. I don't blame you."

It's refreshing to know that there's at least one person in New York City who doesn't blame me for something.

Janek continues, "Hutch tells me that you're teaching yoga these days. My trainer really thinks I should do yoga. Thinks it would be good for my lower back especially. It goes out a couple times a year."

I don't have to sell Janek at all—he's clearly decided to try yoga even before Hutch's plug about my teaching—and we set up a lesson on Monday morning. Client number four, Hutch later reminds me, as we clink shot glasses together—all thanks to him.

This is unquestionably a good thing, but I realize that something feels a bit off. With my three current clients (and my Epitome students), I am basically a blank slate. None of them know anything about me, thankfully, beyond my (entirely projected) guru status. Not so with Janek. Janek, although he's not a particularly close friend, totally has my number. But let's be honest: it doesn't take much to figure me out.

As you might have predicted, I'm ecstatic when, after a night of shagging, Heidi leaves midmorning on Sunday to join her friends—at a knitting club or reading group or something she does regularly that involves brunch and ladies. I sleep the rest of Sunday away, but Monday morning arrives nonetheless, cold and empty-handed.

Rather than choosing an Upper East Side address, Janek's opted for the deluxe Soho pad. It's funny how much difference a twelve-minute walk can make in one's environment; in this case, moving from my dingy Chinatown crash pad to the heights of upscale Soho Pseudo-Bohemian Chic. As with my other clients, Janek's building has only one unit per floor, so when the elevator door opens, you step right inside Janek's amazing apartment. In the upper stratospheres of wealth, even sharing airspace with someone in your building is too plebeian.

Entering the posh loft, I realize I've only been here at night. It's your classic chick-magnet apartment, demonstrating that the owner's very rich, has incredible taste, and yet somehow is still laid back and louche. Looking around, I realize it's maybe even more gorgeous during the day, with light streaming in from huge windows and a set of skylights, endowing it with the spirituality and sexiness of a playboy's cathedral.

This is exactly how I would live, had I the loot: hardwood floors, open space, everything spare and lean. A stainless steel fantasy kitchen with a floating island, most probably for someone who can't cook, but fantastic for parties. Frankly, it's like living in a yoga studio, but with a few pieces of high-end Italian furniture thrown in, and lavish hipster art (beautiful but ironic) covering the huge wall spaces. "Symphony" has an alcove devoted to her framed fashion mag covers. On another wall, there's a series of vaguely S&M, Helmut Newton-esque black-and-white photos that I think are of her and various "friends" (she's masked in them, but the legs and butt seem remarkably familiar). They are one arty step away from Penthouse—not the sort of Nice American Girl you bring home to your Slovakian Mamushka—adding to the aura of upscale chic.

Janek greets me himself. "Symphony" is off to South Beach for a shoot—Vanity Fair, I think, is the title he tosses off—and so we've got the place to ourselves. "Can I get you anything?" Janek asks. Were it not 7 a.m., and were we not meeting to do yoga, Janek would absolutely be offering me a glass of a full-bodied pinot noir. I dismiss this thought, realizing that I must focus on my official identity here as yoga instructor, not my alter ego as someone he was out with until 4 a.m. only twenty-seven hours ago.

"I'm good, thanks," I say. "Let's get started."

Janek's ready to go. He's wearing sweats and a wifebeater, and although this comes as no surprise, his trainer has done a good job conditioning the lean, strong body that nature gave him. With just him to focus on, I notice more fully that Janek really is a good-looking guy, with thick, unruly dark blonde hair that makes him look more like a soap star then a businessman. He's unshaven now, which only enhances the effect of upscale dishabille.

I've already decided that I'm going to go for broke in establishing my identity as yoga guru—three Oms together, the whole nine yards—as though he were someone I were meeting for the first time.

Janek's Om-ing is a little hesitant—I suppose it's a little weird if you've never chanted before in your life, and it's just you and me, two non-monk guys if ever there were ones, stone-cold sober at 7 a.m.—but he's game nonetheless. Unlike Andrew, I can tell he's actually focusing on his breath and striving to understand and make all the subtle adjustments I suggest.

The second we start doing poses, however, is when he really comes to life. Although he's more than a little tight from all the weight lifting, Janek's in great shape. He responds to every instruction with the right mix of eagerness and competition, one that I understand so well. A natural athlete, aware of his body, he takes pleasure in the experience of moving and challenging it.

When we get to Ardha Chandrasana—the Half Moon Pose I shared unsuccessfully with Phoebe—Janek's wildly into it. He takes only a few seconds and needs just a few words of alignment advice ("Make sure the fingers on the ground are about ten inches forward of the little toe so that your arm falls right under your shoulder.") and he's lifting and soaring. He holds the pose for about three seconds, and then he falters—he hasn't learned how to balance in it yet—but without asking, he immediately reestablishes the shape.

I'm impressed. There's nothing I admire more in a yoga practice (or in a dude) than being gutsy and risk-taking. You fall down in a pose, mutter "Fuck that" silently, and get back up. It's the embodiment of everything I believe in.

I decide to throw in two or three poses that I'm pretty confident he won't be able to do just yet, just to show him what lies ahead. (And I admit, also to establish clearly that in this territory, I'm the Big Dog.) I pick some arm balances, which rely on upper-body strength but also require coordination, open hips, and abdominal control. He manages to hover in Crow Pose—something I couldn't do at all when I started—and holds the shape for a breath or two and then falls. He laughs good naturedly when he tumbles out of the shape, but again, is not so amused as to disguise that he's slightly pissed at himself. Of course, as before, he tries again without being asked.

Best of all, I realize, is that this is totally uncomplicated: there are no confessional Andrew anecdotes, there's no Phoebe sexual tension, no Brooke weight-loss hauteur. It's just yoga. I'm teaching him what I know, I'm sharing the power and movement and beauty of the shapes, and he's eating it up. And that is absolutely awesome.

Just before rest, as Janek lies on his back and brings one knee into his chest and then off to the side for a twist, I give him a deep assist. One hand sculpts the head of his arm bone in and down to the ground, and the other catches the top edge of his hip. I direct him to exhale deeply, and as he does, I move the top of his shoulder and his hip away from each other, lengthening out the torso. With my other students, I've totally held back here, using maybe ten percent of the pressure I could put into this. With Janek, I go to about forty percent of my leaning-in strength, asking, "Is that okay?"

"Dude, that's fucking awesome," he answers.

I smile, pleased that I can add a touch more. Releasing, I direct him to center himself so that I can offer him the same assist on the other side.

After a solid ten minutes in rest, when Janek sits up again, his Om-ing is louder and a thousand times less self-conscious. Even if I weren't already confident that the session had gone really well, this seals the deal. When normal conversation resumes, I'm pleased at how totally sold Janek is.

"Wow, I had no idea it would be this tough a workout," he comments.

"And it only gets more intense and interesting, especially when you know the poses well," I reply.

"Awesome. I already feel a thousand times looser. And I feel really relaxed yet ready to go to work."

"It's just the beginning," I assure him. "We'll be able to do some really cool shit together. Seriously, dude, you're going to have a killer practice in no time."

I realize that I've lost any trace of guru-speak, but I don't care. Forget the Rumi riffs, I'm back to just being one dude hanging with another dude, doing whacked physical shit—stunts almost, like drunken barroom dares—and if it leaves us feeling a little calmer and mellowed out but still pumped, that's doubly cool.

Janek asks my fee, and when I tell him $1,500 for ten sessions, he pauses for a second (I fear he's going to bargain me down; he is, after all, a super-successful merchant.) but he counters with, "How about $2,850 for twenty?" He's asking for a five-percent discount for purchasing a larger package (effectively, one free), but since this means more immediate cash in my pocket, I'm overjoyed. As always, whenever anyone pays me for an honest moment's work, I feel like I've won something at the track.

As I grab my coat, there's none of the prom-date awkwardness when I'm leaving Phoebe or the calculated precision of a Brooke meeting. Impulsively, we do the whole grab-each-other's-hand, then pull in for a brief manly chest bump, as though we're two dudes after a Saturday pickup game of b-ball at the park. This is probably not how most gurus leave their disciples, but what the hell; I'm soaring high on the dual wings of yoga and male bonding.

I saunter out of Janek's loft even richer than I thought I'd be, already brainstorming things I can work on with him for next time.

Like Hutch and me going out on the town, Janek and I have a perfect camaraderie, a completely simpatico symbiosis. I feel like the Yoga Gods have given me a brother. Finally, a yoga client who's actually all about the yoga.

Blessed with Janek's check, I'm one step closer to solvency than I ever dreamed possible. Nothing will be disconnected this week, and barring eviction, I'm stable for the moment. It's a sad comment on my last six months, but my new barely-crawling-out of-quicksand status makes me feel quite rich. And thus, I feel empowered to spontaneously quit The Sweatshop.

I wish the scene had more drama. There really aren't any Norma Rae conditions I can protest against. Diane isn't even that big a bitch: she just doesn't like me, probably for all the right reasons, too. But with Janek's check and with a client every morning, more than ever before, this gig seems like a total waste of time.

When I tell Diane that I'm quitting, she has pretty much no response. She just nods, glancing at the scheduling spreadsheet on her computer.

"Your next scheduled shift is four days from now. Shouldn't be a problem to replace you."

"Okay, then. Thanks for everything."

Diane says nothing. No inquiries into what I'm doing or where I'm going, much less your standard "cake break and good luck" farewell moment. I may be a player at night and a guru by day, but here, I'm less than a cog.

And I'm definitely less than a memorable red-blooded man, too. Departing, I bump into Paloma in the elevator, chatting with Pimples and another nameless dweeb from Mergers. I try to catch her eye, but she doesn't really recognize me, and—engrossed in the more virile discussion of the market—she smiles only in my general vicinity. She's probably a nice girl, I think, with civilized and sweet autopilot manners, but since, apparently, I am grossly deficient in banker-level testosterone, I don't even register on her sexual radar.

I exit the building as Dwayne, a tall, gay, black actor who's been working on and off at The Sweatshop for years returns from his cigarette break.

"You cutting out early, Dawg?" he smiles with dazzling teeth.

"More like forever," I reply, prepping to toss my laminated ID into the lobby trashcan.

"Whoa, there," Dwayne counters. "You never know, my friend. What'd you get? A national? A part on a soap?"

I like Dwayne—he's a good guy, and more than once, he's showed me how to convert a column of text or globally replace embedded logos —but I've made it a point to reveal NOTHING about myself to anyone here. The world of all the would-be actors (stage to screen) and dancers (ballet to Broadway) and singers (opera to rock) sharing their grandiose dreams while word processing seem far too precarious and suicidal to bond with. So I don't bother to correct Dwayne, particularly as—however nice a guy he may be—I'm convinced I'll never see him again.

"The first time I got a national tour, I said the same thing myself," he continues. "But trust me, Bro, nothing—not even me in Cats—lasts forever."

I smile and thank Dwayne, departing with a brotherly backslap hug.

The instant I hit the street, however, I throw my Sweatshop badge into the trash. And as I'm walking home, except for a mild boost of elated freedom akin to a Snow Day, I've almost forgotten about The Sweatshop entirely. Diane … Pimples … Paloma … I hardly knew ye.

Walking home past the bridge gallery—where the smoke-blowing hipster couple has been replaced with a gorgeous stained glass of modern Madonnas—for better or worse, my illusions of prosperity allow my thoughts to turn to Shane. Staring into the closed exhibit, I hold my daily pointless reminiscence vigil.

I want to believe that I can make it up to her somehow. At least, I want to try. Even if she'll never forgive me personally, at least I can solve some of the more tangible problems—like the $15,000 I owe her—as a start. I know that the few hundred I might be able to send won't matter much towards the fifteen grand, but at least it's something. That's what you're supposed to do if you're trying to be a good guy—right? Make things right with your ex. So I call her.

I freeze for just a moment after the beep and flirt with hanging up, but screwing up my courage, plunge in. "Hi, it's me—but please just listen to this one. I haven't called since September, and I promise I won't call again if you want … Okay, the thing is, I know I can never make things up to you, but I want to start paying you back some of the money I owe you. It's the least I can do. Things are going a little better for me now. It's only a couple hundred, but I'm going to send you something next month, too, and—"

Shane picks up. "Don't bother" is all she says before hanging up.

Fuck. This did not go well.

I stroll along for thirty minutes, dazed.

Once the heart-racing sting of Shane's hang-up starts to dull, I realize I've also added a further complication into the already messed-up situation. Now that she's said "no" to my offer of repayment, is it better or worse to execute it? Will she regard it as disrespectful if I do, or, on the other hand, will it be viewed as another one of my broken commitments, another sterling example of my lack of follow-through, if I don't?

And how should I pay? I wonder if Shane is hotheaded enough to throw away perfectly good cash—dollars she is rightfully owed—just because she despises the source.

I opt for a check—I want to know if she cashes it—and spend two hours figuring out what the accompanying letter should say. I draft numerous lame opening lines like "I know I can never make up for …" or "Please accept this even though I'm an asshole." Even the short and financially focused "More to come" feels wrong.

In the end, I enclose the check in a blank greeting card—an incredibly neutral Ansel Adams landscape I pick up at an upscale stationers—but I write nothing additional inside. Frankly, Shane's made it clear that there's nothing more to be said.

SUN SALUTES
(SURYA NAMASKAR)

Sun salutes might feel like a kid's game except for the fact that pretty soon you'll be dripping with sweat, and at that point, kids—unlike yogis—usually have enough sense to go back to the video arcade.

There's a rhythm of deep inhales and exhales as you rise and fall and move through the handful of shapes. And there's your basic Western push-up in the middle of all of it, guaranteed to appeal to the Gym Set.

It's this rhythm, this changing and escalating repetition, that warms you up and that builds strength and flexibility. Getting lost in it, you fall into your breath and (one hopes) out of your thoughts.

Frankly, that's the beauty of most rhythms, good or bad, that we establish: you don't have to think. Like some murky jazzy composition best listened to in the wee hours, several scotches into the night, habits will take over and drive you safely home—or on the other hand, they'll lead you to that dangerous, secret place you unfortunately know all too well.

From the moment I spy the "For Lease" sign, I know "this is the one" for my first venture.

I insist on unveiling the space for her in the most memorable way possible, complete with blindfold and theatrical announcement. "Here it is … Our first place together!"

Shane rushes into my arms for a lingering hug that teeters delicately between camaraderie and budding romance, overjoyed by our nascent collaboration.

Plunging in wholeheartedly, we meet every morning, and I always bring her the same Starbucks order—cappuccino with double espresso shots, one Sugar in the Raw on the side—without fail. Once, when our branch is inexplicably out of Sugar in the Raw, I travel five blocks just to get things exactly right for her morning brew.

And when things blow apart and the latte boy (who has a definite crush on Shane himself) still automatically hands me two of our drinks, I decide rather than explain things to him, it's simply best to avoid that Starbucks altogether.

CHAPTER 10

I show up twenty minutes early to teach my second class at Epitome, determined that it will be better than my first one. From the moment I enter the room, however, I sense the energy is different. Last week, the class was packed; you could feel people struggling to make sure they got in before it was too full. This week, there isn't the same "got to find a spot" panic. Not at all. Sadly, there's plenty of room. Five minutes before class starts, I count fifteen students. In the next few minutes, there's a trickle of latecomers. We're up to nineteen. Nineteen left from thirty-six! What happened to the seventeen other people who were here last week? I've lost 45 percent of my—I guess, make that Jasmine's—audience. And I notice that Gay Muscle T-shirt Guy is not in attendance; I've even lost a student who wasn't paying.

Even at Thank Heaven, I've noticed that numbers go up and down, but usually there's an obvious reason, like a holiday or a hurricane, when a popular teacher's class is reduced by half. Hard-core yogis make it a point of showing up to practice. Nothing can deter us from our Downward Dogs.

Unfortunately, of all the students who remain, front row center is Jasmine-Fan, whose gloating smile really gets on my nerves. Even if my debacle doesn't bring about the resurrection of her beloved Jasmine, you can feel her excitement over my failure—and, I suppose, my potential firing. Very Slinky Brunette slips in ten minutes into the class. My feelings are mixed. I hate for a hot little lamb like this to see me looking so lame with this scanty class. On the other hand, at least she brings my numbers up to an even twenty.

As things move along, I feel that this class is perhaps

marginally better than the last, but only by the merest fraction. I'm still a D-minus group teacher: fumbling for words, uneven in pacing, uninspired in my choreography, and offering zero spiritual insight or inspiration. It's just an endless downhill slide into sweaty boredom.

I end on time, and almost as soon as the last Om evaporates, Gay Muscle T-shirt Gary busts in. He's managed to keep his minions quieter outside the door than they were last week, which is particularly impressive given that his followers seems to have gained in numbers. In fact, I recognize three or four little Upper East Side honey dippers who took my class last week, who are now in his fold. I don't know what sucks more: the fact that my class stinks or that I'm letting yoga get trumped by Gay Disco Cardio Funk. Before I can drown in any more self-pity, however, he's blasting Britney Spears or Rihanna or Beyonce or some other disco diva. I think it best I scurry away.

The elevator door closes as I approach but then reopens; Slinky Brunette has held it for me. I don't want to share the ride, but there's no reason I can think of not to enter the elevator with her and descend. I have no idea what to say to Slinky Brunette. Why is she even back in my class? She doesn't seem like a moron—so why can't she tell that it sucks? We don't know each other well enough to have much to say, and the confinement of the elevator space serves to extend the awkward silence as we drop to the ground.

Peripheral glances reconfirm that she really is pretty great looking. But I know that if I start something with her, even a casual drink, it's not going to be a good thing. Not if I want to keep myself well behaved at Epitome.

Slinky turns on her cell phone in the elevator, and just as we exit, it rings. She takes the call, saving us that next uncomfortable moment of stretching the elevator awkwardness towards the street. She's engrossed in her girl-talk conversation, so I smile and wave "bye" and she returns the gesture with slightly more enthusiasm than I put into mine. (I am sulking away in failure, after all.) Tail between my legs, I'm astonished at how eager I am to get away from an interested, hot woman.

And then the last part of the rhythm of my new life falls into place as well: dialing up Monique, now officially my "fuck buddy."

I begin thinking about her on the subway, maybe just out of lust, but also as a way of moving beyond my self-pity and disappointment with myself and the dismal class I floundered through.

It's not like I have that much guilt about screwing around with Monique. Don't get me wrong—there are lots of times I wish I could just shake away all the remaining "decent values" my parents and Catholic school did their best to instill in me and fully embrace the carefree, playboy persona I've worked hard to perfect. God knows, Monique and I are both full-grown adults who know exactly what we're doing, and when it comes to street smarts, she's more than a match for me. Even if there are some rather strong yoga suggestions towards a celibate lifestyle, unlike with my altar-boy upbringing, there's no official sexual "Dos and Don'ts" sin list to consult.

What's mostly weighing on my mind is that I am aware that this will be my third encounter with Monique. I realize I'm entering dangerous territory here. Can Monique—can any woman—really be a fuck buddy? And if so, for how long?

I wonder ... but truthfully, given the 45 percent drop-off rate of my class, I don't care. When Monique shows up at my door, ready to screw my brains out after the merest ten- or twenty-word, superficially polite banter—mind you that, and the fact that no currency is exchanged, are the only ways I can tell that I haven't hired a gorgeous hooker with an MBA—frankly, I've never been happier to see anyone.

In my first few lessons with Brooke, I asked her if there was anything in particular she wanted to do. Brooke's serene answer—"I'll leave it in your capable hands"—provided no information. But in today's lesson, I finally say something that sparks her interest. I say it randomly, too, almost as a thought to myself: "Maybe today we'll focus on the core."

Brooke's eyes light up. "Could we? Are there yoga poses for that?"

"Sure," I reply, a little frightened by the new gleam in her eye.

"I have been trying everything to tone my stomach"—mind you, her stomach is so flat you could cut a diamond on it—"so if we could work on that I'd be very grateful."

Jocks are always doing endless crunches and sit-ups. I used to be one of them. But the yoga stuff involves really deep access to your core. It's about a thousand times harder to learn the way to access the abdominals in certain poses than it is to slug through a sit-up marathon.

Throughout today's lesson, I make almost everything a little harder by giving variations, like one leg lifted in the push-up moment of the Sun Salute, that tax the abdominals. For the first time, tiny beads of sweat appear on Brooke's brow. To be perfectly honest, I wasn't sure she was capable of sweating; it seems like the kind of thing she'd have outsourced or perhaps have had a tasteful operation to remove her plebeian sweat glands.

I marvel at the ferocity with which Brooke approaches yoga today. If I told her it would strengthen her abs to ritually sacrifice her butler Gerard to the God of the Internal Obliques, she'd race to the kitchen for a carving knife. (Actually, she'd probably ring for Gerard to bring her one and then use it to eviscerate him.)

For a grand finale to the abdominal focus, I bring Brooke up into headstand against the wall—she can't quite come up by herself or balance yet, so I assist—but once she's up, she's reasonably steady against the wall, so I introduce the abdominal connection when coming down.

Previously, after a few moments in headstand—only very gradually increasing the length of time in the shape so as not to strain those smaller vertebrae in the neck—I'd direct Brooke to gently soften her knees into her chest and descend. Today, I direct her to explore lowering straight legs together.

When you're coming down from headstand, slowly lowering your legs out straight and together is about one thousand times more difficult then just bending them and swiftly descending. It not only takes tremendous strength in the abs, it also takes a great degree of control, even more so because one must maintain balance.

For the first attempt, I direct Brooke to explore the sensation a bit by just dipping the legs a few inches and then bringing them back up. "Eventually, you'll be able to bring the legs straight down all the way, which, believe me, is about as tough as doing a few hundred sit-ups."

Brooke mutters something. I can't quite hear her since she's upside down and concentrating.

"Okay, time to come on down. You can soften the knees in and—"

"No. I'd like to continue."

By now, I can see that her face is beet red from both the strain and effort in the abs, but also from being inverted for much longer than usual. I don't mind her exhausting herself so much, but I am concerned that this might be a strain on her neck. Fortunately, on her third lowering-down attempt, she loses it. Collapsing, she softly tumbles out of the shape.

The moment she has her breath back, she asks, "Could you show me how you'd lower with straight legs, please?"

I'm happy to demonstrate. It's rather impressive anyway but much more so now that she knows just how difficult it is to lower or lift with the legs outstretched.

"What you find," I explain, "is that it becomes much more difficult the lower you bring the legs. The first quarter of the arc—where you were working—is comparatively easy and more of a balance challenge. It's here"—I travel halfway—"where it gets very exciting and here"—I travel three-quarters of the way down—"that's really like being punched in the gut."

I instantly realize that describing something as "being punched in the gut" is deeply inconsistent with the positive, friendly imagery we're trained to use as yoga teachers, but it just slips out. Unfortunately, there isn't a pleasant way of describing the feeling ("challenging," "intense") that's not watered-down bullshit. This is core abdominal, gut-wrenching stuff. It's impossible to make it seem beautiful, graceful, or effortless until you've totally perfected it.

I finish, lowering down super-slowly so that Brooke can savor my physical prowess. I realize that this demo was not only instructive but deeply satisfying to my ego, and frankly, I'm okay with that. My superior core strength is something that Brooke cannot buy outright, although that must drive her crazy.

"All right then, let's move on to some backbending."

"I'd rather not, actually." Until this moment, Brooke's been a completely compliant student. Mind you, Brooke says this in a way that's perfectly polite, but it's clear that "no" is not an acceptable answer. "I'd like to try the headstand with straight legs again."

I'm a bit startled, and stumped. Thus far, none of my students have requested a pose that's so beyond their range, much less requested returning to it for third helpings. Janek's passionate, but he knows when it's time to move on.

"I am concerned about your neck," I tell her. "It can be a strain to—"

"I assure you my neck is quite fine. Will you assist me in coming up?"

What can I say? Brooke is soon up, finding her balance and ready to again explore the lowering of the straight legs and their tug on the abs. This time, her face is redder than before. She manages three sweeps with the legs up and down, and on the fourth one, she surpasses her own record, getting almost a very shaky third of the way down before collapsing, exhausted.

The room becomes utterly silent and yet charged with energy, with the two of us sitting and simply breathing as Brooke regains her imperial composure. After her breath stills and her face loses its redness, she waits a moment and then reopens her eyes.

"One more time."

Christ, I really hadn't anticipated this. I thought just doing rigorous yoga would be enough in the fight against Invisible Fat Cells. Apparently, I've revealed a new miracle ab-toning treatment, and Brooke wants to gorge herself on it.

Brooke's and my eyes meet. If I say "no" to her, I'm sure she will find another instructor who will let her do headstand sit-ups for hours on end, perhaps exclusive of all other poses.

"Last round," I say, "and we'll save some more for next time." She tacitly agrees as she bounces up yet again.

This time, Brooke only has enough juice to do two of the lifting leg movements and collapses on the third one. She's totally wiped out.

She doesn't fight me now. I'm forced to abandon the heart-opening backbends I'd planned (After all, on Park Avenue, who needs an open heart if you've got washboard abs?) and take the energy down to simple cooling poses and more restorative shapes. God knows, Brooke has done enough for today.

We finish on time (of course), and unlike at the end of our last few lessons, rather than politely dismissing me, Brooke walks me toward the door herself. I feel that this is an honor reserved for first-time visitors (probably to make sure they don't steal anything) and special guests she doesn't want to part with. I feel as desired as only the finest plastic surgeons must be: the ones for whom, no matter how much money you have, you still might have to wait months in order to secure an appointment.

"I particularly enjoyed our lesson this time," Brooke tells me.

"A little too much," I want to say, but instead I merely smile. Brooke's too smooth to say directly, "And next time we need to do this again, and even more of it." She knows that I'm not so inept as not to realize that my job depends on it.

CHAPTER 11

In the ludicrously posh locker room at Epitome—a true manifestation of "them that's got shall get," with fluffy fresh towels and every toiletry imaginable offered for free, as though the Rockefellers cannot afford their own grooming products—I hang up my coat. Somehow Gay Tank Top guy sneaks up on me.

"You go there?" he asks through over-bleached teeth and a January tan. I realize he's referring to my crummy, desperately faded Yale sweatshirt as I remove it to reveal my crisp, black, clean teaching T-shirt underneath.

"Yup." Again, I hate admitting this, but there's no point in lying. But still, it makes me uncomfortable. Frankly, so does Gary. And yet, even though something about Gary definitely creeps me out—it's not the gay thing; it's more his generally airbrushed, spray-tanned style—I actually am happy to see him because maybe this means he's going to take my class this week. Anything to up the attendance so as not to be fired for being Jasmine manqué.

"Want to grab a drink later?" he asks me.

This takes me by surprise. Is this a colleague thing ... or is he asking me out? I don't want to appear unfriendly, but I really hadn't been expecting this.

"I would. But I have to check in with a friend first. We might have plans."

He nods as though he's aware of just how capricious my imaginary friend can be.

"That's cool. I was thinking maybe The Townhouse. Or is that too old school?"

I have no idea what he's talking about. "Whatever. I don't

really hang out in this part of town."

"A downtown guy then?"

"More or less."

"How about G then? Or Barracuda?"

"Never been, but sure, I guess. Anyplace where the vodka's cold is fine with me." He looks at me for a moment, clearly looking for some sign of recognition, which I don't deliver. Then it becomes crystal clear to me—he's naming gay bars and clubs to see if I know them. Fortunately, my authentic ignorance of his scene, and the delay of my recognizing his game, establishes my team. Once again, general cluelessness confirms heterosexuality. He gets it. And in true postmodern fashion, he sees me getting him getting it. We could probably save time by just wearing nametags with sexual preferences and relationship stats, but for now the labeling is complete.

He smiles, but his reaction is mixed. He's seemingly satisfied to have an answer although I sense slight disappointment that I'm not one of The Boys. I've got to admire him though because at least Gay Tank Top Gary has the guts to double-check his research and ask me to my face.

"So, you're straight then?"

"Yup."

"Girlfriend? Single?"

"Very, very single. And happy that way."

"I hear you."

"All right, then," I say, heading toward the exit. "I'll see you in class."

"Actually, I'm gonna pass today. My rotator cuff's been acting up."

Wow—so, he's really here an hour-and-a-half early just to get the 411 on my sexual inclinations? It's kind of flattering ... and kind of creepy.

"Later, then," I say, almost wanting to do something jock-like to underscore my straightness. I can't think of anything that's not ridiculous, so I head off to class.

Moments later, as I'm shutting the door, I see Gay Gary and Slinky Brunette talking. It's a pretty obvious interchange to read (even for me): he's reporting back to her about our conversation. It's like the high school-girl tactic of having a friend do a little undercover work to see whether her far-off crush from geometry class might feel the same way. Except in this case, it's whether I'm into chicks or dudes. Again, it's kind of flattering and kind of creepy. Maybe I should have paid more attention to that sexual harassment video after all.

I do, however, proceed to teach my best Epitome class ever. Hours of preparing it at home have paid off. Indeed, as a group instructor, I am rapidly approaching adequate. How lucky, I think, for the nine students in attendance. If I continue this rate of inversely increasing my performance while decreasing attendance, next week's three students should have the time of their lives.

Maybe I'm a glutton for punishment but I can't stop myself. Removing the postcard from the fridge, I glance at it to find Andrea's website, logging on to see if there are other works depicting Shane or even other people we know together.

I read through Andrea's Artist Statement. It's VERY slick and quite well written although very much teetering on the brink of art-historical hubris, with references to her own work alongside seminal artists. Andrea does speak a bit about her process of finding images from a wide range of sources and then creating original canvases from them, but she provides no further clues as to the source of that haunting Shane image. Like a parent displaying a bad report card to shame a truant child, unable to either frame the postcard or toss it away, I repost it on my fridge.

When Brooke tells me that her dealer wants to start taking class with me, for a second I think, "Is Brooke confessing a drug problem?" but then I realize I've misheard: she's talking about an antiques dealer.

Linney Mooney operates his biz out of a townhouse between Madison and Park, reserving the top two floors for his private residence. The office I'm ushered through is standard "Rich People" décor: plush velvet upholstery and silken drapes with lots ruffles and overhanging swag. Tons of Louis XIV and Biedermeier furniture. Antique paintings of terriers and pheasants and pale Revolutionary War children who look simultaneously mawkish and ghoulish all at once. All very safe, predictable, and status-screeching décor.

When you get to Linney's private floors, however, although the decor is probably equally pricey, you see how much darker, quirkier, and twisted his own taste really is. Every inch of the wall is covered with framed objects ranging from interesting nudes to primitive oils he later tells me were drawn by mental patients. Seemingly casually decorated shelves overflow with interesting objects ranging from Jurassic fossils to animal skulls, from Mexican Day of the Dead paraphernalia to grim Civil War memorabilia. He tends to like things a little worn and rough with recurring themes like crucifixes, both pictorial and sculptural, all with an exposed Sacred Heart crowned with thorns. There are enough of them—and lots of other trippy religious icons chosen for their beauty and perhaps blood-dripping irony— that this might be Mel Gibson's pied-à-terre, were it not for the simultaneous inclusion of various Mapplethorpe prints and other homoerotic art.

I like Linney from the moment I meet him. Brooke arranges things so I teach him twice a week, during his lunch hour. In his sixties, he's highly energized, his compact form probably once quite fit despite a terrible hip injury that he refuses to have operated on. Fortunately, thanks to my sessions with Andrew, I have mastered the art of yoga-lite.

Linney is more fun than any of the other Park Avenue types. Openly gay, super-queeny, and flirty with me in the most obvious and, therefore, most harmless, of ways.

"Oh, God, I hate all you cute young straight boys," is the first thing he says to me. I'm kind of stumped for a response.

"Well, not really—life is better with you than without you," he continues, "but still … it seems needlessly cruel of Brooke to send me someone like you."

He's smiling, and I realize it's all a compliment, so I try to surf above and around it. "I'll do my best not to be too tortuous," I reassure him.

"Don't hold yourself back, Blue Eyes. Are your lashes dyed?"

"No," I say laughing.

"Interesting," he replies. "They remind me of a Shetland pony Brooke had when she was a toddler."

Truly, these are the strangest compliments I've ever received. "You knew Brooke growing up?"

"Peripherally. Our families were briefly intertwined. Brooke's was of course far, far richer—unlike moi, beyond the need to work. But we shared many rarefied childhood moments together about a century ago."

Linney's hip injury limits our practice, but he's actually a highly sensitive student. He's so graceful that I have a moment of wondering if he has a dance background. Then Linney casually mentions, during an easy hip-rotating move I give him to loosen things up, that this reminds him of being a go-go boy in the West Village in the '60s.

"Excuse me?" I really hadn't seen this one coming.

"Oh, back in the day, I had a few moves of my own, dear boy. I wasn't always this obtuse mound of flesh."

"You're hardly that."

"You're being kind. I'm very aware that my days of entertaining the crowds in a G-string are a thing of the very distant past. However, I think you might look rather smashing in my old G-string. I believe it's in the bottom left drawer of my desk, if you'd care to try it on."

I laugh, and so does he.

When it comes time for final rest, he lets go with an amazing sweetness. In his still features, I can totally see the naughty, seventeen-year-old go-go boy escaping from summers on Über-WASP Nantucket to frolic in the West Village, gleefully driving his crusty relations utterly insane.

When we finish, Linney smiles and grabs my offered arm in an assist to help him come smoothly up from the floor. "You certainly know how to sweep a guy off his feet, Blue Eyes," he smiles as he writes me a check.

"Aw shucks, Go-Go," I reply, ducking it into my pocket. He stops me, taking the check back.

"In the trade, it's more like this," he counters as he tucks the check into the safe part of the top of my underwear as though tipping a stripper.

It's a naughty gesture, but since it's not going anywhere, it's pretty hilarious. We both chuckle as he clasps me benevolently on the shoulder. "See you Friday."

FLYING CROW
(EKA PADA GALAVASANA)

If you want to intimidate someone with a yoga pose, just bust into Flying Crow.

I pretty much guarantee that no matter who your target is, they won't be able to do it without a ton of practice.

Your hip needs to be very open, so that rules out a ton of guys. You need real arm and ab strength, which defeats most of the chicks. And even if you're challenging some strangely flexible, buff hermaphrodite, they'll still have to deal with balancing. But once you do nail it, it looks spectacular, like some gravity-defying move out of The Matrix.

Standing, bring your left leg across your right thigh. Bow forward at the waist, trying to touch the floor. Walk the hands a little forward, so the palms are on the ground. Press down and lift your chest forward as you try to bring the right leg off the ground. You're balancing entirely on your hands, one leg bent on top of your arms and the other floating in the sky. You're literally soaring, rising above the ground through your own strength, balance, and focus.

There's only one catch: for the first six- or ten-thousand times you try to take flight, you'll fall flat on your face.

Shane and I move from friends to something more in pretty predictable fashion. Endless time spent together working on Haven (the name we've decided for our first bistro) with the requisite late-night hours and ever-blurring boundaries.

One particularly late night, after one too many glasses of a good bordeaux, exhausted, we're slouching on the half-installed banquette after a lavish tasting menu for two. Shane wants to keep working a bit longer, but half-feigning exhaustion, I recline along the banquette and rest my head on her lap in mock protest. It's a blurry, loaded moment until I reach up to kiss her and she leans in to kiss me. Soon, I'm upright again, one thing leading to another, struck by the newness and the rightness of the moment, both shockingly fresh and completely comfortable all at once. This is so much more than just a lack of impulse control; on this night, surrounded by the beginnings of everything we're creating, the entire universe feels perfect and inevitable.

CHAPTER 12

If not with actual whips and chains, somehow, with her intense investigation of core strength, Brooke and I have entered into an S&M relationship. The trouble is I can't tell who's the sadist and who's the masochist.

Indeed, if someone were to hear only the moans and grunts coming from Brooke, it would seem that I am the master and she is the slave. Appearances can be deceiving. Approaching Brooke's apartment for our usual session, I hope, once again, that perhaps today is the day she'll allow me to modify our lesson to steer a few degrees away from Ab-mania. Yet when I open the door and it's Brooke herself, and not Gerard, who greets me, I know that something truly out of the ordinary must be in store.

"I have wonderful news," she beams.

"There's been an Invisible Fat Breakthrough?" I'm tempted to inquire. "Under the right ultraviolet light, those cells can now be seen through the Hubble Telescope?" Instead, I merely smile and wait. Brooke will reveal all in her own good time.

"Last night I had dinner with Nan Bongiorno who, of course, is the Editor-in-Chief of Grand Central Magazine." It comes as absolutely no surprise that Brooke hangs with the founder of New York's glossiest, most gossipy name-dropping magazine. "When Nan told me she was frantic over their annual 'Stars of the City' issue, I made several recommendations to her, and, well, I'm quite pleased to say that she's going to feature you."

"I'm sorry … what?"

"You're going to be a Grand Central Star."

I almost reply with "star of what?" and then I realize she means as a yoga teacher.

"Really? That's quite amazing." It's all I can think of to say.

"Yes, I thought you'd be pleased." (Actually, I'm more shocked than pleased, but let Brooke interpret my reaction as she will.) "It's all rather rushed to meet their publishing deadline," she continues, "so I took the liberty of saying you'd be available for a photo shoot this afternoon at 2 p.m. I'm assuming that's not a problem." Brooke knows full well that there's very little that I might be doing that would be more compelling. Of course, I'm available.

"I've written down all the specifics, and I can give you that after our lesson. I'm quite eager to work on the core lift in those arm balances from last week. God knows, I need to tone there as well."

She's no bodybuilder, but of course Brooke's arms have not an ounce of flab on them. I say nothing. My compliance is assured. My mistress has spoken. And once again, although she's the one who grunts and groans, we both know as I submit to her will once again, in our little masochism tango, it is absolutely Brooke who brandishes the whip.

There's a sense of barely restrained chaos at the photographer's Meatpacking District loft. The photographer, Dario Something-Exotic-That's-Hyphenated greets me in a barely perfunctory way and then returns to the more important task of ordering his assistants about as they rearrange lights and gels. He's polite enough, but he's pissed, and whether it's with me or his assistants or life in general, I can't tell. It may be his usual mien with everyone; Brooke has made clear that he's "a very important young photographer" and that "we're" very fortunate to have him doing the shoot.

I saunter by the craft services table, flirt with a bagel, but decide it's probably unwise to carbo-load before my first (and probably only) photo shoot. After about twenty minutes of adjusting the lights, Dario seems even more irritated than when he started. He gestures to the makeup/hair dude, who leads me to his table. Sebastian—somehow that's his name, although he seems to be a sweet, totally Bronx-born, ultra-gay Puerto Rican—studies my hair with ferocious intensity, running his fingers through it again and again, lifting the strands vertically and then dropping them while looking at us both in the mirror looking back at him. After a moment, I feel compelled to address the situation.

"Um … can I ask what you're doing?"

"Sorry, just judging your product needs."

I'd assumed that, with a guy on a photo shoot, they'd just comb my hair, cover up any zits, and then we'd be good to go. Sebastian, however, has an entirely different game plan. Space shuttles are no doubt launched with a more cavalier attitude than his determination to even out my skin tone. Mind you, I've never noticed anything particularly blotchy or mismatched about my face, but Sebastian spends a full fifteen minutes blending and perfecting all manner of cosmetics. He veers close in and then away from me to judge his work, constantly dabbing my face. After he's finally satisfied, he begins to artfully muss my hair, incorporating at least four different grooming products. When he's finished thirty minutes later, I look exactly like myself, with my skin being imperceptibly smoother and my hair exactly as mussed up but no longer moving. Sebastian's approach to my grooming is like Brooke's toward her Invisible Fat: monumental effort toward an entirely unnoticeable end.

Frankly, I'm sure Sebastian would still be fine-tuning me to this very moment except that Dario proclaims that he is ready, and therefore Operation Natural-Look must be terminated midspritz. I approach the center of Dario's set, assuming that's what I should do.

"Why isn't he dressed?" Dario shouts to no one in particular. Far from naked, I am entirely clothed, wearing simple yoga pants and a clean, black T-shirt from Banana Republic, my usual teaching getup. No one answers Dario. So, impatiently, he approaches me. "What are you going to wear?"

"This is what I was going to wear. It's what I usually wear to teach."

He looks at me, and then, after breathing in deeply, replies while restraining his desire to slap the class buffoon. "The background is black. We're not doing a black-against-black thing here. I need you in something else."

"Well, I brought a white T-shirt, too," I offer.

Dario can barely conceal his condescension. "White is much too bright for this setup. Can someone, ANYONE, please go out and get him a decent T-shirt?"

There's a tremendous bustle as the assistants scamper, grabbing their coats and bags. Several are dispatched simultaneously, as this is clearly a task requiring extensive manpower.

"All right, you can take ten," Dario says to me, walking casually away in disgust at this unbelievably hideous turn of events. Sebastian appears and tweaks his work, dabbing at my face and fluffing my rigid hair.

"Is he always such an asshole?" I ask Sebastian, who giggles conspiratorially.

"No, he's all right really. It's just ..." Sebastian hesitates for a moment, then whispers, "Well, Dario hates when they pull stuff like this on him. Veronica something was supposed to do this shoot."

The yoga world isn't that large, so I actually know Veronica, a great young teacher who was another important influence on my early yoga life. Totally beautiful, with a sensational practice, she was perhaps my first yoga crush from afar.

"They did a pre-light with her yesterday, but this morning he was told they were using you instead. And confidentially ... I think she and Dario might have been hooking up. I have a sixth sense about these things."

It never occurred to me that Brooke's securing this shoot for me involved getting rid of someone else last night, someone no doubt more deserving than me. Of course, I realize that Brooke has absolutely no qualms about rejecting and sending things back—witness the white rose episode—but I feel a twinge of guilt that I've replaced another, definitely worthier yogi at the last minute. But my reveries are interrupted by Sebastian's long monologue about the plot intricacies of Gossip Girl, and shortly thereafter, the return of the first assistant with a bag full of T-shirts. Dario inspects them, handing one to me to try on.

I yank off my shirt, and as I do, he starts flashing Polaroids. I put it on—it's way, way too small. "Perfect!" Dario exclaims.

"I think it's a little too tight, actually."

"No, the Polaroid." His staff swarms to study the image that has pleased the Master. "We'll do the photos without the shirt."

"What?"

"Shirtless … why—do you have a problem with that?"

I pause for a second as the photography assistants wait nervously. Sharing the Polaroid, Dario exclaims, "See how great your skin tone looks here against the shadow."

His artistic creativity ignited, Dario has undergone a complete Jekyll and Hyde switch to become caring and concerned rather than an arty Euro-bitch. "Trust me," he says, "these photos are going to be hot." Like any good pimp, he's got the switch from total asshole to warmhearted business buddy down pat.

It seems more prudish to protest and refuse to do the shoot without covering up my pecs than it does to just get it over with and comply. After all, I'm no starlet being tricked into nudies that'll destroy my chances of winning Miss America. "If you say so. Let's do it," I agree.

I watch Dario's smile broaden as I start busting out my most athletic poses. Inversions (going upside down) and arm balances are clearly his favorites. They're dynamic, graceful, and impressive all at once. When I bust into Flying Crow, he practically orgasms.

Fortunately, it's a pose I can really do well, although hanging out in it very long is difficult, even for the real pros. I do the pose again from the other side, and he snaps that passionately as well. Then Sebastian comes in and fluffs, spritzes, and powders me, and we do it all again. And then one more time.

Dario embraces me at the end as though we are war buddies reunited. And as we part company and Dario talks about getting together and hanging out sometime soon, I almost believe him.

Grand Central Magazine hits the newsstands every other Wednesday, and when it does, I'm more than a little surprised to find that I've made the cover—part of a collage of six or seven trainers, aestheticians, and a massage therapist—of their "Best of Health and Beauty" feature. Excited, I open to the article inside, seeing that Epitome has made a full quarter page as "Hottest New Spa." But my mind is totally blown when I turn the page and see myself, shirtless and levitating in Flying Crow, occupying one full page of ink.

"Damn!" is all I can say. I have nailed the pose, and man, it is just a really good photo. The light and composition against the dark background make the image very striking. The pose looks impressive, and somehow under those lights, and shirtless, I look particularly buff.

There is a tiny moment of cringe factor, however. When I confirmed the spelling of my name with the reporter for the article, fresh from a Rumi-soaked lesson with Phoebe, when she asked me where I was from, I quoted—more like quipped— from his poem "Only Breath." "My place is placeless, a trace of the traceless." It's a poem about transcendence, but honestly, I just didn't feel like getting into anything personal, preferring to gloss over anything that would link me to Page Six flashbacks. Anyway, the quote is pretty small and inset, and I hope the picture will tell the real story about impressive yoga poses.

I want to show the article to someone immediately, and the only person present is the newsstand attendant, who seems completely not interested in the latest installment of my newfound career.

First I call my mom but get her machine. Then I call Hutch, but it rolls over to voicemail. I leave him a message, telling him to check out Grand Central, page 28. I'll have to mail my sisters and folks copies, as they're not exactly the types to subscribe to this glossy report on what's ridiculously expensive and hip in NYC. (I wonder, though, if this will confuse and further frustrate my dad, another indication of how much I have squandered my education and opportunities for a bit of bizarre contortionist fame.) I shrug this off, though, and pleased with myself, and a little elated, I grab another three copies, stuff them in my pocket, and walk home. The only remaining dampener to my enthusiasm is that, besides Hutch, there's nobody else I can think of calling to share the good news.

"Dog, this is totally awesome," Hutch tells me.

"I have to admit: it is kinda cool."

"Kinda? Are you totally whacked? Do you know what celebrities would do to get a full-page photo in Grand Central? Gwyneth would probably give up Apple for this much ink. And it's a very swank photo, too. You look good. Impressive, but not in a yoga freak-show way."

I laugh. "That's your idea of a compliment?"

"Just proud of you, Dog. You're my main boy, after all. Anyway, drinks on me tonight. I'm not taking 'no' for an answer." Hutch hangs up before I can reply. I've curtailed my going out during the week with amazing restraint over the last two weeks. On the other hand, if a cover photo and a full page in Grand Central aren't worth a clink of the glasses or two tonight, then what is?

Hutch and I arrive pretty much simultaneously at P.J. Clarke's on Third and 55th. The saloon is convenient to Hutch's midtown banking gig and suitable to me because: a) Hutch is paying, and b) they have the best burgers in the city. P.J. Clarke's is over a hundred and twenty years old, and even though the new investors (George Steinbrenner and Timothy Hutton, and some other guys) just renovated it, thank God they did everything they could to make it look like nothing has changed since Sinatra "owned" Table 20, the spot where he ended up after every night of carousing.

After getting texted, emailed, and called in rapid succession, Hutch winces and shrugs, "Dude, I gotta swing by this gallery opening on 57th or Honey will kill me. You in?"

"Why not," I figure, so after paying our tab we walk a few blocks over to your basic Thursday night art gallery wine and cheese opening at one of NYC's most "important" galleries. Honey apparently has been good friends with Celeste, the gallery's founder, since they studied slides from the late Renaissance together, back at Wellesley. The crowd looks sedately middle-aged and affluent although mixed with a few art fiends of a decidedly younger persuasion. As always, I do a quick "safety check" of who is passing the hors d'oeuvres to make sure Shane's on-the-rise catering enterprise hasn't been hired for this gig (which it hasn't). After we take in the art, Hutch and I are calmly calculating how much longer we need to stay in order to honor his filial obligations. It's then that I turn and see Andrea, Shane's artist friend.

Andrea's now a proud Williamsburg loft dweller, having rejected her Beverly Hills rich- kid roots (but not the money from her trust fund, paid for by papa's game show empire). Nonetheless, even in Gotham City, Andrea's expression remains exactly like that of someone who's staring out vacantly at an infinite stretch of freeway.

"Making the scene?" I say, stating the obvious. Andrea remains silent, her features moving just a bit to indicate she's not deaf. "I got the postcard for your show," I continue. (I am not someone who does well with awkward silences.) "Congratulations." This at least produces a begrudging nod and a muttered "Thanks" from her.

Hutch returns with our two plastic-glass refills of red wine. Unlike me, he actually finds Andrea's gargoyle-like demeanor amusing and fun to provoke. "Andrea, baby, what's shakin'? You nailed down your retrospective at the Whitney yet?"

She treats him to a sneer, one that evaporates instantly when Honey and Celeste, the owner of the gallery, appear and fawn over Hutch and me. Hutch makes the intros with almost too much graciousness.

"Honey, Celeste, this is Andrea Bernstein—an up-and-coming artist you should really keep your eye on. She'll probably be on the cover of Art Forum by year's end."

"Are you showing anywhere?" Celeste politely asks Andrea. The Fastest Gun in the West, Andrea has a postcard at the ready. Celeste swiftly examines it, noting the other artists in the show and then studying Andrea's image more carefully with her keen dealer's eye. "Very interesting work." Celeste pauses, then looks up at me and back to the card. "Isn't this your friend, Shane?" Celeste asks me. (Shane and I stopped by an identical such event six months ago together.)

Wanting the spotlight back, Andrea answers for me. "It's based on a found image," Andrea counters, "but yes, it is of her."

"I like it," Celeste ventures. "There's a lot of bite to the work. Nice and edgy. I'm eager to see more." Heading off to mingle with some Prada- and Vuitton-obsessed Japanese, Celeste offers Andrea her card. For the first time in the decade I've known her, Andrea actually smiles. Frankly, it's a little disturbing to realize that papa's game show money paid for Andrea's amazing set of gleaming white teeth, ones that like a comet, appear only on the most stellar, career-advancing occasions.

Twenty minutes later, while Hutch is saying his goodbyes, Andrea and I find ourselves in line together at the coat check.

"Found image, huh?" I inquire.

"Yup, technically that's true," is Andrea's reply. I see the afterglow of Celeste's attention has rendered her unnaturally talkative. "I was helping Shane throw out lots of her junk, and I rescued the photo strip from the trash."

It's only then that I remember where the photo in Andrea's image comes from, and it's the corniest of the corny: four old school photo booth strips, ones Shane and I took together at Otto's Shrunken Head, a tiki bar on 14th Street between Avenues A and B. That joint is about as gnarly as decent folks want to get, but Shane and I had a fantastic night there playing the porn video games and getting blasted on zombies. Nothing happened between us back then, but zombified or not, I vividly remember posing for those photos at three in the morning. Although a lot of rum was involved, it was almost a Hallmark moment. I never thought about those photos again, but still ... Shane's tossing them in the trash hits me surprisingly hard.

"I was inspired by the Warhol Times Square photo booth images he did with Holly Solomon, and of course with his appropriated images in general," Andrea continues. She's quoting from her Artist Statement, totally unconcerned that what she's appropriating are some of my best memories.

"Did you ask Shane if she minded?" I ask her.

Andrea stares at me for a moment. She looks as though I'm asking whether the Pope minded Michelangelo dabbing some paint on the Sistine Chapel's ceiling. "Of course, she didn't mind. She was throwing them out. I cut you out of the picture anyway, so why on earth would she care about my making art out of her trash?"

The next morning, as I emerge from the subway and walk the two Upper East Side blocks toward Epitome, I almost feel like calling out "Dead Man Walking." Maybe Brooke's recommendation is so powerful that even if no one comes to my classes and I just spend the time standing on my head all by myself, Marguerite still won't give me the ax. Or, better yet, perhaps Jasmine can be summoned back from her higher plane of consciousness to restore bliss to the class she was so unjustly dismissed from, a class I am clearly driving straight into the ground. Confidence-inducing thoughts such as these fill my brain as I walk toward Epitome, a scant seven minutes before the class is to begin. I have timed my entrance to the last second so as to minimize the awkward absence of students in the room.

Strolling toward my class, I'm stopped by one of the front desk people, "Martina" according to her nametag—God, how I wish all women would wear them—who seems a little frantic. "I'm sorry, but what's your cutoff policy?" Martina asks.

"Excuse me?"

"How many students will you let into the room?"

"I don't know. Why, is there a problem?"

"Well, Gary closes Cardio Funk off at fifty."

"I'm a little confused. How many people are signed up?"

"Forty-two and we've got at least ten more in line." Is this a parallel universe? I'm besting the ineffable Jasmine, even in February, when New Year's resolutions have long faded.

Martina follows me toward the studio. Upon entering, the room bristles with excitement as though a prizefight, rather than a yoga class, was about to begin. The volume rises once I'm spotted, generating a marked increase in whispering. It's actually tricky to count the students, as people are still entering the room—including Gay Gary, a resurrected student, who, if not lured by my straightness or by the improved quality of my class, is here at least because suddenly it apparently is the place to be at 6:30 p.m. on a Thursday night.

Slinky Brunette shoots me a huge smile and an awkward little "please notice me" wave. I also realize that even though she's about to begin exercising, for the first time ever in class her face is lightly made-up.

And then the obvious hits me. Two things have changed: Obviously, with my Grand Central profile, I am suddenly chic, cool, and happening. Simultaneously, Gay Gary has been hard at work, or else his report back to Slinky Brunette has done its trick in the ladies locker room. Fully branded as straight and single and enjoying my fifteen minutes of fame, I'm now fresh meat—and given my sweatshirt, I'm also fresh, Ivy-League meat—thrown into a cage of rich, hungry tigresses. Suddenly, I'm starting to feel uncomfortable for entirely different reasons.

Less easily distracted and more focused on desk duties, Martina does a quick head count. "There are forty-four students in the room. I think we can let in a grand total of fifty. That should be the absolute maximum. Same as Gary's class."

Satisfied, she scurries to the front desk to make sure my new Sold Out policy is strictly enforced.

Strolling to my place at the front of the room, I notice one student decidedly not present: Jasmine-Fan is nowhere to be seen, no doubt too troubled by my new success to continue her gloating. I almost miss her.

In a last-ditch effort to try not to lose the presumed handful of remaining students from last week, I've gone to great lengths to prepare today's class. In fact, I worked on it over the last three days, going through it first once, and then a second time, each day to make sure my pacing wouldn't be thrown off so that I'd only get to half of what I'd planned. Each time I practiced this class, I knew in my heart that it was just a last-ditch, semimasochistic effort to have a decent final Epitome moment before the inevitable firing for teaching classes no one wants to attend.

Eight hours of preparation to teach a one-hour class is admittedly an impractical ratio, but fortunately it works: For the first time, I teach a class that's actually decent. In fact, it's pretty challenging, more in a slog-through-it, boot-camp way than in a more Gigi-inspirational or Calypso-choreographed sense, but still, for the first time, I can honestly say it doesn't suck. I've kept the poses simple. I leave students in them for just long enough to make them challenging, but keep things moving enough to build up a flow. I am teaching the most basic, no-frills yoga class, but I'll be damned if I don't offer one that delivers a workout.

Most remarkable of all, I find that the energy of the room does shift in the way it should during a good yoga class. We move from slow warm-ups to more intense, faster sequences, finally doing lingering, meditative poses. As individuals, and as a group, the class has been brought from one vibe (frantic, post-work clamor) to another (sweat-drenched calm). They can feel it, and so can I. Finally ... I've managed to do my job here.

When class ends, the ladies thank me and congratulate me on the photo in Grand Central. No one even bothers to play coy about having seen it. In fact, the most brazen students actually bring in copies for me to sign. I find this slightly odd but, bolstered by my newfound self esteem as a decent teacher of group classes, I comply.

It's quite a journey from a lonely nine students to signing autographs for a packed house of fifty. Weirder still, I've leapfrogged my way up the teaching hierarchy; rather than training for years and perfecting my teaching, thanks to Gay Gary's gossiping and one tremendously effective photo spread via Brooke, I've catapulted from novice instructor right to Rock Star.

CHAPTER 13

What do you get your fuck buddy on Valentine's Day?

Do you just ignore the holiday, knowing that it only applies to those saps who define themselves as "in a relationship"? Together, do you laugh at the notion of it all, amused by the idea that people actually shop for heart-shaped objects and purchase corny greeting cards? Do you give each other ironic gifts? Or sexually provocative ones, underscoring the carnal nature of things between you, while at the same time gesturing offhandedly toward the sentimental?

When Valentine's Day arrives, I have purchased nothing for Monique, mostly because I have no idea of when the mood will strike either one of us to hook up again. Monique is such a no-nonsense realist that even the purchase of a box of waxy Russell Stover chocolates from my Duane Reade seems like overkill. Worse, it might offend her that I have, on some level, crossed a line and violated the nature of our understanding.

When Monique calls me at 10:24 p.m. on February 14th, I've frankly forgotten about the holiday. It's just another Tuesday night. And yet it's late, and just the sound of her voice—even the flash of her name on my caller ID—has the Pavlovian effect of getting me horny. As always, without hesitation or fuss, all is arranged in minutes. Within fifteen minutes, she's arrived and we're doing it.

I'm not prepared for what happens next. After we have a solid round or two of going at each other with our usual conviction and gusto, Monique pauses to say she's hungry.

I realize that Monique probably does enjoy the full range of human functions and activities, but in our limited hookup bubble together, I guess I've forgotten that she might do things like eat and drink. "My fridge is pretty empty. Sorry," I apologize.

She laughs, "I thought it would be." In fact, the entire contents of my kitchen are some beer, a frozen bottle of vodka, and, if I'm lucky, in the cupboard there are a few boxes of ramen noodle and mac and cheese packages gathering dust.

"I have some menus in the drawer by the sink."

"I guess we could order in, but I'd rather go out, actually."

I don't know why this startles me. I know Monique has an outside life, but other than the time we first met on New Years (at some event I've entirely forgotten about, thanks to the amnesiac properties of the fermented potato), I've never seen her anywhere but in my apartment.

"Well, I guess we could," I concede.

I realize that it's not that shocking a notion: people who are hooking up can actually go out in public and be seen together—in fact, it happens all the time. And yet, this takes our relationship, such as it is, if not to a new level, at least to a new location.

"Look," Monique interjects, as always cutting to the chase. "This is not us 'going out on a date.' I'm not interested in changing our situation in the least. God knows, I'm not dragging you to a late-night justice of the peace. After twelve hours at the office and another two screwing you, what this is, is me—desperately needing something more substantial than the yogurt I had for breakfast—totally starving."

I realize that I, too, could go for something right about now. "Sold. Where to?"

"I don't know. Somewhere bistro-y. It's a shame Florent is closed. Maybe Blue Ribbon? They close at 4 still, right?"

Perfect. Arguably the finest late-night dining experience in the country, Blue Ribbon's the place where all the serious chefs go when they close their own kitchens, knowing they can indulge in lobster and caviar, or a perfect hamburger and a beer. It's so un-yoga, but true carnivore that I am, I am craving some medium-rare red meat.

We arrive at Blue Ribbon close to 1 a.m. It's still packed, mostly with couples, all needing a late-night bite to eat. The difference is most of the couples are, in fact, couples, rather than two fuck buddies who happen to be out dining on a sappy, greeting-card-industry-created holiday. Fortunately, since they only take reservations for groups of five or more, there's a table waiting for us. I have to admit, at this hour one could do worse than a downtown, dark, candlelit, bistro with stellar cuisine and wine.

I order our steaks, and then Monique takes the liberty of ordering our wine—she's much more of a connoisseur than I am—and besides, as long as I'm on top most of the time, I think it's kind of hot when she's in take charge mode, especially when the focus is our mutual pleasure.

"I didn't want to say anything yet, but I think I might have something that'll interest you," she teases.

"Okay, what?" I reply, assuming she's got some fetish for sex in public places she wants to indulge.

"I'll let you know when it's more concrete, but I think I might have found a way for you to get back into the game." Ah, she's talking nightlife again.

"Monique, I am so out of the game, it ain't even funny."

"We'll see," she says, minx-like, as our food arrives.

And simultaneously, it's just then that it happens—the thing I want most of all and the thing that I'm totally dreading happens … Shane appears.

She's with the guy from her Facebook profile: Frame Boy. And they are being seated two tables away from us.

I realize that Blue Ribbon is at the very top of the list of places one might run into Shane. The Bromberg Brothers own eight acclaimed restaurants, and like all food fanatics in the restaurant world, Shane's drawn to this brasserie's late-night magic just as much as I am. It's not like Shane and I ever divided the map of Manhattan or crafted a list of Mine and Her restaurants and hangouts, but if we had, this one would have been the most contested.

Monique's talking to me when I catch Shane at the very periphery of my vision. The voltage of my surprise is enough to draw Shane's attention right to my gaze. She stops whatever cheerful sentence she was in the middle of, and freezes. We're only one bistro table apart from each other, a distance of probably only four feet, and that, combined with the unexpectedness of the moment, makes it all the more stunning.

Neither of us says anything until I break the silence with a brilliant opener. "Hi."

"Hi, " Shane replies. This is more face-to-face dialogue than we've had in months. I want to view this as a promising beginning despite the complete lack of emotion in Shane's face.

"You look amazing." I don't know why I lead with a compliment, but I do, probably because it's true and it's all I'm thinking, given that I'm not thinking.

Shane does indeed look amazing. She's dressed in a typically Shane way. Nothing about the outfit is calculated to be sexy, but somehow it comes across that way when she puts it on. Maybe it's just the effect Shane has on clothes, on everything maybe. In fact, until the moment she saw me, in her easy laughter with Frame Boy, she was every bit as vivid and passionate in her conversation—frankly in everything—as I remember. Like Gigi's, her enthusiasm splashes around her companions like a drink your favorite bartender has purposefully overfilled, a little messy but joyful, lifting the energy of everyone around her up a notch.

Shane does not respond to the compliment. She does not look away from me either, although I can't tell if this is good or bad. I wonder if she's feeling the same rush of adrenaline that I am. What is that response called? Oh yes, fight or flight. Are those the choices that Shane's contemplating now, or is something else on her mind? Exacerbating the awkwardness, I continue in the same vein of unacknowledged, unwanted compliments.

"I like your hair that way," I tell her.

Shane's hair—once the fastest-growing, wildest mane of anyone I know—is now cut quite short, in an asymmetrical bob of sorts. It looks both very chic and very tossed-off casual. It might be a cut that cost $350 on Madison Avenue (hairstylists used to always stop her and offer to work on her for their books), or she might have done it impulsively herself.

Why I'm going down this banal conversational path, I have no idea. I realize that given our history, a few cheesy compliments will do exactly nothing toward patching things up, but the words are out of my mouth before I can stop them. I speak them to fill the silence, and because, other than endlessly apologizing for our past, I can't think of anything else to say.

Monique clears her throat. I suppose I've been rude, completely disregarding Monique in favor of Shane, the tall, cool drink of a girl seated one table away.

"I'm sorry. Monique, this is Shane. Shane, Monique."

Shane gives her a nod that's just polite enough to extend basic courtesy to Monique without offering me an ounce of encouragement. Frame Boy steps up to the plate to introduce himself around. I can barely register his name, as I'm finding it particularly hard to focus. I give him the once-over. Frame Boy reeks of dependability and sincerity. If he were running for office, you'd feel compelled to vote for him. I realize at once that in the flesh, even more than in his photo, I totally hate him.

The silence is beyond painful, but what small talk is there to make? There is probably no one with a lower opinion of me than Shane—and it doesn't speak well of me to know that there's probably no one else who knows me as well. Shane looks away and leans in toward Frame Boy. She whispers something and then he looks at me (in a very unfriendly way) and whispers something back. She nods, and they stand up to leave, putting on their coats.

Monique, trying to help, leaps in. "Look, this is silly. You guys don't have to go. Can't we all just have dinner in the same restaurant? Maybe there's another table in back, if you want more privacy."

Shane puts on her hat now. It's an authentic Peruvian cap, all handwoven and organic looking, but it's also deeply silly, with tassels and earflaps. It looks like something a child in Lapland might wear. Somehow, its cuteness on her makes this moment all the more ridiculous and tragic. Just as our steaks arrive, Monique makes a fatal, last-ditch effort to save the day.

"Can't we all be grown-ups about this? Look, I have no idea what the story is between you two, but I just don't know why this has to be such an enormously dramatic 'Big Deal.'"

"No, you're right," Shane counters. "It's never a big deal. Nothing is with him. That's the problem."

"Shane, I—" Words fail me, but it's no matter. Her glare, as she and Frame Boy head toward the exit, stops me completely. Spontaneously, she turns for one parting jab before heading into the cold.

"But then again, what was it …? Your 'place is placeless, a trace of the traceless,'" Shane says quietly, making air quotes. She shakes her head lightly at my bullshit Grand Central quote. And then she's gone.

Part of me—and I admit this is not a sign of emotional health—is actually really pleased that Shane saw the article. Like the misbehaving toddler, I somehow prefer any attention over being ignored.

And yet, I note that Shane's last remark is the only time during our encounter that she condescends to show any emotion whatsoever. Frankly, the fact that that emotion is intense disapproval, bordering on disgust, doesn't bother me that much. Given the choice between having her hate me to my face or never seeing her again, I'd rather get what I deserve than lose her completely. Like a badly mismatched prizefighter, no matter how battered I am, I like to think that if I'm still in the ring, at least there's some tiny flicker of hope.

In other words, I'm delusional.

DOWNWARD FACING DOG
(ADHO MUKHA SVANASANA)

Dogs just whip into the pose all the time, instinctively knowing that they need to keep moving in order to stay in the groove.

Humans are a lot less bright. Tight, sometimes seemingly straitjacketed, we need to be reminded, even retaught through yoga, the most basic stretches, the most natural way to breathe.

Not that I'm totally dissing the intellectual benefits of being Homo sapiens. I like Mozart and Bach and the Beach Boys and movies and video games. But our species does not have a total advantage, especially in the physical world.

And when it comes to animal instincts, drives, desires, and urges ... well, if anything, we're even more disadvantaged than those that crawl or walk on all fours. Spending most of our time denying our nature, when we do indulge, it's a constant, losing battle to keep things from blowing up in our face.

Downward Facing Dog, indeed.

CHAPTER 14

If Monique and I had been a real couple, our parting outside Blue Ribbon might have been more dramatic and fraught with jealousy over my unspoken Shane history. As it is, Monique never makes a further inquiry during the rest of our dinner, smiling warmly as she heads off in a cab to her own bed.

The evening's unpleasantness was in no way her fault, but maybe it all stems from my mistake of taking our situation outside the 450 square feet of my apartment. I half wonder if this is simply Nature's way of telling me that the Monique situation has simply run its course. And the part of me that still feels a little guilty about free and easy F-Buddy sex wonders if I somehow brought this on myself.

In any case, I resolve not to call her again although I know that's the kind of resolution I might break easily enough. On some cold March night, when Monique texts me at a quarter to midnight, I know she'll probably be far too tempting to resist.

There is one unexpected consequence to the Monique/Shane episode—one I'm completely bewildered as to how to interpret—but three days later, when I go online, I see that Shane has finally cashed my check for $500.

When I get home from teaching, I'm surprised to find that there's a message from Gigi on my machine. "Give me a call when you have a moment, baby. I'd like to talk a little yoga with you."

To my great discredit, it actually takes me two days to get back to her. I don't know why exactly. I am busier, but I've gone from taking pretty much daily classes at Thank Heaven to now maybe one or two a week. When it comes to your yoga practice, Gigi always quotes Woody Allen: showing up is 80 percent of the job. Still, my not calling her back is shoddy behavior, even for me, and especially toward Gigi, the woman who opened up the door that's given me the possibility of getting my life out of the crapper. Finally, almost as though I'm making amends, rather than calling, I decide to drop by the center and take her class.

Post-class, Gigi alludes, jokingly, to the delay. She's too cool to be that angry, but she's also too much of a straight shooter to let me get away with shit, either. "Things must be quite busy for a yoga celebrity like yourself," she says. "That was an awfully snazzy photo of you."

"I'm sorry. I'm an asshole," I apologize.

"Don't be so hard on yourself, sugar. I'm sure you've got lots of people around you who will be more than happy to scold your bad boy ways. No big deal. I do want to talk to you though."

"I'm all ears."

"Well, you know how tight the schedule has been here at the center. There are so many excellent teachers who come out of the training, and I just can't find spaces to give them all classes. I swear, we're ready to outgrow this joint, and it feels like we just moved in."

Thank Heaven has two large rooms—very decently sized, actually—yet Gigi's right. Classes have been so popular that the center could soon grow into being one of the two or three biggest studios in New York City.

"It's no surprise. Thank Heaven's the best," I tell her.

"Off the record, I like to think so myself," she says. "Anyway, I don't know if you know this yet, but Merissa is going on a six-month retreat to work with Amma's missions."

Amma is regarded by many as a living saint, a true manifestation of the Divine. Basically, she travels everywhere, giving free hugs to the masses. No joke: She hugs you, and many think the simple moment of contact carries a real jolt of mystic voltage. I tried going to one of her events on her annual pilgrimage to New York City, but once I learned that the visit required at least a six-hour wait in line, I jetted out. I've never been one to wait in line for concert tickets; there's no way, saint or no saint, I'm giving up my entire day for a hug.

"Anyway, the schedule's always evolving and I've had my eye on you since yoga school for a spot."

"Really," I exclaim, surprised. "Because of my final?" I blurt out, like a pathetic apple-polishing student clinging to a success. (I aced the yoga school written final with a perfect score, but honestly, only because all my Yale cramming tricks and mnemonics got me through.)

Gigi chuckles. "Are you kidding me? I mean, our teachers need to have the right practical information of course, but the written final's the least important part of it. It's not even your very snazzy practice either. I don't necessarily select the teachers who have the most advanced practices—we're not training folks for Cirque du Soleil—but the ones who really have put their hearts and souls and guts on the line. I've just been impressed with how you consistently keep showing up for class and how much passion, how much focus you put into your practice."

"Thank you," I say, hoping she hasn't checked the class rosters for the last few weeks.

"My pleasure, sweetheart," she tells me. "So, right now I'm happy to offer you a slot. I'd like you to teach Day-Breakers every Saturday at 8 a.m."

Damn! It's not just on Saturday—it's on Saturday morning. Which means I couldn't go out on Friday nights anymore. (I know that like New Year's Eve, going out on the weekends is for amateurs, but now that I'm forced to pretend I'm a morning person five days a week, weekends are my only outlet.)

"I wish I could pay more, but we're offering $25 a class, and then $3 more for every student over ten."

"That's cool. And how many people have been showing up?"

"Usually around twelve, but I'm sure you'll be quite popular. We'll have to get a velvet rope," she jokes.

If I were a better person, the choice would be obvious. It's an honor to be asked to teach at Thank Heaven—a real yoga center, not a cheesy spa—and it's the least I can do for Gigi.

Unfortunately, I am not a better person. Not by a long shot. I'm making $150 an hour teaching privates. My Epitome class with fifty students currently nets me even more. Right now, a Thank Heaven Saturday morning class would be paying me $31. Sure, maybe it would build—perhaps I can do a nude photo spread somewhere and really rope them in—but the low pay, combined with the god-awful hour, are the deal breakers regarding Day-Breakers.

"You know, Gigi, I'm really honored, but I don't know if Day-Breakers is going to work well with my current schedule."

As always, Gigi's bullshit detector is razor-sharp. "Oh, really?"

"It's just that I have this private student I sometimes see on the weekends. If I didn't already have him as a client, I'd totally pick up the class," I explain.

As she takes another sip of her herbal tea, I can tell that she sees right through my rather pathetic lie. It's pretty lame: an imaginary on-again, off-again client whom I didn't remember until after I heard the pay rate. "I'm really sorry," I say to her.

"Well, darlin', whatever journey you're on is great," she assures me. "Come and go as you please. Explore every trail. But know this: You're family. We're always here for you, baby."

I can tell she's disappointed, but at least she's not busting me on my lie when I know she could. And the truth is, while it feels like shit to lie to Gigi and turn down her offer, I just can't see myself getting up early one more day a week for $31.

And yet, if I'm being really honest, it's not the combination of the low pay and the early hour that resulted in my passing on her offer. It's that I'd have to teach far better than I do now at Epitome. With Gigi, there is just no phoning it in. Knowing that Gigi or Calypso might come to my class would mean that I would have to deliver something of quality and substance. Unlike my private students, with whom I can just go with the flow and teach in an improvised style, and unlike my Epitome classes, which are now consistently tough workouts but generic and completely uninspiring, at Thank Heaven I would have to, for my own satisfaction and for Gigi's, consistently deliver something excellent. Not just poses and sequencing, but something with an inner quality. Something that could only come from a deep, authentic place inside myself.

I'm not willing to do that work. It's not so much that I'm lazy per se—it's just that frankly, right now, I'm not sure if I could ever dig that deep.

Just as I'm leaving the center, I turn my cell phone back on and it's buzzing. It's Monique, and, astonishingly, it's not even nightfall.

We haven't spoken since the messed-up Valentine's Day incident, so I take the call more out of curiosity than a desire to get laid at 2 p.m.

"Hi, what's up?" I ask.

"Something interesting," Monique replies. Already, I can tell that this is a different kind of call. Her phone manner has shifted out of full-time flirtation gear; she's blending business and efficiency into her purr. "I have a possibility that might be right for you," she tells me. "A property that's available on the Lower East Side."

"What? Thanks, but I'm not exactly in the market for real estate at this time."

Monique is undaunted. "It's an interesting space for a club that was offered to us. It's wrong for us now since we're focused on expanding the brand into South America, Europe, and Asia. We don't want to dilute our NYC interests with another project. But I thought it might be the right next step for you."

"Monique, you know I've told you I'm outta the game."

"Please stop wasting both our time. This is an incredible opportunity that I'm sharing with you. I wanted to be sure we were passing, but now that we are, I've persuaded them to show it to you first, before it goes on the open market. You need to meet me there in twenty minutes. I'm going to text you the address right now."

It seems that whether we're talking hookups or business propositions, all my Monique encounters are characterized by urgent phone calls and rendezvousing twenty minutes later. Sure enough, she and I arrive pretty much simultaneously at a beaten-down Lower East Side building. Its exterior shows some character (read: "grime"), with a boarded-up front window that indicates some serious neglect. I remain increasingly skeptical about this entire episode.

Walking inside with Monique and the property manager, however, I'm amazed. The space is cavernous, infinitely vaster than the outside would suggest. The ceilings are vaulted and enormous with a tremendous, ornate skylight you'd never have guessed was there.

Monique sees my open-mouthed surprise. "Maybe they were growing weed. Perhaps it was seized by the DEA or something before it got on the market again."

The space even has sections that occur naturally—architectural nooks and crannies, as it were—that lend themselves to VIP rooms, or the like. The place has character that transcends function—like the constantly reinvented space that houses Limelight/Avalon on Sixth Avenue and 20th Street—or like I'm told Area had back when I was breastfeeding.

Last year, I tried (and failed) to open up a small restaurant, one of those places that could handle a twenty-person seating, tops. This place—I don't even know how many it could hold. It's not super-enormous, like the defunct Roxy, but it's impressive nonetheless. Monique then adds the coup de grâce of her selling strategy: there's a working kitchen.

"You'd have to have everything inspected quite thoroughly before you signed anything, but we can check it out now, and you'll see that it seems fully functional," Monique tells me.

This actually is the kind of place I've long dreamed of opening but as my third or fourth venture. This kind of joint would be my step up into the Big Time.

The excitement grows exponentially inside me with every moment. I can imagine running this place. I can see it filled with beautiful women—the best eye candy and total 11s—and cool guys, overflowing with the energy and vibrancy that only New York nightlife has. It's the NYC, amped-up reincarnation of the vitality I first felt when I was old enough to work at The Grill on Saturday nights. The Grill was the only place in thirty miles to grab a decent meal and a beer, and although describing it as "a scene" would really be pushing it, it was definitely the only place where anything at all could remotely be said to be happening.

I try to appear slightly poker-faced around the property manager until Monique and I are alone.

"Well?" she asks, smiling broadly.

"It's amazing! Abso-fucking-lutely amazing!"

If Monique were a dude I'd be high-fiving her.

"I know. Believe me, I'd be all over this if it weren't slightly off-brand. But our pass is your gain," she says.

"I'm happy to absorb Becker's rejects. Tell me what it would need to make this happen."

"Besides knowing me," Monique smiles wickedly.

"Come on. I need some numbers."

"Over a drink," she says. Monique hails a cab and we're whisked off to Brass, one of Becker's snazzy properties—thankfully not Gold, where Shane works. Brass's interior is all sleek perfection: golden chrome and shiny surfaces everywhere.

Monique gets us a great table, orders two drinks, pulls out a legal pad and her laptop, and starts jotting down notes and doing the math.

She knows the costs for these kinds of ventures far better than I do, but she keeps checking in with my vision of things. I have tons of details that are important to me, and Monique gathers and estimates the gist of what it will cost to make them real. She puts everything into concrete financial terms, translating square footage into seatings, calculating how many people the club can accommodate in order to hover between the exclusive limits of the velvet rope and the maximum capacity of the fire laws.

Monique plays with the numbers on her laptop spreadsheet, oblivious to me except when she needs something clarified.

Finally, she seems satisfied, pushes her computer away, and takes a big sip of her drink.

"$3.8 million," Monique concludes.

I don't even know what to say. I'm happy making $150 a lesson, getting caught up on my rent, and—except for a $500 check to Shane—ignoring my $120,000 debt from Failed Venture #1. Thus, $3.8 million feels a tad out of my league.

"What's wrong?" Monique asks, sipping her scotch seductively.

"Not sure if my piggy bank's got that much spare change," I say in a lame attempt at wryness.

"Oh, please, that's nothing at all. You can find the money if you really want this. You're getting an amazing piece of real estate that, if you make this work for you, will become a tremendous income generator for you."

"We're talking about several million dollars."

"Money is everywhere in New York. We're practically swimming in it."

"Trust me, I'm not."

"Oh, you may be a puddle personally, but come on. This is a city with over thirty billionaires. And that's billionaires. God knows how many people with just a few hundred million there are." There's a wild, on-fire look in her eye that, frankly, I don't think I've seen even during our most intense sexual moments. I'll be damned, but more than screwing, talking about money really gets Monique going.

She continues, "This is the business capital of the world. The energy of it is everywhere. Money is being exchanged faster and more furiously than anywhere else in the universe. Think of it—right now, countless transactions, endless exchanges of goods and services via the medium of currency, are happening even as we're sitting here. At this very moment, millions, billions, probably trillions of dollars are shifting hands, moving through accounts and morphing through exchange rates: being soundly invested and squandered. Endless electronic transactions are splashing right through us as we're sitting here. It's like an electrical current, baby. You just gotta let it flow through you."

Monique savors her scotch and the curious eroticism she finds in all this financial talk.

I refrain from interrupting her rapture with the obvious truth that high-voltage electric current is usually pretty deadly. Instead, I refocus on the $3.8-million-dollar problem at hand.

"Very inspiring," I tell her. "I'm just not sure how to get any of that energy redirected my way."

"It shouldn't be that hard," Monique shrugs, signaling the waiter over for a refill of our drinks.

"You think so?"

"Absolutely. It's your destiny."

"I'm glad you have such confidence in me. Last time around, I seem to recall getting myself quite burned with this kind of venture."

"Last time was last time. This time is different."

"Why is that?"

"I'm around this time," she smirks seductively. "These things require two strong skill sets. Yours is the look, the feel, the crowd, setting the vibe and having the vision. Defining and establishing the brand. Mine is corporate: crunching the numbers and structuring the investment opportunity. Interestingly, they rarely coincide in one individual, but each is vital for the success of this kind of enterprise."

I note that we still haven't discussed the extent of Monique's involvement, but knowing her, I'm sure she'll lay out her terms with her usual point-blank, take-it-or-leave-it style.

"Even so, moving back into this world feels vaguely kamikaze of me"

"Look, your teaching yoga is sweet—I've enjoyed a couple of stretchy classes at Canyon Ranch myself—but the truth is, that's not your real nature. Who do you think you're fooling here? You're pretty far from Gandhi."

"Well, I don't wear a diaper, but still ..."

"Look, I don't believe in fate—I think we make our own beds—but even so, I'm still absolutely certain that it's not your destiny to sit around trying to sell wheatgrass shots and the whole peace/love/bliss thing."

"That's not really what I do. I teach poses and breathing and some meditation and—"

"Whatever. You're just like Becker."

Now she's got me. "Go on."

"You're both bad boys who are much smarter than the rest of the pack. Sure, you might later acquire a domesticated, civilized veneer, but deep down, you live for all the endless nocturnal adventures: the ones that are only possible for a handsome devil with plenty of charm who, deep down, every girl knows is bad news but still wants anyway."

"Thanks, I guess." She really does have my number.

"I'm just telling it like it is. Everyone's always broadcasting exactly who they are if you pay attention."

"Oh really? You think so?"

"Absolutely. Take yourself. I'm surprised you can even publicly bluff your way through that spirituality shit without laughing. You're about sensuality and sexuality and fun. You may be able to con some socialites, but at least stay honest with yourself. You're not meant for the yoga mat—you're meant for the prowl."

Maybe it's that I felt particularly like a fraud around Gigi, or maybe it's that I'm sick with myself for allowing Phoebe to keep thinking of me as a paragon of virtue. I know in my guts I'm NOT a real teacher. Suddenly, after many months of hibernation, becoming a force in the nightlife scene is starting to look good again.

I used to dream of Scarface-style money. Dealing with big gobs of cash floating around my desk and out of my secret office safe rather than just billing my current hourly rate. I want to go back to who I was—or more accurately, who I almost was—before everything got so messed up with the investors. And with Shane.

Shane. Now there's a thought.

Obviously, if I came to her now and offered her the position of head chef at my latest theoretical grandiose venture—exactly like I did a year ago—there's not a jury in the world that would convict her if she murdered me on the spot. But this might be the way I could actually start seriously paying her back.

If I really could pull this off, if I really could launch this place successfully, seeing it through to completion, then ultimately I could offer her an incredibly swank opportunity. So what if the first lounge scheme fell through—it would now be totally small potatoes compared to this place.

"You're a million miles away." Monique brings me back to the present. She pretends to be amused, but I detect that she's a little irritated that I've drifted away from her personal charms and even more seductive career lures.

"Sorry. Just thinking about how this could all work."

"Oh, it'll work all right."

I know she means raising capital and profit margins, but my thoughts have shifted from my own nightlife fantasies to the possibility of mending things with Shane. I want this. I want this for myself. And the proverbial icing on the cake is it's my only shot with Shane. Payback of $500 a month simply isn't going to cut it. Frankly, there's no way of knowing, but the truth is, unless I make this work, there's nothing else that could even come close.

I realize I'm ravenous as the waiter appears with another round and some complimentary appetizers. Monique extends her refilled glass towards me.

"Here's to your destiny, Bad Boy," she toasts.

Indeed.

CHAPTER 15

My mind whirls with thoughts of my impending moguldom. Monique has a business dinner, so I walk around for a few hours, window-shopping other possible New York venues that I will someday conquer. On a day like today, the city feels like a place where anything and everything is possible.

Two hours later, I'm hungry again. I swing by Raoul's in Soho. The restaurant has been there since the '70s, but although there's no more smoking and the artists have all fled the neighborhood, the bistro vibe prevails. As do upscale prices. I treat myself to a thick steak au poivre with crispy frites and fleshy steamed artichokes with thick dipping vinaigrette. Savoring the perfect steak—$37 but worth every penny—I contemplate that, soon, this will be my lifestyle. I take another swig of my single malt, $18 scotch.

That night, I can barely sleep. My mind is whirling around the possibilities and also the challenges of how the hell I'm going to pull this off. Come morning, as the prelude to my hitting the pavement and the phones at 9 a.m. to make this dream happen, I'm looking forward to another chaste yet subliminally illicit encounter with Phoebe.

Yet to my complete astonishment, it's Phil who opens the door.

"Hiya, how's it going?" he asks, letting me in. Even Phoebe's smiling entrance doesn't totally dispel this ominous beginning.

"Oh, great, we're all here, then," she proclaims. Instantly, I realize this is the theoretical moment I have silently dreaded but thought would never actually happen: Phil's going to join us for a lesson.

"Yup, it worked out that I could be here today. Moved my shipper's meeting to tomorrow," Phil confirms.

"Great." I reply, as we walk to the yoga room. To his credit, Phil at least seems game. He's willing to give it a shot, more or less.

Phoebe and I sit cross-legged in our regular places. I see that it's really uncomfortable for Phil to sit this way, and rather than torture him (which, I admit, crosses my mind as a way of discouraging his future participation), I opt to play the role of good teacher. I offer him a yoga block to sit on the edge of, thereby letting his inflexible hips relax. He's grateful, and he seems a little surprised that I've managed to effectively solve a body problem so easily.

I direct their breathing, but Phil is wildly restless. He adjusts his outfit. Clears his throat. Fidgets. He can't sit still. I wait for him to settle, but pretty soon it's clear that that moment's never going to happen. If anything, he's getting further and further from stillness with every shallow, wheezy breath he takes. Unlike me, Phoebe seems to be the soul of patience, glowing with the sheer joy of having Phil's twitchy presence next to her.

I don't know whether to basically give up (as I have with Andrew's breathing properly) or stop the lesson dead in its tracks and force Phil to breathe through his nose. It would be a total waste of time for Phoebe although she might respect my attention to detail, my commitment to teaching excellence, if I were to be entirely painstaking with Phil and his congested inhales and exhales.

I flip a mental coin and decide it's best to move on. After all, I was myself an unaware, inept breather during all my early yoga classes. Besides, if I get him moving, at least he'll start to sweat—that seems like progress, and at the very least, he'll register that something's happening.

Okay, then, it's time to get this show on the road, time for what, I presume, will be a disastrous Om-ing together. Perhaps the weirdness of "Om"-ing alone will be enough to drive Phil from the room.

"We'll do three Oms together. I'll start, and you'll

immediately join in," I tell them.

"Don't worry about the chanting or the singing quality. It's simply a way for us to connect with the breath, and with the sound, and with each other. And it'll frame our lesson at the beginning and end, uniting us in a tradition of yoga practice."

"Okey-dokey," is Phil's cheery reply. I say nothing. It's sort of sweet that he's responding to me, even when I'm used to people just absorbing my directions in silence.

I start the Oms and Phil surprises me with an extremely hearty (but off-key) contribution. Usually the guys like Janek and Andrew—and frankly, me, back in the day—are less than comfortable making a loud chanting sound. We sort of sneak it in under our breath, barely participating, calculating the minimum sound we can get away with making.

Not Phil, though. You'd think he was auditioning for the Met with the enthusiasm he puts into his first foray into chanting. Another disturbing thought occurs: What if he actually enjoys the lesson too much? Am I doomed to having him disrupt my spiritually erotic Phoebe vibe on a steady basis? Or can I count on the demands of being the Wire Hanger King to keep him away from our Rumi-infused private practice?

I quickly learn that Phil has absolutely no affinity toward taking directions regarding his body. For better or worse, he looks to Phoebe for constant visual assistance. I can understand that the first time he's in Downward Dog and I say, "Raise your right leg to the sky," that the meaning might take a second to process. He looks to Phoebe and then simply lifts his right leg upward as she does. But twenty seconds later, after I say, "Lower your right leg. Now inhale as you raise your left leg to the sky," he looks to her again. Phil's unwilling to take any chances, cautiously looking to Phoebe before swinging his left hindquarters upward. It's a confidence thing, not wanting to look foolish by making a wrong move. Instead, he winds up looking like he's mentally deficient.

I try to get Phil up and standing as soon as possible so that he doesn't have to strain his neck so much to look at Phoebe for constant input. He's incredibly stiff—that comes as no surprise—but as we progress, I must admit I like his verve. He's more than willing to jump right in despite a complete lack of coordination or anything resembling physical grace. The guy has spunk; I'll give him that. When I say, "Energize your arms in Warrior One," he gets that concept and it's like fire could shoot out of his pudgy fingers.

The funny thing is, more and more, I'm actually liking the dude. He's not wimping out. I've even picked up the pace of the vinyasa because I feel he's digging it. I can tell he likes the rush of the movement and the music—I've moved into light Brazilian on my iPod to give us a little something to move to—and perhaps somehow I've touched some latent athlete within. I dimly recall some anecdote of Gigi's regarding teaching people: if you really work with someone, really accept your student, and offer the best in yourself, something in you changes as well.

I find myself shifting, trying to make things more attainable for him. Adjusting him as I'd want to be adjusted myself. I hate wimpy assists—dammit, if a teacher's going to put their hands on me and apply a little pressure, I want them to go the full, safe distance so that I feel something. When it comes time to complete the more cooling poses on the ground, I give him deep but reasonable assists in the forward bends, fully aware of how tight his hamstrings are. I want him to truly feel the potential to open, but God knows, I don't want them to snap. "Go easy on me, kid," Phil mutters a little nervously.

"Don't worry. This is as far as I'm going," I reassure him.

Phil's sitting down and bending forward. I've thrown a blanket on his sweaty back so that I can first use my hands to invite him further forward. Then, I'm sitting back-to-back against him, using the weight of my own body to push him gently forward.

When it comes time for Corpse Pose, I decide that today, Phil—as a first-timer—gets the use of Phoebe's eye pillow. I start with my usual move—a tender smoothing of Phoebe's brow with my thumbs—and then I press down on her shoulders. She breathes a lovely sigh. Then, astonishingly, when I move to Phil, I find myself transfixed by the beauty of his face. Well, beauty might be stretching it considerably, but nonetheless, I feel something when I look at him. Eyes closed, with a stillness stemming perhaps largely from exhaustion, there is still something truly lovely about this bullfrog's visage at rest. Mind you, it's Chinese-Guard-Dog-Statue-Beautiful, but beautiful nonetheless.

We complete with three Oms together, and Phil, if anything, is even more operatic in his enthusiasm. We bow forward with a trio of "Namastes." Phil waits a respectful moment and then breaks the silence. "Wow, that was really terrific."

"I'm glad you liked it," I reply.

"Yup. I don't think I've sweated this much since back in the day in Newark. I spent my summers in high school working as a mover," Phil continues.

Of course, this is not the profound, spiritually connected response one might hope for, but nonetheless, I'm pleased. Frankly, the fact that I've given a workout comparable to moving furniture up five-floor tenement walk-ups gives me a smidgen of satisfaction. It's the kind of clueless thing I probably said to my first yoga teachers as a compliment, too. More and more, despite myself, I actually find myself liking the bullfrog. Given fifty pounds, forty years, and sixty million dollars, how different are Phil and I really?

"Did you offer him the tickets?" he asks.

"Oh, I forgot," Phoebe replies.

"What tickets?" I inquire.

"For Wicked. You know, the musical. Herb Abromowitz and his wife got them for us. You know the guy from Abe's Cleaners?"

I don't know them, but like most New Yorkers, I'm quite familiar with the "Honest Abe" dry cleaning chain and their annoying, omnipresent ads on local cable.

"Anyway, I forgot tonight's a major UNITE meeting, so we can't go."

"Unite?" I ask. Phil doesn't really seem the type to be involved with any political or humanitarian organizations.

Phoebe fills me in: "Union of Needletrades, Industrial and Textile Employees—UNITE. Phil's on the board."

"Anyway, I figure you guys like those kind of things—

musicals and all—so I figured you'd probably enjoy it," Phil explains.

"I'm sorry?"

"With the hangers and all, I'm on the sidelines of fashion— what a crazy business that is!—but I just figured that it was the kind of thing you might enjoy. And I've got two tickets, so you could bring your guy friend or whoever. House seats."

Now I get it. Phil assumes that I'm gay and therefore the most appropriate recipient to premium tickets to a hit Broadway musical.

My eyes meet Phoebe's. It's only for a fraction of a second, but we share a look of conspiratorial amusement. Clearly my sexuality is not something they have discussed—or if it is, Phoebe has omitted, or misrepresented, the findings of her own, only slightly more subtle investigation. As to the tickets themselves, well, I'm no stranger to theater, but I'm forced to honestly reply, "Thanks very much, but I teach a big class tonight. I just started, so I wouldn't want to get a sub at the last minute."

"No problem. Some other time. People are always giving us cultural stuff like this. Phoebe'll tell you how hard it is to get me to get all dressed up and go out at night. Just not my thing."

Part of me—and it's probably just knee-jerk, residual high school homophobia—is briefly tempted to correct Phil and let him know I like the ladies. I stop myself, though, because: a) it's stupid and none of his business, and b) it might not work in my favor to let him know the man he leaves his wife with every day, the man who runs his hands all over her body, adjusting and assisting her poses, would very much like to have those hands roam a lot more freely if he could.

Then it suddenly dawns on me that Phil still thinks I'm gay, and yet throughout, he's been completely open-minded, allowing me to touch and move and now practically lie down on top of him. The guy is cooler than I thought.

"Holy Toledo, look at the time. Hon, I gotta run." Phil pecks Phoebe quickly, then pumps my hand. "This yoga stuff really is all right," he decides. "I'm away next week, but when I get back, I'm definitely gonna do this again. I'll try for once a month or so to start."

I almost launch into a speech about how steady practice several times a week is necessary for any real progress. But having him around that much is not my goal here. Instead, I just accept the compliment.

Phil heads off to take a much-needed shower, leaving me and Phoebe alone for our parting moments. Unlike soggy Phil, as usual, she's simply aglow. Phoebe walks me toward the door, letting me out herself, as is our ritual.

"Thank you so much," she gushes. "I understand how demanding it must be to teach a total beginner."

"He was pretty fun to teach, actually."

We smile. As always, it goes on a bit longer than necessary, the smile substituting for dialogue we're better off just not saying.

I can tell Phoebe wants to say something more. "About those tickets ..." she begins as I'm waiting for the elevator.

I cut her off. "Very sweet of you both. Maybe some other time."

We smile knowingly. She understands that I'm not insulted by the gay assumption and that I have no need to set the proverbial record "straight" with her husband. And perhaps she shares my sense that it would be strategically unwise as well, potentially interfering not only with our chaste present but also with my barely sublimated fantasies of future dalliances. I enter the elevator, reluctant to leave her serene smile behind.

"Phil's okay." I don't know why I say that. It just sort of comes out, this semi-random endorsement of her husband.

She smiles again. "He definitely has his moments," is her cryptic reply.

"See you on Thursday?" I say.

"Absolutely," she says.

Liking Phil, yet wanting Phoebe all to myself; enjoying teaching him, yet hoping his attendance doesn't become a habit—it's a mixed bag of motivations. As I depart, I'm reminded of a line from Hafiz, Rumi's spiritual cohort: "This teaching business sure ain't easy."

One more reason—thanks to Monique—that it might just be a good thing I'm contemplating getting back in the Game.

CHAPTER 16

I had never felt that I had a future in stand-up comedy until I'd approached five different banks for loans. I am practically laughed out of all of them.

It's not hard to understand why. My personal credit is terrible. I have no assets that could even vaguely be considered as collateral. I lack any financial track record of business successes. And I am hoping to use their money for a ludicrously speculative venture. When asked about my experience in this realm, I can boast only of my tremendous success in hitting on hotties and my spectacular failure of last year. (Of course, I do not say these things, and frankly, by this point in the interview and application process, my fate's long since been sealed; there's no way any reputable institution is going to loan me money for this, or anything else for that matter.)

That leaves the dismal task of hunting down investors, and although my life seems drenched with rich people, I know that they are a difficult quarry. Like the exotic Tibetan snow lion, successfully getting a rich person to invest in a personal project like this has probably never been captured on film.

I won't ask Hutch—I can't afford to risk my only continuous, thriving relationship by doing business together, and frankly, I don't think he's got that kind of loot sitting around just yet. I don't know what he's making now—low- to mid-six figures, probably—but a few years of that does not a spare $3.8 million make. Besides, I don't want to discuss this with Hutch just yet. I'm not sure why, maybe because he'll talk me out of it, but mostly because I think he'll be really into it and disappointed if I fail (again).

Brooke, I feel, would view it as a tremendous breach of breeding. Her Marie Antoinette-ness would make such a conversation unthinkable.

Phoebe thinks of me as a spiritual guru. I'm not sure how she'd handle the news that I'm more interested in resurrecting the spirit of Studio 54 than in Sufi Mysticism.

Andrew? Well, maybe, but it just seems so outside his sphere. I don't know if he's even been to a club since the El Morocco, or the Stork Club, or something else with Rita Hayworth and Jock Whitney. And besides … it vaguely feels like asking my dad for money (would that my real dad had that kind of loot).

Janek? I think about it but decide that I should keep things professional with him, too. And, as with Hutch, Janek might be a thriving achiever, complete with a stunning apartment, but even though he is president of a successful company, he also may not have an extra $3.8 million floating around.

On the subway ride home, I gaze up at ads for ambulance-chasing lawyers and their multimillion-dollar victories for their victim clients. Hitting the street, I half wonder if I should throw myself into traffic and just hope for the best. With a nice settlement, I might be able to attend the club's opening night, albeit on crutches or life-support.

Mostly for his own amusement, Hutch pretty much insists we go to Andrea's opening. Technically, it's not really hers, in that there are seven other artists in the show.

"Come on, Dawg, it'll be hilarious," Hutch says, "watching Andrea try to put the moves on anyone marginally able to buy a canvas."

Knowing full well the primary reason for my hesitation—the prospect of yet another increasingly dismal Shane encounter— Hutch puts his intel on the table. "And Shane's out of town for the week, amigo. No ghosts of Break-Ups Past will be present."

"How the hell do you know that?" I wonder aloud.

"Oh, it was totally easy to get it out of Andrea. She called me up a half-dozen times to get Honey and Celeste to swing by her opening. Practically offered to send one of Daddy Game Show's limos to pick them up. Anyway, brother, just wanted to make sure the coast was clear for you to buzz by."

Andrea has three paintings in the show, and as reflected on her website, only one is devoted to Shane. Andrea is at her most cordial although Hutch taunts her continually that Celeste is texting from her cab that she's dropping by right after she leaves Brice Marden's studio. All is all, the the evening is relatively unremarkable. (Andrea does reveal that her first solo show is coming up at the bridge gallery, barely disguising her ambition to have Celeste offer her an uptown show as well.) Although I'm secretly hoping that somehow I'll stumble upon a deep-pocketed art investor who, captivated by my latest venture, decides to sell a Damien Hirsh and throw the funds my way … I've no such luck.

Curbside, Hutch and I hail a cab to depart—"One tiny nightcap to wash away Andrea's smugness," Hutch insists—and surprisingly, it's Janek who steps out. Warm greetings all around.

We chat for a bit, with the driver getting impatient and doubtless wondering if he should wait around for us or not when Janek's joined by a good-looking, artsy-looking dude who does something for Vilinikov, and having obtained our share of culture, we all head off into the night.

Unlike my fundraising fiascos, my class at Epitome continues to rock. This week, it sells out at fifty students a full ten minutes before start time. Interestingly, Serious and Diamond Cleavage both take class this week. It is Diamond's bejeweled hands that I notice first, as sparks of platinum and diamond catch my eye. Even among the many striking women here, these two are difficult to ignore. Diamond Cleavage—and I can think of her by no other name—has opted for a necklace-free class. She has, however, adorned herself with scads of bracelets: enough to make a minor racket whenever she moves. This is actually rather annoying until I turn the music up. Looking up from Downward Dog, Diamond Cleavage peers up at me, smiles, and mouths, "Hi."

I return the smile without missing a beat, noticing that next to her is Serious Cleavage, whose serious cleavage is, well, even more abundantly on display in both Downward Dog and every other pose, thanks to the most plunging neckline I've ever seen on a fitness outfit. She has, no doubt, had her workout clothes altered to emphasize her most obvious assets. At least this time, she doesn't pinch my ass in passing.

Post-class, as I emerge from the men's locker room, walking down the hush-hush hallway where spa treatments are offered, towards the exit, it's practically a "psst" that draws me toward Serious Cleavage. Standing seductively outside the door of one of the treatment rooms, a meaningful glance conveys that she has something intimate to say to me. I slow my exit to speak to her.

"Let's talk in here; it's so much more private."

The few scented candles flickering in here pretty much add nothing to the visibility level. There is enough light, however, for me to see that Diamond Cleavage, also in a spa robe, sits in a reclining piece of furniture that seems designed for pedicures.

"We loved your class," Diamond Cleavage says.

Both of them, hot as they are, could barely get through the class. They spent most of it in Child's Pose.

"Why am I here?" I wonder, feeling a little trapped in the small room designed for two reclining rich people and two aestheticians seated on stools. In fact, there's nowhere for me to sit now that Serious Cleavage has taken her place adjacent to Diamond Cleavage on their polyurethane thrones.

"The thing is, we were hoping for some private lessons, perhaps," Diamond Cleavage proposes.

"That's cool. I think you're supposed to book those through the front desk," I tell them.

They both softly chuckle, smiling at me as though I'm a

not-so-bright child comically misunderstanding something basic, like the on-off switch for a household appliance.

"Well, we were hoping for something a little less … corporate," Serious replies.

"A little more intimate, if you know what we mean," Diamond continues.

Truly, I'm beginning to feel a lot like that dense child, one contemplating a mystery like how those people live inside the TV set … What the hell are they talking about?

"You see, we admired your photo in Grand Central very much. Congratulations on that," Serious Cleavage compliments.

"And the thing is, we both enjoy doing things together. Privately."

Serious slips her hand on Diamond's exposed thigh. Diamond smiles. Serious starts to run her fingertips under the thick terrycloth robe toward Diamond's crotch.

"But sometimes we like to include someone else in our private times together," Serious says.

"We're very good at sharing, you see," Diamond adds. "And we thought if there's a time we could schedule a 'lesson' together, we might all enjoy exploring some interesting positions with you."

In theory, I'm not averse to threesomes, but even with all my nightlife practice, ladies don't throw themselves at me quite this easily and, frankly, never in bathrobes. Is this the Upper East Side or the Playboy Mansion? Speechless, I'm saved by a delicate tap on the door.

"Come in," Serious says sweetly, as two foreign attendants enter to minister to the needs of the Cleavage Gals' feet.

"Um …" I start to reply, as Serious hands me her calling card. There is, of course, no profession listed. Just her name, address, phone, and email.

"You can let us know anytime," Diamond replies, completing the moment with a relaxed flourish as she waves and gestures me toward the door. They're both so smooth, you'd think they approached guys for ménages à trois all the time.

I swiftly duck out of the room, frankly feeling more like

a sheep than a wolf—something I haven't felt in years and years—and just plain happy to have escaped the clutches of two carnivores that—despite Monique's statement to the contrary—make me seem like Gandhi.

I don't mention anything about the club to Andrew, but when I show him my Grand Central spread, he expresses great enthusiasm and almost paternal pride. "Jesus," he says when he looks at my Flying Crow, "do you think I'll ever get into that?"

I wonder if he's kidding, but then I see that he's not. I don't really know how to answer him although the answer is basically, "Not if all we do is talk about your pity fucks during your lessons, no—not in a million years."

Instead, I diplomatically reply, "Well, it took me a lot of practice."

He nods. A thought occurs to him. "Say, I don't know if I mentioned this but ..." He rummages briefly on the top of his desk to produce this month's issue of Forbes. Andrew is the cover subject. I have a one-page photo spread in a New York glossy; he's the cover story profile of a national magazine.

"Impressive," I say, meaning it.

"Keep it if you want," he tosses off as he lies down, getting ready for his restorative block pose. "They give you a ton of them when you're on the cover."

I leaf through the article as Andrew settles himself down. "So, have you been getting a lot more action?" Andrew asks me. This is startling because he rarely inquires about my love life. We are there to talk about his, after all.

"I always find that after a big public profile," Andrew says, " the ladies come swarming more than ever. Something about the power of the press, I guess. Anyway, it's a narrow window," Andrew continues. "Magazines come out every week or month. Suddenly, someone new is on the cover, and someone new is getting laid. This is your month, or in your case, your week."

Actually, it's my three days, as I realize that the next issue of

Grand Central comes out on Wednesday.

As if reading my mind, Andrew continues his mentoring. "Of course, I'm not advising doing anything foolish," he tells me. "There is one overriding moral principal that you must adhere to. You must insure that you will never, ever be trapped and exposed by your own behavior. Don't allow the satisfaction of your basest desires to undo you."

"Shouldn't we at least try to take the high road?"

"Why?" he asks, totally straight-faced.

I'm stumped for an insightful answer other than a knee-jerk "It's the right thing to do." Andrew, however, is quite well thought out in his convictions.

"It's a matter of being a realist. In fact, I believe that's the single greatest key to my success. Our follies are inevitable. They are probably engraved into our DNA just as much as our eye color and height. The choices you should truly focus on are how you conceal your weakness, your appetites. Do they destroy you, or are you able to insulate and protect yourself from them?"

"The lessons are all around in nature," he continues. "Jaorinia frogs in the tropics hunger for the Clarington beetle, and so they've managed to evolve themselves to blend in perfectly with the local fauna. Species after species has done the same thing, disguising itself so that it can remain undetected and therefore safe from predators."

Usually, I think of myself as the predator, but Andrew's on a roll, so I think it wise not to interrupt.

"Deep inside, you know your true nature, its shiny qualities and its shames, and you are therefore faced with the choice of not only how and what you're going to present to the world but also whether you will let your own underbelly destroy you."

Andrew is mixing so many theories so brilliantly—Darwinian evolution, Jungian analysis, Karma, and your basic PR bullshit—that it's no wonder he's so successful … and yet so tormented. But still, there's something haunting about his words, something almost prophetic. Maybe our follies are inevitable, indeed. And while Andrew tortures himself about his situation endlessly, he also has, in some ways, accepted his nature. His concern is not "good" behavior, it's flying under the radar of those who would tarnish his status or dethrone him. His suffering is real, but it is the torture of a general planning a war, not of a shriveling penitent. Unlike me, guilt seems to be entirely beneath him. He's never expressed a moment's remorse about his liaison with Gloria or any of the others, and while many would question my behavior, at least I have a modicum of internal torment whenever I'm straying beyond the guidelines of Parental Control. Perhaps there's a lesson here: a wolf does not apologize for craving the lamb.

Correctly assessing that he's slam-dunked his case, Andrew returns to his initial inquiry.

"So who's been throwing themselves at you since your photo spread?"

There's something about the way Andrew asks things—totally straightforward and with tremendous authority, much like a good district attorney would, I imagine—that makes it very difficult to withhold anything. I give him the gist of the encounter with the two Cleavage ladies at Epitome. He asks their names. I confess that I never really learned them solidly, but one of them gave me a card, and while it's somewhere in the back of my wallet now, I believe it began with an S—or maybe an S sound. Susan? Cicely? Stacey? And the last name was Baxter? Or was it Boston?

"Benton?" Andrew offers. "Fond of wearing an enormous canary diamond pendant, the Foxbury?"

"Yup. That's her."

"Not so surprising. And the other woman, probably Dick Welles's wife."

"That sounds right, too. Do you know them?"

"Dick and I are on the board of St. Gabriel's together. Benton and I are both members of the Maidstone Club. I've met their wives at various functions. Both very fetching. I've certainly never received such an invitation from them. It's certainly an interesting proposition."

I watch Andrew think for a moment—and I really mean that. In moments like these, you can actually see the concentration, the calculation, occurring rapidly in his brain. He reaches a conclusion. As always, he's decisive and committed.

"I think you should go for it."

"Really?"

"Absolutely. I have no recollection of either of these women having even an inclination of indiscretion whispered about them. They have impeccable reputations that I'm sure they're quite unwilling to carelessly tarnish."

"Still, I don't want to screw up my situation at Epitome."

His laugh is a guffaw. "You've got to be joking."

"No, I'm not."

"I don't mean that you'd want to lose your job there. Of course, you don't. But you can't possibly compare what you have to lose—namely the pay for one class a week, a class, mind you, that you could no doubt attain at countless gyms and spas in the city thanks to your newfound fame—with what those two women have at stake. Lloyd Benton is a senior partner at Morganstern Reid, and Dick Welles runs Stoneheap Hedge Fund. Conservatively, Lloyd's pulling in twenty million, forty million, maybe even a hundred million a year. In a good year, Dick probably does that easily, perhaps even double. There is no way those women are going to do anything to jeopardize their lifestyle."

"You don't think sleeping with me jeopardizes it?"

"Getting caught does. Sleeping with you is incidental. And if this is indeed something they've done before, I'd argue that the risk is severely reduced."

"Really? You don't think they're more likely to get caught over time?"

"No. Law enforcement would love you to think that, but career criminals are much more successful than first-timers. Like these ladies, they clearly know how to manage things discreetly. They've developed systems to keep their shenanigans safe from prying eyes."

"They're pros, in other words?"

"Well," he smiles wryly, "you might look at it that way. As with everything—including perhaps especially, deception—

practice makes perfect. The point is, as with any investment, if you're going to indulge in anything risky, I think you're much better off with a partner—and in this case, plural partners—with several hundred million reasons more to be cautious than you have."

I ponder this for a moment. It feels like reality.

"It is, of course, true," Andrew summarizes, "that to take no action has extremely little risk involved. I doubt severely that they'd be so offended as to cause some kind of problem for you based on your rejection of them. But my sense is that this kind of no-strings-attached offer is usually too difficult for anyone to turn down. You should conceive of this as a trip to a sexual Disneyland: plenty of safe adventure, complete with two fun rides, all of it completely independent from a real-life context."

And as with Disneyland, I want to add, there's nothing particularly romantic or even human about it—in fact, it's a little creepy—but still it does sound pretty hard to pass up.

"Thank you," I say, genuinely grateful for the Über-Wolf mentoring.

"Don't mention it," Andrew replies, his vast analytical resources turning back to his favorite subject: himself. "By the way, I don't know if I've mentioned her before, but did I tell you about Kendall Morrison, the associate handling the Cincinnati merger?"

As always, Andrew's back on his own trail, forever hunting, tormented perhaps, ever ravenous, but very, very much the victor.

When Monique calls me at 5 p.m., again I know this is not about sex.

"How's the fundraising going?" she asks.

"Less than stellar," is my understated reply.

I've spent the last three days going through the numbers on my Rolodex—okay, actually it's a shoebox of business cards—along with the handful of numbers I've entered into my cell. Unfortunately, 90 percent of my cell numbers are chicks

I've met while out on the town, who are not going to want to hear from me now, much less invest in my creating another hunting ground.

"Well, you better step up to the plate fast with something," Monique warns me. "You know Becker insists on an exclusive three-week window to evaluate these deals, and you should thank me for sweet-talking them into another two-week extension. Once that's over, I can't help you. Of course, the property could theoretically remain unsold for a year, but given how that area is booming and how low the asking price is, I think someone else will snatch it up."

"Two weeks. Okay, thanks, I guess." I can't disguise the dejection in my voice.

Monique's voice shifts. I can feel her dismissing her assistant so she can shut the door and give me your basic high school coach, no more bullshit pep talk.

"Listen, I'm not about to suggest that you watch The Secret but you've got to fucking change that defeatist attitude right now if you're gonna pull this off. I never said that someone was going to just hand you the check. I just said that it's absolutely possible to raise the money if you put your mind to it. Focus on it. Create a Vision Board if you freaking must, but don't let yourself down."

I try to sound resurrected as she signs off without ceremony.

Minutes later, the phone rings and it's my sister. Immediately, I know I'm in for my second mini-lecture of the night.

"Why haven't you gotten back to me about Dad?"

"What's up with Pop?" I ask.

"Uh … his sixtieth birthday is tomorrow. Did you not get the invite I mailed?"

Oh yes, that invite I put on the fridge, the one I've totally forgotten. I've also forgotten that my five-year-old niece left me a message three days ago. Somehow the "adorable quotient" of it all blocked it from my frontal lobe's to do list. (Or maybe, having Andrea's Shane postcard in hand, I just erased the entire day's mail delivery from my memory.)

"I'm sorry, Sis. I have it in front of me. So, tomorrow

at five at The Grill. The Old Man actually wants to cook on his birthday?"

"You know Pop. He loves The Grill. So … you'll be there, right?"

I hesitate. It's not just that every day counts if I want to raise money—since I've run out of ideas, what does it matter? No, it's more that time at home with Pop is never a stroll through the park. Of course, the highlight of my failures, in his eyes, was blowing all my savings and the investor's money on my failed first venture, but frankly, ever since I can remember, in one way or another, I've been disappointing the dude.

"Listen, he really wants you to come. It means a lot to him."

It might mean a lot to my mom, and to my sister, and to my grade school nieces and nephews, but other than archiving the event with a complete family portrait that he'll put on the cash register, I can't imagine Pop would care. Still, since the majority of my family is pretty awesome, and somehow, every conversation with my Mom helps just a little bit, I agree. If necessary, I will sit through one of Pop's terse but to-the-point statements that I "really should look into law school for next year. It's still not too late."

"Okay. Sure. I'll take the bus up tomorrow morning," I promise.

Funny, but sometimes when I tell Manhattanites, "I'm from 'upstate,' they look at me as though that's slang for prison.

I arrive in Goshen, NY, and get off the bus just before the party's set to start. My sister and her three kids throw their arms around me. For a moment, I'm actually glad I'm back.

Even though it's only an hour and a half from the city, I realize that I haven't been here for over a year. I blew off last Christmas and Thanksgiving, telling my folks I had to stay in the city and work, which was only half true. Diane, of The Sweatshop, bless her heart, was willing to let me have a few days off, but I just couldn't, just didn't want to return home. Too many concerned questions to answer about my disastrous first venture. Plus, my family never got the manual for good wives of unfaithful political husbands; they will not stand at the podium nodding politely and "forgiving" any and all "indiscretions." It would be more in character for my father to cuff me across the head and after berating me soundly, tell me to "straighten up and fly right." Not only am I not living the life he wants for me, I am also failing at the one I have chosen against his wishes.

It's not far to Pop's joint, The Grill (even the name has no imagination), but since it's suburbia, of course we drive there. As we pull up, I see that, as I suspected, nothing has changed except that there's a hand-lettered sign on the door saying "Private Party."

Mom hugs me. Pop's strategically placed behind the counter, near the grill, surrounded by well-wishers. Smiling, he waves to me, his spatula in one hand. I wave back. We won't hug unless it's unavoidable.

Over the next few hours, the place gets packed but not in an insane hot spot way. It's just full to the brim with folks who come here all the time, and rather than paying $5.95 for a burger, they're getting one for free along with a complimentary T-shirt with a drawing by one of the grandkids of Pop over the grill. It's pretty cute actually. And Pop really does look happy.

It's near midnight when the crowd disperses. These are decent folk and I think they already feel quite decadent being out this late. The crowd boils down to Mom, Pop, and three grandkids who are asleep in a booth. Mom and my sister try to get their coats on without waking them. It's Pop's moment alone with me. He approaches with two open beers.

"Here's to you," I offer, as we click bottles and sip. "Happy Birthday."

He sits at the counter, and I join him. We're physically close, but at the same time, we mostly look straight ahead. It's only occasionally that we turn our heads and meet the other's eyes.

"Nice party," I say.

"Thanks. Good folks here."

"Yup."

We both smile at my nephew's sleepy protests over putting on his jacket.

"How's work?" he asks.

I pause, as I'm not sure what he's asking exactly. True, I sent them the Grand Central article via my sister, but I don't know if he understands what yoga is, much less my whole teaching career. The idea of spas and private yoga teachers and standing on your head is pretty foreign here.

"You opening a new joint anytime soon?" he asks me.

I turn to look at him. As always, his gaze is eagle-eyed, dead-on.

"I've thought about it," I confess to him.

He nods, taking another sip of his beer. "Good. I think you should."

"Why?" This is not the line of conversation that decades of sparse small talk and awkward lecturing have led me to expect. My hope was that since he probably presumed I'd fail, given my bounty of shortcomings, we'd skip the lecture and just exchange banal pleasantries until my bus ride home. Or maybe he'd get Mom to slip some MBA program brochures into my duffle bag.

"Well, you always were good at it," my dad continues. "Remember how you used to work here after school and in the summers? Always thinking of things to make the place better. Like that Breakfast Combo." I basically suggested that the menu incorporate something that's standard on diner menus throughout the known universe, but to Pop, as with any change, it was revolutionary.

"You always had a good feel for chatting with folks when you worked the register. And you always remembered what people ordered before—folks like that. Helps turn them into regulars."

"It wasn't that hard."

"I don't know, son. Not everyone can do that. Me, I'm pretty good at the grill, but I guess I've always felt you had a real shot at something more. A man always wants more for his son. You know, something bigger. But anyway, you hang in there if you want this. You're a smart kid. It'll work out."

I'm stunned. This is more praise—frankly, more attention—

than my father has paid me in decades.

Especially given my failures, I do admire that the old man has made this place such a staple of the community. Sure, there's not much competition—there's no Page Six, Pan-Asian fusion hybrid about to appear on the next street corner—but still, it's an accomplishment. In a world where 90 percent of restaurants fail in the first year, people actually want to come here, tonight and every night. In this greasy-spoon version of Oedipus, I just want to play in a different league, to step up to the Big Time.

"I'm glad you came," Pop says, as he clinks bottles with me one more time. His arm floats over my shoulder for a nanosecond before he gets up to close up The Grill.

"Me, too," I add, as I help him lock up.

CHAPTER 17

Usually when the Greyhound bus pulls up towards Manhattan, a small-town boy's elation at returning to the Big Time hits me right away. It still does today, but then there's a queasy feeling and a gripping sensation in my chest: Where the hell am I going to get $3.8 million? Sunday's cold April rainstorm does nothing to lighten the mood.

As promised by the Wire Hanger King, on Monday, Phoebe and I have our next lesson solo. The rain pummels the windows, and even with their Park Avenue insulation, you can feel the brutality of the weather and the chill outside.

"This weather is incredible," I remark.

"I actually enjoy the rain," Phoebe replies. "When I was a little girl, I used to like to pretend I was in a Brontë novel."

"Which one?" I ask, knowing yet again that this is not a conversation she could ever have with Phil.

"Wuthering Heights mostly, although sometimes Jane Eyre," she confides, as though it's some great big secret that she shares the literary dreams of all shy, bookish schoolgirls (and, I suppose, some schoolboys).

"Cathy and Heathcliff." I smile knowingly in response. My memories of the novel are murky, beyond a lot of tramping on the moors. I remember the gist of it: the childhood passions gone awry, the faulty marriages, and mostly the loneliness and disappointment. And, of course, there's the entire conflicted bad-boy romantic fantasy around Heathcliff, although the dude's far too tortured to be a role model for me. Still, especially these days, I realize that I can relate. I, too, have been taken in by the upper classes without really fitting in—and, I suppose, I know a little something about the pain of loss, as well.

Phoebe looks at me, and God help me, with the miserable weather still brewing like the devil itself outside and this talk of romantic novels, I can't help quoting a little Rumi to her.

> *When it's cold and raining,*
> *you are more beautiful.*

> *And the snow brings me*
> *even closer to your lips.*

She looks at me with total vulnerability and with absolute devotion. Time freezes. And then she's kissing me.

Like Cathy embracing Heathcliff on the moors, it's actually Phoebe who rushes into my arms. And while I look down at her face longingly, it's she who reaches upward and plants her lips on mine. Not that it matters—we're equally complicit, immediately kissing each other with complete abandon and freedom. Once ignited, there is no hesitation in the brushfire.

As you may have gathered, I am not one to postpone or deny pleasure. In fact, until recently, about 99.9 percent of my energy was directed toward seeking it out. For a Player like me, making out with a hot woman is pleasurable but par for the course. Each time, everything responds as is anatomically correct, but these days—even I feel a twinge of guilt afterwards—I never feel that nervous flush, the newness and adolescent thrill to it all.

Yet somehow in this moment, I realize that my heart's pounding right out of my chest. I haven't felt this kind of intensity when just kissing someone for so long, it takes me by complete surprise. And therefore, I know that this has got to stop. I gently put my hands on Phoebe's slender forearms and move a few inches away.

It is not guilt, or trying to be good, or—God knows—loyalty to Phil. Rather, it's the fact that my heart is pounding this way that makes me pull the plug. It's the non-jadedness of this encounter. Without the usual numbing effects of vodka, dim lighting, club music, and only a vague sense of my quarry's name, there's just something a little too honest in this situation.

As though this were a heady new drug disorienting me, I'm not willing to just surrender control and go with the whole trip. I pull back gently but in a way that indicates that I mean business.

Phoebe looks intensely wounded. Just as I'm about to cave in, grab her tightly, and escalate things until we're devouring each other—partially because not to do so seems like it would be an advanced and unusual form of cruelty but mostly because every fiber of my being wants to—something happens. Bizarrely, a look of complete understanding comes over her along with even more devotion, if such a thing is possible.

"No, you're right," she says. "Even if there is some kind of physical connection, you're right that it's so much wiser not to act on it. What we share is so special it's best kept as a spiritual friendship. It's so much better to keep things at your level."

She's elevated my motivations so that I'm even more of a poet-saint. The truth is that I'm not sleeping with Phoebe because I'm an emotional dwarf. Never, ever have I rejected a woman when the wanting of each other was so mutual. And today, the first time I do it, it only serves to make her think better of me.

"I ... maybe we should stop and call it a day," I say. I don't know how it would be possible for us to continue the lesson—particularly with all the hands-on assists—without both of us feeling completely out of sorts.

"Yes, I think so," she replies with sheepish guilt. "I ... I'm sorry," she apologizes.

"You've got nothing to be sorry for," I reply, for once being honest.

"No, this is my fault. I let my loneliness get me carried away. I shouldn't have involved you in something like this. You've been nothing but a real teacher and a true friend to me, and I took advantage of that unfairly. I'm sorry."

"No, you shouldn't say that ... I, I ..."

I'm about to reveal my entire sordid, guilty life history, letting Phoebe know just how much of an utter wretch I am, but I find myself speechless. Maybe I just don't want to knock myself off the ridiculous and fraudulent pedestal she's placed me on, but my priority becomes to get out of the apartment before I can mess things up any further, most probably by sleeping with her.

"I … I should go, " I manage, heading toward the door. Phoebe merely nods.

I see myself out. Phoebe doesn't bother to walk me to the door this time.

She's letting me make a clean exit. I don't feel great about leaving her this way, frustrated and alone and embarrassed in the Zen perfection of her yoga room.

But as the door shuts behind me, I'm absolutely sure that, if I stayed, I'd soon feel even worse.

I thought life sucked with just my dream slipping away, but I'm feeling even more like shit from my encounter with Phoebe, and I don't know what to do about it. I try to take in a movie. I stroll into a Union Square theater and into something involving vampires. But even all the blood and gore doesn't have the power to transport me away from myself. I walk out before the ending, not caring if the pretty heroine is going to be saved in time or whether the young lead's going to have to put a stake through her heart. Maybe the vampire melodrama's just too close to home. Cape or not, I've pretty much trashed my Phoebe situation, luring it away from the safe morning light toward the dark side.

Even though it's barely noon, I grab lunch at the Union Square Café. Although for nine unprecedented years, it's been voted the most popular restaurant in the city, you can still get a decent seat at the bar. The food rocks and unlike the bistro places I usually gravitate towards, the place has a light, airy feel. I order the Hot Garlic potato chips to distract from the "drinking at 12:15" low to which I've now sunk.

When I get out my wallet to pay, I stumble across Serious Cleavage's card. I hold the card in my hands for a few moments, turning it around and playing with it, almost as though it's going to offer me more information than just Serious's digits.

In the end, my decision's pretty obvious. Right now, to quote Andrew, a trip through a sexual Disneyland seems to be exactly what I need.

I leave Serious Cleavage a message, embarrassed that suddenly I'm actually speaking in adulterer's code: "I'm calling about arranging … the yoga lessons. As it is, I have a free space in my schedule."

Nonetheless, however canned my message sounds, it is quite effective. Two hours later, Serious calls me back and says, "Everything is arranged," and gives me a time and address: tomorrow afternoon at 2:30. At, of all places, the Harvard Club.

The irony that their husbands are being cuckolded by a Yale man is not lost on any of us. "I'm so glad they let an Eli in," Serious says to me.

I barely remembered that one needs a jacket and tie in the public areas of the Harvard Club and threw myself together as I left my shabby apartment.

"It's an unusual place to meet, don't you think?" I say, as Diamond hands me a scotch. She doesn't ask me if I want one, mind you; she just pours me a glass.

In a way, this gesture summarizes her style: There's a saucy confidence that anything she's going to offer you, you'll obviously take—and frankly, she's right.

"Our husbands are both members, so it's only natural we'd lunch here, " Diamond says.

"Trust me," Serious says, as she removes her Chanel jacket to reveal her always-startling figure. "There's nothing like hiding in plain sight. No one suspects a thing."

"Lloyd pays for lunch, and I have my own account through Radcliffe to charge the room. In the extremely unlikely chance that Lloyd were ever to inquire, I was feeling a little flushed from the wine at lunch and decided to take a nap."

"Even though you live at most twenty minutes away?" I'm dubious.

She laughs and kisses me sweetly. "Believe me, I've established a history of decadence. Spending a few hundred dollars on a two-hour nap is nothing."

Diamond kisses me with far more subtlety and sweetness than the situation would suggest. "Besides, the Harvard Club is much too staid for anyone to suspect a thing. For a tryst, one would assume the Plaza—well, at least back in the day."

"Or the Carlyle."

"Or the Mercer, if you're going downtown."

They kiss each other. Diamond loosens my necktie as she speaks. She leaves it on.

"Everyone goes for the obvious in a clandestine affair. They practically wear trench coats and sunglasses, begging to be noticed," Serious says, as Diamond undoes her friend's blouse.

"But this place is so deliciously dowdy, no one would suspect a thing."

Serious begins to undress Diamond, who, true to form, has her magnificent pendant afloat on her magnificent breasts.

Serious, meanwhile, has stepped out of her skirt to reveal an incredibly lithe body, with perfectly toned butt and thighs— thanks, no doubt, to all the Centrifugal Force at Epitome.

"And in the end, what could possibly be more innocent than lunch and a little spending spree with my shopping buddy?"

Diamond and Serious giggle but only for a moment as they start nibbling, then segue into French kissing each other rather passionately.

I stand there, scotch in hand. Serious and Diamond are now nearly totally naked and making out, with only my tie loosened. This is their game and they've invited me to join, but I don't quite know the rules yet. Hand in hand, they walk over to the bed, their perfectly contoured bodies increasingly and effortlessly intertwined.

I stand back, happy to watch, yet unsure what's expected of me. After a moment, they look up—as though I've passed some kind of test—and smile at me.

"Would you like to join us?" Serious asks, as Diamond seductively fingers the platinum chain of her necklace.

"I thought you'd never ask," I reply, as I move toward the bed, rapidly shrugging off my jacket and shirt.

"Not so fast," Diamond smiles. Clearly, they have this down to a science. I sit down on the edge of the bed.

Serious begins to undress me as Diamond produces a blindfold from the pillow. "It's more fun this way, trust us."

"Just let yourself get lost, " Serious instructs.

I say nothing in reply. I sense that there's nothing they need from me, beyond acquiescence. Oh, of course they want a compelling erection that lasts, and lots of enthusiastic use of it, all of which I'm happy to supply. They really just want to use me as a condiment to their adventure together. The blindfold, meant to add to the eroticism, accomplishes that, but it also makes them impersonal to me—and me to them, too. I can tell Serious from Diamond only when I'm touching their breasts. Otherwise, they blend into one shimmering, invisible, erotic creature. I don't know who I'm kissing. And when their mouths move over every inch of my body, I have no idea about any personality, any individual attached to any of it. Before, during, and after, I am fundamentally no one to them, and in the midst of the most intense physical pleasure, they've made sure they've become no one to me. It's just pure erotic bliss, and it's fantastic. In the end, we've all three gotten exactly what we wanted.

The two of them have gotten a naughty adventure to tide them over between lunch and more shopping. And me, well, for a few hours, I haven't had to think about my woeful miscasting as a guru. Or my pimped-out Epitome class. I've put my S&M relationship with Brooke, and my therapist role with Andrew, on the back burner. I've valiantly striven to distract myself from how I've complicated Phoebe's life, and perhaps even more important, I've managed to block out that heart-pounding feeling from kissing her. Most importantly of all, I haven't been thinking about my failure to raise bank, and that this is probably the last nail in the coffin for my Shane forgiveness strategy.

Basically, trysting blindly with the Cleavage gals, I've gotten a chance to vanish.

In the end, I am my own pity fuck.

Once I'm outside the lobby of the Harvard Club—there's no cell phone use, although apparently a ménage à trois skims underneath the radar—my cell starts vibrating. I get a phone call from Sassy, this chick who's now making a name for herself as a teacher at Thank Heaven. She's obsessed with anatomy and precise alignment and knows a ton about all that shit. Early on, I attended some of her classes and I believe (shades of Phil) that I told her that I sweated my ass off—back in the day, it was my highest compliment.

Anyway, Sassy wants to know if I can be an emergency sub for her. She's got a last-minute audition for a Broadway show. Sassy gives me way too much information—apparently she knows the director and he requested her, and she's right for the role because she once played the first revival of it and ... Anyway, there are about four million other details that make it incredibly URGENT that she show up and strut her stuff onstage.

I just want to go home and sleep—actually, I'd rather go out and get smashed but it's only 4 p.m.—but other than that, there's no practical reason I can't sub a 5 p.m. class at Thank Heaven.

"Sure. I guess I can do it. No problem."

Sassy is profoundly grateful, and thankfully, I've showered the adulterous sex scent off myself before leaving the Harvard Club.

I head straight to Thank Heaven. Especially given my early, dismal misadventures with replacing Jasmine, I'm aware that it's always weird subbing a class. It's like going to the movies and finding out that your flick is sold out; there's usually something relatively decent to see, but it takes a minute or so to switch out of erotic thriller expectations into a sophomoric comedy mindset.

After countless hours taking classes and doing teacher training at Thank Heaven, it's a little trippy to actually be teaching here. However novel this is, I'm utterly blown away as Gigi herself plops down a mat in the back of the room. I'm surprised at how much dread I feel as I go right over to her. She wraps me in the warmest of hugs.

"Darlin', I was just dropping off the paychecks," she says, "and I found out you were teaching. So I thought I'd stay."

"Great," is all I can think of to say. 'Damn it, but why can't you have direct deposit like Epitome?' is what I think.

Under any other social circumstance, I'd be probably be thrilled to see Gigi, yet now I'm scared shitless. The teacher I respect most is taking my class, a class I didn't know I was teaching until forty-five minutes ago.

There's no time to plan anything. There's no time to panic. It's time to get started.

I'm thankful that Gigi's positioned herself in the back, something I've observed she always does whenever she takes class. If you know she's in the room, it's hard not to notice her, but it is a consideration to the teacher so as not to steal her (or his) thunder. There's no need to remind the employee that the boss is on the premises, or the understudy that the superstar watches hawk-like in the wings.

I decide that my strategy is to keep it simple. No bravura moves or sequencing, I intend to offer nothing out of the ordinary. I just want to get through a standard hour class and have my performance be unimpeachable.

Right from the start, everything feels false. I offer up nothing spiritual, nothing heartfelt. As with many yoga centers, there's a monthly focus that teachers can riff around, giving a coherence to all the classes. Unfortunately, having been largely absent for this month (and the last two), in more ways than one, I have no idea what the spiritual focus is. I'd like to be able to speak from my experience, but having just exited the Harvard Club after a threesome with two married women, which involved being their blindfolded plaything for two hours, there's no doubt in my mind that I'm absolutely the least spiritually grounded person in the room.

I spend a lot of energy trying to ignore Gigi even though

she takes the class just like any other student. It's perhaps not the best focus, since when I look at my watch, I realize we're forty minutes into the one-hour class, and I've just gotten started. The time has completely gotten away from me again. This is exponentially more problematic since I know about Gigi's insistence on good sequencing. I need to make some decisions quickly. Although Gigi's own classes run over, she's built that into the schedule; there's never anyone directly after her who needs the room. After this class, however, there's another one in fifteen minutes. In other words, I must end this on time.

I can probably get away with a five-minute Corpse Pose, but we're nowhere near where we should be for that. We haven't done a single backbend or twist, and God knows we're not getting near any inversions. The class has become a big, messy spill of rudimentary poses that I realize I have only a few minutes to clean up.

I get through the rest of it somehow. The class and I Om together. Heads bow with a "Namaste," and the class is complete. Students who bump into me as they exit thank me politely, but I can tell that there's little enthusiasm. This was a particularly slipshod performance for a Thank Heaven class, especially since they're used to Sassy's no doubt super-plotted offerings.

If only there were a way I could sneak out of the center without Gigi noticing me. Maybe there's a yoga emergency that needs tending. Of course, she's waiting for me by the front desk. She gives me another warm hug. "Thanks for class, teacher."

"You're welcome. Not my best, but …"

"Well, we can talk, if you've got a minute."

"Sure," I say out of knee-jerk honesty. If only I were more sensible, I'd have fabricated something incredibly urgent that would prevent the conversation for the next six, maybe ten, years.

Gigi and I retire to her office, a small affair but with enough room for us to both sit on the floor on oversized batik Indian cushions. Instead of launching in, always the teacher, like Socrates she begins with a question. "So, what did you think of your class?"

It's better for me to man up and admit that it sucked than for her to have to tell us both. "Not great," I say. "I suppose not being prepared is a lame excuse, but I totally lost track of the time."

"Happens to the best of us, God knows," she replies. "What else?"

"Well, mostly stuff I didn't get to."

"Such as?"

"Revolved poses. Backbending. More forward bending than just Baddhakanasa."

"I see."

"Am I missing more?"

She pauses for a moment. "Well, poses aside, I guess the main thing is I wanted to see a little more of you in your teaching."

"How do you mean?"

"Well, there was nothing particularly wrong about anything you said—you did forget the second side once or twice during the sun salutes and standing poses—but there was nothing particular about you that came through. Anyone could have recited facts about those poses like you did. I want to see a little more of your own practice, your own journey."

"I'm sorry that I didn't have a spiritual theme prepared. They discourage that at Epitome. And I honestly didn't know what the focus was this month," I explain.

"Well, 'spiritual' is such a loaded word. I was thinking more about 'personal,'" Gigi counters. "I don't care if it's an anecdote, or an expression, or the music—anything that really excites you. Trust me, the most personal things always turn out to be the most universal, the most 'spiritual.'"

I hate that my first class for her sucked. Gigi reads the dismay in my face. "Please don't look so hangdog. I don't want to be too hard on you. This is only the kind of stuff that will make you a much better teacher."

Technically, to become a "better" teacher, I'd have to be a good one first—but I don't correct her.

"What I loved about the physical part of your teaching final," she continues, "was that it was totally you all the way.

I connect with Nina Simone; you connect with U2—and you made me connect with them during your opening sequence. Everything came from your own experience on the mat, not a Rodney Yee DVD."

She waits to see if this registers with me and then continues.

"Anyone can teach the poses 'correctly,' but that's not what keeps people coming back for more. We're not here just to work folks out; we're here to offer a little uplift." As she says this, she touches my arm; it's a warm and friendly gesture and would have a soothing effect if I didn't feel unbelievably shitty to begin with. I feel like I'm having a postmortem with a spiritual Sherlock Holmes; will she be able to detect the faintest traces of scent of Diamond and Serious Cleavage that linger post-shower? Or, maybe—besides defying gravity when she moves through poses—can she also read everything in my presumably filthy aura?

When I don't offer more, she speaks again: "Please don't take this so hard. I've always thought you had the makings of a really fine teacher, and I still do. I just think for you to move to the next level, you need to incorporate more of your own practice—more of yourself—into your teaching. You've got to let us in. That's the only way you can really uplift your students." I take this in.

"Well, in terms of offering anything uplifting—I just don't know … if I'm in a place where that's possible for me."

"How do you mean?"

I look up at her, and I see real interest and true compassion in her eyes. I've got her undivided attention. It's funny, but for a second, I flip back to what my students might possibly think of me. Gigi is a truly amazing person, but this is also partially attributable to the context in which I know her. As always, she is my teacher first and foremost. She bears the mantle of this relationship whenever we're together, no matter how seemingly casual the chatter. In other words, I might not have any of these intense feelings about confiding in her had we met, say, on line for an action movie; I met her when she offered her spectacular practice, her blazing energy, and the heart and soul of her life experience via her yoga class.

I swallow and feel myself about to toss everything in my life out on the table for her to fix: my indulging in a flirtation and Phoebe's subsequent advance, the dalliances with Serious and Diamond Cleavage, my fuck buddy Monique, Andrew's yoga-as-therapy sessions, Brooke's abdominal obsessions, and my basic feeling that, despite offering a few decent sweaty practices at Epitome and instructing some physical breakthroughs with Janek, I'm a complete fraud. I'm ready to even cap off the whole litany of my troubles with my screwing over Shane. God knows I so desperately want to tell Gigi everything and have her just make it all go away for me, or at least to tell me what to do. And frankly, I'd bite the bullet no matter what she suggested. If it means a mountaintop in Katmandu, I'd be trudging there barefoot through the snow. But at that very moment, when I'm about to spill my guts, one of the front desk karmi-girls knocks on the door.

"I'm sorry," says Cute Karmi #461, one of an endless stream of fresh-faced, beautiful twenty-four-year-olds working at the front desk in exchange for free classes.

"What's up, Liz-Beth?" As always, I marvel that unlike me, Gigi remembers everyone's name.

"Calypso's on the phone. She's waiting for you downstairs and she's double-parked."

Gigi looks at her watch, "Damn. Why is it so easy to lose track of time?" She looks at me intently. "Are you all right?"

"Yup. Totally fine." I lie.

"We have to pick up Calypso's niece for her surprise birthday party. Otherwise, I'd—"

"No, you go. I'm good."

"Are you sure?"

I nod, trying to appear together and not like someone she should be worried about.

"This conversation is to be continued. I don't mean the critique part. That's over and done. I want to hear what's really going on with you, my little Flying Crow Yoga Celebrity." She hugs me, and maybe it's just the extra lingering beat of it, but I detect concern with the compassion.

"I'd love to have you swing by on Sunday. Maybe we could share a chai after class?" she inquires.

"Definitely." I love Gigi's Sunday noon class—she calls it "Good News" and floods the room with gospel music, harkening back to her New Orleans roots.

"Okay, then. Sunday noon. Chai at 2—unless I run over!"

She blows me another kiss and she's gone, leaving me alone in her office for a moment.

Looking at the schedule on the office's dry-erase board, for the first time I wonder if Sassy got the part; frankly, her last-minute audition couldn't have gone any worse than mine.

I leave Thank Heaven more convinced than ever that, despite my packed Epitome class and photo spread, I am woefully miscast in the role of teacher. And as a club owner, I am once again emerging stillborn.

Indeed, I'm beginning to wonder if there's any world—Nightlife or Yoga or anything in between—where I truly belong.

CHAPTER 18

I'm not sure what to expect when it's time for Phoebe's next lesson. At least she hasn't cancelled. I realize on the elevator ride up that I'm actually quite nervous. Maybe concerned is more like it. Unlike with all the "relationships" (i.e., hookups) I actually consummate, I'm worried that this fragile bubble with Phoebe might have burst with nothing more than a kiss being exchanged. I steel myself for the inevitable awkward moment of seeing her again—but it's Phil who answers the door.

"Hiya, how's it hanging?" he asks as he pumps my hand and ushers me in.

"I'm good, thanks."

Phil starts us toward the yoga room. "It's just you and me today, kid," he tells me.

"Really?" This is certainly a new, unforeseen twist.

"Yeah. Phoebe just wasn't feeling well—one of those 'lady troubles'—so she told me to just go ahead and take the lesson while she slept in."

"Okay, then. We'll make do," I manage, both relieved and frustrated. I suppose it's theoretically possible that Phoebe's period might be causing her enough discomfort to cancel her lesson, but the obvious explanation—that she's feeling awkward around me—seems much more likely.

I begin teaching Phil, and once again, I find myself liking him more and more. He's awkward and stiff as a board, but he's intelligent and focused. He's willing to plunge in, like Janek, but without any of the grace or athleticism. Since, frankly, I've never particularly connected him to Phoebe in my mind, other than as a bizarre obstacle, I'm actually able to focus on Phil and his needs without any resentment or distraction. In the end, teaching Phil solo—a good-hearted, scrappy student—is actually totally enjoyable.

Phil walks me to the door. The model of cordiality throughout, as with the Broadway tickets, it's obvious that he knows nothing about what passed between Phoebe and me last week. "I think I gotta be in Detroit again, so probably Thursday it'll just be Phoebe," he tells me. "But, kid, I really enjoyed myself. Definitely coming back for more the next time I'm in town."

"Terrific," I reply. A pumped-up handshake and we're done, our business successfully transacted, and yet, as I descend in the elevator, I really am more at a loss as to what to do next than ever.

The next morning, I share one of my signature moves with Janek: a one-armed handstand.

It's damned impressive, if I do say so myself. I do it for him against the wall, demonstrating how if you send the hips a little in one direction and widen the legs a bit, you can maybe (just maybe) take the opposing hand off the ground.

When I assist it, however, I actually do the lion's share of the work. I frame and hold the edges of his hipbones up, actively lifting him so that he won't topple over. It goes off without a hitch. Thanks to his natural athleticism and all the weight training, Janek's a strong dude, so for the second round—now that he's felt it in his body, via the assist—I suggest that he try it on his own. Always fearless, Janek's game. He manages one side and then the other.

"That's so awesome," Janek beams once he's upright once more.

"It's a helluva party trick, I'll give you that," I reply. "I'm not sure what else it's good for, though."

I don't know why I blurt this out. It surprises us both. Probably just me losing focus for a moment and letting my generally negative default mental state slip into the lesson. But even though, more and more, I like Janek—thinking of him as a hybrid of friend/client and late night, party-going comrade—I really had no intention of dragging my problems into his lesson.

"Something wrong, man?" Janek inquires.

"Nope. Sorry."

"No, it's cool. What's up?"

Obviously, I can't go into much with him—the club slipping away from me, the Cleavage Twins, much less my feeling like a yoga impostor, or my sordid Shane saga. But Janek's a cool guy, so I don't want to lie or blow him off.

"Nothing that can't be fixed," I tell him. "Don't want to drag it into your lesson time. I'm here to teach you, not bitch about my problems."

"Okay, man. Just know that I'm willing to listen."

"Thanks, I don't think it's listening I need. Just some answers. But I keep coming up empty-handed."

"Really? Even a yoga guru like yourself gets stumped?" he asks.

I wonder if he's being serious or even semi-serious. Surely, Janek must know I'm just a fit dude with some helpful information that can enhance flexibility, balance, and strength.

"Trust me, dude—I don't have any answers," I reply. "None, whatsoever."

Janek takes this in. "Hasn't the yoga helped you though? I mean, not in sitting in a cave and meditating way but …"

He's being sincere. I respond in kind. "Honestly, man … yes, definitely," I reply. The words reveal themselves to me as I say them. "Not so much that I feel one iota more enlightened. Definitely not in this lifetime. I guess I feel, I don't know … I suppose it's sort of like, by getting good at this shit—like armed handstand—I've mastered something I never thought I could do. Or even just a simple 'touch your toes' forward bend. I can do it now but man, that used to make my hamstrings fuckin' scream. Now I'm pretty open there. Even though it's just lengthening out tight muscles, I learned that if I can just focus and let go for five lousy breaths, a change is gonna happen eventually."

There's a moment between us, one where we both realize

that this is really pretty enormous. For once, I realize, I'm actually teaching something directly from my experience.

"The thing is," I say, "I'm not good at all that flowery yoga shit, the stuff that comes naturally to all those willowy girl teachers. I just know about sweat and frustration. And that what I once thought was impossible somehow doesn't always stay that way permanently. One day it's suddenly easy and accessible, and mostly because I've stopped struggling against it. I've just accepted where I am, keep showing up, and then the change just happens."

The moment is instantly complete. There's nothing more to be said.

"Headstand?" I offer.

We're back on the mat.

Rather than call Phoebe to discuss our situation, I opt for the path of least resistance: the totally neutral confirmation email. I write: "Hope you're feeling better. Just confirming Thursday at 9." I'm hoping it conveys clearly the subtextual question, "Can we please pretend nothing happened and that it's back to yoga as usual?"

Phoebe responds a few hours later with, "Feeling much better. See you tomorrow."

I take this as a good sign. I read it as a tacit agreement between us to move forward and pretend nothing's happened. Even if that doesn't really reflect the truth of our situation at all, at least we're sharing a common position: denial.

Phoebe herself opens the door for our next lesson. It's less awkward than either of us had imagined. Or, with the aura of romantic tension between us, maybe it's that it's always been slightly awkward; it's not that much different now that someone's made a move.

"How are you?" I ask.

"Much better, thanks."

Banal pleasantries are good. We're off to a strong start back toward normal. We walk to the yoga room together. Phoebe makes some remarks about the warmer weather. I concur. Soon we're Om-ing, and the lesson has begun.

I'm careful to do just enough touching in the assists that it doesn't feel like I'm retreating from my hands-on role. At the same time, I go out of my way to avoid any poses that require more intimate contact.

Fortunately, the framework of the lesson gives us something to fall back into. I don't have to worry about words or conversation. More than I usually do, I share all the information I have about alignment. Channeling Sassy, I have plenty to say about the poses, which can fill up any awkward silences that arise. I give endless info in Triangle Pose: spin the heart up, soften the top hip, lift the quads up in the front leg, lengthen the spine, and on and on. Right now, I am extremely grateful for all the alignment information I can draw from memory. If Sassy were here, she'd be so proud.

It's only after Corpse Pose and the final Oms, when conversation is forced to resume again, that I can't continue filling the space with details about the shoulder blades and tailbone.

As always, Phoebe walks me to the door. There's a pause. It's unavoidable. Someone has to say something.

"I …" She begins. I wait. "About last time … I'm sorry."

"There's no need to apologize. I … I think it best that we just let the whole thing fade into the past. Treat it like it never happened."

I guess that since—like Serious and Diamond—she is a married woman, then, according to Andrew's thinking, she's the one with much more to lose than me. But I think it's not the loss of creature comforts and status that she's concerned about; it's clear to me that her distress comes from the feeling that she's jeopardized our relationship. More specifically, that she's disappointed and distanced me, her Poet-Saint and Guru, by failing to live up to my (nonexistent) high standards of personal conduct.

"That's so generous of you," Phoebe says. "I'm so sorry that I reduced things to a more base level. That I took advantage of the higher-level friendship you were offering."

This is torture. My "higher level"—when I'm not out hitting on chicks at late night lounges—consists of spending my spare time screwing Monique and the Cleavage Twins.

The look in Phoebe's eyes tells me that she wants something more. Astonishingly, she wants true forgiveness from me. Distracted, I notice that a few wisps of hair have fallen out of her ponytail and into her eyes, and God help me, but unthinkingly, I brush them gently off her face as though—channeling my altar-boy roots—I'm giving her absolution.

"Thank you." Her gratitude is excruciating. My offering her forgiveness is so inappropriate for the context of the situation—much less my entire life's modus operandi—that I'm amazed I'm allowing this to continue.

"See you Tuesday?" is all I can muster in reply.

"Absolutely."

As Phoebe shuts the door, as always, she looks particularly beautiful: "Just Fucked" but also Just Forgiven. It's a good thing the elevator door shuts on me when it does. Otherwise, I might never have left this weird sanctuary where I am valued for virtues I do not possess.

FULL WHEEL
(URDHVA DHANURASANA)

Full Wheel is a very dangerous pose: they say it opens the heart.

You simply lie on your back with your knees bent about hip width apart. Your hands flank your ears, palms down, and fingers point toward your toes. Breathe in, and exhaling, straighten your arms and try to lift your torso off the ground. If it actually happens, then suddenly you're in a huge backbend.

The pose is quite difficult for people for lots of different reasons. Some people just aren't strong enough in their arms to press down and lift themselves up. (Push-ups, anyone?) Others—especially gym dudes—have the opposite problem. They've built up such tight shoulders that despite arms that could punch through solid steel, they aren't flexible enough to rise more than a half inch off the ground.

And others, well, they're just plain afraid. Like my childhood chocolate lab, you're showing your belly. It's a position that's good for tummy rubbing ... or potentially getting stabbed straight through the heart.

Getting caught cheating on Shane—with the investor's wife, no less—is so awful I want to recoil from the retelling, knowing that no matter how much I confess it, there's no absolution.

Why did I stray? I don't need therapy to know that what I had with Shane was so good, so surprisingly real and natural, that I just couldn't handle it. I'd never spent all this time with a woman before—certainly not as best friends and then lovers— working together to build a now-shared dream. Like Andrew "confessing" that after a deluxe spa week at Canyon Ranch and losing eight pounds, he felt compelled to stop his limo at the nearest Wendy's on the way back to the city to binge, I find myself craving "junk sex."

So when the investor's boozy, cougar wife hits on me, I hesitate but find myself giving in without a fight. And though I have no conscious strategy for getting caught, the whole thing is so ill-executed—Boozy Cougar and I tryst while the investor and Shane travel to Jersey for equipment buying, returning an hour earlier than expected—it borders on bedroom farce. The key difference, however, is that real emotions are involved. Shane is furious and devastated, and I'm doomed forever to attempt to earn forgiveness that I don't believe I deserve.

Unlike Andrew's broken spa regimen, the consequences of "junk sex" can't be repaired.

I've broken something that can't be fixed, no matter how hard I try.

CHAPTER 19

Andrew's sessions continue as always: tons of therapy with a few poses thrown in for show. He is, however, quite pleased when—while he's resting on the block in Half Wheel—I decide he's ready to move in to a more intense angle. The work is still restorative in nature but nonetheless deeper, and it demonstrates a measure of progress. As soon as he settles in, I can tell he feels he's getting his money's worth.

Naturally fearless, Janek's backbending gets stronger and stronger. Today, we've done a full-blown Wheel rather early, so I decide that it's time to take it further.

When he's in his third Wheel, I stand in front of him, positioning myself so that I'm grounded as I place my hands on his hips. Framing his back, I direct Janek to breathe in deeply, and when he exhales, I bring him up to stand from the Full Wheel.

Now we're ready for the next part. Janek stands; I direct him to exhale as he bends backward; and I support his fall back into a Full Wheel. My job is to frame him and slow down his descent. Even so, falling backward is always an extremely scary feeling.

I pride myself on a rather fearless practice, and yet I still feel something pretty intense whenever I get ready to drop back into a Wheel. I still can't do it totally on my own—I succeed fifty percent of the time, and the other fifty percent, I fall back too fast, my hands aren't ready, and I bump my head on the ground. It's never that much of a painful landing (beyond my easily bruised ego) but, nonetheless, one is very aware of having fallen, of losing balance and perspective and dropping as though blindfolded.

It's funny, but I will always remember the first time I dropped back. It was, of course, under Gigi's capable hands.

The physics of it require you to get quite close to the person you're dropping back into the Wheel, even traveling part of the way down with them, towards the ground. When Gigi brought me up to stand, her hands were on my hips, and she leaned in quite intimately to lift me. Being dropped back into Full Wheel is what I can only imagine it feels like to be dipped low in an Argentinean tango. I can even remember the song that was playing: Sade's "By Your Side." Truthfully, there was something a little romantic about it all; Gigi and I having "our song," as it were. I let go into trusting her, and it worked beautifully. It was a total rush, enhanced by my fear, and I loved it.

It's funny, but I realize that I'm standing much closer to a guy and holding one in a way I never have before. It's still totally athletic and cool, but it's interesting how for a flash, I'm acutely aware of both our proximity and his vulnerability.

Janek takes to it brilliantly. I'm pleased that I can tell that he totally trusts me despite the basic level of fear the enterprise is going to engender in any sane person.

I complete two more cycles of up and down with Janek. It's admittedly a lot of backbending, but I think it wise to have the experience register as reaching a new level, a new skill, than as some kind of a one-shot fluke.

When we finish, Janek is particularly pumped up and excited. "Dude, that was intense."

"Good, I'm glad. It's a little trippy the first couple times, especially if you're not sure what to expect."

"Yeah, sure, a little scary—but awesome, too," Janek agrees.

Would that I could have been this ferociously brave with Shane and not screwed things up—but that's another kind of courage entirely.

It's Friday night and I'm really running out of time to raise funds for the club. A full week has passed, and I've explored every loose connection from my past and entertained every harebrained scheme I can conceive. Other than lottery winnings (and yes, I did buy ten tickets in the local, smoke-filled Chinese convenience store), I see no hope of financing that space. I know the world won't end for anyone but me as a result of my failure, but still, I feel like shit.

Hutch, on the other hand, has closed some sort of big deal and, pumped up from that, he wants to go out. It seems like the perfect antidote—make that distraction—given my sorry situation.

The evening begins steadily enough, with Hutch ringing me at 11:30 p.m. as he's nearing my hood in a cab. I head downstairs to meet him, jump in, and we're off to an unmarked, newly opened Lower East Side bar he hears is hot. Revved up, this night is about volume and speed. When out carousing, it's one drink, max, per watering hole. The goal is to cover maximum territory, having maximum fun along the way.

Unfortunately, we're off to a rough start, as hot spot #1— Fountains, apparently, is its name—is so unmarked, we totally can't find it. It's lucky this is our first joint of the night. If this were four hours later, I've no doubt we'd be stumbling into various random lobbies, convinced we were inches away from the fun but merely irritating anyone sane enough to be in bed before 4 a.m.

After ten minutes and several pissed-off phone calls to the banker colleague who tipped him off to this place, Hutch finally uncovers the locale. The place is starting to fill up, but again, that's a minor accomplishment, given that it's smaller than my apartment. Despite the decent crowd, I think the whole place is a big mistake. The central fountain takes up way too much space, and with bad lighting, is really just annoying. Although I respect someone going the distance with a theme, I think the minor fountains they've got are uninteresting and too small. Lots of miscalculations of size and effect here, and if I had to bet, I'd put my money on this place having three weeks of novelty success and then vanishing.

Nonetheless, the crowd tonight is pretty hip, the mood is cavalier, and the dynamic is like bedding the right sort of beautiful woman: they've made a virtue of being just hard to get enough to whet the appetite without frustrating the libido with a night of blue balls.

The crowds at joints two, three, and four are far less successful. I do get the number of a very cute gallery assistant who's embraced the cliché that if you put your hair in a ponytail and wear thick black glasses, no one will notice that you're a hot blonde sexpot underneath it all.

We travel to Jadis, a wine bar I like on Rivington that's less of a pickup scene but has some good bottles going. Hutch has to wish a colleague happy birthday, so we grab a drink at the bar—where Hutch spots a gorgeous dancer/actress/model type who seems to have combined the best of all races in her appearance, including a wild, Pam Grier mane. Afro Chick is falling out of a snazzy jumpsuit—like her hair, retro '70s— revealing a sensational body. Like many women who go to great lengths to bare their assets in public, she's resentful that anyone has noticed the goods she's put so blatantly on display. Afro Chick interjects at one point, to nothing in particular Hutch is saying: "I have a boyfriend, you know."

"Is that so? Well, when you're ready for a man-friend, you can give me a call." Hutch delivers the corny line with rakish bravado, and she actually laughs.

"Besides I'm not the boyfriend type and," he continues, "a girl like you is all wrong for me, anyway."

"Oh really?" she counters with indignation that pretends to be mock but has more than a tinge of curious irritation toward his preemptive rejection of her.

"Yeah. I never do well with actress types. Too self-involved."

"Unlike yourself? And by the way, I'm a lawyer."

At least she's not letting him get away with shit.

"Touché—although frankly, lawyer or not, I'm more concerned that I couldn't keep someone like you in the style they want. Maybe if I'd been banking back in the '80s, but they only pay so much in Mergers and Acquisitions these days. Yeah—I'm all wrong for you." He's noticed her purse now. "You need one of those senior banking cats if you're gonna shop at Louis Vuitton all day. I could introduce you to some if you want."

"This?" She leans in and whispers, "Big secret: Chinatown knockoff. Completely fake."

"At least the rest of you isn't," he comments, glancing at her breasts but quickly resuming respectful eye contact. "I like that."

He clicks glasses with her, I'm not sure why, exactly, but it's conspiratorial. He's somehow turned her fake designer goods into a compliment about not having had a boob job.

Soon, I'm almost at the end of my scotch, and so is Hutch. He knows he's got to wrap this up and keep things moving. "Would you like to kiss me?" he asks.

She rolls her eyes, but she's leaning into him. "You're a shy one."

He shrugs it off, and once again, twists it around. "Well, it just seemed you were looking at me like you wanted to, that's all."

"Oh, was I?" she counters.

Hutch pulls out his Mont Blanc pen and a business card. "Let's debate it ad nauseam ..." Afro eyes him for a few seconds, her irritation now totally mock, and then writes her digits and name on his card, handing it back to him.

Hutch smiles and slips on his coat. He looks at her for one moment, then gently caresses the side of her face with one hand. She does not resist.

He tilts her head slightly upward and then gives her a sweet, simple kiss, but one that is full of just enough implication as to leave her wanting more. And then we're off ...

It's toward the end of the night, and I've lost count of how many stops we've made and how many drinks we've had—four? five? six? Could we have been to seven places? By now, the evening has taken on a very sweet, hazy quality. We stop outside a Turkish kabob place on Houston and Avenue A, grabbing some Mideastern meats for our empty stomachs. It's 1:30 in the morning. Hutch downs his $3 falafel with as much relish as he would a $37 steak at Raoul's.

"Okay, Dog. One more joint and we call it a night."

We return to Fountain, where we began the night. Now it's positively bursting at the seams and has somehow, in the last four hours, become the place to be on a cold April night in New York City. In fact, there's even a small line out front with a velvet rope.

Note: this is always going to be a pain in the ass for two dudes. Beautiful women have the advantage here completely. You can't even bribe your way in, as most doormen would rather slug you than deign to accept a hundred bucks to let some loser into their venue.

We're in luck though, as I actually know Tony, the massive doorman. All I've ever done for Tony was listen to his wife and girlfriend troubles over scotches one aimless night when I ran into him at some dive bar. The dude was hurting, though, and now—as though I were Androcles—he greets me like a brother, slaps me on the back, and ushers me and Hutch past the velvet rope.

As I'm thanking Tony, however, who should I see but Nathaniel (aka "Pimples") and his Dweeb Banker Posse, no doubt condemned to wait for all eternity. I guess word of a cool club spreads through even the nerdiest banking circles. Pimples starts waving frantically and pathetically in my direction.

What the hell, I think. Maybe it's kindness or my attempt to earn some good karma points, but probably it's to let my ex-Sweatshop Taskmaster know that in this world, I have more clout than he does. I want Pimples to know that in this zip code, I'm king and he's begging by the gate. (I only wish that Paloma were here to see my rise from Lowly Graphic Pauper to Prince of the Night Realms.)

I whisper to Tony that I "sort of know" that guy over there. Tony wants to help and asks Nathaniel how many are in his party. When Pimples says "six," I realize it's out of my hands. There's no way that a Dweeb Sextet is getting in here tonight. Maybe one of them had a shot, but six—no way any self-respecting nightspot is going to let in a gang of losers, no matter what their business cards say. I shrug at Pimples to say,

"I tried," and entering with ease, I'm both amused and saddened to see Pimples's look of profound despair mixed with sincere, mystified admiration.

It's all behind me when, from across the packed room, I spot my target, hovering innocently around the bar. Well, not that innocently. Her dress is backless—a racy and rather daring choice, given the twenty-degree New York weather—and her body is totally hot. She's in profile to me, her hair slithering around her face when she laughs with her two, only slightly less hot friends.

I point her out to Hutch, who seconds my opinion and follows me as my wingman. We approach. As they turn, I'm floored to see that my focus is, in fact, Very Slinky Brunette from Epitome. Maybe it's the last four or five drinks, and maybe it's the backless dress, or maybe it's the magic of 4 a.m. and mood lighting, but she looks even better than she does post-yoga. In fact, she looks amazing.

"Hi," she smiles, equally surprised and seemingly very happy to see me. Slinky introduces me to her friends as her yoga teacher, and I fold Hutch into the mix. Hutch casts his rakish charm over all of them, but I can tell that my boy wants Slinky's blonde friend. With the intros made, and having meshed our way so easily and completely into the group, there's no need to even officially release him from his wingman duties. It's now every man for himself.

Slinky is a class act, but it's very apparent that the lady's into me. Everything in her body language telegraphs just how much she wants me to have my way with her. I lean back, and she follows. I say something that's barely amusing and she laughs sweetly. I stroll my hand along the curve at the small of her exposed back, and she doesn't move away. Rather, she pulls in closer, inviting more touch.

She smells totally great, too. I haven't really noticed her scent before—there are so many strange herbal and therapeutic and just plain sweaty smells at Epitome—but whatever she's wearing is going straight to my seven-drinks-to-the-wind brain.

When she touches my hand, lightly brushing the tiny,

almost invisible hairs and the edges right where my wrists begin, I feel a shiver up my spine. I want her too, and badly. And yet even when I am absolutely sure that if I invited her back to my place, she'd come without hesitation, I'm somehow not issuing the invitation. Yet another sexual/spiritual conflict for which sadly, there is no twenty-four-hour helpline.

Even Hutch notices my sorry state. He interrupts himself as he's making his moves on the blonde and pulls me aside, which lets the ladies regroup and confer.

"Dog, what the hell is wrong with you?" he asks.

"What do you mean?" I say.

"You did not just meet this girl. This is not a night where you only number close and get her digits. You guys were at the 'get-a-room' stage ten minutes ago. Why are you still fuckin' here?"

And the answer is … I don't know. Has my mantra of "Don't fuck this up" by not hitting on my students actually taken effect? Has common sense really permeated my brain so deeply that when a hot, available woman totally wants me, I've conditioned myself not to respond to my loins? Question one: Can this be true? Question two: Is this a good thing or even more screwed up than my usual mindless cavorting?

Hutch is waiting for an answer, and he is not one to wait for anything.

"Shit, Dude, I just don't know. She's totally hot, but—"

"But what?"

"She's my student, man. I teach her."

"Look at her, Dude. Believe me, I wouldn't mind teaching her myself."

"I'm serious. You're the one who told me not to fuck up my yoga career."

This gives Hutch a rare moment of pause. He scrunches his face up a bit, as he gives this heavy matter his deepest, seven-scotches-into-the-morning thought. "Listen, Dog, I could go either way on this one."

"How do you mean?"

"Well, she's not a private student, right? So there's no major financial loss to you once it's over, right? At most, she's worth

$3 a week. A measly $150 a year, even with perfect attendance.
You make that in one lesson with a private student. On the other
hand, do you think she'll screw things up for you at Epitome
after you dump her?"

"Hard to say. I really doubt it, though."

"Well, Dog, it's a tough call. She's so hot that I wouldn't
fault you, but it is a calculated risk since Brooke got you that gig.
In and of herself, her direct economic impact is marginal, but
she could have a majorly negative trickle-down effect for your
bread-and-butter gigs."

"Thanks for reducing my ethical dilemma about getting laid
tonight to a pure cost-benefit analysis."

Hutch laughs. "Dog, I gotta play to my strengths."

I return to Slinky. She smiles at me eagerly and then looks
up at me with innocent doe-eyes. And that does it. This is
suddenly way too intimate and personal.

"I should really be going," I manage reluctantly. She
looks devastated.

I can't help it. She's looking at me with that Phoebe
vulnerability, that look of lust perhaps, but with so much
admiration in it—admiration for a spirituality and a depth
that I frankly do not in any way possess—that I can feel my
resolve evaporating.

And then I feel like shit because I see I've made her feel
like shit. I don't know what to say either. She couldn't be hotter
or sweeter. In fact, that's the problem. Like Andrew does, I now
feel that it's almost high-minded of me, compassionate even, to
carry out the one-night stand in order to spare her feelings. But
just as I'm about to completely cave, Hutch, as always, comes
to my rescue.

Appearing with our coats, he turns to Slinky and whispers
something. She seems concerned and then relieved. She
rushes up to me, impulsively throws her arms around me, and
kisses my cheek.

"You take care," she says.

"You, too," I reply as Hutch practically drags me out
of the club.

Once we hit the fresh air, I exclaim, "Dude, what the fuck did you tell her?"

"That your mom or your sister, I don't know, someone and I'm pretty sure it was female, was in a hit-and-run accident two weeks ago. That Mom or Sis has a fifty/fifty chance of recovery. That I had insisted you go out tonight, you know, forcing you to rejoin the living."

"What? Are you out of your goddamn mind?"

"Look, Dog, at least this puts her on hold. She clearly knows you're not gay, and that's good, but you can't reject someone that hot without some kickass excuse."

"But a dying mother—"

"Or sister—I honestly can't remember."

"This is pretty messed up, even for you."

"What's the big deal? She seemed like she was about to cry when you were going to ditch her. Now she feels good about herself and sorry for you and your tragically unlucky relatives. She doesn't feel rejected. If anything, she wants you more."

"True, but—"

"There are no buts. The odds that she's ever going to meet your family and take a head count are pretty much nil. You're in the clear. And if you want her in two weeks, it's up to you if Mom or Sis recovers or not. Either way, she'll jump you like nobody's business."

"I guess."

"Trust me. Problem solved. Everybody's happier, thanks to your potentially dying mother."

"Or sister."

"Yeah, I should probably have been a little more focused there. Well, when she asks, you can just wing it."

"I suppose. Well, then, thanks, I guess. I mean it." And I do. Slinky's rejection was about to break my no-student-seduction resolve—I've justified that the Cleavage Twins are somehow an exception—until he stepped in.

"Look, Dog, that's what a wingman is for." Hutch grabs me with a brotherly hug and lets loose one more howl of the night. I join him, and for a few seconds I do feel better, until he grabs a ready cab and speeds off. Then I'm back home for the sleep of the frustrated. But fuck it—imaginary-accident-victim relative or not, for once in my life, I may have actually Done the Right Thing. Rather than feeling virtuous and glad hearted, though, I am only now learning that Doing the Right Thing feels, well, lonely.

CHAPTER 20

Next morning, Janek calls me. Since it's Saturday, I'm surprised. We really haven't expanded our relationship beyond our yoga lessons or group drinks. Maybe he's canceling our Monday appointment? I wonder.

"I have big news," Janek announces. "Synnove and I are getting married."

"Wow! Congratulations." I'm not a total idiot. I know that's what you're supposed to say. But, still, my most authentic response is "Marriage? Are you out of your motherfucking Slovakian mind?"

"Yeah, man. It's awesome. So, listen, we're inviting some friends over to celebrate. Are you free? Like, around 10 tonight?"

"Absolutely. I'm there." For a party at Janek's swank pad—cohosted by a model whose friends are, no doubt, all models as well—I can get past my knee-jerk anti-commitment prejudices.

"Awesome. Just about to call Hutch, too, of course. Great to have you both there to celebrate."

Up until this moment, I've been totally envious of Janek's whole lifestyle—I could even deal with the live-in girlfriend (she is a supermodel, after all)—but a live-in girlfriend is not a wife. Granted, it's not a life commitment, a life commitment being something that pretty much cancels out Rule #1: Always Be On The Prowl. (Unless, of course, you are Andrew, who plays entirely by his own set of rules.) Nonetheless, given my track record it feels wiser to remain single than risk hurting someone that badly again.

For a few seconds, part of me wonders if I had anything to do with this sudden advancement of their relationship. After a huge breakthrough of heart-opening Wheels, the next thing I know, he's proposing marriage. For better or worse, could there be a little yoga magic influencing his sudden romantic leap of faith? Is my prize student suddenly attracted to dropping back into an even deeper kind of oblivion, namely marriage? I shudder to think so, even as I awake from my nap to shower and shave for the supermodel bounty that Janek has so generously lain before me and Hutch.

I arrive before Hutch and the party is rocking, but in a super-sophisticated way. Janek's hired excellent last-minute caterers, and within seconds of arriving, attractive waitstaff take my coat, bring me a glass of champagne, and offer me really good appetizers. I survey the scene, extremely pleased with the crowd.

Janek spots me across the room and approaches. Gives me a brotherly hug.

"Congrats, man."

"Thank you. I'm very happy."

I limit further comments because I feel it would be in particularly bad taste if I continue to mispronounce his fiancée's name at her engagement party.

Janek's pulled away by other guests, and I start to circulate. I'm caught eyeing a sloe-eyed blonde colleague of Symphony's by a vaguely familiar, good-looking guy wearing the kind of thick-framed black glasses that are so ugly, they're stylish. His look telegraphs architect/designer/Arthur Miller Wannabe.

He smiles and walks right over to me. "You're the yoga teacher, right?"

"Yup. Guru on the go," I say, although I'm not sure how well I'm representing any spiritual path, given my double martini and my leering.

He extends his hand. "I'm Jeffrey Alston. We sort of met at that art opening last week. Janek has great things to say about working with you." I recognize him as the dude who was in Janek's posse as we departed.

"He's a great guy. And a pleasure to teach," I reply.

"I'm sure. I designed the lights for the new showroom. Best creative and business experience I've ever had." So, he's a designer, then. The look works and all, but I guess these guys just feel they have to unpretty themselves up when they're too classically handsome, as though they can't look like a matinee idol and still know where to artfully install track lighting.

Just then, Hutch arrives, throwing a big, public bear hug around me. I introduce Jeffrey. And then Hutch introduces Jeffrey to what seems to be his date, the beautiful Afro chick we met last night.

Hutch reintroduces us, but we both remember each other, although, of course, I've totally forgotten her name. It's "Etta," I relearn and instantly forget again. Afro Chick is looking good and reeks of style. She's reigned in her seventies retro vibe a bit, and while still urban and edgy, she's doing it up a little more elegant, a little less club scene. The girl has taste, in other words.

We hang out a bit—Hutch, Afro Chick, Jeffrey, and me—until Jeffrey gets dragged away by what looks like a roving gay design posse. When Afro Chick runs into a colleague—despite her Jackie Brown persona, or maybe because of it, she works as a junior district attorney—the two of them head off to the ladies room together, leaving me and Hutch alone.

"So, how you doing, Dog?" Hutch asks. He signals for martini refills.

"I'm cool, man. But I gotta ask ..." I wait for him to explain the Afro Chick situation. He doesn't have a clue.

"Okay, ask what?"

"Dude, Afro Chick is—"

"Her name is Etta," Hutch corrects me without reproach, although this is definitely the sort of slip on my part that he's pretty much continuously ignored for the past decade.

"Okay, sorry. Anyway, Etta is really hot and actually surprisingly smart and cool, but why have you brought her here?"

"What do you mean?"

"Duh ... We're at a party given by a fuckin' Scandinavian supermodel for her friends. Bringing a hot chick here is like bringing sand to the beach."

Hutch laughs easily, but nonetheless, he doesn't offer any explanation. Afro Chick—I mean, "Etta"—is a beautiful woman, and yet the city is teeming with them in endless varieties and combinations, especially in the present 3,000 feet of prime Soho loft space.

The next few hours become a happy blur of perfect martinis and digits exchanged with beautiful women who probably have trouble counting higher than their weight in kilos. In fact—and I never thought I'd say this—it's almost too easy here, like shooting fish in a barrel. Janek and Symphony have stocked the room to overflowing with babes while creating the perfect trusting, cozy atmosphere. Unlike with a cold approach in a bar or a club, there's almost no challenge to hitting up the ladies successfully, especially when they ask how I'm connected to the party, and I tell them I'm Janek's yoga instructor. Since every hot model is addicted to yoga, it's almost as good as bringing a puppy you rescued from a burning building. Once again, given the ease of gurus' getting laid, I make a second "Note to Self" about starting a cult.

Since the quality of my prospects is so high, I decide to focus on quantity. I set a goal for myself—obtaining a dozen model phone numbers, enough to tide me over for the next two months until the summer's here—and proceed to exceed it by 1 a.m.

Nothing here thrashes my buzz except for Hutch and Etta's departure. From halfway across the room, I see him helping her on with her hip fake fur. I've seen him make all sorts of moves on the ladies before, but there's something particularly tender, protective even, as he folds her into her coat. And I suppose there's the fact that he's not bothering to find me to say good-bye. He's done that before, obviously, when we're out and the night has sent us to opposite ends of a large club. Hutch is not consistently sentimental in his comings and goings; his bear hug hellos and good-byes coexist with sudden vanishings from clubs with that night's hookup, him texting in a cab, "Outta here, talk tomorrow." But in a situation like this, where no hasty departure seems necessary, I'm surprised he doesn't venture around the corner for a fond farewell. Having enveloped Etta in her coat, however, he looks up and our eyes meet. He smiles, waves warmly, and they depart without further ceremony.

Around 1:30, I decide that I should probably leave. The night feels complete. I already have a pocketful of numbers to pursue. I'm pretty buzzed without being shit-faced. Even the twelve-minute walk home seems strangely attractive.

Except, however, when I snap out of my posh party denial and remind myself that I'm about to lose my second—and probably final—chance at my dream.

Like staring at Andrea's postcard, or walking past the bridge gallery, I renew my gluttony for punishment. In fact, my wandering home turns westwards towards the Blue Ribbon Brasserie, the site of my Valentine's Day encounter with Shane.

Our appearance there last time was technically Monique's idea. But now I'm on my own. There are, of course, about a million other places I might grab a nightcap before bed, many directly between Soho and my pad. I can't even bother to pretend I'm not hoping to run into Shane again, which I know makes no sense whatsoever. Like drinking to get drunk, sometimes when things look grim, you want to darken them up even more.

In days, the property goes on the market. Of course, Monique might be right—in this economy, it could easily take months before it's purchased. What does it matter? It's not like I'm going to unearth a long lost billionaire uncle. I guess somehow the lingering feeling of lost opportunity wants to snowball into more misery. Before I know it, I'm seated at the bar at Blue Ribbon, nursing a scotch.

I'm about to give up hope—a truly ironic word in this context—when Shane and Frame Boy and two other friends of hers I vaguely recognize stroll in laughing.

As usual, I don't really have a game plan here. I suppose knowing that I'm going to lose this last chance to make things up to Shane somehow requires that I see her again. But whether slightly smashed or stone-cold sober, my rational brain knows that no good can come from another carbon-copy contrition conversation.

A wave of common sense and cowardice washes over me, so I head to the men's room before I can be spotted. Maybe a few splashes of cold water on my face will sober me up and drive some sense into me. Or, at least, maybe I can get out of here before I make an ass of myself.

No such luck. Exiting the bathroom, I run directly into Shane, who's by herself and waiting outside the door. We're both equally taken aback. She recovers first, and unlike her cool manner last time, there's real anger in her voice.

"There are other restaurants in New York," she glares.

"I know. I guess I was hoping to run into you."

"Why? What the hell for? How clear do I have to make it to you: I don't want anything to do with you."

"Shane, I—"

Her voice rises, much louder than normal. "Look, I don't care what you have to say or how many apologies you want to make. Whatever it is you want from me, it's not ever going to happen. So spare me the crawling-on-your-knees, 'I'm so sorry' bullshit. Accept the truth: I am NEVER going to forgive you."

I take this in.

Her voice is quieter now but no less firm. "So please … just leave me alone."

She pushes past me and shuts the door to the bathroom behind her.

Fortunately, given the crowded restaurant, I'm able to slap a twenty on the bar and slip past Frame Boy and the rest of Shane's friends unnoticed. Outside, going through my pockets to double-check if I have my keys and cell, I find a couple of loose cigarettes. In all honesty, I'm a failure as a smoker—only when I've had a scotch late at night do I even want to light up—but tonight's definitely one of those nights. I round the corner, and seeing a homeless dude vacate his park bench, I indulge myself.

I'm a handful of drags into the cigarette when Shane and Frame Boy round the corner. Even at a distance of thirty feet, their choreography makes the scene clear: she's left the restaurant without her coat and he's hurrying after her. He gets her to stop—which is quite fortunate, since she would soon be stumbling towards me, the source of her misery.

Their body language tells it all. He's tall and comforting and after a moment of resistance, she folds into his arms. Shane's not angry anymore—I'm not around to provoke her—but from the shadows, it seems like she's still acutely vulnerable, maybe even crying. This becomes clearer when he brushes away what must be a tear.

Frame Boy seems to be the soul of patience, a fantasy of the good guy who chases after you and somehow makes things all right again. He's the opposite of me, the one who fucks things up in the first place. A few moments later, it seems Shane's recovered, and as they hold hands, Frame Boy leads her back to the restaurant.

It's funny but I realize that I'm not even jealous. Instead, I feel something inside me shift. Until now, I've wanted Shane to forgive me so that I can feel a little less guilty, so that I can feel a little better about myself. But seeing how angry and how hurt she still is, my motivation shifts. Forget about the forgiveness I'm craving; I just want Shane to feel better. I want her to be free of me and all my screwups.

Unfortunately, more than anything in the world, getting Shane to feel better is increasingly and utterly beyond my reach.

The Cleavage Twins are, as always, a welcome diversion. Serious and Diamond are not interested in blindfolds today, which is fine with me. This time, they want to tie me up. It's really not my thing—you may have gathered by now that I like to be in control—but never having had a threesome before that involved a little bondage, I decide to play along. You never know …

As before, the ladies are experts with their tongues and hands and every other part of their bodies. In fact, they're so skilled that I almost wonder if either or both of them did this professionally before. It wouldn't be the first time a high-class call girl married money. I don't voice the question, however, less out of politeness than simply because conversation isn't the point here. Meaningless sex is.

We manage to spend two hours together, every moment of the encounter as technically perfect as a player piano pounding out soulless music no one wants to hear. Despite my increasingly depressed state, I've been fully functional—hell, I think I've performed admirably—but when it's time for us to depart (separately, of course), Serious notices something's amiss. Serious gets, well, serious for once.

"Is something wrong?" she asks.

"What? Oh, no. Just a little distracted is all."

"No, really, baby. What's up? You don't seem quite yourself today," Diamond concurs.

These chicks are very observant. I guess they've had to be to get and stay where they are despite their naughty transgressions.

"It's no big deal. Just a little frustrated by a project that's not working out," I say, trying to skim over it entirely.

"Really? It sounds intriguing. Tell us more," Diamond coaxes.

"It's pretty lame actually. And I don't think it's going to come together."

"Why not?"

"Financing. I need investors for a new venture, and I'm coming up dry. I can't get anyone with cash to hear me out."

They both giggle—well, it's less than a giggle but yet another of their amused interchanges that make me feel like the slow child again.

"What's so funny?" I'm slightly pissed that my rapidly falling-apart dream amuses them.

"Well, neither one of us is exactly an MBA—" Serious starts.

"Or even a CPA, for that matter," Diamond interjects.

"But we are matrimonially affiliated with two rather splendid gentlemen who excel in such matters," Serious continues.

"Yeah, but it's for a nightclub venture," I tell them. "And not the kind of thing they're probably used to dealing with."

"Our boys like all sorts of unusual investments, provided, of course, that the risks are reasonable," Diamond adds.

"And the profit potential is huge. How much are we talking about anyway?" Serious asks.

"$3.8 Million." I say, with a little hesitation. They have no reaction. I might as well have told them that I need $7 for a pack of cigarettes or $12 for cab fare.

"Tell us about what you want to do."

I hesitate for a second. I really hadn't seen this coming. In fact, I contacted the Cleavage Twins because I wanted to escape from my inability to make this happen, not to discuss and dissect it. "Really?" I wonder aloud.

"Really," Serious replies, handing me a fresh scotch.

And so, I tell them everything. The amazing location. The concept. Its uniqueness. The daring architecture required. My entire vision for the place. And they listen, only occasionally asking a few pointed and surprisingly intelligent questions, all of which I have reasonably coherent answers for. As if they'd rehearsed this, Serious and Diamond nod to each other. "Well, then, I think this is something our Boys might want to hear about."

"Really? Are you kidding me?"

"Trust me, there are two things we do not joke about: Money and Our Men." I'm sure those are the truest words Serious has ever spoken.

In minutes, it's arranged. I'm invited to come out the following weekend to the Hamptons—Diamond and Serious want to go out before the season starts on Memorial Day to get their houses in order. A luncheon meeting for Saturday at Diamond's house is set. Serious writes down the address. As I'm leaving, I have a twinge of uncertainty.

"What is it?" Diamond asks.

"Nothing. Except ... are you both sure about this

being wise?"

"You mean, do we want to mix business with pleasure?" Serious says. I nod.

"Darling," Diamond says as she kisses me out of the room, "for the professional, business is pleasure."

More in need of advice and less of a handout, I tell Andrew everything—well, almost everything—and he listens with superb intensity to all of it.

He thinks the venture sounds promising, but, of course, he makes not even the slightest gesture toward getting involved financially. There's something eerie about this, actually, although perhaps I am the only one feeling that. Neither of us addresses in any way the fact that he has plenty of exactly what I need: Money.

I mean, I'd expect him to get invested in the situation if I were on fire and he were holding a bucket of water. Of course, I realize that my speculative venture isn't fully parallel to a dire emergency. Yet even without the sense of life-threatening urgency, you'd think he'd still feel compelled to address the point that he possesses the very thing I lack in vast amounts.

I wonder, if like Brooke's and Andrew's interviewing style, this is something they teach the very rich in some kind of Outward Bound program. "If a fierce grizzly confronts you in the wild, just freeze. Do not attempt to run away. Do not offer him anything of yours. In fact, do not acknowledge his existence in any way. Simply be still, and wait until the moment passes, and said grizzly will most likely leave you unharmed." Substitute "person who genuinely needs some of your money" for "grizzly bear" and you pretty much have Andrew's reaction.

And this strategy works, of course. I don't consider asking him for money for one second despite our bonding and shared confidences and the fact that he probably wouldn't even miss a few million dollars here or there.

Andrew does generously volunteer some free advice, however. "When you visit them, have someone financial with you. Doesn't matter who as long as it's someone with an MBA from a good school, preferably one of theirs."

"Okay." I agree.

"And why don't you take the Jag," Andrew proffers.

"Excuse me?" I ask, wondering what I must have misheard.

"I think it's better if you drive there, rather than have them pick you up at the train. That reads as needy, summer-guest-for-a-weekend behavior."

"I could just rent a car," I venture.

"Why? The Jag's just sitting right next to the Bentley in the garage. Frankly, since Danielle and I go out every weekend after Memorial Day, the car practically drives itself there."

"That's very generous of you. It's an awfully valuable thing to loan."

"It's insured. And you're a good driver, right?"

"Yes." And I am.

"It's settled then. People will only invest in something if they think you don't need the money. You've got to create that impression—that you're jaunting out to the Hamptons, gracing them with your presence, instead of accepting any of the dozens of other investor invites you've received. It will add just a little extra splash to your whole presentation, to the impression of thriving self-sufficiency that you need to project in order to get anyone to help you."

"Thank you." And I mean it wholeheartedly.

"It's nothing. Remind me, before you go, to tell Phelps at the garage that you'll be picking it up and to leave you a key. Now let's discuss your wardrobe. What time is the appointment again? Lunch?"

Andrew rapidly tells me what to wear and drink and which programs on CNN to watch in the next three days to appear knowledgeable, essentially putting me through a ten-minute crash course in How to Fake Success. I'm flashing on the possibility of a Mogul Makeover reality show when Andrew finishes his final presentation tip—brush up on modern art, specifically the ton of it that one of the Cleavage Boys has been buying at various auctions. Then he launches right back into his favorite topic: his perpetually turbulent personal life. "Now, did I tell you what happened with that Forbes reporter when …"

I update Monique on my progress, including Andrew's suggestions, without naming my source. Somehow, it seems tasteful to keep his name out of the conversation with Monique, even though I'm revealing nothing personal and giving absolutely no hints, much less any details, about his indiscretions. And, of course, even though Monique's whole schtick is that there are no demands, limits, or commitments regarding our relationship, I still think it best to be discreet regarding Serious and Cleavage, referring to them merely as "friends from my yoga world."

"I think those are excellent points. The Jag is the right car for you—or the you that you're trying to sell them on. And I'm sure they'll love me," Monique volunteers.

"Excuse me?" This is news.

"You should definitely have an MBA around, and last time I looked, mine says Harvard."

This is a new development. Now that we're this far along, I was actually considering asking Hutch to come—although he'd be distracting, rakish catnip to Serious and Diamond—but Monique has thrown me a curveball. She's made such a point of her independence, and her loyalty to Becker, that I guess I never pictured her involvement extending beyond hooking me up with the space.

Even I can see, however, that way beyond her Harvard MBA, as the right-hand man of Anderson Becker, one of the most successful nightlife impresarios ever, Monique is indisputably the best possible choice for this mission. Who could be better able to persuade two banking guys to part with their money than someone who's worked side by side with a guy who's made a fortune doing exactly this—and someone who, on top of it all, is not so bad on the eyes?

"Are you offering to come? That's great," I agree.

"Of course. Totally my pleasure."

"Well, I'm picking up the car at 9, so I could pick you up at 9:30, and, at this time of year, I think we'll have no trouble making lunch at 1."

"Sounds like a plan. Later, then." Monique is about to hang up, but I stop her.

"Wait a sec … I need your address."

"Oh, right," she laughs. "You've never been here before."

She gives it to me—heart of the West Village, at Perry and Hudson—telling me to call her when I'm five minutes away, and that she'll be waiting outside. While I am a little curious to see Monique's pad, showing it is clearly not something that interests her in the least. We do best, it seems, safely confined in mine.

I realize that, given our last public venture and the Shane disaster, perhaps I'm compounding the folly enormously by not only seeing Monique outside my apartment, but actually taking a road trip with her outside Manhattan. On the other hand, she is the best candidate I can think of to accompany me, and at this point, now that she's decided she's going, I bet it would take a crowbar to pry her away from the trip.

More and more, like driving along a badly marked highway at night, moment to moment, each of my decisions seems to make sense. And in my darkest moments, that's been a source of hope: you truly can make the journey of a thousand miles seeing only ten feet ahead of you. At the very least, the path seems familiar most of the time.

(On the other hand, while sometimes you arrive at your destination safe and sound, unfortunately sometimes you never know for sure if you're lost until you're really lost.)

The car ride out to East Hampton is perfectly pleasant. Traffic is with us, and the May weather is a pleasant sixty-two degrees. Monique has brought a wide range of interesting CDs, and we enjoy adult conversation on topics like music, books, and films.

We briefly discuss the meeting strategy, with Monique outlining a basic game plan, and her informing me she's "done her homework" and is quite satisfied with the financial specs she carries in a slim Hermès leather binder. We never discuss exactly what Monique's role is in this venture, and yet somehow that feels right—or it may simply be that I've no desire to explain or define all the nuances of my relationships with the Cleavage Gals and Monique. This blending of business and pleasure has already gotten way too complicated. I just hope I can remember their real names in order to introduce all my fuck buddies.

We find the house ten minutes early, so we drive around the block twice. Frankly, there's not much to see, as high hedges obscure most of these homes from the road. Three minutes before the appointed time—once again, I am consistent in my handful of virtues—we pass through a gated break of hedges and toward the driveway.

Monique, who has spent considerably more time in the Hamptons than I have, is impressed with the address. "It's not Lily Pond Lane, mind you, but trust me, this is far from shabby."

That's an understatement in my book, as we wind our way up to the end of the driveway, where an excessive number of luxury cars seem to be parked for a lunch for three couples. There's a Rolls, a Bentley, and two Mercedes convertibles. Andrew was right: the Jag fits right in, while a Ford Tempo rental would really have sent the wrong message.

I'm pleased that Monique also set the right tone with her appearance: a ladylike spring dress, crisp and straightforward, but also clingy enough to reveal a tremendously sexy body underneath the businesswoman's navy silk jacket.

The Cleavage Twins and their husbands have been playing doubles, it seems, and have wound their way around from the tennis court to greet us as we exit the car. Given all the complex romantic entanglements, complete with a country-house setting, I feel like I've drifted on to the set of a Noel Coward play. The ladies each give me a peck on the cheek and perform the introductions, with me filling in Monique's identity.

The husbands seem like okay guys. Although, from the moment that Serious introduces them as "Our Boys," I can only think of them as, ironically, the "Boyz." Both Boyz are mostly bald, late forties/early fifties. Neither one is particularly good- or bad-looking. They're trim, fit, and intensely wired in a slightly neurotic, vaguely accountant-like, but ultimately masculine, way. Maybe it's just that they both seem pretty confident—which makes sense, given that they're filthy rich, have super-hot wives, and we're on their fabulous turf—and while they don't seem like they should rush out and run for political office, they also don't seem like chumps whose wives have invited a guest with whom they have an ongoing ménage.

Diamond volunteers a tour of the house, and Monique and I readily accept. It seems the polite thing to do, and besides, I'm always a little curious how the other half—I mean, the other 0.5 percent of the population—lives.

I'm struck by how easy this seems for both Diamond and Serious. They are totally at ease, indicating not the slightest inkling of any awkwardness toward me, and this, in turn, gives me the cue to maintain my own performance. If I didn't know any better, I'd swear I really was in fact only their yoga teacher and that they were merely taken with the business merits of this opportunity.

The property is luxurious, and Diamond's delight in showing off certain details is rather endearing. She's genuinely excited about all her renovations, things involving Italian tile and marble apparently stolen from under the feet of the Medici (I'm making that up; I wasn't quite listening.). Diamond has one of those mechanical clothing racks, like at a dry cleaner's, for her walk-in closet that she's rather proud of as well. I see a look from Monique that exemplifies pure envy as we pass through Diamond's temple to her shoes. It's really just another large walk-in closet with lots of shoes on various pedestals, but something about the room's design evokes a bizarre, almost hushed reverence—even from a totally uninterested shoe oaf like me.

The entire house is one of those basically all-white affairs that looks great in magazines but is impossible to maintain (without live-in help) if you have children or if you do anything other than pose for magazine shoots of your living room. The art against the beachy, white gallery walls is particularly spectacular. Mr. Diamond Cleavage, to his credit, does seem to have a genuine interest in the paintings he's purchased, beyond their value to appreciate above the Dow Jones Average. Thanks to Andrew's coaching about Mr. Diamond Cleavage's recent purchases, I'm able to interject a few thoughtful sound bites gleaned from the Internet. A few De Koonings, one Rothko, a whimsical Klee, and two Frankenthalers later, and we've arrived at the patio, where a table is set for us.

Lunch is superb—a perfectly poached salmon, wild rice, and grilled vegetables, all so delicious that the fact that it's all very healthy too is almost obscured. Fresh berries with a side of sorbet complete the meal.

Conversation is buoyant throughout. Everyone seems to have a very chatty temperament although no one gets anywhere near the topic of the point of the visit. Instead, topics range from the obvious cultural events of New York to a tasteful hint of limousine-liberal politics. No one here evidences the slightest desire to offend anyone else.

The Boyz, though, of course are good at getting the basic résumé facts out of a person. Monique isn't shy about her Harvard MBA or her triumphs with Becker. Mr. Diamond and Mr. Serious clearly respect Becker's financial savvy, and while they tacitly admit that they do not frequent any of his hipster establishments, they are keenly aware of their property values and profit potentials. There's a solid—and I suppose, very helpful—round of Harvard Business School bonding, and as Monique and the Boyz get rather macho in their in-joke financial swagger, I almost feel like retiring with the ladies to needlepoint and crochet. I suppress this left-out feeling, as clearly part of this whole trip is for Monique to bond with them as part of the Old Boys (and now, Hot Ladies) network. Monique, by the way, is doing almost too well here, commenting intelligently on everything from the art to the champagne.

"I love the hazelnut and apple scents," she comments, as

Mr. Serious refills her glass.

"And how extremely long it is in the finish," Mr. Diamond adds.

"Funny, being extremely long in the finish is also my favorite attribute in a man," Monique replies, and everyone chuckles at her bawdy PG-13 pun on connoisseurship.

I do wonder when we're going to get down to business although it occurs to me that perhaps the conversation is taking place under my nose, and I'm just not aware of it. Maybe it's all subtext, and after a lot of confidence building, they just write a $3.8 million check because we've all got the same secret handshake and an Old School tie in the back of a sock drawer. On the other hand, no matter how freely the 1999 Louis Roederer Cristal Brut flows during lunch (and it flows at about $300 a bottle retail, thank you), I can just as easily imagine that there will be endless flow charts and cost-and-profit analyses required by these guys.

Soon enough, and I'm sure that the Cleavages must have orchestrated this all in advance, Serious and Diamond announce that they've got tennis lessons at the club and remind their spouses about some dinner they're all attending that night. My curiosity about the nature of their tennis lessons (versus our "yoga lessons") is stifled because clearly their departure leaves the Boyz, Monique, and me alone to talk business.

As the Cleavages get up from the table, the Boyz suggest we talk in the living room, also giving us a chance to escort their wives toward the front hall. Somehow, the logistics of departure are such that the Cleavages and I trail behind the Harvard MBA trio.

The Cleavages have been impeccable throughout—frankly, I've almost forgotten that we'd been banging furiously, in increasingly obscene ways, scarcely seventy-two hours ago—but as we near the front door, Serious takes my hand and squeezes it, and Diamond brushes hers across my ass. This contact takes mere seconds, and to the casual observer might think it means absolutely nothing other than a naughty bit of contact after a champagne lunch. But Monique, as though she has some kind of radar for illicit, mindless sexcapades, somehow half cocks her head and might just glimpse the import of the moment. I can't tell. While her smiling at the Boyz's banter seems entirely continuous, I wonder if she's grasped anything of significance, anything out of context in the ladies' fleeting, flirting gestures of wishing me luck. Nothing in her face or manner indicates that she has.

The Boyz kiss their wives good-bye. There are some stock jokes about their wives' spending patterns and needing to start moonlighting in order to keep them in the style to which they've become accustomed. And then, with the Cleavage gals gone, it's time for business.

Monique has coached me extensively beforehand. "In the end they will invest because this is a sexy proposition. That's entirely up to you to sell them. I'm there more or less for reassurance that it's not a crazy investment. But it's up to you to pitch them with enthusiasm, with passion even, gauging how receptive they are. Just be ready to just shut up and let me take over whenever they decide they want to talk numbers or track record. But remember: this is your sale to win or lose, not mine."

I spin out my whole concept, sharing everything that excites me about it and will make it a huge success. I've come up with a name and a concept for the place that I love and so does Monique: Diwali. Monique was thrilled by the vaguely yoga connection, believing it will get us even more press since my Grand Central spread. Diwali is a festival of lights that spans many Eastern cultures, and that's basically all about good winning out over evil. Since it comes in October or November, depending on the yearly lunar calendar, it's also great since that would coincide with our theoretical opening.

I like the name, too, because it doesn't sound like other places. Most of these joints go for either something that makes them sound hipster ironic (like Happy Ending), vaguely Euro (like Pastis or Cielo), or masquerading as a gentlemen's club (One Oak). Diwali is memorable and multi-culti in a good way. Plus I think it would allow tremendous potential for us to play with the lighting—everything from candles to oil lamps to lasers—and maybe some Kama Sutra murals. It could be sexy and exotic without being heavy-handed or arbitrary. And even if we did offend someone by naming a nightclub after a religious festival, we'd get a ton of invaluable press from it.

I compare and contrast tons of other places—some of which they've been to, and most of which they've only glimpsed in Grand Central or on Page Six—and I feel that my enthusiasm is indeed spilling over to the Cleavage Boyz. I try to remain sensitive to my audience's interest level. Monique nods, subtly encouraging me to keep going, so I start getting into more details: the menu, the entertainers, the way the dividers will slide away to open up the floor, even my vision for the ceilings, the mirrors, and the linens. I'm far from exhausted—and they seem totally into it—but Monique soon indicates that it's time to move into the practical side of things, and I feel that, too. Leave them wanting more.

Monique, now fully inhabiting her role as sexpot MBA, is stunning. Conveying total fiscal responsibility, she outlines the entire investment possibility with clarity, coolheadedness, and charm. The Boyz ask many pointed questions regarding rate of return, deadlines, and real-estate values, and when they start getting into details of the limited liability corporation's structure, I feel like excusing myself to grab another bottle of Cristal. However, realizing that might not be exactly confidence inspiring, I pretend to listen.

I wish I'd had Monique on my side when I tried this before. Oh, I got the money from my investor in the end, but it was more in spite of myself. I immediately resolve to get an MBA in my spare time or at least to occasionally glance at the financial section of the Times.

Suddenly, after we've talked for about an hour, there's a pause in which it seems the Boyz have exhausted all their questions, and Monique, and I to a lesser extent, have answered everything adequately.

Picking up my cue from Monique, I do the quick recap of my pitch—hitting the keynotes of "Vision" and "Excitement"—that she felt should follow her turn at bat. Not overselling, mind you, but just reiterating a little passion, a little sizzle, now that their calm, rational banker's brains have been sated and they can officially relax. There are far safer ways for them to make money; this will only work if they feel this adds some spark, some excitement to their lives (and portfolios).

I finish—again, leave them wanting more—and there's a moment of stillness in the room. It makes me nervous, but Monique warned me to let this moment happen. Let them fill it with "Yes," or "Not for us" or "We'll have to think about it."

The Boyz look at each other—clearly, like their wives at the Harvard Club, they've done this before—and communicate agreement. "Sure. Sounds good. We're in. Have the papers sent to Dick's office and we can have a check for you midweek."

I'm amazed. Monique beams, and we all do pumped handshakes with hands on the shoulder, like affable ex-presidents greeting each other. I am quite thankful that the next bottle of Cristal is swiftly opened without my having to ask for it. One tasteful glass and then Monique indicates that we really need to be heading back to the city.

There are no protests from the Boyz. If you speak the language—namely, you arrive in the right car with the right date/investment advisor—everything here really does run like clockwork. In fact, in just under two-and-a-half hours, you can walk away $3.8 million richer.

Monique and I drop off the Jag at Andrew's garage. We hail a cab back to my place. We're barely able to keep our clothes on. We have the best sex we've ever had—and that's really saying something. I wonder if it's because there's a greater connection between us (I can almost hear Monique responding, "God Forbid!") or whether it's simply the shared triumph of the day, of a job well done, and a goal achieved. Or, perhaps, it's just that Monique finds my new bank balance—okay, it's not mine, but my project's—more stimulating than anything I can do in the sack.

In any case, whether it's the quality of our time together, or the day's victory, or just increased capital, Monique falls asleep and actually stays at my place until morning.

She's seemingly not embarrassed by this breach of our Fuck Buddy contract, and I certainly wouldn't dream of asking her to leave, but I can't help but wonder if this means we're embarking on a Mom-and-Pop mission together. Am I—or is she making me into—Becker Manqué?

In any case, at 7 a.m., Monique awakens leisurely, smiling at me like the lovely Cheshire cat she is. "Good morning, mogul," she says and kisses me.

"Not yet," I reply.

"Soon," she says. "Soon."

CHILD'S POSE
(BALASANA)

When you can't take it any more in yoga class, rather than getting up and grabbing a cigarette in the lobby, you're supposed to put yourself in Child's Pose.

You kneel, then send your hips back to your heels, letting your head melt towards the floor.

Unless your hips are insanely tight, it actually feels pretty good. Even the most demanding teachers know that they sometimes have to let their students chill, pausing after a series of challenging sequences before beginning another.

As an adult, however, I've found so many more potent ways of checking out.

I sometimes wonder if Shane would have continued with our restaurant even after my betrayal, dutifully holding up her end of the bargain. The investor's withdrawal, however, immediately put a halt to the entire venture.

I still bitterly recall the moment where I gathered up the few things I'd left behind, like my laptop, as the rusty grate came down and the "For Lease" sign went up. I particularly recall the stinging sadness of the landlord, already irritated with my sudden evacuation, slapping Shane's vintage Escoffier back into my hands. The perfect gift has been handed back to me unread, a metaphor in more ways than one.

I left a half-dozen messages that went directly to voicemail, agonizing that I was compounding things by now harassing her in my pathetic quest for forgiveness. We both had keys to each other's places, but I wasn't about to break in, yet I strayed dangerously further into stalker territory by waiting outside her building. Soon, I realized that she wasn't there; she must have returned to her folks in Virginia or decided to stay with a friend. She'd made it clear that she wanted nothing to do with me.

And of course, I couldn't fault her in the least.

I don't want anything to do with me either.

CHAPTER 21

Totally back in character, the next morning Monique prepares to depart almost immediately upon awakening. As she dresses, she casually reveals her Sunday plans, also something she's never done before.

Her day consists of Pilates, lunch with someone named Simone (whom she's never mentioned, as we never talk about the people in our lives), going into the office for a few hours, and packing before she leaves for Becker Business in Rio for two weeks, then London, and then a month in Asia.

Just before leaving, as though it's an afterthought, she gets down to business. "I'll follow up and make sure the first portion of the $3.8 million is in hand by Wednesday. They'll definitely want to structure something in partial payments to make sure it's all going according to plan. That would be standard. Do you have a lawyer you want to draw up the LLC and do the filings so that we can get the bank accounts open?"

Since my lawyer is threatening to sue me for nonpayment post Haven debacle, the answer is a resounding "no."

"We can use my personal attorney then. You'll love her, actually. As ruthless as they come. When we were renegotiating my contract, I swear she's the only person alive who's ever made Becker break a sweat. Oh, and about my deal," she purrs—here it comes, finally—"obviously, I can't really run this for you. I've no time of course, but it does sort of feel like a potential conflict of interest with my day job."

"I get that."

"This really is your baby. I'm happy to advise as needed, of course, but I really think you mostly need me to initially structure things from a financial and legal perspective, and, of course, to handhold your investors until the money's in the bank. Once you launch, with a good accounting and management structure in place, I'm certain you can run the day-to-day operations on your own."

"I agree," I say, wondering when she's going to get to the dollars-and-cents punchline.

"So, think of it as a finder's fee, but I think my receiving a standard ten percent of the initial offering seems reasonable. Don't you agree?"

Even I can do that math. That's $380,000—and, actually, that seems like a helluva lot of money, but who am I to argue? Without Monique's help, I'd still be getting laughed at by glorified bank tellers.

I do have one concern, however. "Isn't that going to topple the budget?" I ask.

"Nah," Monique smiles with breezy confidence as kisses me and heads toward the door, "I built it in."

The next two weeks fly by.

Although Monique's largely in Rio, she keeps totally on top of everything. I find myself needing to log on hourly to check my emails from her. Each one is precise, never straying from her brisk, businesswoman mode. In business or in bed, Monique doesn't like to waste time.

Papers are drawn up remarkably swiftly, papers I do mostly read, but frankly, without a law degree, I'd have to ask so many questions that the legal fees to explain them to me might exceed $3.8 million. Upon signing, the first payment (for one quarter of the offering) plus Monique's ten percent finder's fee, arrives in the new account for the LLC Monique's set up. I can't believe it. Suddenly, I have over one million dollars at my disposal.

Not really, of course. Until we're up and running, Monique has sole authority to dispense the funds. It actually does make sense because not only is she the financial brains behind this, it's also her professional standing, her attorney, and her accountant who make everything happen like magic.

There are a few moments—like with the Boyz—where I almost feel ancillary to my own vision, but then I stop myself. Monique may know how to make the numbers sing on the spreadsheet, but it's my vision—a million tiny choices about obsessive details and broad design and getting in the right crowd—that will make or break this venture.

At midnight, I get a text message from Janek canceling our next lesson. No explanation, just a brief apology. It's unlike him, but I'm not concerned. In fact, I'm grateful for the double benefits of getting to sleep late and being able to charge for the late cancellation.

Andrew and I don't spend that much time talking about progress, but he makes a point to inquire during each and every session, usually picking up exactly where his last query left off. He's genuinely interested, and he is completely focused when we discuss my venture, often offering immensely helpful practical advice. Nonetheless, as soon as possible, he winds back to his primary focus—himself.

Indeed, everything with Andrew has its own established routine. Board meetings, annual reports, and tennis clubs—in short, everything except his secret extracurricular activities— reflects an almost royal predictability. I have somehow become part of that comforting routine. For example, twice a week, I wave at the doormen, and they nod, calling up as a mere formality. Usually, I'm halfway down the hall and walking toward the elevator before Andrew or Danielle answers their phone.

So I'm quite surprised when I show up to teach on Tuesday and the doorman, named "A. Gomez" (Their nametags are, strangely, first initial and last name only, as though more than that would be too familiar and lead to a social revolt.), stops me. "I'm sorry, sir, but Mr. Harding isn't here."

"Really? He didn't call me to cancel. That's unlike him,"

I respond.

I suppose there could have been some business or family emergency, and it is true that every now and then a voicemail does get lost. I leave a message saying I assume there was a miscommunication, and that I'll see him on Thursday.

Two mornings later, when Thursday arrives, I'm even more surprised. Surrounding the exterior of Andrew's building there's a slew of paparazzi milling about. Cameras are poised, and reporters are at the ready.

I have no idea what's going on, so I elbow my way through the throng until A. Gomez catches my eye and lets me pass into the lobby.

"What the hell's going on?" I ask, thinking that this is not the kind of building that would ever sanction any new-moneyed tabloid starlet, no matter how much cash she offered them.

"You don't know?" Gomez asks.

"Know what?" I continue in my clueless way.

A. Gomez seems pained to share with me verbally, gesturing instead to the New York Post headline on his desk. The cover photograph and headline assault me. There's Andrew himself with a bold headline, "Harding Shoots Himself ... Again!" placed over a cupid's arrow and a photograph of what looks like an attractive woman sneaking out of a hotel room. From previous yoga-lesson confessionals, I realize this is the attorney on the Cincinnati merger.

"Jesus," I mutter under my breath. I barely skim the article although its point is overwhelmingly clear. The Über-wolf's been caught in a trap.

Inside the paper, there are photographs of Danielle as the classic "wronged woman," wearing sunglasses, looking down and downtrodden, but nonetheless ravishing. I suppose she is devastated, and the $10 million she'd be entitled to after nine months of marriage is apparently not going to cut it. It seems Danielle wants her tragedy lifted by contesting the prenup and getting a full third of Andrew's assets, which the Post conservatively estimates at $1.4 billion.

"Do you know how to reach him?" I ask. "I just want to

talk to him as a friend. See how he's doing."

With what I read as genuine sympathy, A. Gomez nods. "Sorry, sir. I honestly don't know where he is. Mrs. Harding is upstairs now, but she's told us no visitors are allowed except her mother and her lawyers."

That's fine. I am fond of Danielle, but I have no need to see her now, and I suppose I am officially more on the groom's side here.

I'm not sure what to do. I've only got Andrew's home phone, not his cell. I suppose I could track down his office and call there, but it might be quite a challenge to get through the barrage of reporters who are no doubt pursuing him for the story. I feel that, as his unofficial therapist, it's my responsibility to check in on my patient rather than just allow our counseling sessions to terminate this abruptly. Yet truthfully, unless Andrew contacts me, there's really nothing I can do.

The press takes a few pictures of me almost by default as I exit—clearly, I might be someone connected to something just because I gained entrance to the building—but there's little fuss or calling after me. The press isn't willing to risk following me, someone who's perhaps not even a real player in this drama, when at any moment glamorous victim Danielle or how-the-mighty-have-fallen Andrew himself might appear.

It is, however, an amazingly beautiful May day, and as I walk aimlessly along Park Avenue, despite my concern for Andrew, I'm struck by how gorgeous the manicured perfection is. Quite soon, however, as I'm strolling along, that sense of being stared at begins to build. It's a very funny feeling, and while I'm sure there are a handful of creditors from the last venture and a score of disgruntled chicks who are potentially angry enough to stalk me, I doubt that's the case.

When I turn around, I see a sleek limo moving a little slower than the rest of the traffic. I stop, and the car slows. I turn right, and the gleaming vehicle follows me. This seems like rather cloak-and-dagger stuff, but then my annoyance gets the better of me. It's 10 a.m. and I'm on Park Avenue in broad daylight; I want to know who the hell is tailing me.

I stop, and the limo pulls up alongside me. The tinted black glass window slides down, and there's Andrew. "Hop in," is all he says, and I, of course, comply.

"I'm afraid things are in a bit of a mess," he rather understates as we whirl around the block, going I'm not sure where.

"I'm sorry to hear about all of your troubles," I empathize.

Andrew launches right in to the latest saga, most of which I already know from our previous yoga-as-therapy sessions and from skimming the Post.

What's striking about the conversation is that this is exactly like one of our old yoga sessions, with two differences: 1) we've dispensed with the pretense of any poses, restorative or otherwise, and 2) I'm not getting paid. Or at least, I don't think I am. Andrew, however, makes that point clear as he dives into the next chapter of his travails.

"And most unfortunately, I'm quite frankly rather broke," Andrew confesses.

"Really?" I don't disguise the surprise in my voice. After all, this is coming from someone cruising around aimlessly in his chauffeur-driven Bentley.

"Danielle's hired Vanessa Miller, who's perhaps the most aggressive and ruthless divorce attorney I've ever met. How I wish she were representing me. As it is, all my assets—every credit card, every bank account—have been completely frozen. Of course, I still have a few friends and connections. I've got a suite at the King James since Clifton there is a dear old friend, and he knows I'll settle up the second this is over."

"And you've got wheels." I still find it hard to believe that Andrew is broke. The two concepts "Andrew" and "broke" seem entirely alien to each other.

"Well, for the moment, I may be in possession of a Bentley, but I've barely enough cash to fill the tank."

I'm sure Andrew is being relatively truthful regarding the overall situation, but still I find it hard to believe that he's anywhere near panhandling on the subway. I can just hear his pitch: "Brother, can you spare ... well, $25 for a martini at the Four Seasons?"

And yet, when he looks at me with those hangdog eyes, I see that he really is in pain. But damn it—worst-case scenario, Danielle gets half of everything, leaving him with what ... seven hundred million dollars? Being a little less than a billionaire myself, I feel that that's the kind of suffering anyone should be able to bear.

For the first time, I'm feeling annoyed with Andrew, perhaps—curiously enough—because I'm no longer pretending to teach him yoga. Although I am no one to give anyone advice or lecture to anyone, particularly on the ethics of sexual indiscretions, I find myself ready to launch into a "Snap Out of It" moment. Seeing him screw up his perfectly awesome life— zillions of dollars, vast respect, gorgeous young wife, acres of sowed wild oats—actually pisses me off. Although I have zero credibility in this regard, I want to give him a tough-love speech about not trashing his life with endless mindless indiscretions.

Maybe that's the problem, I think. Maybe no one has had the guts or the opportunity or the inclination to tell Andrew the truth: that these problems are entirely of his own making, and that it's high time he stopped indulging in such chaos.

Just as I'm about to attempt my first ever "it's time you grew up" speech, I'm utterly thrown when Andrew—my Role Model—his baronial composure lost, actually chokes up. Seemingly on the verge of sobbing, he holds himself back but reaches for the perfectly triangulated pocket square in his suit pocket and unfolds it. He wipes his face, obscuring the question of whether or not any tears fell, although it seems like perhaps a few were shed.

I'm silenced. The dude's in pain. His suffering is real. He doesn't need a lecture from me. This whole incident would obviously be enough of a wake-up call for anyone. What he needs now is just support. I throw a filial arm around his shoulders. It feels both a little awkward and yet totally right.

A moment later, when Andrew's fully composed, I remove my arm with a double tap, an oddly comforting gesture as though I'm burping a baby.

We drive ten or twenty blocks through Park Avenue green

lights, circling pointlessly around our country's highest per-capita-income zip code. Andrew looks away, trying to stabilize the waves of emotion coursing through his stately frame.

"Thank you," is all he says.

I nod, trying to convey that I'm there for him. "This must be very difficult," I say to him.

"Yes. It certainly is." There's a weighty silence. Andrew fills it. "But there is one thing I've learned."

I wait, extremely glad that my speech was unnecessary and eager as always for Andrew's wisdom. He turns to me, that intensely vulnerable look still in his eyes.

"I never should have sent the Cincinnati lawyer flowers. It always stands out on a credit card statement."

I have no response. That's the lesson? That's all he's learned from his downfall. Andrew continues, unaware of my reaction.

"Other things—jewelry, for example—you have to pick out in person and can just pay for in cash," he continues. "You'd be surprised how many reputable jewelers will even give you a significant discount when you do. And obviously, any trip or dinner or hotel room just seems like a normal business expense. But flowers on your AmEx statement: that starts ringing bells. Any wife is bound to eventually to put two and two together."

I take this in. He's not capable of learning to avoid the folly of his ways. As always, he's only interested in one thing—not getting caught.

The chauffeur rolls down the glass partition that separates us. "Where to, Mr. Harding?"

Andrew looks at me. I don't have any answers for him. I have no idea where to go. Andrew makes his own decision. "Back to the King James then, Fenton. That is," he turns to me, "unless we can drop you anywhere?"

"That's okay. Wherever you can pull over is fine."

"Are you sure? Really, it's no trouble."

"No, it's a beautiful day; I'll just walk."

I can't explain it, but I've got to get out of the Bentley as soon as possible. Suddenly, its luxurious interior feels like an inescapable, mobile prison cell. The chauffeur obliges, slowing to a halt on a spectacular corner of prime Park Avenue real estate.

I'm not sure what I can say to Andrew in parting. Of course, I'd never turn my back on a friend—and despite it all, I really do consider Andrew a friend—but at the same time, I'm not sure what I can really do for him, what anyone can do for him. I realize then and there, perhaps more than anyone I know, he is what he is. And nothing is going to change that.

Impulsively, I give him a bear hug before departing, which he accepts and returns. Again, I don't know why, except perhaps that part of me realizes that this might very much be our good-bye moment.

I know that Andrew will weather this storm. If necessary, he will manage to scrape by with a mere seven hundred million dollars. He'll make the money back. He'll marry again, no doubt to a woman just as beautiful as his current/soon-to-be ex wife and even younger and increasingly disproportionate to his own age.

I just somehow think that yoga won't interest him any longer. And I'm not sure if or when he's ready to resume lessons again, I'll be available, either because of my own impending moguldom or because I just can't listen to his bullshit any longer.

CHAPTER 22

It might just be that with Andrew gone, I need to fill his voided role of client/confidante. No, it's not really that. It's true that with Andrew, it was 95 percent about Andrew—although I must admit that, in those fleeting moments when he did briefly turn away from his own escapades and laments to offer me advice, Andrew's contributions were brilliant and invaluable.

When Linney asks some simple, typically flirty general inquiry about my life, I'm surprised to find myself volunteering all about Diwali. With his limitless witty repartee, Linney's always a blast to talk to, but I realize soon that he's actually truly interested in this topic. He's asking questions about details, and although he's not a restaurateur, there are overlapping areas of knowledge.

"You know, Blue Eyes, please do think of this as a come on, but this is definitely the kind of project I could sink my teeth into," Linney says. And of course he winks broadly.

"Really?"

"Well, one can only create so many 'I'm ludicrously rich and want you to know it' Park Avenue sitting rooms without going mad. Besides, no one ever asks me to the downtown parties anymore. And to think of all those West Village Walks of Shame I remember so fondly—well, this might be my way back in."

I laugh, but I also realize he's serious. "Listen, I don't know if we can afford your Park Avenue prices just yet. I'm making most of the creative decisions—"

"As well you should," he interjects. "I think your vision is both cutting-edge and also somehow comfortable. It's all Very Global. Very Now. Très Chic."

"Thanks."

"I just think I can lend a hand, here and there. I know tons of suppliers and vendors. The salary is incidental; maybe give me a few profit points or whatever those things are called."

Like finding a wallet you're not sure what to do with, this is an unexpected but not entirely unpleasant turn of events. Still …

"You really want to head below 59th Street and roll up your sleeves on the Lower East Side?" I ask Linney.

"God, yes. I'm craving an adventure, one with a little more creative edge to it than matching swatches of fabric to Grandma's needlepointed throw pillows. You would not believe the ghastly horrors I have to contend with on a daily basis. Maybe you'd let me try my hand at the VIP back room."

I glance up at the extraordinary display of serious art, kitschy paraphernalia, and outright pornography on the shelves directly in front of me. "I can only imagine what you do if I let you have a free hand in the back room."

"Hah! Feel free to slap my wrists whenever you need to. Actually, Blue Eyes, I think I'd kind of like that."

Linney proves to be a dynamo of creative energy. His wealth of experience with all aspects of interior design and décor proves invaluable. Whether it's the right lighting or the wall coverings, I know exactly what I want, but Linney knows exactly how and where to get it cheaply. "No, throw that catalogue away," he'll say. "Those vendors NEVER deliver anything as promised or on time. We'll get it far cheaper from the Farconi Brothers warehouse. Come on … Road trip to Jersey!"

And he's invariably right. I realize just how much fun I'm having one night when I look up from our half-emptied bottle of bourbon, amidst piles of hardware catalogues, to realize that Linney and I have spent almost four hours discussing possibilities for the large front window we're unboarding next week.

Monique's MBA solidified the funding, and now Linney's décor experience is bringing it all to fruition with dazzling style and efficiency—my own Nightlife Dream Team.

MONKEY GOD POSE
(HANUMANASANA)

A Full Split is definitely the worst pose ever invented.

Totally unnecessary—unless, that is, you're contemplating a career as a cheerleader, which I decidedly am not—and totally torturous.

Hanuman is this semi-divine chief of an army of monkey warriors in Hinduism. He rescued Sita, consort of the major god Rama, from an evil demon king. The pose dramatizes Hanuman's famous leap from the southern tip of India to the island of Sri Lanka. In other words, the dude certainly knew how to stretch his hamstrings.

Nothing gives the hamstrings a wake-up call like a full Hanuman. The first thousand times I forced myself to move towards it in class were torture. It's never gotten any better.

As you begin to slide out the front leg, you can use blocks or other props under your hands to give you some height so that you don't feel like you're going to collapse and tear anything in your nether regions.

Gigi always says that the poses we'd give anything to avoid are the ones we most need to practice. We need to hang out and explore where there's resistance and tightness if we're ever going to move through it. But even though this sounds all well and good, I'd rather go through life without feeling like I was being torn and split in two, about to be ripped open at my groin. Really, wouldn't you?

CHAPTER 23

I have no plans for this Saturday night—Hutch and I trade messages, and he's unspecifically "totally booked"—and since none of my invitations sound spectacular, and I know I have a model's digits in escrow, I opt instead to order in Chinese, stream some mindless films on Netflix, and have a totally satisfactory night in.

It's a surprisingly warm mid-May Sunday morning, so when I get up, sans alarm clock, after breakfast at the Knife & Fork, I decide that a long walk to the West Village and reading the paper in some mini-park is in order. As I'm prowling around, enjoying the feelings of a crisp, clean Sunday, I walk past Pastis.

Of course, it's totally crowded with yuppies and poseurs and all sorts of avid brunchers, and since I'm not at all in the mood for such a scene experience, I'm planning just to stroll by. However, dining at a corner table, I spy Hutch, who smiles (a little sheepishly) and waves. Across from him is Etta. Hutch waves me in, although I'm not sure if I should intrude. But having a mouthed conversation through the glass is corny, so I enter.

The place is buzzing. Hutch and I do our usual brotherly hug. I give Etta a simple kiss on the cheek and tell her she looks and smells great, which is absolutely true. To demonstrate to Hutch that I've absorbed the four letters of her name, I make sure I greet her as "Etta." I can tell this pleases him.

Interestingly, they don't invite me to join them. Yes, the restaurant is packed with hungry folks milling about trying to bribe the maitre d', and they are sitting at a café table for two. But more the point, I am not the wingman here; my buddy is flying solo. I spare them the awkwardness of my hanging around and volunteer that I'm off to take Gigi's noon class, something that, until this moment, I'd completely forgotten about over the last few weeks.

"It's already 12:45," Etta points out.

"I'm meeting the teacher afterward for chai," I counter, suddenly remembering my already-broken promise to Gigi. I bid Hutch and Etta good-bye, yet deep inside I know that I'm not going to show up. I realize I'm going to blow Gigi off.

I mean, it's not like I'm leaving Gigi waiting on a street corner in a blizzard. Her class will be packed and she'll either hang out with someone else or probably just go home to Calypso … but still. During the worst of my unemployment, my nonexistent calendar only had her classes on it. And the phenomenal gift of yoga school has utterly transformed my life. Now, when Gigi's actually reserved some of her valuable time to give me the benefit of her counsel, I'm blowing it off.

As if I'd made an appointment with the dentist when a tooth throbbed but found when I'd arrived that it no longer did, I'm going to cancel without ceremony. Of course, the decay hasn't miraculously eradicated itself, but for the moment, the pain isn't piercing enough to make me seek the cure. When I get home, I'll send her an email, apologizing and yet again asking to reschedule. I know this is lame, even for me.

I flash on Linney and his bum hip. He will postpone the surgery, it seems, until he can no longer walk at all. Experience shows that, like Linney, I'm the type who needs the root canal as a wake-up call. Only when the nerve's removed will the pain really be gone.

Monique returns from Rio and goes directly from the airport to my place. We have a torrid reunion and then immediately head to Diwali to check out the progress there. Even though Monique's been traveling among Becker properties in South America, Europe, Australia, and Thailand, I definitely get the strong sense that the NYC construction crew is a little frightened of her.

Monique is pleased, however, with pretty much everything at the venue, including almost all of my decisions and Linney's executions. She has a few quibbles (the font on the menu is a point size too small; there are obvious omissions on my VIP wish list for the opening), but nonetheless, she seems quite satisfied with our progress over her six-week absence.

Mind you, the place is far from being ready and thus, the club looks a bit like a war zone. Nonetheless, under Monique's stewardship, we are totally on track for a soft opening that coincides with this year's Diwali festival. More and more, like a statue emerging from Michelangelo's hunk of raw marble to reveal its perfect form, Diwali is becoming real before my eyes.

This time, the dream will become a reality. I can feel it.

Monique has other, unspecified plans, so I grab one drink at a local dive in order to unwind after a day of decisions. As I exit, it's raining torrentially, but I'm lucky enough to snag an available cab for the ten-minute journey back to my pad.

The cab pulls up to my building and I get out, ready to make an impossible ten-foot mad dash to the door without getting drenched. And then I see Janek, of all people, standing there, suit collar turned up against the rain, which does nothing to help. He's completely soaked.

"Janek? Dude, what the hell are you doing here?" I exclaim.

He doesn't really reply and it doesn't matter, as I'm scrambling to open the door and let us into my building. My building has no lobby, mind you, much less a doorman. You walk in, get your mail immediately to your left, and then if you still want to, after viewing the height of it all, you can climb the five flights straight up to my apartment. Many ladies wince at the thought of making it up all those stairs—and, mind you, most of them spend countless hours on their StairMasters. It may be that, as with many things in life, seeing the steps laid out directly before you makes them somehow more intimidating then if you are merely marching blindly ahead, circling mindlessly.

"I ... can I talk to you?" Janek mutters.

"Sure." Away from the battering of the rain and under the fluorescent lights, I'm surprised at how sadly disheveled Janek looks, especially for a guy who's practically the hottest stylemaker in New York.

"Man, you look like shit. You must be glad your publicist can't see you now."

Granted, it's not the most sensitive thing to say, but I'm not used to being sensitive, period, especially not around Janek. He's like Hutch. Unlike with almost everybody else in my yoga world (and even in my forays with investors), I don't have to censor myself. I can pretty much just say whatever's on my mind.

"I, er ..." Janek hesitates. It's more than just his being soaked. It's more than the cold and the rain. He really is a mess. And he's miserable. It even looks like he's been crying. Whatever's going on with him, whatever's caused him to miss our last two sessions—I'd almost forgotten that he texted me again yesterday to cancel without explanation—must really be eating away at him. The dude is really hurting. He needs to talk in a big way.

"Are you okay?" I ask him.

"Yes ... no ... I—just thought." He stops himself. "Forget it. This was a stupid idea. I should get outta here. It's late, and—"

He turns to exit and head out into the rain, so I grab his arm to stop him. "Whoa. Slow down, bro." Janek looks more and more like a drowned rat and less like someone who allegedly turned down a modeling career. "I don't know what the fuck is wrong with you," I tell him, "but let's get the hell out of the rain."

I realize this is the first time Janek's been to my apartment. Frankly, besides yoga, it's the first time we've done anything alone together.

We're about the same size, so first things first. The dude's got to get out of the wet clothes. I trade his drenched Prada suit for my cleanest set of sweats.

"You want to take a hot shower? I think I have a decent towel somewhere," I ask.

"No, that's okay. I'm okay," Janek shakes his head.

"Can I get you anything?"

"No, I'm fine. Well, actually, do you have any tea?"

I so wish I were the kind of person who offered people tea in a crisis. Sadly, I'm the kind of person who offers people vodka.

Rummaging through my nearly empty shelves, the cupboards are indeed quite bare, so I offer Janek a shot of Grey Goose, my one luxury.

He thinks for a second, then says, "What the hell—sure, why not?"

We each toss back a shot. I refill our glasses as we plunk down in my living room, a dismal affair if ever there was one.

"So, dude … what the hell is up with you tonight?" I query.

Janek looks miserable and uncomfortable.

"What is it? Symphony?" I press.

He doesn't even bother to correct my mispronunciation. "Sort of. No, not really."

"Okay." I pause, unsure not only of Janek's undefined problem but even of the most basic things, like what is my role here? I mean, I really love teaching Janek—my purest, truest student of the poses—and more and more, I think he's a great guy. I enjoy hanging out with him socially. But as of today, quite frankly, I'm surprised that I even made the short list of friends to call in a crisis. (My own list only has one name on it—Hutch.)

Although I've been resolute in never using yoga clichés with Janek, I'm tempted to spout my usual bullshit: "Do what you can. Don't push it. Focus on the breath." Even if it's all bullshit, at least it might be moderately helpful.

"But she's okay, right?" I manage.

"I don't know. She didn't take it that well."

"Take what?"

"When I told her our engagement was off," Janek reveals.

"Oh. I'm sorry, I guess." That seems like the right thing to say—or is a better response more of a backslap, a "plenty of fish in the sea" remark?

"Thanks. It wasn't easy." It's hard for anyone to dump a supermodel, I suppose. Janek stares into the depths of his empty glass, and I refill it. At least I am a good host when it comes to beverages. I refill mine, and we click classes.

"Na zdravie" he offers. "To your health, indeed."

Then Janek just stares into infinity. I try to wait patiently for few moments but—

Okay. I've had it. "Look, Dude, I'm up for sitting here all night, not saying a word and getting shit-faced drunk if you want. But fuck it, Janek, if you've got something on your mind, and you think I can help you in any way, you gotta start talking."

He refills his own glass (generously) and tosses it down.

"Oh fuck it—the truth is ... I'm gay."

There's a long beat of respectful silence after he says it. Both of us instinctively feel the moment deserves a little something.

He waits for some kind of reaction from me. I'm not sure what he's expecting or hoping for. I've never been in this situation exactly, but I'm trusting raw instinct to see me through.

I refill both our glasses. "Dude, that's totally cool. Be whoever the fuck you are."

It's as you'd suspect: the weight of the world's off his shoulders. Suddenly, Janek looks, well, like Janek. Or at least more like the Janek featured in every style magazine known to man and not the flailing, waterlogged creature I dragged in off the street tonight.

Our glasses refilled, we toast again. I'm not sure what I'm supposed to do next. No one's ever come out to me before. In a way, I feel totally honored. And also a little perplexed. I mean, do I seem like the kind of sensitive guy you'd run to in order to reveal your secret inner demons? Bolstered by the vodka, Janek expands on his confession.

"I broke things off with Synove yesterday," he says. "I had to. I couldn't go through with the engagement any more. It was killing me. And besides, there's someone else. Someone I have feelings for."

There's a heavy pause, and I wait. It goes on a beat too

long until … suddenly I begin to wonder, is Janek talking about me? While I've been dancing my little tango of feelings for Phoebe and all my other comely students, have I totally missed that someone else has had the same yearnings for me, cultivated and expanded during our times together, through all the tactile contact—Oh, Jesus. This is something I totally hadn't factored into the mix.

Janek takes another hit of vodka, screwing up his courage, no doubt, to confess the depths of his feelings for me. "Anyway," he begins, "I was wondering—"

I cut him off. "Look, dude, I'm totally flattered. Really, I am. But I just don't swing that way. But you know if I did, I can totally, totally see it."

He looks wounded for a second, then bursts out laughing. "You think … Oh no … I can see why, but no. No, I'm not into you."

"Really?" I'm a little taken aback.

"Don't look so hurt."

"I'm not. I just. Oh, forget it. Who the hell is it?"

"Hutch," he confesses.

"What?"

"You heard me."

"Hutch?"

"Yup."

"Why the fuck Hutch and not me?" I blurt out, my insane Alpha-male competitiveness clearly on autopilot. I'm competing with my wingman for a liaison that's not even in our playing field. Janek laughs heartily, and after two seconds, I join him.

"Okay. Okay. I couldn't resist. I'm sorry, but neither of you two bad boys is the object of my affection," Janek smirks.

"Well, that makes it simpler. But there is someone, though, right? Someone gay, I hope."

"Yeah. His name is Jeffrey Alston. The lighting designer. I think you met him at my party and that art opening. He redid our showroom, and he was brilliant. And cute. And sweet. And … Oh I don't know what the hell I'm saying …"

"But you know he's definitely gay, right?"

"Totally out."

"So, what's the problem?"

"It's funny," Janek continues, "I've pursued all these women, dated all these models, had all these beautiful girlfriends. But when it comes to this guy, it feels like I'm a train wreck."

"Don't be, man. Unless this Jeffrey dude is totally deaf, dumb, and blind, he's totally gonna want to hook up with you. Gay or straight, you're totally Alpha, man. And that's something I'll drink to."

I top off our glasses one more time. I'm going to feel like shit when I have to teach in the morning, but what the hell? How often do I get to be gay godfather?

"Man, it's totally cool you're here. But I still have to ask you, though. Why me? Why did you pick me to come out to?"

"... Honestly?"

"Of course."

"Well, when I hauled myself out into the rain tonight, down through the squalor of Chinatown, I was sort of wondering that myself."

"And ..."

"It wasn't anything you said, so much. Not that you ever go overboard with all the spiritual stuff when we work together. That's part of what I like about it, actually. I mean, I love the poses, and the breathing, and the challenge, and how open you feel afterward. So, that was part of it. That openness. That freedom. The release of tension in the body. I associate all that with you. And I suppose I just wanted to do that to my mind."

"That's cool," I reply.

"But it wasn't just that," he continues. "It was that, well, you're not faking anything. You're ... sincere."

I try to take this in, but "sincere" ... Me?

"Are you shitting me? I don't know anyone who'd say that sincerity is my strong suit," I counter.

"Well, sincerity, maybe that's the wrong word. 'Authentic,' I guess," Janek goes on. "I always felt that when you were with me you were just yourself. You weren't trying to be some fake spiritual guy. You kept it totally real with me ... and still, it was spiritual without even trying. It's just that—no offense, but you're pretty much the least likely guy in the world I would ever think would be teaching anyone anything even remotely spiritual. I mean, you're out all the time, constantly hitting on a million different women."

"I hear you."

"And all the drinking and carousing. Totally superficial. Shallow. All the posing and posturing. Just interested in screwing around and a quick good time, without any emotional connections or—"

"Trust me, Janek. You've made your point."

He smiles, silenced. "And yet, the yoga was totally real for you. The poses. The breathing. Even the stillness. All of it. You just made it work for you. You didn't try to make yourself seem like what everyone must think a yoga teacher should be like." Janek downs his shot. "And, I guess, when you talked about stopping struggling with a shape and you said that maybe things that seemed impossible could become possible ... well, saying that—and you just being your very, very flawed self—made me feel that maybe I could, too. That I could start trying to be who I really was, instead of forcing myself to be someone that I'm not."

I'm entirely drawn into his explanation and, more interestingly, shocked that it actually makes sense that somehow my behavior, what I said—things that came from me, a dude totally obsessed with his own immediate gratification—could actually be a positive inspiration for someone else's growth. That somehow my litany of selfish vices has served as a springboard toward a good end—even possibly being the turning point for Janek's life—is, well, rather mind-blowing. My student with whom I was most honestly myself—and what a highly flawed, not necessarily spiritual, self that is—focusing almost entirely on the joys of the physical practice, has mysteriously become the student I have affected most deeply and genuinely. Bizarre, right?

"So, what you're saying is, if an asshole like me can somehow get away with calling himself a yoga teacher, what's the big deal about being gay?"

"More or less," he laughs.

"Thanks … I think." But I'm smiling, and I know he means all this as a compliment. Otherwise, he wouldn't be here. This teaching business is a funny thing, indeed.

Janek and I more or less talk the night away. Post-confessional chilling with Janek is just as easy and effortless as our physical practice has been, maybe even more so since I'm no longer on the clock and concentrating on teaching him. We're just hanging out. Somewhere around 4 a.m., we doze off, until my alarm wakes us both. In my first week of teaching, I went out and bought the loudest alarm clock I could find, one that I religiously remember to set each night before going out so that—no matter what disorienting adventures I find myself on—I'm brutally awake and on time in the morning. And this morning, I've got to get to Brooke's to teach.

In a way, having Janek crash here feels oddly natural, even though he has, amazingly, now topped even Andrew in terms of impassioned, shared confidences. Now I feel even closer to him, like Hutch, or another brother.

Wearing my old, grubby sweats, he gathers up his still-soaking Prada suit and I put it in a Duane Reade plastic bag.

"We're on for Monday's lesson, right?" he asks.

"Totally."

"Okay, then."

"So, see you."

Impulsively, at the doorway, Janek grabs me and hugs me, deeply and without reservation. It's miles away from the usual male backslap moments. I can completely feel his gratitude and relief. The emotion in him wells up as I hug him back. I let him decide when it's time to pull away. After a few solid moments, he seems complete and draws back from me. He initiates our usual basketball court, secret-handshake gesture, not bothering to disguise his moist eyes. He starts out the door and then turns back.

Janek—whose soul I've touched, whose life I have forever altered by virtue of my example; Janek, to whom I am actually a legitimate guru—before heading off into the dawn, has these parting words: "You know, your apartment really sucks."

He says it smiling, bounding down the five flights of concrete steps, down to the street.

"Fuck you, pretty boy!" I call after him.

He doesn't turn around but continues springing down the steps, waving one hand up to say good-bye. It's cool. I don't need to look at his face to know he's smiling.

I return from teaching Brooke—another session of abdominal overdrive which, thankfully, I can do on autopilot—and decide that forty winks are in order. I'm happy to have helped Janek, but that vodka heart-to-heart really broke my curfew, and I figure I can get an hour or two of sleep before heading to Diwali to make up for it. Thirty minutes into my nap, however, there's a frantic buzzing of my doorbell.

I ignore it, knowing I have no deliveries scheduled or friends who'd be dropping by now. All the scenarios I can think of in which someone might want to reach me are one-night-stands-turned-stalkers and creditors disgruntled with the court system, and there's no need to welcome those possibilities back into my life at 11:30 in the morning.

The stalker keeps buzzing, so knowing my nap is going to be trashed completely unless I deal with whoever it is, I march to the intercom, totally pissed off.

"What!" I bark.

"Delivery," the disembodied voice answers.

"I fuckin' haven't ordered anything!"

"Slip says it's paid for. Maybe it's a gift."

"What is?"

"Look, we're double-parked and we ain't gettin' any younger out here. Ya gotta just buzz us in."

I comply. Whatever this is, there's a note of authenticity in the pissed-off quality in the delivery guy's voice. I slip on sweats and open the door to my apartment, expecting … I don't know what. A tasteful fruit basket—maybe stuffed with a rattlesnake? Instead, three burly movers heave a huge blob of something wrapped in brown paper up the stairs, straight to my door. The delivery dudes are unfriendly, thug-like, and straight to the point. "Where do you want it?"

"What the hell is it?" I demand.

"A loveseat."

"What?"

And then I see the logo on the packing slip: Zilinikov. This is from Janek.

"Over there, I guess."

Another three guys make their way up the stairs with a smaller item as the crew in my apartment unwraps a gorgeous chocolate brown leather loveseat. These guys are thugs, but they know how to move furniture like nobody's business. Before I know it, a matching leather chair is being unveiled before me.

"How many are there?" I ask.

"We have eighteen pieces. Two armchairs, a coffee table, two floor lamps, two bookcases, two area rugs—you want I should keep reading?" the guy holding a clipboard answers.

I'm speechless.

"Oh, and the packing slip says we should take away the old stuff at the same time," the delivery guy adds.

"Sure, I guess." "Never Look Back" has always been my philosophy, especially regarding my casual flings, and now towards beat-up, secondhand furniture. This shit has got to go.

I scramble for my cell to get Janek on the phone. His secretary puts me directly through.

"How do you like the chocolate brown? I thought better than your basic black," Janek launches in with what I know must be a smirk.

"Dude, what the fuck are you doing?"

"Classing up your joint, player. How you ever managed to get laid with a pad like that is beyond me."

"You're out of the closet for ten hours and you're already Queer-Eyeing me?"

Janek laughs.

"Seriously, I appreciate the thought, Janek, but this is way, way, way too much."

"I owe you, man."

"No, you don't. I didn't do anything."

"I'll be the judge of that."

"Still, this is way too generous in the extreme."

"Nah. We've got warehouses of this shit. Besides, this stuff is just a combo of floor samples and discontinued series, anyway. You got lucky because this week we're changing the floor displays. Anyway, I put everything together this morning from cast-off stuff. There are a few scratches and scuff marks—nothing too trashed, though, but not merchandise I can sell at full price. It would just have gone to waste."

I don't know if I fully believe him or not, but as my ratty old furniture gets cleared, and Janek's absolutely excellent pieces (floor samples or not) replace them, I don't care. I feel as grateful as a game show winner—although I'm trying not to act as giddy.

Interestingly, even though the movers seem like total thugs, the foreman is a genius, intuitive decorator. The crew doesn't just dump stuff and run. The foreman directs them where to place everything, and it works perfectly. I've misjudged these guys by their burliness and outer-borough accents. Rugs are unfurled, sofas and armchairs perfectly angled with artistic precision. Somehow, even during his confessional breakdown, Janek managed to calculate and envision the perfect scale and style for redecorating my apartment. Well, at least this cliché of gayness works for me.

"I'm glad you like it. Listen, I gotta hop. I'm late for a meeting with In Style," Janek explains.

"Go for it."

"See you Monday morning, right?"

"Definitely."

And, more or less, we're back to normal. Nothing has changed. Except, of course, that thanks to Janek, my apartment, instead of looking like shit, actually looks like a million Zilinikov bucks.

Oh, yeah, and one other little thing—for the first time in his life, Janek can really be himself.

CHAPTER 24

It's Monique's last night back in town before Round Two of her Asia Brand Expansion Tour, so she and I have dinner at Platinum, another Becker joint. Not only is it totally excellent, Monique also manages to expense the entire feast. Afterward, we walk a bit together.

"Listen ..." Monique begins as we stroll.

Already, I can tell something is different. This is a tone I've never heard her take before. There's an element of—could it be?—seriousness in her voice. Damn it! We're going to have the relationship talk, the one she's promised we'd never have.

"It's not like we didn't know this day would come," she continues.

Monique is an incredibly attractive woman. Plus, she's amazing in bed. And I doubt that there is another woman of her level of hotness who would offer the purely physical exchange we have going. All this, coupled with her instrumental spearheading of my career, makes her an unbelievable find. With her, I have hit the emotionless fuck-buddy jackpot—and now she wants to talk relationship.

"Maybe it's that we've been working together—and extraordinarily well, I might add—but ..." She takes a deep breath. "But honestly, I'm ready to move on."

"Excuse me?" This is a major conversational U-turn.

"Well, of course, under any other circumstances, I wouldn't bother with this conversation. If there's one thing I hate, it's those moments with a man where one has to 'define' things. So endlessly tedious."

"You mean you're officially breaking up our non-relationship?"

"I guess you might put it that way," Monique smiles. "We're so close to completion, and of course I will be 110 percent on top of all those details."

"Okay, but I'm confused. Why exactly?"

She pauses, then her face becomes a blank canvas as she says simply, "It's not you, it's me." A moment of silence.

Then suddenly, she cackles wickedly. "God, how I've always wanted to say that." Recovering, she continues, "Our situation's a little tricky in that I can't do what I usually do—stop returning calls and emails, I'm sure you know all those moves—until they take the not-too- subtle hint that it's Capital O Over. But with our little business venture going along swimmingly, I need to keep things clear on all fronts. I just feel that the shelf life on our hooking up has pretty much expired."

"You're bored? Is that it?"

"Awww, don't look so wounded, Sport. It doesn't suit you," she continues, purring. "I have my own set of rules about these things—and no, I'm not going to share them—but I've already frolicked with you far longer than I ever thought I would."

"I see. Okay, I guess." And the funny thing is, the reverse is also true—this has lasted far longer and gone infinitely further than I thought a New Year's Eve one-night stand ever would. Nonetheless, I guess my face reveals my perplexed state.

"Wow, you really aren't used to being on the other side of this," Monique smirks with perhaps just a hint of compassion. She even tries for a joke: "Anyway, it's sort of like that Kenny Rogers song. You know ... 'you've got to know when to hold 'em, know when to fold 'em, know when to walk away, and know when to run.'"

She kisses me thoroughly, and since this is presumably for the last time, I feel an odd sense of finality.

"Suddenly you're quoting country music?"

She shrugs. "Seems a fitting exit line for a sweet girl from Georgia."

"I didn't know you were from the South."

Monique hails a cab.

"Sweetheart, we were fuck buddies," she says. "You barely

know the tip of the iceberg."

And with that, she gets into her taxi, starts furiously text-messaging on her Blackberry, and without once looking back, departs.

CHAPTER 25

Monday morning, bright and early, Janek and I are back on schedule.

Janek answers the door, all smiles. Moments later, Jeffrey emerges from the bedroom, his hair wet from a shower, as he tucks himself into his crisp white shirt and jet-black suit. Polite "hellos" exchanged by all.

I ask to use the bathroom in order to give them as much privacy as you can have when a third party has suddenly entered your morning-after-sex space.

Jeffrey's halfway out the door as I return. He waves me good-bye and departs with a kiss for Janek.

"So …" I start, figuring that even though I don't really want to intrude, I am sort of the Cupid figure here. I deserve a little update.

Janek smiles. "Well, what can I say?"

"I guess the feeling was mutual."

"Definitely seems like it is."

"Cool."

Not much more needs to be said. With this short exchange of just a few phrases, we're already back in the groove. Unlike with Andrew, I am never going to be Janek's full-time therapist.

We have one of our best, sweatiest lessons ever. When the lesson's over, we part with the same friendly, guy on b-ball-court style, and then I'm off. It's amazing. Even though he's gone gay, Janek is still my most straightforward client.

If anything, in absentia Monique plunges herself even more deeply into her remaining duties as General Manager of the Limited Liability Corporation (I did actually read through some of the contracts), determined to get everything done perfectly on schedule.

Still not sharing anything of my plans and schemes with Brooke or Phoebe or Janek—or even Hutch—I swing by the site every day, arriving midmorning after my teaching is complete. The only void in my schedule is Andrew's empty slot. I'm sure that, if I asked Brooke, she'd find a new super-rich client for me in a second, but I don't ask. I'm not sure if it's because with my new venture moving so rapidly, I shouldn't be taking on new clients, or whether I want to "retire the jersey" of Andrew's timeslot. In either case, I keep his Tuesday/Thursday slot free and arrive at Diwali-in-the-making a little earlier on those days than others.

Over the next four weeks, nearly every morning when I arrive to teach Janek, Jeffrey is on his way out. It all feels totally natural, as though it's always been this way. It's a surprisingly effortless adjustment, but then again I never really knew "Symphony." At least I can remember and know how to pronounce Jeffrey's name.

In fact, given the clutter-free loft, the only things that are visibly different in the apartment itself are the missing photographs of Symphony's magazine covers. And, maybe it's just the light today, but now that I have a second look at those S&M photos, it's not the masked Symphony who stands out, but the nebulous male bodies that were always lurking in the background.

The next few weeks—an intense blend of juggling my yoga teaching with the demands of setting up the club—fly right by. It's a good state of being too busy. Like being in one of Gigi's classes—which I realize I haven't been to in two months now—my life suddenly demands complete awareness and commitment. I'm still high on the juice of entrepreneurial creativity, and before I know it, May's almost over.

After Janek and I finish our lesson, he tells me that he and Jeffrey are going on their first trip together.

"That's cool. Where?" I ask.

"Fiji. We're going for two weeks. We're leaving next Monday after our lesson," Janek reveals.

"Wow. I was expecting maybe a cozy inn in Vermont or something."

"Nah. When I do something, I tend to do it all the way."

"I get that," I reply, sincerely smiling at the miracle of gay fast-track romance. I wonder if, perhaps, it's a big step for me to root for the "happy ending" here. I certainly do not want to see Janek dumped in any of the ways that yours truly (or Monique, for that matter) has perfected.

Later that afternoon, Hutch rings me up. "Dude, think you can handle life without me for two weeks?"

"What's up?" I query.

"Etta and I are heading out to Fiji."

"That's a weird coincidence—so's Janek."

"I know. We're going together."

"What? Are you kidding me? When did you guys start double-dating?"

Hutch laughs. "Fifteen minutes ago, actually. Janek told me about this awesome villa situation. It's just the edge of the peak season, but still pretty gorgeous. Anyway, I checked out the flights online and well, it makes sense."

"Well, have fun, I guess. Be careful scuba diving; I think there's a law that pasty preppies like yourself are only allowed to sail."

Hutch chuckles, but there's the slightest hesitation in his response. I can tell that he's got something else on his mind.

"Is there something else?" I decide to ask.

"Well, yeah, there is. And I wanted you to be the first to know."

Since "first to know" always makes me think someone is pregnant or dying, I am curious about what Hutch has to share.

"I was calling Janek in the first place to see if I could scam a discount on some new furniture. Time to class the place up. You see ... Etta's going to be moving in."

Now, this I hadn't foreseen. This is still, after all, Hutch we're talking about. Having a Sunday brunch with a chick is one thing, but asking her to live with you is another. It's still one giant step away from marriage, kids, and country-club memberships—but honestly, to me it feels like a death knell.

"Wow," is all I can say. I'm trying not to sound disappointed or disapproving, but I suppose I am a little of each.

"Yeah. We've been talking about it—she's been here pretty much every night for the last two months—and well, instead of bullshitting about that kind of thing, like everybody else does, it's actually happening."

"Amazing." And I mean that. Have I stumbled into some bizarre, parallel universe, I wonder? One where my best friend and my best yoga client have both plunged into blissful romances, started double-dating, and are now embracing cohabitation? Why is everybody redecorating their lives? Did I miss the "It's Time to Settle Down" memo?

"And, look, Dog ... I don't know how to tell you this," Hutch starts, "But ..."

"But what?"

"I think she's the one," he confesses.

"One what?" I say without thinking. And then I realize what he's talking about—"The One."

There's a momentary beat in which Hutch waits for me to figure out what he's saying—that he's found that fabled "soulmate/only one for me" fantasy connection. This is just not the kind of thing I'd ever imagine Hutch would ever say. This is the kind of phrase he'd scoff at.

"Are you shitting me?" is all I can manage.

"Nope."

I honestly thought that Hutch and I would be the last of the holdouts. I guess whatever Butch-and-Sundance fantasy

I've always had about us—and I do vaguely recall that they die offscreen at the end—has been busted.

Hutch isn't looking for a second opinion, much less a point-counterpoint discussion of the merits of the bachelor life. I know that I'm supposed to say positive things about their future together or at least compliment Hutch on his luck at finding such an amazing woman. Suddenly, it's crystal clear that if I don't want to blow the last ten years of friendship, I'd better say the right things fast.

"Dude, I'm really happy for you," I reply quickly.

"Thanks," Hutch says, sounding more than a little relieved.

"Having personally bunked with you for two years, I can vouch that if Etta can stand your snoring and all your other nasty personal habits, she's might very well be 'The One.'"

Hutch laughs. The awkwardness has been smoothed over. Our friendship's preserved. Someone buzzes him about a prospectus or a merger or something else urgent and financial, and he's got to get off the line.

Don't get me wrong: I realize that neither Janek nor Hutch is jumping off a cliff into oblivion. They're just settling down, willingly and happily. Nonetheless, I suddenly feel like some kind of lone holdout.

All this compulsive cohabiting truly makes me understand why wolves are considered an endangered species.

CHAPTER 26

Usually when I arrive to teach Brooke, Wallace the doorman and I have a friendly moment. Sometimes we exchange a few pleasantries about some safe topic like the weather or sympathy for a natural disaster. It doesn't go much deeper than that, although I freely admit that, alongside Hutch, I credit Wallace with launching my newfound career as a yoga stud. Truthfully, there's just no way that Brooke would have hired me and written that all-important first check had Wallace not basically hosed me down before the interview. The guy is, if not my friend, at least solidly on my side.

Wallace is always quite scrupulous about not letting me up until he's rung up to officially confirm my welcome, but it's a formality at this point. The model of upscale efficiency, he's always on the phone to Brooke's lair by the time I've moved past the building's exterior doorman and toward his desk.

Today, however, Wallace has not only not touched the phone, he's making no moves toward it. And he's not offering his usual upscale, service-oriented smile either.

"Hey man, good weekend?" I ask. Who knows what's off with the guy—fight with the missus, kid failing trigonometry. Could be anything.

"Good morning, sir." Although Wallace never refers to me as "dude" or "dog," the "sir" is a little formal.

"What's up, Wallace? Something wrong?" I ask.

He is entirely stone-faced, neither angry nor sympathetic. "I'm afraid I'm unable to let you up today."

"Oh, is Brooke canceling?"

"I'm afraid that Ms. Merrington has informed me that she

no longer requires your services." What the hell?

"Excuse me?"

"Ms. Merrington will no longer be employing you as her yoga instructor."

"Wallace, I … I'm sorry. I don't understand. I've been fired—why?"

Wallace looks at me, and I think I see a flicker of pity and understanding creep in—but he also has own neck and (I imagine) a wife and six daughters in Queens to think about. "I think it would be best if you were to leave, sir."

Wow. Suddenly the lobby I usually breeze through seems not only utterly inhospitable, but incredibly cold. "You're throwing me out?" I ask in disbelief.

"Ms. Merrington has asked that you leave immediately."

"Wallace, dude, what's going on here?"

"I'm very sorry, sir."

I don't think that Wallace has a secret panic button at his post, but perhaps he does, as two other doormen saunter toward us. I realize that these guys—while not overbuilt, macho bodyguard types—nonetheless reflect a kind of muscular solidity. They're my height, and although they're a little soft around the middle, when all three of them stand up near you, they do have a presence.

"Oh, and Ms. Merrington said that you may keep the remainder of your fee for the unused lessons," Wallace adds.

I hadn't thought of that. Brooke is always several steps ahead of me in every financial transaction—and it's a good thing, as that money has now long been spent toward overdue bills. Yet even with this building's doormen strongly "encouraging" me to leave via their presence, this matter feels far from settled. I'm both curious and pissed off as to what I did to deserve such an abrupt dismissal. Have I, like the white roses, suddenly developed an unacceptable odor? Yet, unlike those white roses, I will not be sent silently away in the service elevator.

I could, I suppose, call Brooke myself from my cell, but if Brooke has determined to get rid of me with her first line of underlings, I don't think she's in the mood for taking my call.

Clearly, she views my transgression as such that it's unworthy of apology or explanation, deserving no second chance. (But obviously, if we're being honest, Brooke has never struck me as someone who, in any scenario, is big on second chances.)

Pissed off but not interested in getting into a fight with these guys, I shrug and head toward the exit. Wallace accompanies me all the way to the street. Outside the door to the building, for one last time, I try to recreate a man-of-the-people vibe.

"Why, Wallace? Can you at least give me a clue about what I've done?"

Wallace hesitates for a moment, unwilling to betray whatever orders he's been given from Brooke. "I'd check today's Post if I were you. Page Six, to be precise."

It's a simple phrase about Page Six—an entirely disposable gossip section of a trashy tabloid—but right now, given my history, it feels like a death sentence.

I travel off Park Avenue back toward Lexington in search of a newsstand. My pocket change at the ready, I'm prepared to see what could be have caused Brooke's summary dismissal. I scramble for Page Six to find myself. I do, in the "We Hear" section of the gossip pages:

WE HEAR … that a certain Bad Boy, who's allegedly gotten all spiritual lately, has not only been canoodling with his Park Avenue "private clients," he's actually gotten two of the ladies' husbands to invest in his latest nightlife venture. Apparently, a lot of this action originates at the Upper East Side's most exclusive spa and exercise studio. And, apparently, said Bad Boy and his glittery ladies make quite a merry threesome … Nice going, Guru!

Fuck. Fuck. Fuck. Even without any names being mentioned, this could only be about me. There are maybe a dozen or two straight male yoga instructors in New York City, and I'm the only one I know at the Upper East Side's most exclusive spa and definitely the only one with a Bad Boy past and a nightlife venture in the works. Fuck. Fuck. Fuck.

My cell's vibrating, and I see that it's Epitome calling. It's mostly a numbed reflex, but I figure, what the hell—I might as well answer. Anjeli in payroll cuts right to the chase. "I just wanted you to know that I'm rushing your paycheck into direct deposit this Friday, just to make everything official, but we won't be including tonight's class since obviously you won't be teaching it."

"Uh, okay, but don't you think someone, like maybe Marguerite, should call and fire me first?" There's a pause on the line, as Anjeli stammers a bit. Apparently, she's been a bit overzealous in wiping me out of the system. "I'm sorry," she says, "I thought you were already informed." Suddenly I feel bad for the accounting staff, ironically as I am the one who's just been fired.

"Don't worry about it. I'm sure they'll get around to calling me," I half apologize. And, actually, they are, as I see I've got a call waiting from another extension at Epitome on the other line. I flip over to it.

"It's Marguerite. I'm sorry to tell you this, but—"

"Look, I understand," I cut her off.

"Good. I'm sorry, but we have to deal with this kind of thing as directly as possible. We can't afford to ignore the ramifications."

"Well, except for the Post, I think everyone wants this to just go away."

"For your sake, I hope that's true."

"What do you mean?" I'm a little confused.

"Epitome is fully insulated. You signed a release confirming the required viewing of the sexual harassment DVD along with a compliance form regarding our zero-tolerance philosophy. We could, of course, sue you ourselves, but we generally prefer to let this kind of thing die as quickly as possible. The other parties involved may not feel the same, however."

"You're kidding."

"No. Although I think you're right that it's unlikely they're going to file any kind of charges—still, they might. Teachers in nonacademic settings are a gray area of the law. But they could still argue that they felt vulnerable and harassed."

This is going from bad to worse. First banished from Brooke, and now exiled from Epitome. What's next? And then it hits me: Phoebe.

I basically hang up on Marguerite with some dimwitted, halfhearted apology so I can figure out what do to about Phoebe. Brooke, I know, is a lost cause. I am thankful that Ms. Merrington, Queen of Park Avenue, will probably draw the line at murder, but otherwise, I'm sure she'd do everything in her power to have me removed from her known universe. Fortunately, since that means the six square miles of the Upper East Side, she might allow me to still live in Manhattan. Maybe.

But Phoebe—if there's anything I can do to salvage things there, to plead my case, pathetic as it is, I'm more than willing to grovel. Opting for the strategy of the desperate, I feel compelled to race over to her building to try to explain things in a way that's somehow less damning than the mention in the Post would make it seem.

I realize I am practically jogging the seven blocks from the newsstand back up to Park Avenue toward Phoebe's, but I can't stop myself. I feel like every second in which I haven't defended myself to Phoebe solidifies the impressive case against me.

Arriving at her building, I'm sweating from the combination of the jog and my anxiety. I'm also on a friendly basis with the doorman here, as well—there are no nametags, so I have no idea what the hell his name is—but he also does not seem particularly overjoyed to see me. His usual friendly manner has been replaced by this glacier formality, as though I were a Jehovah's Witness or a Hare Krishna, not someone he's admitted twice a week for the last five months. Clearly, Phoebe has warned him, although this whole scene reeks more of Brooke's "off with their heads" style.

Taking my cue from my previous encounter, I leave the building before I'm thrown out, but I will not give in. Brooke can vanish from my life if she wants, but I'm determined to see Phoebe. Somehow. Some way. But there's just no way I'm going to be buzzed up today.

It may be delusional, but, as always, I cling to the hope that no matter how damning my crimes may be, if I can somehow plead my case in person, that will somehow make the crucial difference. Nothing in my life experience supports this. This strategy has obviously been a complete failure regarding Shane. In fact, each time I see Shane, I make things worse. Nonetheless, I feel a face-to-face is my only chance. I will find a way ...

I walk around for the next two and a half hours in a daze, wondering if there's anything I can do to remedy the situation. Absolutely nothing comes to mind.

I show up for my lesson with Linney, pretty sure of what the outcome's going to be. I am grateful that at least I can enter his showroom without going through a doorman security system. When he sees me, he looks genuinely sympathetic—crestfallen, even—but fortunately his wry, gay humor supersedes all.

"Tsk tsk, Blue Eyes. You've been a very bad boy. Were it not for this bum hip, I'd like to spank you myself."

"The whole situation sucks."

"I can imagine. I'm sorry, but of course, you realize ..." he trails off, less willing than the rest to vaporize me from his life.

"That it's over between us," I finish for him.

"You make it sound so romantic. I like that."

Despite myself, I smile against my will at his autopilot flirtation. He continues, downtrodden, "Although I'd like to think that given our vast, epic, and intertwined family histories, Brooke would never see fit to use her considerable influence to discourage and diminish my clientele, I can't afford to kid myself."

Even though it's only noon, Linney pours us both stiff tumblers of bourbon. "She absolutely would. She's not a woman who likes to be contradicted."

"I understand."

"Ah, Blue Eyes, don't look so sad. You'll get through this." At this point, I'm beginning to wonder, but Linney continues, "Now of course, if you were willing to consider running away with me, I suppose I could close up the shop, sell off everything, and probably we'd have just enough for us to retire and live modestly but happily on some tropical isle together. We wouldn't have more than enough to pay for a set of matching sarongs, but I think you'd look rather dashing, like a young Clark Gable in Mutiny on the Bounty."

"I find it somehow strangely comforting that despite the fact that my life is falling to pieces, you can still flirt with me," I half smile, sipping my bourbon.

"Oh, dear boy. Don't take it so hard. You're not a condemned man. And Brooke's not God."

He thinks for a second as he sips his drink. "Well, at least not below 57th Street, she isn't."

When I leave Linney three hours later, bolstered a bit by the pan-fried foie gras lunch he impulsively makes, topped off by crème brûlée, we exchange a long, comradely hug. It may be the three or four bourbons we've washed the foie gras down with, but I feel myself about to tear up—until he grabs my ass, and we both laugh. It's a fitting ending—heartfelt but irreverent, harmlessly flirtatious to the last. I think it's best I get going, as I've got a busy agenda of aimless wandering planned, with much stopping in taverns along the way.

God, how I wish Hutch were in town or even remotely reachable. Disregarding the fact that Fiji's probably in some completely unfavorable time zone, I actually try his cell phone. It rings for a second and then goes dead, not even spiraling over to voicemail. It's not encouraging that I can't even leave a message about my colossally messed-up predicament. I try Janek's as well, and the same thing happens. Clearly Fiji is somehow not covered under either of their calling plans.

After my third bar visit, I decide to take the fourth call that's come in from Monique's lawyer, prepared for the inevitable. Not surprisingly, the Cleavage Boyz have backed out of the deal.

"Can they do that?" I ask Monique's lawyer.

"Did you read the contract?" she barks condescendingly. Frankly, I more or less skimmed it, trusting that Monique was looking out for every business angle with her ravenous eagle eyes.

I'm told straightaway that they absolutely can back out based on paragraphs x, y, and z, and subsection this and that. And here's the kicker: they want their first $1.333 million back—nearly all of which has been spent, of course—except for Monique's finder's fee, which is protected and nonrefundable under any circumstances.

"No problem. I'll be down there in twenty minutes with my checkbook," I sneer.

"This is not a joking matter. According to the terms of the deal you signed, this is completely within their rights," Monique's lawyer tells me sternly.

"How is that possible? I can't even get store credit at the Gap without a receipt."

"It's unfortunate for you, but they are entitled to a full refund of their money."

"Yeah, except of course for your client Monique's finder's fee."

"Well, honestly, why should my client suffer just because you blew the deal she got for you? Besides, hasn't something like this happened to you before with investors?" the lawyer asks. I can't tell if she's asking rhetorically, just to salt the wound more deeply, or whether she really wants to know for some valid reason.

"Sort of. Why do you ask?"

"I just thought you might have paid more attention to that section of the contract, that's all. These situations have a tendency to repeat themselves," she comments pointedly.

I almost correct her: they don't repeat—like viruses, they mutate and multiply. Instead of getting caught with one investor's wife, I've been caught with two. And instead of losing

$120,000, I'm out over a million. Tired of being lectured, I decide it's easier to just hang up.

Via her assistant, I actually manage to reach Monique directly in Thailand.

Ten thousand miles away, she's fully abreast of the sorry situation. Her no-nonsense manner is running full throttle.

"I'm sorry but I don't see how I can help you," is how she answers the line. "I've already called Richard Johnson at The Post to see about a possible retraction, although those things never do any good. Anyway, it doesn't matter because although he won't reveal them, he assures me his sources are impeccable."

"Sources?" I question, noting the plural.

"Yes. Could be investigators from one of those jealous husbands eager to make some extra tabloid loot. Maybe one of the more vengeful ladies in the legions you've casually tossed off. Or maybe just some lucky dirt someone dug up on you while covering one of your celebrated private clients."

Monique is neither angry nor rude, merely straight to the point.

"Certainly, I suspected that something like this might be going on, but I hoped that it would remain entirely discreet. It seemed a calculated, reasonable risk."

Another thing I did not know about Monique is that apparently, she speaks Thai. For a few moments, she barks orders to underlings before returning to our conversation.

"Although sometimes this kind of tawdry exposure can bolster something's appeal, unfortunately I just can't imagine anyone who would take this on right now. I am afraid that the property will go back on the market, and you'll have to face the liability issues alone."

She issues more directions in Thai, working towards manifesting another five-star Becker triumph. "Well, anyway, I still wish you luck," she says. "You're going to need it."

There's a pause. Despite trying to be all business, I can feel a transcontinental wave of compassion wash over Monique. "Look, I really do wish I could do something more for you," she says. "or offer something comforting. What's the thing they say in yoga classes … 'Remember to breathe.'"

"Yeah, that's what I say whenever I don't have a clue."

"The bottom line is that no matter how bad this gets, you're not dead. While there's life, there's hope. And when there's hope, there's always the possibility that something will work out. Most of the time, it usually does." And with that, she signs off.

Having started at noon with Linney, I watch the hours pass as I wander the streets, grabbing drinks at various bars. Once happy hour hits, every now and then, while bellying up to the bar, I run into someone I vaguely know, which I take as a cue for immediate departure; when your world is falling apart, sometimes you really do need to be alone in the crowd.

By the time it's nightfall, I'm moderately hammered—not so bad that I'm staggering but enough so that I'm not exactly thinking clearly.

I stroll back toward Phoebe's building. Seeing her, pleading with her to try to understand, has become dominant in my thoughts. Perhaps it's because the $1.333 million is too staggering a problem to wrap my mind around. Or, perhaps it's because hurting her reminds me a little too much of hurting Shane all over again.

During the afternoon, I've called Phoebe a dozen times, caller ID be damned. The first eight or so times, I just hung up. Then I left a generic message asking her to call me so I could explain. Then, I believe I left two different messages in which I started to explain, tried to delete my false starts from the voicemail system, but may or may not have hit the key to mark them "urgent" as opposed to getting rid of them entirely. How limitless, I wonder, is the possibility of things getting totally fucked up?

You know, Park Avenue is not an easy place to stalk someone, I realize drunkenly. It's all very exposed, something I assume to be the antithesis of the stalker mentality. There are no nooks or crannies, no places to hide and view from afar. Just big buildings and doormen and stretches of sidewalk. From across the street and a little down the block, I keep monitoring Phoebe's windows—even though I'm not sure what I'm looking for.

I do see lights go on and off occasionally in Phoebe's apartment, but I have no idea what any of the flickering means. Is it Phoebe's maid doing a final dusting … or is Phil searching for sandwich crumbs? How many hours are appropriate for a stalking? Am I required to stay here until I am escorted away by the police or the local sanitarium? When it starts to drizzle lightly, I am even more confused. Getting soaked to the bone and dying of pneumonia seems a fitting end, but I'm not sure if even I have the masochistic endurance required to take another pummeling today.

For better or worse, my musings are cut short when I see a figure that, even through the blur of alcohol and from across the street, is unmistakably Phoebe, appearing in her building's lobby.

Barely glancing at the traffic, and nearly getting sideswiped by a cab in the process, I race across the street to her.

I realize it's the first time I've seen Phoebe in anything but a yoga stretch outfit. Dressed now for some formal function, she looks like a pint-sized goddess in a flowing gown and all the jewelry that wire hangers can buy. She waits underneath the awning as the doorman attempts to hail her a cab in what is rapidly turning into a downpour. This is a night-shift doorman, and thus someone I've never met, who seems just as surprised as Phoebe when I race forward toward her.

"You've got to talk to me," I blurt out.

The doorman looks like he might be reaching for a handgun, or at least pepper spray, but Phoebe holds him at bay. Somehow, she manages to signal him that while police intervention is not in order, he should nonetheless not stray too far.

"I shouldn't be speaking to you," is the first thing Phoebe says me.

I want to ask, why "shouldn't?"—is it because whatever she's feeling is too painful or simply because Big Stepsis Brooke has forbidden it—but I don't.

Though half drunk, I try to stay focused. "I need to explain everything to you," I start.

"I don't think any explanation is going to help much."

She's probably right—there's not really much I could say that would improve, much less fix, the situation—and more to the point, despite patrolling outside her building for the past few hours, I haven't prepared anything particularly compelling to say in my defense.

I don't even know where to begin. Should I start by explaining that the Cleavage Twins were just meaningless, diversionary sex?

Or should I confess that, despite her unique, high-minded view of me, I am possessed of a deeply if not hopelessly flawed character, and that perhaps my greatest mistake was letting her think well of me?

Or do I lead my defense with an admission of true and intense feelings for her, feelings that made me run straight from her willing and loving arms?

Or do I have to start from the beginning, spilling my guts about my entire story, knowing that the only way to perhaps forgive me is to understand my entire pathology?

"I ... I ... It's not like you think," I fumble again.

Phoebe looks at me, and I fancy that her eyes are pleading me to make things right. "So, it's not true, then?"

I'm silent. This is was clearly the wrong tactic.

"It's all lies," she continues, hopeful yet worried. "Seducing students at Epitome. Sleeping with your investors' wives."

I can't lie to her, so I say nothing. She continues. "Rejecting me, not because you're some ethical person, but because ... because ..." Phoebe's holding back tears, unable to fill in the blanks about why I turned her away so abruptly when I am clearly a base, horny dog.

I realize it is not without irony that this is perhaps the singular incident in my life where I have made matters worse by not sleeping with a woman.

I'm not sure what I can say to her that doesn't involve endless explanation, and even then, it might not be forgivable or made right. I'm spared this next failure, however, as Phil waddles toward us, dressed in what is probably a $3,000 Armani tux that manages to make him look like, well, a bullfrog in a $3,000 tux.

He stares at me, surprised. Then he reads the choreography of my positioning with Phoebe—turned close to her, my hands gently on her upper arms in intimate, forgiveness-beseeching mode—and his face goes beet red. Clearly, today Phil has had a rude awakening not only to my true sexuality but also to the possibility that his lovely wife was perhaps an available tender morsel for this carnivorous wolf.

"You better get out of here, son." Phil says, standing between us. Even though my advantages include a foot of height along with thirty years and forty pounds in my favor, Phil manfully steps up to bring Phoebe behind him, away from my sullying hands.

Despite hours of brooding, I've somehow not thought any of this through. I'm not sure what I'm supposed to do here, or what I can say. Technically, no adulterous crimes were committed with Phoebe. I want to reassure Phil of that while simultaneously also convincing Phoebe how much I genuinely want to make love to her—that even now, drunk and disgraced, I want her even more. Not even the most experienced diplomat could rescue this situation.

Phil puffs up his chest—bullfrogs do that—and I flash on the crazy street fighter Phil must have been to have clawed his way up to the top floors on Park Avenue. The look in his eyes conveys both eagerness to duke it out with me and a reasonable level of reservation at the prospect of taking on someone with much greater physical advantage.

I look at Phoebe, who just seems utterly lost and confused. If only this were a clearer, cleaner situation. If only I'd admitted something of what I was feeling for her rather than running from it the moment it nearly rose to a boil. Then the fight we'd be having would make sense. I, the Lancelot interloper, stealing the fair Guinevere would be entirely deserving of a pummeling from this Bullfrog Arthur. Instead, my crime is wimpy omission: I've passively allowed Phil to think I'm a show-tune-loving gay guy and Phoebe to miscast me as a mystical poet. For entirely different reasons, both seem rather unglued by their parallel revelations that I'm a run-of-the-mill heterosexual with dubious moral standards.

Backing away, I know there's no way I can fix things here today. I have no choice but to add Phoebe to my ever-growing list of "People to Whom I Need to Redeem Myself." Phil seems both disappointed and relieved. "I'm sorry," is all I can muster toward Phoebe.

"I'm really sorry," I repeat numbly as I exit from underneath the safety of the awning into what can now only be called a downpour. I fantasize that Phoebe's lips silently mouth, "Me, too." But truthfully, she seems only sad, yet grateful, to see me go.

As I travel downtown to the site of Diwali Almost, needing one more dose of misery, I stop by the bridge gallery. Sure enough, it delivers. Close to a year ago, I saw Shane herself here at Andrea's show, and as I'm approaching, there she is again. Well, almost. There's a huge painting of her on the wall, a new work that's the centerpiece of Andrea's solo show.

I stare at the canvas through the glass. Maybe it's that I'm already haunted by Shane, but even at this distance, the painting is striking and evocative. I don't think Andrea's woven me into the imagery, and frankly I don't care. I'm sure if I wanted, I could take partial credit for the fiery yet wounded look in Shane's eyes. What the fuck does it matter?

I head off for my graveyard march to Diwali.

Someone—I suppose someone from Monique's lawyer's office—has let the crew know that that the jig is up. As if the building were ruins leveled by an ancient volcano, it seems that the workers have fled midday, abandoning everything they couldn't take with them.

Besides all the money that's been spent here, I don't even want to think about all the items that have been placed on order and all the unpaid work already done by the architect. Will anyone, contractor or tile maker, be willing to just forget about the whole thing? Or am I going to be stuck with seventy-five barstools that will take up more than the space of my apartment? Just then, I realize that I've ordered close to another million dollars' worth of shit that will be arriving over the next few weeks; who knows how much of that I'm liable for.

Sitting around—squatting on the floor, actually—I'm quite convinced that this must be rock bottom. Like a co-ed who's trapped by the killer in a horror movie, I realize I'm at that moment in which I think things can't possibly get any worse.

I have had the forethought, however, to have nabbed a bottle of Jack Daniels on the way, figuring I can at least have a parting drink with any remaining members of the unfortunate crew that my publicized philandering has rendered unemployed. But with the site abandoned, it's just me and the bottle. I'm learning there is no camaraderie at rock bottom.

I've gotten a strong head start on getting totally smashed— I've scheduled the final portion of my descent for tonight, alone in the dark and brooding. So, after about thirty minutes and the consumption of the contents of a nearly empty pint-sized bottle, I rise from the floor, look around the space, mutter "Fuck" a half-dozen times, turn off the lights, take the proverbial "one last look," and depart.

Shutting the door behind me, and fumbling for my keys, I flirt with leaving it unlocked. It occurs to me that maybe if things are stolen, insurance will help me off the hook with those seventy-five barstools. My minor responsibility instincts dominate, however, and I decide to lock the ruins of my dream away from potential roving bands of nightclub looters. As I'm drunkenly stooping to pick up the keys that have slid from my hand to the ground, I'm tapped on the shoulder, and turning, my face meets up with a rather solid right hook to my jaw and then another dude's punch to my gut.

I think I say something insightful like "Jesus" or "Ugh," and wincing, collapse into a fetal curl, looking up to see my attackers.

I find that the urban thugs attacking me are astonishingly well dressed. And they're middle-aged and balding. And then I realize that they're the Cleavage Boyz.

They are, of course, very angry, and acting in a street-brawler way that I assume is out of character for guys who rake in multiple millions a year. Well, the screwing-someone-over part may be totally in character, but I doubt that physical blows are frequently traded.

They've got me down, and while I hesitate to use the phrase, "I'm a lover, not a fighter," it's more or less true. I suppose that given my athleticism, I might be able to bluff my way through a fair fight with one of them. But given that I'm already three sheets to the wind, taken by surprise, and knocked on the ground, the two of them have a decided advantage over me. And while I'd have guessed as much, I soon learn that these are guys who are not afraid of exploiting their advantages.

In a way, I'm almost grateful that at least someone's finally confronting me to my face, even if technically what they're doing is pounding said face. It hurts like hell, but it's a more real experience than Brooke's imperial dismissal from her moated castle on Park Avenue. No more implied threats. Finally we're getting down to business. It's refreshingly direct and primitive.

Through some combination of whiskey and being messed up by the Boyz, I feel myself slipping out of consciousness. Part of me resists it, but on the whole, passing out and descending into oblivion doesn't feel like such a bad idea at this point. Things get kind of blurry, and I drift away.

The next thing I know, I feel myself being manhandled again, and it might be the indeterminate nap I've had—perhaps it's only been minutes, but I could easily have been passed out for hours—but when I resurrect myself, I find I'm actually quite angry.

Eyes half open, a little caked with blood from a cut on my

forehead, I'm up on my feet, starting to swing back blindly and wildly. Although I can't really see what's going on, I'm punching like crazy. There's no strategy here—just dim recesses of survival instinct operating—but it feels like the right thing to do.

And then I'm out again. This time, much more suddenly, and without any time to contemplate the slide into oblivion. Just BAM—I've been clubbed or shot or chloroformed. My last thought is a realization that as I've hit the ground unconscious yet again, there can be no mistake this time: I've literally hit rock bottom.

Okay, once again I was wrong. I keep finding new lows. I wake up to find that, not surprisingly, I've landed in jail.

Technically, I'm in a holding cell. Apparently my burst of pugilism was unfortunately targeted at the New York City cops who were trying to revive me. I suppose my being battered and bloody, reeking of whisky, and collapsed in a fetal ball from my first beating from the Cleavage Boyz didn't convey the best upstanding-citizen impression. The officers were no doubt merely trying to see if I was alive or dead, or perhaps just shaking me to encourage the wretch to "Move it along." And thus, it was not so great that my first response was to blindly start swinging at them.

I stagger through my arraignment in front of the judge. Fortunately I have no record—well, at least not a criminal one—but still, assaulting a police officer is a serious charge and quite frowned upon in law-enforcement circles. I'm told this repeatedly during the arraignment by the judge and the junior DA—who, although cute in a Law & Order way, is not Etta. I am partly glad that Etta is off in Fiji with my boy Hutch so as to spare myself further embarrassment, but even so, I'd trade anything for a friendly face.

Anyway, bail is set at $15,000. Not much in the grand scheme of things but still more than I can handle, given my pathetic fortunes and utter lack of collateral.

Sitting here in a holding cell that's more like a sterile high school broom closet (albeit with bars) than an episode of Oz, I flail about and wonder who I can call to get me out of here. Hutch (or even Janek) would do it in a second, but those boys are unreachably windsurfing. Andrew probably would, as well, but he has vanished into his own legal hell. Even if I could reach him, I wonder if the court system would take his marker as readily as five-star hotel owners do?

Brooke and Phoebe—well, there's no need to even go there. I might as well call Shane (who is probably the only one likely to show up, merely to confirm her opinion of me and delight in how low I've fallen). On the other hand, I'd then owe her another $15,000.

I make the only call I have left—the one I should have made a long time ago.

FULL FORWARD BEND
(PASCHIMOTTANASANA)

For most guys, this is pure torture. Tight hamstrings and a tight lower back can make bending forward totally impossible.

Ask your average jock to try it, and no matter how much they try to move forward, it'll seem like they're sitting bolt upright.

If backbends, with all their heart-opening action, make the body aware of opening up into the future and encountering the new and the unknown, then in the primal symbolism of body movement, bending forward means going within, diving into your thoughts, and exploring your past.

No wonder they're such torture.

CHAPTER 27

To her credit, Gigi says next to nothing when she bails me out. I know her finances aren't infinite, but she's always been solid around money. You can sometimes just tell that about a person, just as you can usually predict who's going to be utterly insolvent—myself a key case in point.

It's Thursday afternoon, and Gigi offers an invitation to her place in the Catskills, an hour and a half from the city. That's not quite right. It's more like she pretty much tells me (gently but firmly) that we're going to their place upstate and that we'll be back by Sunday for her always sold-out "Good News" class. I don't bother to protest. She's parked their convertible Saab two blocks from the jail. Before I know it, we're whizzing up the Henry Hudson Parkway and out of the city.

It doesn't surprise me that Gigi is a mad, twenty-miles-above-the-speed-limit driver. I'm trusting that the superb coordination she's demonstrated in thousands of yoga classes extends to the moments with her hands behind the wheel.

We say very little on the ride upstate. I've never been to Calypso and Gigi's cabin—that's what they call it—and I find myself slumping in the front seat, curving into the space, letting the scenario wash over me. I'm only dimly aware that it's the most beautiful June day ever.

In just under two hours, we're somewhere else entirely. It's amazing what a little geography can do.

When Gigi zooms her Saab convertible up the path to their cabin, winding her way up the long driveway, I see that the cabin is, indeed, a cabin, I suppose, but one that can sleep six, all wooden and flagstone, very rustic and totally gorgeous. I've heard the rumor that Gigi bought it with the royalties left to her post-plane crash by a legendary rocker's classic unplugged ballad about their on-tour summer romance. I've never inquired if this is true, but in any case, it adds to the mystique of this lakefront retreat.

Calypso emerges on the porch and hugs me deeply. We all unload a few bags of groceries that Gigi picked up from Whole Foods. Were I not a recently sprung ex-con, this might be the start of a delightful weekend in the country.

The living room spills into a dining area with a rustic table that looks like it's made from craggy logs. Although it's June, the stones keep the place cool, and Calypso has already built a small fire in the huge stone hearth that dominates the center of the living space, more for effect than for warmth. The whole house is one of those Architectural Digest affairs in which the living room is two stories high with a landing on the second floor that looks downward on the open areas.

There's a classic rustic feel to the place (except that, as hardcore vegetarians, they've omitted the stuffed moose's head that would typically go over the huge stone fireplace) and they've added tons of cozy—I hesitate to use the word "lesbian," but the homey, no-frills, rough-hewn cliché works here—touches. Everything is shabby chic and inviting.

Walking upstairs, Calypso offers me a choice of rooms. I select one less because of the view of the lake and more because the bedding looks like I could sink into it and sleep for a million years.

In fact, that's pretty much what I do. I shower in the guest bathroom and then decide I'm going to take a short nap. It's not even noon, but I figure I'll be fresh for the explanatory conversation that's inevitable, no matter how long Gigi's willing to postpone it. If you bail someone out of jail, you deserve a little backstory.

When I wake up, I'm startled to realize it's pitch black. I look at my watch and see it's 11 p.m. The catnap of the damned, indeed.

Realizing I'm starving, I head downstairs cautiously, hoping not to wake Gigi and Calypso in case they've already gone to bed. After years of teaching early-morning classes and living the yoga lifestyle, like reverse vampires, I assume they get up at dawn and go to sleep as soon as the sun sets.

Quickly the sound of their casual laughter reassures me, guiding me to the large dining table where they're sitting together. It's obvious dinner was completed hours ago, but they've left an empty place setting for me. Seeing me, they smile warmly.

"I'm sorry. I just passed out completely," I apologize.

"No worries. Sleeping is sweet in the country," Gigi replies.

"You must be hungry. I'll get you something," Calypso comments, getting up from her place.

"Thanks, but I don't want you to go to any more trouble."

"It's easy. I'm just reheating dinner."

She leaves Gigi and me to talk.

"Merlot?" I'm slightly surprised that Gigi offers. I didn't know she drank at all. Most serious yogis don't (or at least say they don't).

"Recent incarceration experiences have suggested that maybe I should give up drinking for a while."

"Suit yourself," she shrugs. "Every mystic has to find his or her own path."

"I'm hardly a mystic."

"That's what you think," she continues as she refills her own glass. "Anyway, baby doll, a taste of wine won't kill me. My crazy partying days are ancient history. They renounced me long ago."

"How do you mean?"

"I've never been a big fan of giving up things. If there's one thing my momma taught me," and here she gets really down home as she amps up her Creole accent, "it's that 'a body's gonna do what a body's gonna do, until they's don't gotta do it no more.'" There's something inherently funny in her larger-than-life imitation of "momma," which gives us both a small laugh.

Then she's back to her hip, NYC persona. "But, damn it, she was right about that. When you're ready, all the so-called vices just give you up. There's no allure to the nonsense anymore." And then she quotes Rumi, yet again: "'Let yourself be drawn by the greater pull of what you really love.' That's always worked for me."

"At the moment, I'm only aware of my gift for screwing things up massively."

"Well, you do seem to have abundant talent in that regard," she chuckles. I find myself smiling, too. Things seem a bit less dismal here in the country with Gigi and Calypso—but I guess compared to being drunk, beaten up, and arrested, what doesn't?

Gigi looks at me with a teacher's quiet prompting. No matter what, no matter how relaxed I am around her, I still always feel that I'm there to learn. That she's willing and available to teach me. I can almost feel it coming, the lecture I've been anticipating and dreading, and yet somehow, I want to just get over with. It's high time that Gigi—or, frankly, anyone—talked some sense into me.

As though she can read my mind—and sometimes, I swear she can—she shakes her head "no." "Babydoll, I am not your momma. I ain't gonna lecture you. That's just not my style." God knows it's not and yet, I want … I realize I can't even articulate what I want.

She waits. I stumble.

"Honestly … I have no idea what 'the deeper pull of what I really love' means anymore. It's all so fucked up. Everything is. I don't know. I guess deep down what I want is what everybody wants," I manage.

"And what is that?"

"The power to change the past."

"Hmmm," she says, peering into her wine. "Not everybody, actually, because that is something I decidedly do not want."

"Really?"

"Yeah, really."

"Even to talk some sense into 'beautiful corpses' of rock stars back in the day?"

"Haven't you been listening?—it wouldn't have done any good! 'You gonna do what you gonna do, until you ain't gonna do it anymore.' Besides, it's every twist and turn that got me here today. And I am grateful, baby, to be here right now. I mean, sure, there are days I'm glad I don't have to live over again, let me tell you. But I have no desire to redecorate my past, cleaning it all up, getting rid of the bad stuff. That's how I got to the good stuff now."

Funny thing is, I believe her. She's come to peace with things, and somehow it shows in the quality of her life.

"Yeah, I hear you," I agree. "I suppose 'Never Look Back' has always been my philosophy, too."

"Now that's bullshit." I'm surprised at the blunt intensity of her response. "'Never look back,' my ass."

"What then?"

"Yoga is about accepting life—all of it. The stuff you don't like and the stuff you're crazy about. Sure, we don't want to dwell on the negative, but the way you say it, I think 'never look back' means ignoring stuff you don't like. The thing you're ignoring is the thing that ends up running your life. Same for whatever you're holding on to—it takes complete control of the wheel."

The words hit me hard. I'm not ignoring Shane with my gallery drive-bys and cyber stalking. I think about the $15,000 I owe her on an hourly basis—and that's only because I can't think of any way to deal with the deeper wounds my betrayal has caused her. In one way or another, making things right with Shane has been running my life since I messed everything up—and yet I haven't told a single person about the heart of it, not even Hutch. Or about any of the other shit I've been going through lately.

When Gigi speaks again, I startle a bit. "Hit a nerve, did I?"

"What?"

"You were a million miles away a moment ago."

"Sorry."

"Never a need to apologize for what you're going through. Want to talk about it?" She reaches for the bottle and refills my glass.

I hesitate for a moment. In my gut, I know I can stay stuck as I am forever or tread one millimeter into that plunge forward. I make a decision. And once I start, there's no stopping it.

Suddenly, I'm telling Gigi everything.

Somehow I finish my story, getting right up to the present day, somehow even including how I feel like a sham as a teacher, particularly with Phoebe. I even include the entire sordid mess with the Cleavage Twins, Epitome, Monique, and Diwali. Somehow it all comes out in a gusher, and at some point I realize not only am I choked up, I'm swallowing tears.

I also realize that somehow, Gigi has moved from warm touches here and there to actually hugging me—I'm not even sure when she started. All I know is that I'm grateful she's not letting go.

CHAPTER 28

The next morning, I wake up way past noon, having slept another twelve hours. I emerge downstairs, feeling slightly guilty. I don't know why; it's not like they need me to chop firewood or anything, but it just doesn't feel right to sleep away this time in the country when you're the houseguest of the person who has bailed you out of jail. As always, Gigi and Calypso are unperturbed, amused even, by my habits.

"You're very good at keeping rock-star hours," Gigi says. "You might consider that as a fallback career."

"Believe me, I used to keep them all the time. But I never needed quite this much sleep," I counter.

"First sign of old age," Gigi laughs, but we all know that rather than just country living, it's more like collapsing after an emotional exorcism.

Calypso's made some amazing vegetable tempura for us, and we wash it down with Pellegrino. (I guess the merlot is saved for evening meals.) Dessert is some fantastic health-food mélange of barley, yoghurt, berries, and honey. I eat heartily and thank them sincerely again and again for their incredible hospitality.

We drive into town, which is mainly a square with several streets of shops. After living in New York City for so long, everything seems very open and spacious, yet very limited. There's no multiplicity of choices, but that's okay. Today I feel as though as though any of my needs would be handled within this quarter-mile radius of shops.

As we're walking idly back to the car, we stop for a moment by the small pond in the center of town. Gigi and Calypso say that they always feed the ducks here. I join them in this perfect, suspended moment. We drive back to the cabin in a deep, incredibly comfortable silence.

I manage to survive the rest of the afternoon without a ten-hour nap. In fact, come dinnertime, my offer to help with the cooking is accepted. I'm drafted into peeling vegetables for some quasi-Tibetan stew that Calypso loves.

Calypso is back in town, choreographing a piece for the local dance company, which is mostly made up of teenage girls thrilled to have a former Alvin Ailey dancer working with them. Gigi and I hang out, preparing the meal for her return.

It turns out I'm right about the red wine. It's a dinner-in-the-country thing. Gigi even tells me she doesn't drink in the city. "Just doesn't suit me" is her simple reply when I ask why.

An easy stillness falls over us, with mild bits of conversation inserted about the meal- preparation tasks at hand. Gigi has some refined Glenn Gould recording playing in the background. (I almost want to ask if she knew him, if her provenance of rock-star legend extends into the classical world—but decide it would be too forward.) If she wants me to know, she'll tell me. Once most of the meal is set for a long simmer, waiting for Calypso's return, Gigi refills my glass.

Gigi looks at me curiously. I guess she's probably wondering if I'm able to handle any more opening up without falling into a coma.

"You know, there was one thing you said last night that I feel the desire to respond to," she begins.

"Only one?" I respond, surprised.

"Yup." I'm curious what one thing sparked her interest. "That whole thing about being a wolf," she offers.

"Right. Pretty lame, I guess. I'm more like a mangy mutt from the pound."

"No, it's not that. Wolves are magnificent. I have a lot of wolf-inspired things here." I had actually half noticed that already—things like a coffee table book and some kind of

National Geographic calendar in the spare bathroom off the kitchen—but I had assumed they were just countrified decorating touches.

"You may think you're a wolf, but you know nothing about them. Wolves have nothing to do with keeping a rock-star lifestyle or being romanticized loners. At least not to the Native Americans. Do you know what the wolf represents in lots of those traditions?"

"No."

"The teacher."

"Really?"

"Yes, really. Do you have any idea why that might be?" I shrug, clueless as usual.

"Wolves are the pathfinders. It's the nature of the alpha wolf to want to go out and explore, to learn all the ins and outs of trails. And yet, wolves don't prowl for the sake of prowling. They're not about mindless adventures. The wolf finds the path, but then he or she shares what's been learned."

Gigi tastes the stew, then hands me another red onion to peel and chop.

"Take their howling. It's true that wolves howl sometimes for the sheer delight of making a loud noise. But most of the time it's about communicating something important to the rest of their pack. Like the right way on the path. Or how far they've roamed, so their pack doesn't get as lost as they did. It's always some vital information necessary for survival."

"That makes sense, I guess."

"Wolves aren't just some fun group of bad boys out for a good time or a random chase. They know how hard the wilderness can be. They're acutely aware of the struggle to survive. That's why the lone wolf is pretty much a myth. It's extremely rare. Wolves are intensely involved with each other as a community. Except maybe at some crazy hippie ashram, you'll never find a group of beings who appreciate and depend on each other more than a wolf pack."

"I've always thought they were such beautiful animals," she continues, sautéing the onions, retasting the stew, and then giving me three more cloves of garlic to mince. "And when I dug a little deeper, I felt so drawn to them as a model for what a teacher is, or what a teacher can be … For what you are."

"Well, I think my teaching's been pretty much called into question these days," I remark wryly.

"Your teaching's just beginning."

I'm astonished that she might view it that way. I know her standards for teachers, and I know how totally I've violated almost all of them. It's incredible that she thinks I might still be cut out for anything educational—except perhaps as a poster boy of "Yoga Don'ts."

"You're kidding, right?"

"Do I look like I'm kidding?" she replies. "Better, I think if you could chop the garlic a little finer."

"You're cut out to be a teacher," she continues, "because you're always missing the mark. Always failing. Again and again. But you get up and try one more time until you eventually succeed. Hasn't anyone ever told you that the greatest saints were the greatest sinners? Back in the day, Momma used to say that to me all the time; took a while for it to sink into my thick head. Now, I'm not sayin' that sainthood's coming anytime in your or my future, but the sinnin' part we got down," she chuckles.

Equally intent on the stew, she fine-tunes the seasonings almost microscopically now.

"And I don't think anything in the past was sinnin'. Not at all. That's how you learn where the trails lead. There are lots of places you and I do not want to visit again. The alpha ones have got to go out and find the wrong ways, so they can tell the pack about the right ways. It's like that saying about Edison finding ten thousand ways how not to invent the lightbulb before he did. The light gets found by the person who's willing to travel all the paths that don't lead to it."

I keep trying to take all this in. "I don't think I've found anything yet."

"You've discovered more than you think. Look at all those fancy poses you can do now. Especially the ones where you fell flat on your cute little ass the first couple hundred times you tried them. We all did. Yoga doesn't get graceful and easy and loose and free for a good long time. And that's the point. You can teach a pose not just because you can do it; you can teach it well because there was a time when you couldn't do it."

"Poses, maybe, but—"

She cuts off my objection, passing me another onion to chop. "Poses. Life. It's the same shit. Good teachers are the ones who got lost the most but didn't give up. They know—we know—all the paths that lead to nowhere. Now our job is to steer the pack away from those." She closes her case, "And I'd add that I think you have a few clues about the ones that lead somewhere, even if you haven't gotten all the way there yet, Trailblazer."

Calypso returns home. Gigi brightens.

"Here, taste this, baby." Gigi offers Calypso the ladle.

"It's perfect. Just needs more cumin," Calypso comments sweetly.

"You're right," Gigi agrees, foraging for spices. It already smells amazing. Cumin added, the stew is pronounced ready for serving, and we retire to the dining table. We stay up late talking that night, but it's neither confessional nor therapeutic. It's just conversation among friends from the same pack.

That night, I finally sleep like a normal person. I awake eight hours later (instead of twelve) ready to return to the city and try, yet again, to find the right path toward making things right. If Gigi's even half right, then knowing all the wrong paths should make me an awesome trailblazer indeed.

OM

Like some Kool-Aid-drinking Hare Krishnas high on ecstasy, *Om* is what almost all yogis chant at the beginning and end of classes.

Om is the audible expression of the transcendental, formless ground of reality, the "primordial seed" of the universe, dissolving into the silence that the yoga scriptures describe as "tranquil, soundless, fearless, sorrowless, blissful, satisfied, steadfast, immovable, immortal, unshaken, enduring."

But what the hell is this monosyllabic mumbo jumbo, really?

Yogis believe that everything is vibrating and in motion. The ultimate cosmic buzz really does turn out to be, in fact, *Om*. It's not just the password—like "Open Sesame"—*Om* is the frequency of the universe itself.

We chant *Om* because it brings the class together, connecting everyone through the most primal of sounds. It reminds us that we are not alone.

We chant *Om* because it brings us inside ourselves, fine-tuning the body/mind connection. It unites us within.

And the ending of *Om*—where that last *M* sound leaves the lips buzzing, moving into silence—is like the dissolving into ultimate reality. Letting go. Releasing. Forgiveness …

All of those things that are just shy of impossible. But sometimes, maybe not.

CHAPTER 29

Becker's office is exactly as you would expect: gorgeous and stylized, a huge understated proclamation that he is the kingpin of cutting-edge, hip luxury.

I don't know exactly why he consents to seeing me—I don't have an appointment—

I chalk it up to a glimmer of recognition that I might be a Young Turk worth talking to, but mostly to good luck—some Japanese meeting has been postponed at the last minute. Simply put, I show up, and since he has five minutes free, I'm granted an audience. I don't waste time. "I have a proposition for you," I state.

"Really?" Becker eyes me. His famously salt-and-pepper hair—a thick mane that has been that color since his twenties—gives him a lupine look. But, no, there's nothing hungry in the man anymore. There's something about the way he stares at me, confident and detached and somehow deeply penetrating, that's more owl-like.

I let the numbers do the talking, dropping on his desk a reconstructed and modified version of all Monique's handiwork. He glances through it.

"And what is this exactly?" he asks.

"A venture that I think you should take on," I propose confidently.

He eyes the numbers, then starts skimming through the concept section. Because we'd worked on the club for three months, this proposal is much meatier—full of fully executed architectural plans, down to the details of barstools, fabric swatches, and menu fonts—than the pitch Monique and I made to the Cleavage Boyz.

I let Becker take his time. He moves through the material at his own pace, asking a highly pointed question—"You're getting the banquettes from Avanti's in Jersey?"—every now and then.

He gets to the last page, closes the proposal, and leans back in his chair, his hands interlaced behind his head. He gazes off—presumably into the future—as he contemplates the venture I've laid out in front of him. After a few moments, he turns to me, staring at me with those owl-like eyes. "You know, I don't really invest in other people's establishments."

"I know. That's not why I'm here."

"Really?" I can tell he's intrigued. On a business level, Monique did an awesome job of the plan initially, and all the work I've added has made it particularly flushed out and compelling—well, it should be, given that the joint is half-constructed. Yet Becker's interest in the deal's possibilities might just run second to his curiosity about why I'm here and what exactly I'm putting on the table.

"You don't want me to bail you out, becoming a silent partner?" he asks.

"No, I can't imagine that you'd do that," I reply.

"You're right. Okay—what then?" He peers at me. Somehow I've stumped the Owl.

"I want to give it up. Specifically, I want to give the whole thing to you." Becker takes this in, his face completely neutral.

"Why? I mean, it's no secret that you are in a rather nasty jam with your investors."

"That's putting it mildly." I concur.

"I'm not negating that it's a major crisis you're dealing with right now. But on the other hand, I also think, given how far you've come, you might be able to find a true silent partner out there who would bail you out. You could still make this thing work."

"I know that. But my perspective has changed. I'm interested in something else."

"May I ask what?"

I knew this moment was coming. The deal itself is

inherently quite appealing. Monique has made the numbers work beautifully, enough to impress two shrewd Wall Streeters like the Cleavage Boyz. Financially, it's solid, and if it suits Becker's brand and his business strategy, he might just do it. But that's not enough. Someone like Becker is going to want to know what the proverbial catch is. Why else would I be here, giving away such a potential opportunity?

"There is a catch, if that's what you're wondering."

"Please enlighten me." Becker leans back again. He's wary, of course, as to why I'm potentially being so candid, why I might actually be putting my cards on the table.

"Under almost any other circumstances, you'd be right. I should just dust myself off from my latest ass kicking, find new backers, and carry on."

"Agreed."

"Initially, I wanted to launch this venture for all the obvious reasons. To make a lot of money. The rush of nightlife. Getting laid often and easily."

Becker nods knowingly. No smiles from him—these are just statements of fact.

He waits for further explanation from me. Despite my playing this over in my head ten thousand times last night, I realize that there's no choice but to plunge in.

He knows the business gist of both my recent failures—the investor's wife, and wives that keep getting in my way—but I need to tell him more. I condense my whole Shane saga, plus the stuff about my dad, and dreaming of the Big Time, and all my obsessive nightlife knowledge. At some point, I realize I've gone way over the sanctioned five-minute slot he allotted early on, but both of us somehow know I can't be stopped. It's only after I've completely finished that Becker says anything at all. "And the catch is?" he inquires.

"That you buy the club and offer Shane the position of head chef. Or at least a significant promotion."

He takes this in. "So that she'll know you made it happen for her." Becker nods in understanding, but not necessarily agreement.

"No," I reply, "I don't want her to ever know. I don't want anything to do with the club or for her to ever know that it came from me or through me."

"May I ask why?" Becker seems genuinely surprised.

"If she knows I'm part of it, she would never accept the offer. She might even quit if she finds out I'm involved later on. She deserves this despite me, not because of me. This only works if she thinks it comes from you."

"And you're willing to give up your interest in this enterprise just to make this happen? You're going to walk away and sacrifice this opportunity, simply to even the score?"

"More or less. I don't think it evens things at all—but at least it's a start."

Becker takes this in silently. He picks up the proposal, pulls a laptop out of a drawer from his pristine, sleek desk—the kind you wouldn't think had drawers to begin with—and starts confirming the numbers.

Nothing happens for what feels like an eternity, but is probably more like ten, fifteen minutes of Becker double-checking Monique's work and adding some variations in a spreadsheet. I sit there, waiting as patiently as I can.

First, Becker finishes with the numbers. Then, he spins his chair away from me and stares out the window into the city. I've no idea what he's thinking or what manner of divination shapes his decision-making process. Again, it feels like all eternity as I wait—even longer when he turns his chair slowly around toward me, still not speaking.

Then he says, "I think you're a fool for giving this one up." That's not really an answer. He keeps me waiting even longer.

Finally, he speaks. "The deal does make sense to me. Provided, of course, that Shane is up to the job—I'll need to confirm that and find some way of explaining the promotion, but I'll manage. God knows, I've explained away more."

"Good. So, it's settled then." I'm more than pleased.

"Yes." I sense he wants to ask me something more. He's not a man who hesitates for long. "And this is Monique's work, I assume," he asks, referring to all the spreadsheets and projections. I'm not sure if there's some particular Monique signature to the flowcharts, or whether she'd disclosed all of this to him already. I nod.

"Typical" is all he says. There's a universe of meaning behind the single word, but I think it's obviously wise not to ask any further.

Becker picks up the phone and alerts his lawyers and accountants to the gist of things, telling them that they need to move quickly. We're as good as done, and I'm heading out the door.

It suddenly strikes me as funny—being this close to the man I once would have given anything to become. I always fancied myself "the New Becker," hoping to become rivals or partners or best friends, depending on the success fantasy du jour. Now, rather than soaking in his wisdom or partying together on one of our yachts, I'm just eager to be done with it all.

But a moment before I exit and vanish from his sacred and chic stratosphere, one hand on the door, he calls me back. "Look, I'm not a man to second-guess the other guy in a deal, especially when it's going my way … but you're sure about this?" he asks. "You're really sure you want to let this one go?"

I need no time to reflect. For once, I am certain of something.

"Absolutely."

The door shuts behind me, with no regrets.

CHAPTER 30

Linney prides himself on knowing "all the best rich broads in Gotham who can still hold their liquor." Opening his Old School Rolodex last week, an hour of phone calls is all it takes to gather a roomful of boozy dames armored in Chanel at his townhouse to celebrate God knows what. Although I'm roughly thirty years younger than any of these zesty ladies, I actually wish I could have attended his bash. Brooke Merriman, however, would never have approved. So I slip in through the proverbial back door. With a clear cocktail hour cut-off of 9 p.m., I arrive just as the last guest leaves.

I'm trying to minimize the drama—I really wish I didn't have to step out from behind the curtains for a Big Reveal Moment—but I don't know how else to make this work. So I wait in the wings of Linney's top-floor personal apartment until Shane knocks and enters.

"Come in, come in, my dear. Everything was simply splendid—although I am going to hold you personally responsible if those fabulous crab cakes add a single centimeter to my famous wasp waist."

Shane smiles at the compliments and hands him the final invoice for the catering. Linney looks at it, nods and hands her the check he's already made out. "This should cover it."

Shane glances perfunctorily at the check. The amount startles her.

"I'm sorry, but there must be some mistake. Even with the most generous tip, this is way too much."

"Is it?"

"Yes, it's about … $15,000 too much."

Cue my entrance from the alcove. I try to sound reassuring and not overdramatic. "No, I think it's exactly the right amount actually."

Shane doesn't move. At least the element of surprise is working for me here. My deal with Becker may have provided just enough to pay off some old debts, but nothing can guarantee that Shane will actually stay in the room, much less accept the money.

"I'll let you two have a moment alone," Linney says, as he exits. "I assume there are still a few crab cakes those girls haven't devoured. Oh well, another dozen sit-ups tomorrow"

"Why?" is all Shane asks when we're alone.

"Well, the amount is pretty straight-up: I owe you the money."

"Yeah, but …" Shane lets the awkwardness linger in the air. At least she's not bolting.

"Shane, please just take the check. I owe you the money. You shouldn't have lost your entire investment because I fucked things up."

"I suppose you think you've made your 'Grand Gesture' and now you want me to reassure you that everything's cool between us. But even you ought to know that the money is the least important thing to me."

Here and now is probably my last chance with her, and God knows how I don't want to blow it. A deep breath before I launch in. "Look, Shane, I know I screwed up with you, with us, with everything. I fuck things up all the time. I'm an expert at it. But you're the one who'll be screwing things up here if you keep holding on to this."

"Oh, so you think I should just accept a little cash and then shrug it all off and go right back to being BFFs."

"Much as I'd like that, no I don't. Not at all."

"What then?"

"Shane, I want you to forgive me so that you can stop wasting so much energy hating me. Maybe even enjoy a memory or two of us instead of throwing everything out in the trash. A couple great years of hanging out, of a real friendship, gone just like that. As though nothing good ever happened between us." There's a pause. At least she's hearing me out.

"Look, I know I probably don't ever get to be your friend again and more than anything that totally sucks, but Shane … I want you to forgive me so that YOU can have a little piece of mind. So that you can let go and move on. God knows you deserve better than me, but you certainly deserve a helluva lot better than being haunted by my screwups."

Shane takes this in. Troglodyte that I am, at least she knows I'm not a liar. For once, something is actually not entirely about me and my needs.

"You can rest assured," I continue, "that even if you do cash this check, I will still feel pretty miserable about us, pretty much all the time."

An eternal beat—I can't tell what the hell she's thinking—and then …

"Well, that's some small consolation, I suppose." There's a lot less bite to the sarcasm, however.

Shane looks at me intently. Like Gigi, her intelligence and her bullshit indicator have always been razor-sharp.

"You know, I received an interesting offer today."

"Really?"

"Yeah, a promotion. Becker's newest place."

"That's awesome. You deserve it."

"Well, actually, I don't. What I mean is, they don't know that I do. I haven't proven myself there yet." I don't say anything, trying to reveal nothing in my expression. In this poker game, I want Shane to keep the winning hand.

"It's a rather bold stroke of good luck," Shane says.

I shrug. "I wouldn't question it. You know how unpredictable the business is. Who knows what internal politics go on behind the scenes? Or maybe they just dug out your old résumé and remembered that you graduated at the top of culinary school."

"I suppose," she replies, unconvinced. "Still, it's as if I had a little help on the inside. From someone high up on the Becker corporate ladder. As though someone upstairs really likes me."

I scan her face. There's no rancor or accusation. Instead,

there's a softness, an openness—something I haven't seen in over a year.

"Well, I'm sure somebody does," I reply, grabbing my coat. "Probably more than you'll ever know," I add heading towards the exit.

I don't want to press my luck here any further than I already have. I'm halfway out the door, but Shane isn't quite satisfied.

"You know, it's funny but it seems like the kind of place you always wanted to open."

"Used to want. Feels like that was a long time ago"

"I had a tour yesterday and if I hadn't known better, I would have sworn that you had a hand in practically all of it."

"Probably just a coincidence. I've … I've let go of that world for now."

"Well, it seems like a pretty big thing to just give up." Shane looks at me intently. We both know what she's really asking.

I shrug, trying to seem casual. "Other things are more important. At least for right now. Oh and"—I try to make this seem casual—"I'd still like you have to have this."

I can't remember the last time I prayed, but I'm praying now that she accepts the vintage Escoffier I offer her, the perfect gift regiven for the second time … The moment seems eternal. She makes a decision.

"Thank you," she says accepting the book and folding up the check in her apron pocket.

"You're welcome."

I want to hold her. I want to kiss her. But my mission here is accomplished. Beyond the fifteen grand, she knows I'm behind the promotion, and she knows I know she knows. And, most importantly, she's accepting it. Shane has let go.

Fortunately, before I can screw anything else up, I manage to make my exit. Nonetheless, looking back, I spy something I never thought I'd see again: Shane's actually looking at me and rather than a look of scorn or hurt or judgment, a soft smile of forgiveness flickers across her face.

EPILOGUE

For the past few months, I've been totally looking forward to Thank Heaven's annual New Year's Day class. This year, however, I'm teaching it.

Gigi and Calypso are off leading a retreat in Costa Rica, and—although no one says this, it's my theory that it's only because all the better teachers are away—astonishingly, they've actually entrusted the joint to me for today's bash.

Last night, I had a tasteful glass of champagne with Hutch and Etta, and even though they invited me to tag along for their evening, I know when three's a crowd. Nine months in, they're still in the first flush of romance. The weather's decent for New York in December, so I walk from Hutch and Etta's back toward my place.

I am tempted to divert myself and walk past Diwali—rechristened "Glitter" to better fit Becker's glistening brand of jewels and metals—just to take in the energy from the outside and to know that Shane is happily ensconced in the kitchen. Becker's unexpected promotion—which Shane had already found a little hard to swallow—was followed by a "surprise" departure of the head chef for Thailand. Shane was given the culinary chance of a lifetime, and surviving the heat of the moment, she did not question this adrenaline rush of opportunity. Instead, she rose to the challenge. The opening reviews were good to great, and like all Becker ventures, this one too (though secretly the embodiment of almost all my best ideas) seems blessed with his Midas touch.

I stand safely across the street, enjoying the bustling of celebratory diners coming in and out, wishing that I could ask them about their experiences inside, experiences in cuisine and music and lighting and design that I shaped and created for them. Crossing the street, I move closer but keep my safe distance.

Nearing the large front window, there's an intense moment, one full of pride and regret, when I see Shane, in chef's garb, approach a satisfied table. She graciously receives their compliments, and though I find myself truly happy for her, I restrain myself from entering. Instead of walking up to her, as I long to do, before she can look up and spot me, I turn away and walk towards home. Shane will be there, thriving, for a while. The day may well come when I'd consider going inside, but it is not yet here.

The cold air feels nicely bracing. The evening finds me more or less comfortably at home. Except for friends like Hutch, I've imposed a loosely structured six-month moratorium on going out just to add digits to my address book. So I miss the midnight moment that marks the year's end, and only after the fact do I realize it has happened.

I sleep until 8 a.m., which feels felt incredibly decadent, given my teaching schedule these days. For three months, I've been teaching Day-Breakers—Calypso's signature 7 a.m. class—four days a week, while she's choreographing for the Wallo Company. Initially, Sassy had been her designated sub, but when, lo and behold, Sassy got cast in an Off-Broadway musical and married a dentist with three kids, Gigi offered it to me.

This morning, I practice for two hours—really just moving around and opening up, more casual stretching and breathing than anything formal—before heading to Thank Heaven. Once again, the weather is moderate enough, especially now that the snow is falling, that I decide to walk to the center.

And now, here I am, seated in front of this class.

It is sold out. I know that's less because of me than because it's an annual event. I recognize many of the faces—I am getting better with names—and there are, of course, a bunch of New Year's resolution types who may or may not last more than a class or two. As always, only time will tell.

We Om together, and it's amazing. So much more mystical

juice here than anyplace else, I think.

My favorite part of class these days are the moments after the Om-ing, those seconds, perhaps even a full minute, in which the teacher says nothing. I like to just sit there, digging the charged stillness.

Sometimes there will be a major fidgeter in the front row, which interferes with the vibe for those not naturally serene (i.e., me). Flashing back on my Catholic school nuns, I want to smack them with a ruler. But most of the time, it's just all of us soaking in the silence, a silence made all the richer by our having filled it moments before with resonant Oms, truly the sound of everything.

Today, I let the silence play out a little longer than usual. And I do something I never really do: I open my eyes before I tell the class to do the same.

I stare out at their faces, all of them with their eyes shut—all but one, a pretty redhead in the back row who meets my eye and then furtively looks away, as though I've caught her in some terribly wicked transgression. Amused, my smile is just for me; like any scolded student, she's already re-shut her eyelids.

I look out at the faces, faces that manifest different degrees of serenity, but in this moment, they all appear indescribably beautiful to me.

Soon those faces will be dripping with sweat. In fact, for the next two hours, there will be endless varieties of changing expressions of strain and release, resentment and laughter, a myriad of shifting emotions beaming from them. But right now, it's mostly contentment and patience I see reflected back at me. They're waiting, I think ... Waiting to be served. Waiting to be taught. Waiting to be transformed.

Good, I think. It's time to begin.

A NOTE TO THE READER

The author has taught yoga privately to several hundred individuals in New York City and many thousands more in group classes. This story was partly inspired by what he learned and experienced.

The writing about yoga poses and philosophy is accurate, although highly personal and delivered via the protagonist's individual and highly quirky interpretations. Nonetheless, it reflects an informed understanding of this ancient and eternal practice for evolving body, mind, and soul.

Downward Dog, however, is entirely a work of fiction. Any resemblance to actual events or persons, living or dead, is coincidental. Many New York City landmarks—ranging from restaurants, bars, and clubs, to celebrities—are mentioned and are used exclusively to further the story.

And yet, on the other hand, as Lord Krishna in the Bhagavad Gita tells us, "all worlds, all beings, are strung upon me like pearls on a single thread" for "infinite are the forms in which I appear."

In the end—even when we fight most desperately against it—in fiction and in life, the imperishable, unchanging Source of the Universe connects us all.

Hari Om Tat Sat

ACKNOWLEDGMENTS

I cannot thank enough all those who have helped bring this book to life, but I'll certainly try.

Sarah Finn, Producer and Friend, whose faith in this project has meant everything.

My agent, Beth Vesel, who brought the project to Mary Cummings and everyone at Diversion.

Rebecca Gradinger, for wise early insights and support.

All of these wonderful friends who read drafts of the manuscript and offered invaluable comments, corrections, and perhaps most importantly, enthusiasm: Amy Ahlers, Jeff Capodanno, Marie Carter, Kevin Dewey, Katey Hassan, Tamer Hassan, Sarah Herrington, Julie Hilden, Nina Lourie, Genevieve Lynch, Anne Miano, Adrian Pineiro, Valerie Ross, Daniel Scranton, Emily Stone

I must also thank those whose helpfulness and kindness particularly shone during the time I was writing this book:

Three very excellent roommates over two coasts: Gro Christensen, Daniel Seagan, and Jude English.

Two old friends, Amy Adler and Hillary Kelleher.

The Phleger Family.

Val and Clark Tate for hosting various screenplay readings.

My Mother.

Roger Gonzalez.

Dan Miller.

Dawn Davis.

Cristy Candler, Bryn Chrisman, Kiley Holliday, and Jamie Watkins for their shapely yoga modeling.

Elizabeth Devita-Raeburn, my first Creative Client, and Ellen Yo, my first Platinum one.

And, when it comes to my life as a yoga teacher, special thanks must go to …

Dana Flynn and Jasmine Tarkeshi, founders of the Laughing Lotus Yoga Center. My teaching there—particularly my time studying with Dana Flynn—gave me the wings and foundation for this book.

Stacey Brass for lending me notes for the yoga school final.

The anonymous copywriter at Bloomingdales who described me as a "legendary yoga master" for the New York Times.

Douglas Boyce, without whose referrals my career would never have taken off.

Nela Wagman, whose steadfast faith in my yoga teaching truly made everything possible.

Patricia Scanlon & Hugh Palmer (my very first students).

Priscilla and Jamie Goldman (my first paying students).

Terrence McNally, for inspiring by example.

And, of course, Belle—the greatest yoga teacher of all …

Finally, I have to thank all the students I taught privately and all those who came so faithfully to my classes.

Truly, more than you will ever know, you taught me.

ABOUT THE AUTHOR

PHOTO BY JONATHAN POZNIAK

Edward Vilga writes many things—books, plays, and films—and makes a little art on the side.

He is also one of America's leading yoga teachers, having taught thousands of group classes (including one in Times Square), hundreds of individuals privately, and countless students through his bestselling yoga books and DVDs.

Edward Vilga lives in New York City with Belle, his chocolate lab.

He is a Yale graduate.

Please visit **www.EdwardVilga.com** for updates, offers, and to stay connected.

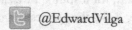 @EdwardVilga

 www.Facebook.com/EdwardVilgaIndustries